NOBLE WARRIOR

ALSO BY ALAN LAWRENCE SITOMER

The Hoopster

A Teacher's Guide—The Hoopster

Hip-Hop Poetry and the Classics

Hip-Hop High School

Homeboyz

The Secret Story of Sonia Rodriguez

Nerd Girls—The Rise of the Dorkasaurus

Nerd Girls—A Catastrophe of Nerdish Proportions

Caged Warrior

BY ALAN LAWRENCE SITOMER

HYPERION
LOS ANGELES   NEW YORK

All rights reserved. Published by Hyperion, an imprint
of Disney Book Group. No part of this book may be
reproduced or transmitted in any form or by any means,
electronic or mechanical, including photocopying, recording,
or by any information storage and retrieval system, without
written permission from the publisher. For information
address Hyperion, 125 West End Avenue, New York,
New York 10023.

Printed in the United States of America
First Edition, July 2015
10 9 8 7 6 5 4 3 2 1
G475-5664-5-15091

Library of Congress Cataloging-in-Publication Data
Sitomer, Alan Lawrence.
    Noble warrior / by Alan Lawrence Sitomer.—1st ed.
      pages cm
    Sequel to: Caged warrior.
    Summary: "Mixed martial arts phenom McCutcheon
Daniels is recruited to help the FBI but then he is disavowed
by the government and abandoned in one of America's most
notorious prisons"—Provided by publisher.
    ISBN 978-1-4847-0528-5
    [1. Mixed martial arts—Fiction. 2. Prisons—Fiction.]
I. Title.
    PZ7.S6228No 2015
    [Fic]—dc23   2014041680

Reinforced binding

Visit www.hyperionteens.com

Dedicated to Wendy Lefkon
for her excellence, for her faith, for her awesomeness

With special thanks to . . .

My brother Roberto, for sampling the boo-boo
pancake and being the absolute KEY to
getting this book right. Love you, dude!

Terry Kaldhusdal, for making countless hours of deep,
challenging discussions feel like mere pleasantly passing
moments of good conversation with a good friend.

Jeremy the Warrior, for teaching me about
the true nature of fear and the true nature of
strength. (A shout-out to the men, too!)

Al Zuckerman, for being so much more than
a literary agent . . . a prince among men!

And of course, to the ladies who live under my
roof: Sienna Brynn & Quinn Bailey, for teaching
me the real meaning of true love and showing
me the unequivocal joy of fatherhood . . . and for
Tracey, whose tremendous dedication to our
home is the straw that stirs our family's drink.

Plus, a HUGE shout-out to G-money . . . without
his solarium, Wi-Fi, car, cell phone, printer, sushi
companionship & couch time, none of this gets written.

"IF AN INJURY HAS TO BE
DONE TO A MAN IT SHOULD BE
SO SEVERE THAT HIS VENGEANCE
NEED NOT BE FEARED."

—Niccolo Machiavelli

ONE

cCutcheon "M.D." Daniels ate like a caveman. Raw food, raw power. After switching to an exclusively Paleolithic diet nearly three years ago he felt immediate benefits in each realm of the fighter's holy trinity: body, mind, and spirit. Physically, by cutting out all the crap he used to eat, M.D. recovered more quickly from the vicious toll cage wars take on the human body. Mentally, like most serious mixed martial artists, McCutcheon sought to carry his discipline off of the mat and into his life, which meant that saying no to tasty foods like pizza, burgers, fries, and cake meant saying yes to deep reserves of mental strength. In the sphere of spirit however, McCutcheon owned wounds. Deep ones.

How could he not be scarred after all the senseless violence and pain he'd already witnessed in his young life? He once saw a neighbor get shot in the face. Saw another overdose on heroin and drown in his own puke. Watched a girl stumble around like a drunken hobo with a knife sticking out of her eye after she'd been stabbed during a robbery gone bad. Yet despite seeing all this and more before the age of seventeen, McCutcheon still deeply believed in religion.

The religion of being a warrior. In its nobility he found truth. Living by a code wasn't a burden to M.D.; it was his church.

"We're closing in fifteen," a waitress said. "Here's your check."

McCutcheon clicked a red cigarette lighter and torched up a bowl. "Thank you," he said exhaling a plume of thick white smoke.

"Pay at the front."

"Shall do."

Putting toxins in his body was entirely out of character for M.D., but the waitress didn't know that. To her and everyone else in the establishment, McCutcheon was just another guy lighting up on a Friday night.

Which, of course, he wasn't.

He gazed out of the corner of his eye across the dimly lit, smoke-filled room at his six-foot-one-inch tall target and took another soft, sweet hit off the brass hookah pipe resting in front of him. The chocolate-skinned Somalian he spied—male, eighteen, typing on a laptop—didn't lift his eyes from the glowing bluish screen. Arabs had been smoking from hookahs for well over five hundred years, but M.D. hadn't come to Mystic Wonders to puff.

He'd come to fight.

His mission: apprehend a teenage terrorist who had plans to blow up the senior prom of the largest high school in the state. Biggest obstacle: the chances of a radicalized

Al-Shabaab soldier simply coming along with an undercover federal agent without putting up a fight landed somewhere between zero and no fucking way.

The clock ticked to 1:47 a.m., and two girls, one with mysterious brown eyes, the other with swollen, perky breasts, rose from their table, threw their purses over their shoulders, and exited through the dark green front door, their men following right behind.

A brass bell, cheap and tinny, jingled as the door closed. McCutcheon pulled another hit off his pipe and waited seven full minutes before making his move. His training had stressed the importance of allowing a battle theater to settle into stillness before initiating action, and no one trained with more diligence, dedication, or balls-out mettle than the soldier who didn't even officially exist—Murk Team recruit Agent ZERO X1.

M.D. walked to the front counter. His target sat on a black bar stool, a woven Persian tapestry hanging on the wall behind him, a twenty-four-inch touch screen digital cash register sitting on the hard wooden counter directly to his right.

"You paying cash or credit?"

"I'm looking for Ibrahim Ali Farah."

A pause. Eye contact as the North African's gaze slowly moved to meet M.D.'s. His fingers froze mid-stroke, he turned his head and waited. It was almost as if he expected someone else to come out and answer the question for him.

Which is exactly what happened.

A bloodred curtain parted and a muscular silhouette

appeared from a private back room. Penetrating, threatening eyes sized up McCutcheon.

"Zuri. Come," the shadowy figure called out over his shoulder. "Trouble."

A second silhouette emerged, tall and lithe, and two men stepped forward into the dim light. They both glared at M.D. with coldness. One stood thick and stocky, biceps like bank safes rippling underneath a white V-neck tee. The other was six feet three inches tall, had a goatee, lean physique, and a two-inch scar above the corner of his left eye.

Just two? McCutcheon thought. They weren't as prepared as he'd expected. Nor as they would need to be. Not if they were going to deal with M.D.

Not tonight.

Prior to getting the green light to strike his target, McCutcheon had been having a rough evening. Extremely rough. Ever since he made the decision to abandon his girlfriend—no good-bye, no explanations, no "talk-to-ya-soon"s or "I'll-be-in-touch"s, just *Poof!* he disappeared— emotional hurricanes of sadness, regret, and anger had been washing over him. As with all elite soldiers, M.D. knew his job was to put his emotions on a shelf and go do the hard work that had been set in front of him—no excuses, no complaints, no bullshit—yet tonight he felt edgy.

M.D. was in no mood for messing around, and though discipline, patience, and the science of being a poised and methodical warrior usually steered his decision making, frustration, tension, and an urge to just rip through somebody with the rage of a lion raced through his blood. A late night dance with a couple of evil-hearted partners, he thought, might be just the bucket of cold water M.D. needed to douse the flames scorching his wounded heart.

As much as McCutcheon loathed his father, Damien "Demon" Daniels, an ex-prizefighter who washed out of pro boxing and then fell into an abyss of crime, drugs, gangs, and whores, it was all playing out just like his dad had once told him it would: "Relationships'll just fuck a fighter up." McCutcheon dismissed his father's warning back when these words were first spoken as nothing more than the BS of a jaded man. But this was also before M.D.'s heart had been spiked by Cupid's arrow. The truth hurts, but when the truth comes from the lips of a person you despise, its sting yields twice the pain.

Nerves tingling, his fists curling into the heads of hammers, M.D.—too tightly wound, too eager to deliver a beating—readied for war.

The short, muscular guy fiddled with his hands underneath the counter. Despite his view being blocked, McCutcheon didn't make a preemptive move. Instead, M.D. just breathed in and breathed out, calm, even, steady breaths. No need to waste energy, he thought.

The tall one raised an axe handle. Hickory. Four feet long. A stick like that, M.D. knew, would leave marks.

McCutcheon stood his ground as if carved from stone. Confidence in his skills had never been a problem for Bam Bam, the legendary teenage cage warrior from the projects of inner-city Detroit. M.D. had put enough people in stitches, casts, and hospitals to know his own capabilities.

The real battle for him was not one of mustering up enough aggression to go to war, but rather of summoning up enough restraint to see if bloodshed could be avoided. "I said," M.D. repeated, working hard to remain composed, "I am looking for Ibrahim Ali Far—"

"He's not here," the tall one interrupted.

"And who's the fuck is you?" asked his thick, squat associate.

McCutcheon glared. "It does not matter who I am," he said. "It matters that I think that you"—M.D. pointed at his original target, the guy sitting behind the cash register—"are in cahoots with Ibrahim."

"Cahoots?" came the reply. "I do not know this word. Are they a type of pants?"

The three Somalians laughed.

M.D. took another long, slow deep breath. In front of him stood Massir "Max" El-Alhou, the CyberFang of Al-Shabaab, a digital Houdini that the U.S. government had been unsuccessfully trying to apprehend for more than two years. An innovative piece of NSA software had mapped his Wi-Fi fingerprint and tracked him to the state of New Jersey. After two weeks of covert hunting, M.D. had tracked him here.

"No," McCutcheon answered. "It means that you are an associate of Ibrahim's, a conspirator." M.D. pointed at the laptop. "And I have a feeling your computer contains a lot of cahoot-like information, so I am going to ask that you pack up your things and please come with me. I have a minivan. It's parked out back."

Silence. No one moved. Menacing looks lasered in on McCutcheon.

"You'll be comfortable," M.D. added. "It's got leather seats."

The beefy kid cracked a defiant smile. "Oh, yeah," he said. "Well, cock you."

Cock me? M.D. thought. I don't even know what that means. The musclebound guy with a neck as thick as a fullback's thigh stepped from behind the counter and McCutcheon saw what had previously been shielded from his sight.

Knucks. Brass ones. Scuffed, sturdy, threatening from his left hand.

Brass knuckles have always been a favorite of soldiers because they hold the power to transform a glancing blow into a knockout punch and a knockout punch into a cerebral hematoma. But only wearing them on his left hand? Dude shoulda just made a sign, M.D. thought: *Look at me, I'm a southpaw!*

The muscular guy squared his stance, raised his fists, and cocked a big left hand. M.D., quick as a cougar, spun and fired off a low Muay Thai shin kick to the inside of his opponent's back leg and *CRACK!* a violent pop exploded through the air as his enemy's knee snapped. With his freshly torn anterior cruciate ligament unable to sustain his body weight, M.D.'s foe buckled forward face-first.

Into an exploding palm strike.

The blow shattered his nasal bone and like a work of art being splashed across a canvas, blood splattered against the white wall in a shower of speckled red dots. Slowly, his enemy's eyes rolled back into his head and, after an involuntary parting of his lips, a soft sigh, and a gentle exhalation, there was a thud.

Boomph! He hit the ground.

Night-night, M.D. thought. One target down.

The tall guy launched an assault, and as if by instinct McCutcheon ducked underneath a strike aimed at his temple a tick before it would have knocked him out. His fierce enemy followed with two more blows, swinging the ax handle expertly, not like a street fighter wildly waving a baseball bat but rather like a martial artist who had been schooled in the skill of stick fighting. Concise, focused, swift strokes aimed at M.D.'s core, head, and then knees caused McCutcheon to backpedal.

M.D. kicked aside a chair, clearing some space, and *Thwwwwisshh!* the wind of another strike sailed by the front of his face. The angular, fierce Somalian refused to give him an inch.

McCutcheon knew he was going to have to absorb a blow. His challenge, he recognized, was to make sure it'd only be one shot and not multiple whacks. After that, M.D. told himself, he'd have him at a disadvantage.

As they say in the cage, everyone's got a plan until they get punched in the face. McCutcheon knew the time had come to see if his tall stick-swinging opponent owned any balls.

His enemy struck from the left; M.D. slid to his right and absorbed a smash to the ribs and groaned. Then M.D.

countered. From the inside. Once the two adversaries were only three inches apart, McCutcheon maneuvered both of his elbows above his foe's forearms, which made the ax handle about as helpful to him as a mosquito net.

Head butt—*Boom!*—just above the eye socket. Few blows are more crippling. As if in slow motion, the sense of alertness in the tall Somalian's eyes shifted from clear to glazed.

Spleen shot, forearm shiver to the face, a knee to the chin that hit like a brick, and *Bang!* second enemy down.

Only one task remained: apprehend his target.

McCutcheon straightened his spine, stepped around a tall brass pipe that had been knocked over in the melee, and advanced toward the front counter. The time had come to stake his claim. M.D. looked up, ready to take his man into custody.

And found himself staring into the barrel of a gun.

TWO

Delivering Ibrahim Ali Farah's lead cyber operations officer to the clandestine command center alive was the reason McCutcheon went to Mystic Wonders in the first place. This was not a "dead or alive" mission; only alive would do. His orders were simple: capture the technology coordinator behind a new-era sleeper cell that had been created by teens, was recruiting teens, and, most terrifying of all, was targeting teens for upcoming bloodshed. These "kids," he was informed, were pretending to be regular students, working late nights, studying computer science, wearing blue jeans and so on, when in reality it had been discovered they were actually a group of young chaos causers plotting mayhem on American soil. Their leader, Ibrahim Ali Farah, functioned as an underage operative for an international terrorist organization known as Al-Shabaab.

In Arabic, the name *Al-Shabaab* means *Movement of Striving Youth*. McCutcheon Daniels got recruited to the world of hunting them after his own underground mixed martial arts career in the ghettoes of Detroit. His father had pimped him out like a violent whore to make money.

Pound for pound, M.D. was the best young mixed martial artist the Motor City had ever seen. Maybe the best ever. Undefeated for years and unmatched in his dedication to training, M.D. had taken out some of the best underground fighters from coast to coast. However, a street gang named the Priests lost a very large sum of money betting on M.D. the night he absorbed the first loss of his career.

A loss that could have been—and should have been—a victory until McCutcheon purposefully threw the fight. M.D. had only done it to escape his father's abusive clutches, but the Priests didn't care about stupid little father/son squabbles. They'd lost a lot of cash fronting money for uncovered bets made by McCutcheon's dad, and according to the code of the streets, the only way to pay someone back for such a giant loss of green was with the spilling of a large amount of red.

The High Priest, the gang's kingpin, sought revenge.

Payback for the Daniels family began with having Klowner and Nate-Neck, McCutcheon's two closest friends and MMA training partners, butchered. A hollowed-out eye socket, necks slashed to the white of the bone, ears carved off with a hacksaw—gruesome, merciless street executions had been carried out on both men. Of course the High Priest had also put a green light out on Demon Daniels, M.D.'s dad, but he slithered away before hit squads were able to take him out.

As the leader of a criminal enterprise growing more influential by the month, D'Marcus Rose, the High Priest, understood that most people feared death. But what people feared even more than death, he knew, was excessive, prolonged pain.

This knowledge led him to create a campaign of terror aimed directly at Detroit's most impoverished residents. Targeting the poorest made good business sense because the down and out were the most easily victimized and the least well-protected by law enforcement. With their fear came power.

Once Detroit became the largest American city in history to declare bankruptcy, opportunities opened like flower buds in the springtime. Fewer cops. Less resources. Virtually no chance to stop the Priests.

Rose became the city's biggest shotcaller. As the High Priest he held only one aim: own Detroit. Anyone who tried to stop him found themselves in either a wheelchair or the morgue.

McCutcheon's mom, baby sister, and M.D. ended up being whisked away in the dead of day and put into protective custody by the U.S. Marshals' Witness Security Program. Once the whole family was safe in Bellevue, Nebraska—like who in the world moves to Bellevue, Nebraska, from the projects of D-Town?—some black op government guys, fans of McCutcheon's unique skill set as a cage fighter, began recruiting M.D. to a covert, anti–domestic terror unit nicknamed the Murk.

Like so many other adults in McCutcheon's life, they too wanted him to fight. But for something more. Something bigger. Something worth fighting for.

America. Freedom. The red, white, and blue.

After all the betrayal and all the violence during his childhood years, McCutcheon hungered for something positive to latch on to. Corny as it sounds, the whole idea of being one of the good guys appealed to him. M.D. was a badass. He knew he was a badass. He'd been raised ever since the crib to be a badass. At three he was shadowboxing, at seven he was executing heel hooks, and by the age of nine he was punching the ticket of thirteen-year-olds who outweighed him by more than fifty pounds. There was never a question about McCutcheon Daniels being a great and mighty warrior; the question, as posed to M.D., was "Can McCutcheon Daniels be a great and mighty warrior who fights for a great and mighty cause?"

A gravel-voiced guy named Stanzer envisioned M.D. as a prototype for the next generation of soldier, the kind that could handle the challenges of fighting the next generation of terrorist.

"The enemy doesn't have an age limit," Stanzer barked. "Why should we?"

M.D. was young. He was skilled. He was the type of lone wolf that could get into places only teens could gain access to and then do some serious damage in an under-the-radar style.

All in the name of saving American lives. On the inside of Stanzer's left forearm the colonel wore a tattoo that rationalized it all:

People sleep peaceably in their beds at night only because rough men stand ready to do violence on their behalf.

Beneath these words rippled the image of an American flag. To Stanzer, his ink wasn't just body paint; these words gave meaning to his life.

"Fact is," Stanzer said to M.D., "sometimes good people have to do some very bad things."

Few teens if any had ever excelled in the world of mixed martial arts to the extent that M.D. had. But his whole life he'd been programmed by his piece-of-shit father to fight for personal, self-centered reasons. Demon Daniels taught his son to dream of winning a belt. Of becoming a world champion. Of living a life of luxury and material wealth. Stanzer spoke of something more.

Duty. Honor. Service. A higher calling.

McCutcheon loved him for it.

Like legions of others who sign on the dotted line, warring for something bigger than himself rang true to McCutcheon, and M.D. decided to accept the challenge. His country, he was told, needed him.

It didn't take long for Stanzer to recognize that McCutcheon was unlike any other recruit he'd ever seen. Yet for all M.D.'s physical skills, perhaps the most impressive quality Stanzer saw in McCutcheon was the manner in which he respected the theater of battle. To M.D., the mixed martial arts were more than just a system of fighting; being a warrior meant living by a set of principles.

Honor, strength, humility, respect. These weren't just ideals to M.D.; these were his ethics, on display morning, noon, and night. A lot of MMA fighters worked hard to build their physical skills in a wide range of the martial arts's fiercest of fighting styles. M.D. had, too. Yet, as Stanzer noted, Agent ZERO X1 also worked just as hard to embody the warrior's ethos of dignity. McCutcheon approached his training with ferocity, his teachers with humility, and his foes with a combination of respect, bravery, patience, wisdom, and unrelenting aggression.

He stood out as a once-every-decade type of soldier so the colonel fast-tracked him and covertly schooled McCutcheon in the art of modern-day urban assault. Weapons, lock picking, phone hacking, disappearing like a ghost—McCutcheon proved to be a remarkable student, and it wasn't long before the military had a teenage warrior on their hands who could slide into house parties, hip-hop shows, high schools, and hookah bars without anyone batting an eye.

The fight against domestic terror had a new weapon: an underage war machine, perhaps the first of its kind. And Stanzer believed that before McCutcheon's time was over his impact on those that would seek to do America harm would become legendary. As far as the colonel could tell there was only one weakness—the memory of the girl. McCutcheon carried it around like an overpacked suitcase.

"You gotta slay that dragon," Stanzer would say. "Cut its fucking head off and leave its carcass for the flies and rats."

"My dragon died a long time ago," M.D. responded.

"Being wounded and being a corpse are two different things."

"I'll try to remember that," M.D. said. "Then again, you know how I feel about murder."

No matter what Stanzer tried to explain to McCutcheon about the true, dark nature of the job, M.D. still continued to hold on to two nonnegotiable rules for himself when it came to his participation in the Murk.

Number one: no killing. Yes, M.D. was an expert in the art of hurt, but he refused to take another person's life. Capturing them with a bit of stank on it? No problem.

Number two—and this was the big one for M.D.: come summer, he planned to break cover, ditch the false Wit Sec identity that had been created for him—as a new-to-Nebraska homeschooled student from Pittsburgh named Jarrett Jenkins—and go back to his true hometown, Detroit.

Why?

To see his girl.

McCutcheon had been forced to leave her at a moment's notice in order to make sure his mom and sister were safe, but Kaitlyn Cummings had never left M.D.'s heart. Sure, ladies had been throwing themselves at "Bam Bam" ever since he was twelve years old—that's what happens when you're a hard-bodied underground celebrity cage warrior with long, thick eyelashes and a six-pack of ripped, granite abs. But when it came to Kaitlyn, things were different.

M.D. was sprung for her. Totally and completely. Kaitlyn was the girl of his dreams—smart, beautiful, took no shit—and he wanted her back. Desperately. The first month without her was hard. The second torturous. By the end of month seven, not seeing her, not smelling her, not feeling the soft, tenderness of her skin burned in M.D.'s heart and grew into a rage.

Time had not healed this wound.

To their credit, the Witness Security Program owned an unblemished track record when it came to keeping those in their custody safe from harm. Literally, never once in the history of Wit Sec had someone who'd come under federal protection ever been harmed or killed while under the active protection of the U.S. Marshal's Service. Of course Wit Sec's first and foremost rule for achieving this was that a person could never return home; and while M.D.'s head might have said *yes* to his current arrangement on a moment's notice in a high-pressure, no-time-to-really-think-about-it situation, now that McCutcheon was actually having to live out the terms of the deal, he was dead set on breaking the contract. In fact, it had gotten to the point where M.D. missed Kaitlyn so badly that he'd begun taking chances. Chances he hadn't told Stanzer about. Chances that could have had immensely negative consequences.

But these were prices M.D. was willing to pay. For the opportunity to be with Kaitlyn, no cost felt too high.

Four times during the previous three months McCutcheon secretly slipped out of Nebraska and drove ten hours into Michigan to do some intelligence gathering on his girl. Essentially, he stalked Kaitlyn. Not with any ill will, of course. Adding fuel to the fire, he still felt awful about the way he'd been forced to leave her as she stood less than twenty yards away crying, *"McCutcheon, McCutcheon!"* as he coldly climbed into a white government van and disappeared forever.

He hadn't turned around. He hadn't said good-bye. He hadn't explained the circumstances or anything. He just left—that abruptly, that unresolved, that icy and heartless.

Yet he knew it had to be that way. For Kaitlyn's safety. So she didn't get mixed up into any trouble with the Priests and they didn't target her. But now that things had settled and everyone was safe, McCutcheon hungered to see her again. He wanted to set the record straight, to fix what had been broken, to go see a movie, hold her hand, and then, like any other red-blooded American boy, find a nice quiet place to cuddle up and go turn out the lights.

M.D. knew that if he didn't see Kaitlyn again soon he'd explode.

Of course Agent ZERO X1 was trained to know better than to allow Kaitlyn to catch sight of him on these secret sojourns, but each time M.D. snuck away he felt more and more tempted to initiate contact and reappear in her life like a long lost ghost.

Their reunion, he imagined, would be like the final scenes of a great romance movie. Passionate. Filled with joy and happiness. And never again, once reunited, would McCutcheon ever let her go. That was a promise he'd made to himself.

His hunger to be with Kaitlyn turned the logical side

of M.D.'s brain to mush. M.D. had come to learn, over long periods of isolation and deep stretches of loneliness, the heart wants what the heart wants, and it rarely gives a shit what the mind has to say about it. Were these secretive trips to see Kaitlyn logical? Not at all. Were they essential? Absolutely, he felt.

It was just like Demon said: "Love, it'll fuck a fighter up."

Now that M.D. was about to deliver on his fifth successful mission he felt he deserved official permission from Stanzer to go meet up with Kaitlyn face-to-face. That was the deal. Or at least, that was the deal as M.D. understood it to be, even though Stanzer had never agreed. Once McCutcheon bagged tonight's target, however, he planned to cash in his chips and make rendezvousing with Kaitlyn a reality. McCutcheon gazed down at the pools of blood forming around each of his two fallen opponents lying on the hookah bar's floor, but he didn't allow himself to feel good about the victory. Taking pleasure from hurting people was what bullies and tyrants did. Martial artists who conducted themselves with honor sought to avoid conflict. To win without fighting, as the ancient texts said, was the highest form of triumph, and McCutcheon knew if he started taking pleasure from violently devastating his adversaries it would open a vault of blackness that had been buried deep inside of him.

M.D. owned a dark side. And it scared him. It was as if he possessed an inner beast, one capable of very grim and savage deeds. He kept the creature shackled, hidden and locked away from the rest of the world, but deep in his soul McCutcheon knew he had to contain this monster because if it got out, well... he feared no man, but as his skills advanced, M.D. had come to fear his own capabilities.

Being with Kaitlyn had always quieted the inner howls. But now Kaitlyn was gone.

M.D. inhaled a long, slow, deep breath, centered himself, and resolved on the spot to return to his core principles. Ibrahim Ali Farah's cyber commander Massir El-Alhou would come with McCutcheon in the minivan, but his apprehension would be all business: no emotion, no pleasure, and no physical altercations if possible. If conflict could be avoided, M.D. vowed he would take the path of not causing his enemy any harm. And if there was to be a battle, M.D. would only use the minimum amount of force necessary to properly execute his mission.

"Don't make me shoot you," the Somalian warned from behind the counter.

"Hand me the gun," M.D. said.

The North African looked at his bloodied friends lying motionless on the floor.

"Stay back," Massir said as McCutcheon moved to within three feet. "I'll shoot." M.D. took note of the details: the unsteady look in his adversary's eyes, the trembling barrel of the revolver being pointed at his face, the white of his enemy's knuckles that were not quite white enough considering the caliber size of the weapon in his hand.

"I'll give you one more chance," M.D. offered.

"You're giving me a chance?" the Somalian said. "I'm the one who has the..."

Then it happened, quick as a flash.

Before the next three weeks were over the only two rules McCutcheon had set for himself—no killing; reunite with Kaitlyn—would be violently and viciously broken.

THREE

"**I** told you it had leather seats."

As the white minivan sailed through the night, Massir made eye contact with McCutcheon through the rectangular rearview mirror from his belted-up position in the backseat. His retina could have been detached. Blood could have been leaking from gashes on his face. He could have been missing his incisors, the ability to grip a pencil, or a functioning windpipe.

But he wasn't. Massir El-Alhou was as healthy as he had been when the evening first began.

Aside from the small bit of discomfort he experienced from the black flexicuff twist tie locks keeping his wrists bound behind his back, there wasn't a scratch on him. Disarming a computer geek, who thought that merely raising a gun was the same thing as attacking someone with a gun, required very little skill from M.D. A strike, a step, a slash, and the revolver went skittering, unfired, across the hookah bar's floor. McCutcheon's biggest challenge had come from showing restraint instead of aggression.

"Let me know if you want me to turn on the air,"

M.D. said. "We probably won't be there for another thirty minutes."

Massir replied with a grunt. Of course if the North African had been thinking clearly he probably would have shown a bit more appreciation to McCutcheon, because the next destination on his journey was sure to be filled with people who weren't going to be nearly as considerate of his comfort. Captured domestic terror suspects were more likely to have their testicles electrified than they were to be offered leather seats and climate control.

The white minivan cruised down the highway, maintaining an average speed of sixty-seven. Going two miles per hour over the speed limit enabled McCutcheon to keep up with the light flow of traffic, but it wasn't too fast to draw the attention of any state troopers. Though he was on a mission for the U.S. government it wasn't like M.D. owned a badge, and being pulled over for driving too fast would have been amateurish.

McCutcheon always worked hard to pay attention to the small details. Though he'd never been introduced to any of his peers in the world of covert ops—because Stanzer always kept M.D. isolated and independent—he'd been told he was the youngest member on any of the underground teams. To M.D. this meant that he'd get cut the least amount of slack when it came to youthful mistakes. It was a world where a kid was not allowed to be a kid, but for McCutcheon this was not that big of a deal. Ever since he took on the role of being the breadwinner for his family at age eleven, it had always been this way. He'd been fighting in gloveless cage wars for years knowing that suffering a loss didn't just mean a chink on his record and a busted body; it meant his baby sister didn't eat.

Pressure breaks many fighters. Others it lifts to unprecedented heights.

M.D. also understood that good reasons existed for Stanzer to keep him separated from everyone else. That's because everything about McCutcheon's work was illegal. More than just illegal; entirely unconstitutional. Putting the lives of teens at risk in order to hunt domestic enemies might have made sense on the battlefield, but it would never wash on the halls of the Senate floor. If word got out about Agent ZERO X1, heads would roll. First among them, Stanzer's.

"You are an experiment, a disposable trial, which, if Uncle Sam has to cut loose, he will. Any problems with that, son?"

"If you're gonna be able to sleep at night, Colonel, so am I," M.D. replied.

Stanzer smiled. "You like playing in the big leagues, don't ya?"

"I don't know if *like* is the right word. A part of me feels as if, well . . . I was born to do this. Like I'm fulfilling my destiny."

Stanzer nodded. Partly out of admiration for his protégé, partly because he felt exactly the same way.

Thirty-three minutes after the white minivan departed the parking lot of Mystic Wonders, McCutcheon approached the clandestine command center where he'd been instructed to deliver his prey. He noted the details of the building: an optometrist's office, a box-and-ship store, a nail salon, and two office spaces still for lease, each and every business not yet open for the day. M.D. had been sent to a very specific location that was noteworthy only for how commonplace it appeared. It was exactly the type of unremarkable, forgettable destination black op officers loved to use when they ended people's existence and wiped them entirely off the map.

But this was Massir's karma, M.D. thought, not his. McCutcheon had completed his assignment, prevailed without serious injury, and through the apprehension of Massir El-Alhou, probably just saved scores of American lives.

Kids who never even knew they were in danger had just been made more safe. This, M.D. felt, was work worth doing. If the mission wasn't honorable, he refused to take it on.

M.D. parked the minivan in an underground parking garage, grabbed the laptop he'd confiscated, and led Massir to the service elevator. As the doors opened on the third floor, Stanzer appeared, his ice-blue eyes processing data even before McCutcheon had escorted his target completely out of the elevator car.

"The CyberFang of Al-Shabaab. Welcome." Stanzer reached out and twisted Massir's face, turned it side to side as if he was inspecting a horse. "No engagement?" he asked surprised to see unblemished features.

"No need."

"He didn't fight?" Stanzer asked.

"He had a gun." McCutcheon reached around to the small of his back and handed the revolver he'd taken from Massir over to the colonel. "But then he didn't."

"Was he alone?"

"Two others. Neither on our list. With them there was engagement," McCutcheon said. "But it was brief."

Stanzer didn't ask any further questions about the two others because he didn't need to. He knew McCutcheon well enough to understand that a couple of bodies lay broken somewhere.

"You take any shots?"

"They took more."

"Let me see."

"I'm fine."

The colonel glared. He wasn't going to ask again.

McCutcheon opened his jacket, hoisted his shirt, and showed Stanzer his ribs. A giant splotch, the size of a dinner plate with streaks of purple and black covered the side of McCutcheon's chest.

"Those ribs are broken."

"Maybe not."

"Cracked for sure."

M.D. allowed his shirt to fall back down over his body. "I also secured his computer and phone."

"All right, you," Stanzer said turning to Massir. "Come."

The three men walked twenty-five feet down a quiet hallway that gave the impression that nothing of significance went on behind any of its boring brown doors and stopped at Suite 253. Stanzer turned the silver handle to the right and the three entered. The door closed behind them and the quietude of the corridor gave way to a burst of feverish activity.

Agents swarmed. Some wore suits, a few wore jeans or khakis, and screens of laptops, cells, tablets, and desktops glowed like digital fireflies inside of a rectangular conference room.

Two athletic-looking men in navy-blue blazers raced up to Massir and roughly hooded his head with a black cloak. Neither showed a hint of concern about having jammed an accidental palm into Massir's nose as they secured the bag around his neck. Eyes shrouded, vision eliminated, the disorientation of the Somalian's senses began immediately.

An office chair rolled up next. It smashed behind Massir's knees, and arms the North African never saw forced Massir downward by his shoulders into a hard gray seat. Three more agents, efficient and precise, raced to the government's new prize with urgency. One tied down Massir's left arm, another tied down his right, and out came a sequence of sterilized hypodermic needles. The first took blood; the second administered a barbiturate. In less than sixty seconds they tubed three blood samples, landed ten fingerprints, and snipped enough hairs from the North African's forearm to archive his DNA.

Restraints around the waist, a collar around the neck, and a pair of black earmuffs—large and almost cartoonish in size—that muted all sound were placed over the sides of

Massir's hooded head. Just like that the CyberFang of Al-Shabaab had been drugged, vacuum-packed, and readied for transport.

"Spooky, huh?" said a blond-haired, barrel-chested man who'd sidled up next to McCutcheon.

"Such is the fate of those that would fuck with us," Stanzer answered. "Come on. Let's go get those ribs looked at."

As Stanzer walked M.D. over to the on-site medic, a door in the back of the conference room flew open and a team of six agents wheeled Massir off to a place where McCutcheon would never see him again.

Most, in fact, would never see Massir again. Not his family, his friends, his government diplomats, and most assuredly not his network of online radicals. The only connected device Massir El-Alhou would touch in the next ten years would be a light switch.

A female doctor approached.

"Show her," Stanzer said. McCutcheon's eyes answered the request with a look that said *I'm fine.* "Show her," Stanzer repeated.

With the grace of a cougar McCutcheon hopped up on a table and lifted his shirt.

"Ouch," said the doctor in an attempt to be sympathetic when she saw the giant bruise. "On a scale from one to ten, with ten being the highest, what number would you assign to your pain?"

"No offense, doctor, but I'd just like to grab my grub and get some nutrition in me. Beyond that, I'm good."

"Give her a number," the colonel said.

"You bring me spinach or arugula?"

"Would you give the doctor a number please?"

"One."

"An injury like that is only a one?" the doctor asked. Ribs that had been smashed like M.D.'s made it painful to even breathe, much less gracefully hop up on a table. "That's gotta be at least, I dunno, an eight."

"No, I would like to start by eating one decent meal, please. It's been a while since I've had any decent food. Plus, I had to smoke. Disgusting."

"Why do you have to be so difficult?" Stanzer asked. "She's a licensed doctor; let her treat you."

McCutcheon rolled his eyes.

"Take a nonsteroidal anti-inflammatory every six hours, alternate ice and heat, refrain from heavy lifting, get rest, try not to cough, and if there's blood in your urine or stool come back for an X-ray immediately. Am I close?" M.D. said.

The doctor nodded. "Young man might take my job one day."

"Young man might take all our jobs one day," Stanzer replied. "But until that moment comes I'm still the boss. Can't you tape him up or something?"

"They don't really tape"/ "We don't really use tape any more," M.D. and the doctor replied at the same time.

"He's a little old school," McCutcheon explained to the lady physician. "Now, can I have my salad please?"

"It's four seventeen in the morning, son. Where in the world am I supposed to get you a salad at this hour?"

"From that green and white Whole Foods shopping bag sitting next to your briefcase on the counter at oh-eight-hundred."

All eyes turned to the grocery bag sitting on the other side of the room.

"And why would you suspect there's a salad in there for you?" Stanzer asked.

"Why else would there even be a Whole Foods bag in this room right now?" McCutcheon answered.

M.D. hopped off the counter and crossed the room. "The only thing I am not sure about is if you brought me spinach or arugula."

McCutcheon opened the bag and removed a fresh green salad. "Kale?" he said popping it open. "Keeping me on my toes, huh?" McCutcheon fished a fork out of the bag and took a nice big bite. "You want some superfoods, Colonel?" he offered, extending a fork. "They're good for you."

"Son, if God intended me to eat that shit he would not have invented Philly cheesesteaks."

"Or nachos," said the tall, barrel-chested man who'd sidled up to McCutcheon a few moments earlier. "Hello son. Name's Puwolsky. Colonel Nathan Puwolsky. Nice to meet you."

Puwolsky extended his arm for a shake. McCutcheon, mid-chew, looked to the colonel before returning the gesture. Agent ZERO X1 wasn't supposed to be making friends. Ghosts like him didn't even exist.

"I'm sorry," Stanzer said, stepping in front of his soldier. "Don't take this the wrong way, but who the fuck are you?"

"I just told you, name's Puwolsky. But I'm not here for you, Colonel. I'm here for the kid."

McCutcheon remained wordless.

"And unfortunately, son, I bring some very bad news."

FOUR

A cold moment hung in the air between the two colonels. Puwolsky owned a strong frame. Looked like a former tight end who played Division I college football at some point in his life. Big hands, wide shoulders, an air of cockiness about him.

Stanzer possessed the skill set to rip the tongue from a man's head for even thinking about burping in his mug like that. He was a Krav Maga guy, a real-world situation type of soldier who didn't give a shit about style points when it came to fighting. Efficiency and brutality guided his strategy for confrontation. Make a threatening gesture toward Stanzer, and his philosophy was "neutralize and pulverize." McCutcheon knew from the way the colonel carried himself that he'd put more than a few bullets into the back of people's heads.

Stanzer was a man who knew what he was fighting for and knew why he was fighting for it. If something needed to be done it got done, fuck the collateral damage.

"I'm from the DPERS," Puwolsky said. "The Detroit

Police Elite Response Squad. They call us the Dopers, for short. I know, ironic, right?"

"You're a long way from Detroit, Doper."

"Detroit's what brings me here," Puwolsky responded. "Demon's back."

"My father?"

"Yes."

"I'm not sure you understand exactly what I am communicating to you right now, Officer Poo-Fart-Skee," Stanzer said. "Refrain from addressing my soldier. Immediately. This is the wrong place, this is the wrong time, and unless I give you the right to speak with him, you do not have it."

"Actually, these little colonel birds I wear on my shoulder give me the right to speak to this young man," Puwolsky said.

"And these little colonel birds I wear on *my* shoulder give me the right to say, 'Eat my ass.'"

The two men moved nose-to-nose, Puwolsky owning a couple of inches in height plus a couple of pounds in weight, but not an ounce when it came to what always mattered most.

Big. Furry. Balls.

"Hmm," Puwolsky said, not showing much zest to mix it up. "Two colonels, questions of jurisdiction; why don't we let the kid decide if he wants to hear? After all, it's his girl they plan to target."

"What!?" McCutcheon pushed his way around Stanzer. "What do you mean my girl?"

"Do I have your permission, Colonel?" Puwolsky asked.

It was a bullshit move executed in a bullshit way, but Stanzer knew he'd been boxed in. Tell Puwolsky to go blow, and McCutcheon would be a useless operative until the situation was resolved. Allow Puwolsky to spill his story without even knowing what McCutcheon was about to hear, and all sorts of cans of worms might be opened.

Cans of worms that might never be closed.

How many times have I told him, *You gotta slay that dragon*, thought Stanzer. And how many times had McCutcheon replied that it was already dead. *Yet at the first mention of this girl's name he pops his top like a schoolgirl?* Stanzer could only shake his head.

"Make it tight," Stanzer said. "And spare us the fluffy bullshit, would you?"

"Just remember one thing, Colonel," Puwolsky said to Stanzer. "I'm doing you a favor here, too."

"Yeah? How's that?"

"What, you think this whole thing is still a secret right now? Look around; you had fourteen people in this room tonight." Puwolsky gave a wide sweep of his arm. "You got NSA, FBI, New Jersey Department of Special Investigations. You think this many folks can keep an operation this significant on the down low? Lid's been blown on your whole little teenage soldier program since your third high-profile snatch—that wanna-be mall bomber in Portland. Shit, a guy as smart as you thinking Bam Bam Daniels is still under the radar? How delusional are you?"

Stanzer didn't respond because he knew it could be true. He'd done all that he could to keep the Murk off the grid, but the more impressive M.D.'s work became the harder it was to keep the cat in the bag. Stanzer, like all officers, had bosses, too. Bosses who liked to boast, bosses who liked to drink, and bosses who liked to secure more funds to finance their most successful programs by drinking and boasting in the private clubs of Washington, D.C., where they lobbied for extra funding. More teams with more teens had been floated down Stanzer's pipeline by the brass above a few times already. If there was one kid from the ghetto who could pull off these sort of missions, perhaps there were more.

"Not so lippy, are you now?" Puwolsky said to Stanzer. "That's because you know if this shit spins the wrong way, you'll get slammed so hard it'll feel like you've been gang-banged by federal gorillas."

Stanzer's eyes narrowed, but McCutcheon quickly intervened, determined to hear the news. "What's the situation, sir?"

Puwolsky, knowing he had his audience right where he wanted them, began."Ask yourself, on the streets of Detroit, who has the most soldiers? Who has the most guns? Who has the largest war chest?" he said. "That's right, the Priests. And in jail, they have the largest army, too. But one-on-one, they're getting their asses kicked."

"What does this have to do with Kaitlyn?"

"Or his father?" Stanzer asked.

"Fuck my father," M.D. snapped. "Tell me about Kaitlyn."

"They're tied together," Puwolsky explained. "Your dad got pinched and sent for a bid to the same jail where D'Marcus Rose is also serving time. You know the name D'Marcus Rose, don't you?"

"I do," M.D. replied. "He's the High Priest who put out the hit out on my family."

"Correct," Puwolsky said. "And they're both in Jentles State Prison right now, a.k.a. the D.T. Nickname stands for the Devil's Toilet. Place is downright inhumane, but since nobody has two hundred and fifty million dollars to build a new penitentiary, and no one in society really gives a fuck about what happens to these street animals once they get locked up, it's a world where anything goes."

"So?" McCutcheon asked.

"So they got this sick guard staging gladiator wars between all the rival gangs, and some cat from Brooklyn is fighting for the Princes of Mayhem, the Priests' biggest rivals in the state of Michigan. Can't nobody touch him. They call him—"

"The Brooklyn Beast," M.D. said, filling in the blanks.

"You've heard of him, I see," Puwolsky said.

"You could say that," McCutcheon replied. Back when M.D. was being pimped out by his father to fight in Detroit's underground cage fighting wars, the Priests had set up a blockbuster fight, Bam Bam versus the Brooklyn Beast, a war to prove once and for all who the best really was. But the battle never happened because the Brooklyn

Beast got pinched for armed robbery just before the show-down was about to occur.

"There's lots of money involved," Puwolsky continued. "But more than that, a gang lives by its rep, and with the Priests being punked time after time, it's affecting their street cred. Which could affect their business operations. Which is a multimillion dollar criminal enterprise. And so when Demon gets tossed into the tank, the High Priest doesn't want the money he's owed anymore. He wants a fighter who can win for the Priests. In other words, he wants you."

"But since his father doesn't have him," Stanzer deduced, "Demon offers up the next best thing he can in order to save his own ass."

"Exactly. He tells the High Priest that he knows how to flush you out," Puwolsky said. "Demon told the High Priest that the way to get Bam Bam is to go after his girl."

"What exactly does that mean, 'Go after my girl'?" M.D. asked.

"With the Priests," Puwolsky replied, "you don't want to know."

McCutcheon, lost in thought, rubbed his chin.

"And how'd you find out about this?" Stanzer asked.

"Wave hello, Oscar," Puwolsky said.

A thick-necked guy sitting in a swivel chair staring at a computer monitor raised his arm and waggled his middle finger at Puwolsky.

"That's Oscar Larson," Puwolsky said. "I work with his brother, Dickey Larson, back in Detroit. The Priests floated a balloon to our side of the fence, got a message to Dickey that unless Bam Bam resurfaced within the next seven days they were gonna, well, like I said, you don't want to know. However..."

"However what?" Stanzer asked.

Puwolsky smiled a big shit-eating grin. "This is fucking perfect."

FIVE

op martial artists always operate from a space of inner peace. The world outside can be swimming in chaos, but to the devoted practioner of the warrior's path, the way is best walked in a calm and balanced manner. Just as seas may rage with waves and choppiness on the surface, underneath the ocean is always steady and serene.

It's one of the reasons McCutcheon always felt so confident in his ability to ultimately triumph. On the outside he was strong, but on the inside he felt immovable.

Until Kaitlyn. She became the lever that opened a swirling drain.

"Is my sister safe?" M.D. asked. Roughly ten months earlier the FBI had offered M.D. a take-it-or-leave-it ultimatum: your sister or your girl? McCutcheon chose his sister. Was it the right choice? Absolutely.

McCutcheon had raised Gemma, protected Gemma, and sacrificed for Gemma. His six-year-old sister always came first. Her dimpled face, her lopsided pigtails, the way she could make M.D. giggle and smile and laugh when the rest of the world only wanted bone and blood and flesh.

Gemma's well-being was the only thing that had gotten M.D. through all those long nights of training, all those brutal poundings, and all those nasty, gloveless wars on all those violent Saturday nights.

Your sister or your girl? Was his sister the right choice? Absolutely. Then again, he always wondered why it had to be either/or.

He wanted them both.

"I have no idea about your sister," Puwolsky replied. "Only Stanzer knows your family's whereabouts. Just a stroke of pure coincidence that I even found you."

M.D. turned to Stanzer.

"She's safe," the colonel affirmed. "Your mom, too. But your use of the word *perfect*, Colonel," Stanzer said, directing his attention at Puwolsky, "is a bit puzzling."

"You're correct; nothing's perfect," Puwolsky admitted. "But this is damn good. Gives us a chance to slip an agent inside the D.T. and break this whole thing wide open."

"Not sure I follow," Stanzer said.

"Ever since Detroit went bankrupt, things have gone to hell. Crime is up, schools are down, and they keep slashing our police department budget in ways that make it impossible to function. My guys' cop cars," he said, "they don't get oil changes. Ain't got no money. And what happens to a car that don't get its oil changed? Fucking engine seizes. Feels like we got more vehicles sitting in the shop than we do on the street, so my guys, they buy their own Quaker State. And they get pink-slipped anyway. R.I.F. notices come every three months. You know, Reduction in Force. Whole thing is bullshit."

The passion of Puwolsky's words turned his cheeks red. As the man in charge of overseeing a special forces unit whose primary goal was to keep the Motor City safe, the colonel's team had been through the ringer. Fewer officers meant fewer arrests, which meant more violent offenders on the streets, which meant more victims on the crime ledgers and more bodies in the morgue.

"We've always felt like we've had to operate with our finger in a dam," Puwolsky said. "Now we got our dicks in it, too."

Puwolsky sniffed his nose, rubbed a meaty paw over his chin and got to the real reason he'd traveled to New Jersey in the first place.

"We want you," Puwolsky said to McCutcheon, "to assassinate the High Priest."

Neither McCutcheon or Stanzer replied.

"Like I said, it's almost perfect," the colonel continued. "They're fucking asking for you, and this D'Marcus guy, he's gotten too large, too big, he's in control of too much," Puwolsky said, growing more and more animated. "We need to decentralize power. When the gangs war within themselves or war with one another, it's the soldiers who die. However, when they're unified, it's the civilians who pay." Puwolsky flashed soft eyes. "Like your friends David Klowner and Nathan Wachowski from your MMA gym. Like your girlfriend Kaitlyn Cummings. This guy, the High

Priest, he's like a fucking terrorist, and right now you're the only one who can end his reign."

"Might I remind you that murder is illegal?" Stanzer said.

"Everything you're doing is illegal, Colonel," Puwolsky replied. "The question is, would it be immoral?"

McCutcheon didn't speak. Didn't reveal any emotion. Didn't touch his salad, either.

"Just think about it a sec," Puwolsky said. "You get to eliminate an enemy of the state, you get to avenge the murder of your friends, and you get to save the life of your girl. Whaddya say?"

"No," he said.

SIX

Puwolsky spent the next twenty minutes firing below-the-belt shots saying anything he could to coerce McCutcheon into accepting the mission.

He appealed to M.D.'s sense of duty.

"This is what agents like you do. They deliver justice to the dark corners of our country, where the courts can't reach."

He appealed to his sense of guilt.

"Why do you even think your friends Klowner and Nate-Neck are dead? Because of you! 'Cause you never let 'em know what was really going on with the Priests the night of your last fight. You got 'em to be your cornermen and they paid for their friendship and loyalty with their lives. And you just let that slide like some little bitch? Own it, son. Their blood is on your head."

He appealed to McCutcheon's sense of heroism.

"Detroit needs a champion. Detroit needs someone who is willing to step up on behalf of all the good and decent people who are being terrorized in this city. Aren't you a victim of that terror? Didn't you come from the

ghetto, the belly of that beast? And now you're going to turn your back on all those little kids, on all those helpless mothers, on all the people who need someone to fight for them because they do not have the power or ability to fight for themselves? Kid, you may be one of the baddest mixed martial artists in the history of the sport, but deep down underneath it's pretty clear to me that you're nothin' but a little sissy bitch."

Puwolsky came at McCutcheon with every hurtful arrow he could fire. And Stanzer just sat there letting M.D. take it. He didn't intervene. He didn't stand up for his man. He didn't once say the words, "All right, that's enough."

Why? Because this was M.D.'s dragon and no one else could slay it for him.

"You have my answer," McCutcheon said in a polite and even tone. "May I be excused, sir?"

His cheeks flushed, Puwolsky snorted, pissed that he'd gotten nowhere. *What the hell is wrong with this kid?* he wondered.

"You may," Stanzer said to McCutcheon. "I'll be in touch."

M.D. exited the building and walked to the downtown bus station, knowing that two other agents had already scrubbed and ditched the rented white minivan. His mission done, it was time to head home.

If he could even call it that. Bellevue, Nebraska, was about as different from Detroit, Michigan, as orange juice was from a kangaroo.

McCutcheon preferred taking the bus back to the Corn-husker State as opposed to an airplane because the long ride gave him a chance to sleep, think, and recover. As he settled into a window seat and tossed his hoodie over his head, M.D. reflected on all the venomous things Puwolsky had said.

None of it bothered him. Sure, the colonel's words were harsh, but no one had harsher words for McCutcheon than McCutcheon had for himself. On the inside, M.D. understood something about who he was, a truth so raw that it made Puwolsky's words pack all the punch of cotton candy.

McCutcheon owned secrets. Dark little dirty ones he kept hidden from the rest of the world. He found them so terrible he felt ashamed to even acknowledge their existence.

Deep down, and I hate to admit it, I'm scared. I'm really, really scared.

Beneath his chiseled surface, fear, hurt, sadness, and shame swam in a cesspool of putrid inner funk.

I'm not as strong as everyone thinks. It's just an illusion. I'm actually weak and worthless. A fraud.

The Noble Warrior mask I wear is a lie. People think I am good and decent, but I know the real truth is I'm just a worthless piece of shit. Savage, violent, and guilty of having done many horrible, hurtful things.

The Greyhound made its way east on Interstate I-80 as the inner tape recorder playing inside McCutcheon's head spun round and round on its negative loop.

I suck, I'm scared, and in this cruel and brutal world I

am all alone. But that's what I deserve. Because I'm hideous, I'm a monster.

The rain tapped against the window next to his head, soft plops playing a gentle lullaby, but Mother Nature's peaceful music did nothing to calm McCutcheon's storming soul. A map of scars across M.D.'s flesh told the violent tale of a life lived at war, and provided all the evidence McCutcheon needed to prove to himself that any emotional pain he suffered was all much deserved. He looked at his hands, large, scarred, and raw. Each lesion came from a different battle, each gash occurred during a different era, yet all of them were united by a common thread.

Bam Bam Daniels destroyed people. This was his gift. Not music. Not poetry. Not photography, painting, or graphic design. McCutcheon's talent came in the form of delivering pain. Deep in his heart he wanted the opposite. M.D. hoped to help people. To heal them and protect them and make them feel safe and secure in a way that he never was.

This is why he joined Stanzer's unit. McCutcheon hungered to bring justice, light, freedom, and protection to the world because these things were always absent from his own life, and he knew how much people who didn't have these things starved for them.

Yet now he was being asked to kill.

Why did all of his good intentions end up in a sewer of piss and garbage? Only one answer made sense.

Because I'm trash. A worthless kid from the ghetto who deserves all the horrible suffering he gets.

McCutcheon clutched on to another buried secret, as well. One worse than any other. In his heart he believed beyond a shadow of a doubt that if he ever did take his first life it would lead to the taking of many, many more.

If I taste the blood of death, it's over. I know me. It will be all over.

Bury enough anger in a warrior's heart and like gunpowder it one day explodes.

You can't do it, M.D., McCutcheon told himself. *You can't. A single death will lead to dominoes, and only I can contain myself.*

No, he would not kill. Not even for Kaitlyn.

After eighteen hours and forty-five minutes, the silver Greyhound cruised across the Iowa border and entered Nebraska. Sleep escaped McCutcheon the entire trip. Too many thoughts. Too many concerns. Too many worries.

Too much awareness of the idea that most people become the thing they fear the most.

SEVEN

"**D**oc's home! Doc's home!"

McCutcheon's baby sister Gemma rushed to M.D. and threw her arms around his neck with a giant squeeze.

Gemma loved Bellevue, Nebraska. She loved the swing sets at the parks, the pies at the diner, and all the nice neighbors who never scowled and only locked their doors at night.

But most of all she loved Doc. He was the big brother who tickled her tummy, did push-ups with her sitting on his back, and had gotten them out of D-town. Escaping the projects of Detroit used to be their mantra, their chorus, their dream.

"*Who's tough?*"

"*I'm tough.*"

"*How tough?*"

"*So tough.*"

"*And why are we tough?*" McCutcheon would ask, a steely look in his eye.

"*'Cause that's the way we get out.*"

"*Gimme a kiss,*" M.D. would say, and Gemma would peck him on the cheek.

They'd spoken these words to each other a thousand times. When their father stole the grocery money for drugs and left them with nothing but ketchup in the refrigerator for dinner. When their mother disappeared from their lives without a note, a wave, or even a hug good-bye. When birthdays came and there was no money for presents, when snow came and there was no money for coats, when the storms of life crashed down on them, and there were no adults anywhere to provide safety and protection, they'd speak these words to each other because these words were all they possessed.

Somehow, like Jack's magic beans in the fairy tale, they'd worked. Gemma and M.D. did get out, and when it came to Detroit, Gemma prayed nightly that she'd never go back.

McCutcheon, of course, felt differently about the matter.

"Wanna see my habitat? Do ya, do ya?" Gemma, still in her koala bear jammies, pulled her brother by the arm and dragged him into her yellow and pink bedroom. With M.D. home, Sarah—McCutcheon didn't call her *Mom* anymore, he called her *Sarah*—left early that morning for the pre-school where she worked as an early childhood specialist. It was Back-to-School night there and a thousand things still remained needing to be done.

It's true that Sarah once abandoned her kids, but she said she only did so in order to save her own life. Maybe theirs, too. Back in Detroit, Demon was turning his son into a savage cage warrior, and once some real money started to roll in from M.D.'s underground battles, Sarah stopped being a fan. Too violent. Too dangerous. Too illegal.

But Demon only saw stacks of green, and when push came to shove, he put a knife to his wife's neck and said "Leave or be carved." High on a combo of speed, coke, and booze, he'd do it, she knew. As a former boxer who grew up in a violent home himself, Demon had been knocking Sarah around for years. Even hospitalized her a few times. To call the police seemed stupid to Sarah, though. Cops in Detroit weren't even able to keep up with all the murders, so how were they going to help with a tiny little domestic dispute?

With nowhere to turn, no one to phone, Sarah fled. Just packed a hasty bag and disappeared, fearing for her life.

When the FBI finally found her, Sarah leaped at the opportunity to rejoin her kids and enter into the Witness Security Program; she was thrilled at the idea of getting a second chance to be with her children. McCutcheon expected to adore having his mother back in his life.

He didn't.

People fight for what they love, M.D. thought. And she ran. If she really did care for her kids she would have been willing to die for them. Just like M.D. was willing to die for Gemma. But spooked, Sarah turned tail and bailed to go save herself, and as a result McCutcheon and Gemma went through years of abusive hell. The next time they did see their mom, Sarah had put the broken pieces of her life back together, landed a new job, and scored herself a cushy downtown condominium with a panoramic view of the skyline.

Good for her, M.D. thought. Really fucking happy for ya, Mom.

In Bellevue, the Daniels's town house boasted trimmed hedges, a nicely painted red front door, and a flower bed near the entryway that made the outside appear charming. Yet it was all a facade. Behind that nicely painted red front door, wars raged.

"You fucking left us."

"Yes, I did."

"Picked up and ran."

"I have no defense."

"Real mothers don't do that. Selfish, horrible mothers do."

"You think I don't feel guilty?" Sarah said. "I've felt it every day since the moment I left."

"Don't make this about you. You're a piece of shit."

"You're angry," she said, tears pouring from her eyes. "But also," Sarah lowered her head, "you're right. I'm a terrible mother, an awful person, Doc."

"Don't call me that. Only one person is ever allowed to call me that and it's not you. Got me . . . Sarah?"

McCutcheon's mother didn't try to defend her actions. She hated herself for taking them. When the family first moved to Nebraska, Sarah tried to put on a brave face. Tried to pretend the past was the past and that the family could move forward with smiles in their hearts toward a bigger, brighter future. But deep down she knew her cowardice had caused McCutcheon and Gemma incredible, unforgettable pain.

Good mothers don't protect themselves at the expense of their children. Good mothers, good people, she knew, do what's right despite how hard it might be. Gemma may have been too young to understand all of this—but not M.D.

He'd lived it. And he loathed her for it.

Every time McCutcheon thought about his mother's decision, anger surged in his heart. From this rage he felt strength—battle strength—yet he knew that drawing ferocity from the toxic well of anger would end badly. Drinking from the cup of hate never ended in positive outcomes. Yet still his fury flowed, a silent rage that quietly but constantly fed his shackled inner beast.

He didn't have to look hard to see how his monster had been born. He and the beast were at war and yet, they were one.

Before five weeks had passed in their new life—a life filled with safe playgrounds, and nary a sound of gunfire—McCutcheon and Sarah spent almost no time together. The happy reunion each one envisioned turned out to be fantasy. Delusional dreams the two held while apart, gave way to the reality of being together. McCutcheon did not respect his mom and she did not respect herself, so when one of them was home, the other would find a convenient excuse to leave.

Like departing extra early in the morning to go prepare for Back-to-School night.

You fight for what you love, McCutcheon believed. *You fight for it to the death.*

Then a question crossed M.D.'s mind.

But do you kill for it? Dying for something and killing for something are not the same thing.

"I was gonna make a desert habitat, but I made a jungle habitat instead, although I could have done something with fish." Gemma held up a shoe box she'd converted into the plains of Africa as McCutcheon tried to shake the fog of his wandering thoughts from his head. "Desert is spelled with one S. Dessert has two. That's because everybody loves dessert so the word is longer 'cause there's more of it and I think my lion is really cool, don't you? Are you taking me to school today?"

"I am," McCutcheon answered, trying to keep up with Gemma's constant stream of words.

"Well, we need to be on time because Mrs. Regali is a stickler for being on time, and she's a stickler for capital letters, too, but in math it's okay to make mistakes as long as you learn from them. I'm gonna go brush my teeth. You didn't say you liked my habitat."

"I do."

"And my lion?" Gemma asked.

"King of the jungle, right?"

"Reminds me of you."

McCutcheon wrinkled his brow.

"Strong, handsome, wants good things in the world for other creatures, and always tries to be polite," Gem responded. "Other than to zebras. Lions eat zebras but

53

even though you don't eat any zebras, you still try to be polite like a lion, Doc."

"No, I do not eat zebras," M.D. said with a smile. His six-year-old sister always saw the best in him. But if she only knew the truth, he thought.

"You don't even eat pizza," she added.

"I am gonna eat you if you don't hurry up," M.D. said.

Gemma rushed back into the arms of her big brother. "One more hug," she said, squeezing M.D. tight. "I missed you, Doc."

"I wasn't gone that long."

"A day without my brother is like a day without the sky. I wrote that in my journal. Are you staying a long, long, long, long time before your next trip?"

"I'm not sure if there are going to be any more trips, Gem."

"Yay!" she exclaimed as the doorbell rang.

"Now hustle up and go get dressed before the mighty lion has to use his CLAWS!"

McCutcheon picked Gem up and spun her around with a *whoosh*. Her smiled beamed a thousand watts as M.D. whirled her like a toy. Nowhere did Gem feel more safe than in the arms of her brother. Many kids had siblings; Gemma had her own private wolf.

Gemma bounced off to the bathroom to get washed and brushed for school as M.D. crossed to answer the front door. In Detroit, M.D. always looked through the peephole before answering. In Bellevue, without dope fiends or thugs to worry about, he didn't see the point.

"'Morning."

McCutcheon exhaled a sigh. "That was quick."

"You're the one who takes the bus. I fly."

"You've come to convince me?"

Stanzer stepped through the doorway.

"Actually," he replied, "just the opposite."

EIGHT

cCutcheon left Stanzer back at the town house and walked Gemma to school. Cruising to class hand-in-hand had always been their special time together. The colonel had already stolen enough of their hours this month. He could wait.

As Gemma blabbed away about motorized scooters, cats, and pancakes, M.D. tried to still his mind and stay in the present moment. He knew the right answer about what to do would come to him. If he trusted himself.

Easier said than done.

"And of course a squirrel is going to choose a peanut over a taco. Really, how obvious is that?"

McCutcheon grinned. "You're not too old to still give your brother a kiss good-bye, are you?"

"You can have ten of them," Gemma answered as they arrived at the front gate of Crested Ridge Elementary. She began counting; between each number his sister smacked her lips against M.D.'s cheek. "One, *peck,* two, *peck,* three, *peck,* four, *peck,* five, *peck,* six, *peck,* seven, *peck,* eight, *peck,* nine, *peck,* ten, *peck.*"

Gemma's smile shined like a second sun in the morning air. And so did McCutcheon's, although his was accompanied by a brief sadness as he realized it was the first ear-to-ear beam he'd felt on his face in far too many days.

"Okay, go fill up your brain. See ya at three."

"WAIT!" Gemma exclaimed. "I forgot to tell you, I got my first wiggly." Gemma opened her mouth and proudly showed off her first loose tooth. "G'head. Feel."

McCutcheon gently examined Gemma's mouth.

"Wow," M.D. said. "Before you know it the Tooth Fairy will be here."

"And I want a hundred bucks."

"What?" M.D. said. "Setting your sights a little high, aren't you?"

"First tooth, doesn't get more special."

"Well, that's between you and the Tooth Fairy," McCutcheon replied.

"You watch, Doc," Gemma said as she got ready to head inside. "I betchya she comes through for me. I can just feel it in my bones."

Her purple backpack bouncing up and down, Gemma skipped through the school's front door. McCutcheon wanted to join her. Wanted to rewind the clock on his life, return to being in first grade and enter into a clean, safe classroom himself, the future a blank slate and a place where having a loose tooth didn't come as the result of someone having loosened it for you with their foot or their fist.

M.D. idled home, in no rush to talk with Stanzer.

Though he tried to remain calm, he found himself hunting in vain for an answer about what he should do.

Action always felt easier to him than waiting.

When McCutcheon approached his front door, he found Stanzer sitting on the wooden bench in front of his town house eating leftover lasagna from a plastic container.

"Your mom's a great cook."

"I make my own meals."

"Still tension between you two, huh?"

"Just feel free to raid our fridge any time you like."

"I guess that's a yes." Stanzer rose from his seat and licked his fork clean. "You realize she's happy I'm eating this, don't you? Good cooks appreciate good eaters. Whether she admits it or not, she wants me to gobble these goodies."

"Always in people's heads, aren't you?"

"Come on, let's walk."

Stanzer set the empty Tupperware on the arm of the bench and led M.D. down the driveway. They turned right and walked down the middle of the street. People in Bellevue often walked down the middle of the street because traffic in town was minimal and drivers always slowed to wave hello to folks taking a stroll, even if they didn't know you.

In Detroit, pedestrians who walked in the middle of the street got honked at, given the bird, or run over.

One America, two different worlds.

"You're set up nice here, son. Maybe you should just

go back to high school or junior college or something. We could even get you credits at Harvard if you want."

"I bet you could," McCutcheon said.

Stanzer chuckled at the long reach of the feds. It stretched further than most U.S. citizens imagined. Background information, financial history, any and every digital transaction stood within their grasp to view, tweak, or entirely fabricate. Say the word and M.D. could be given a PhD in molecular astrophysics before Stanzer had eaten his morning muffin.

"Maybe this is why there are age limits for what we do," the colonel continued. "This whole thing, well . . . You're still a kid."

M.D. scowled.

"No offense. And no shame either," the colonel said. "Look around, this place is nice. And that little princess of yours is in hog heaven. Girl's getting big."

"Maybe *she* could move out here?" M.D. said. "You know, with the others."

Stanzer stopped. *Others?* Of course McCutcheon had figured it out, the colonel realized. M.D. was too sharp. The Daniels weren't the only family Wit Sec had ever moved to Bellevue. Sure, different locations on the national map existed, plenty of them, but when things worked well for government programs they often repeated them, and M.D. had been trained to spot small, telling details that, to a keen agent, lay all over town. The holes in people's stories. The avoidance of direct eye contact when talking about their past. The cryptic way some folks in Bellevue didn't really speak about their relatives in other cities when holiday time rolled around, or the fact that some families never hosted out of town guests for the weekend. To the untrained eye, Bellevue represented a change-of-pace type city where people found it nice to move and set up shop. To the skilled eye, however, Bellevue existed as a dumping ground for people who needed to vanish.

"She?" Stanzer asked. "She who?"

"You know who," McCutcheon replied. "If her life's in danger, then just put her in Wit Sec like you did me and let her join all the other nomads who call this town home."

"It's not that easy."

"Sure it is," M.D. replied, becoming more animated. "In fact, it'd be great. She'd already know some people, which would make the adjustment pretty smooth, and I could...well, I could even go out and get her. Like be the one to go to Detroit, explain what happened, and bring her out."

"She'll hate you for it."

"You don't know her like I do. You don't know what we have."

"You mean had."

Anger flashed in M.D.'s eyes. He refused to believe his relationship with Kaitlyn only existed in the past tense.

"You're living in a fantasy world, son," Stanzer said. "And you need to slay this dragon before it slays you."

"It's not a fantasy."

"You're delusional."

"I love her, sir. And she loves me, too."

"How long's it been since you've even had a conversation with this girl?" Stanzer asked. "Since you looked her in the eye? Held her hand?"

"I made a mistake," M.D. said. "And I believe once I explain it all to her, she'll take me back."

"I'm not going to argue logic with someone who is being entirely irrational."

"That's the beauty of love, sir," M.D. said. "The fact that on one hand it makes no sense at all and yet on the other it makes all the sense in the world."

Stanzer grunted. "Very poetic."

"Not just poetic, true."

"It's like talking to a fucking wall right now."

"Please." M.D. looked at Stanzer with soft eyes. "I've done everything you've asked. Can you just do this for me? Can you put Kaitlyn in Wit Sec?"

Stanzer rubbed his chin and considered his response. As the colonel deliberated his next words, visions of how wonderful life could be floated through McCutcheon's head. Sunsets on the hill. Friday nights sharing ice cream. Gemma getting a big sister of sorts.

Kaitlyn moving to Bellevue would be an unequivocal home run.

"You are so fucking delusional I don't even know where to begin. Why you don't get this?" Stanzer threw up his hands. "You think some girl you haven't seen in ten months is gonna just want to up and leave her life to move to corn-loving Nebraska in order to play a game of puppy love with

61

the kid who turned her into a target for murder? What about her family? Her friends? Her entire goddamn life? Kids like her don't go into Wit Sec."

"But kids like me do?" McCutcheon said.

"Her father went to college with the fucking lieutenant governor. Families like that, shit works different."

"So what are you trying to say?"

"I'm trying to say that you gotta let this girl go. Take yourself off the hook for whatever might happen to her. Maybe take a year or two off from our unit, too."

"You're cutting me loose?"

"I have no more assignments for you. Go clear your head. Get your spirit right and then see if what we're doing is still what you really want to do in life. You've been spared so far, but at some point every last one of us who does this kind of work gets bloody with stains that don't wash off."

"I know what you're doing," M.D. said. "This reverse psychology shit you are pulling. You're telling me not to go because you know that it's going to make me want to go even more."

Stanzer shook his head. "Unbelievable," he muttered.

"'Cause you know I gotta do this," McCutcheon said. "Because if something happens to Kaitlyn, that's more blood on my hands. Like I already don't have enough."

"That is not what I am saying at all."

"Tell your boy Puwolsky, I'm in."

"He's not my boy."

"Tell him I'm in."

Stanzer reached out and grabbed M.D. by the arm. "McCutcheon, listen to me."

M.D. scowled at the colonel, his eyes clearly sending the message, *Take your hands off of me.*

Stanzer released his grip.

"Listen, son," the colonel said in a softer voice. "This thing they are asking you to do, I can't find out squat about it. All I know is, this shit's the belly of the beast."

"You don't think I can handle it?"

"What I think is that once you go into that penitentiary, the same person is not going to come back out."

"Can the cops protect her?" M.D. asked.

"In Detroit? Versus the Priests?" Stanzer shrugged. "Right now they're on her round the clock. But next week? Two weeks? A month from now?"

"Exactly," M.D. said, a disgusted look on his face.

"That's why I am saying you gotta let this girl go. Take yourself off the hook. You're not responsible for the fucked-upness of the entire city of Detroit; and this relationship you think you still have with her, it's gone. Over. Dead."

McCutcheon threw his hoodie over his head. "Downtown Detroit bus station at oh-nine-hundred the day after tomorrow. Have your boy meet me there," McCutcheon said.

Stanzer knew he couldn't control M.D. No one could. But still, he tried.

"Son, wait..."

"I have waited. Now I'm clear. And I need a hundred bucks."

M.D. extended his hand, palm side up. Stanzer scrunched his face.

"What?"

"One hundred dollars," M.D. said. "Do you have any cash?"

The colonel tilted his head sideways, not understanding the request, but McCutcheon's arm remained outstretched. M.D. was entirely serious.

After a moment of strained silence, the colonel reached into his back pocket, fished out his wallet, and counted off some bills.

"I imagine twenties will do?" Stanzer said sarcastically.

"Actually," M.D. replied, "I'd prefer a single note."

Stanzer nodded his head. "Of course you would."

The colonel squinted his eyes, fiddled around inside his wallet, and passed McCutcheon a hundred-dollar bill.

"Do I get to know what it's for?"

"The Tooth Fairy."

Stanzer folded over his wallet and put it back inside his rear pocket. "Prices have skyrocketed, I see."

"It's not the tooth I'm paying for," McCutcheon answered. "It's the heartbreak."

M.D. turned.

"Oh-nine-hundred," he repeated and then he walked away.

Next stop: prison.

NINE

Fat plops of rain pelted the sidewalk and bounced upward off the cement from under a gray and dreary sky. McCutcheon didn't bring a bag to the bus station because he knew he wouldn't need one. Prisoners enter jail like a baby enters the world: naked, traumatized, and completely dependent on another entity. Newborns get the warm and tender breast of a mother. Inmates get the cold and bitter tit of the Department of Corrections.

"Did he try to stop you?" Puwolsky asked.

"No."

"Did he tell you you'd have any support?"

"No."

"Did he go over any aspects of how to execute this mission, any strategies, plans or directives?"

"No."

Puwolsky rubbed his chin. "And you don't find this odd?"

"No."

"Why not?"

"Because Stanzer either shows one-hundred-percent

support or none at all," M.D. said. "He's an all-in or not-in type of guy. This is my thing."

Dickey Larson sniffed. "A man of principles, huh? I eat fuckers like that for breakfast."

"Kid, meet Larson, my partner in the narcotics division," Puwolsky said. "Larson, be nice and try not to foam on our friend. He's on our side, remember."

Dickey Larson stood six foot three inches, two hundred thirty pounds, and sported trapezius muscles the size of meteorites. With his hulking upper body so exceptionally disproportional to the size of his calves, and a wild, revved-up look in his eye, it took McCutcheon all of two seconds to get a bead on Puwolsky's partner. The distended stomach, the immense lats, the red-speckled acne traveling around the side of his neck and most assuredly down his back, all were telltale signs.

'Roid monster. No doubt.

"So this little twig is the fucking legend I've heard so much about?" Larson scoffed. "Gotta say, I'm sort of disappointed."

Larson circled M.D., sizing him up. He sniffed, unimpressed.

"With all the shit I've heard about you I expected you to be about seven feet tall with a thirty-inch dick."

"You were misinformed," McCutcheon said. "My penis is only half that size."

Larson took a moment to do the math and then his glower turned into a laugh.

66

"Aw, lemme have a go at the smart-ass, boss," Larson said to Puwolsky. "Before we drop him in. A beast like me deserves a crack at the champ, don't ya think?"

Larson flexed his sixteen-inch biceps like a bodybuilder showing off a championship pose and then got right up into M.D.'s face. The two locked eyes. McCutcheon had no idea who this pit bull was, but steroid users were notorious for erratic, crazed behavior. Whacked-out body chemistry plus overinflated egos, mixed with too much time staring into mirrors, wasn't psychologically healthy for anybody, and this guy Larson proved no exception to the rule. But M.D. had dealt with this kind of nonsense before. Many times. People had been challenging McCutcheon for years to fights for no other reason than they wanted to measure up against a guy with a huge rep. Most of the time, the challengers were idiots with big mouths who turned out to be all bark and no bite.

Yet occasionally M.D. would have to, like a lame horse, put a guy down. His rules about when to do so were simple: Talk all you want, but touch and you pay.

"Get yer head out of your ass, Larson, we're doing business here." Puwolsky clicked his key chain and beeped open the door to a white Cadillac Seville. The car sported a high-end enamel paint job and special edition silver rims. "Get on in. I got no time for this shit."

Larson reached for the door handle.

"Not you," Puwolsky said. "Just him."

"I thought I was goin'?"

"Negatory."

"Why?"

"Because," Puwolsky said. "Nothing personal, Larson, but sometimes you act like a brain-dead meathead and I don't want you to mess any of this up. There's too much riding on it."

"That's bullshit."

"You have other talents. Important ones, too," Puwolsky said. "But going for long, uneventful car rides is not one of them." Puwolsky nudged his head as if to say, *Trust me, I got this.* "And that's what I need this to be," Puwolsky added. "An uneventful car ride."

It took a moment but Larson let go of the door handle, stepped back, and did as he was told.

McCutcheon climbed into the Caddy and glanced around. A black-and-cream interior. A polished wood steering wheel. An all-digital panel and stitched leather seats.

"My wife's," Puwolsky explained. "She owns a waxing salon. You wouldn't believe how much women pay for their fucking eyebrows."

"I bet I wouldn't."

"You don't believe me?"

McCutcheon buckled his seat belt and waited for the car to drive away. Stanzer had lobbied, made his case, made a great many arguments to try to change McCutcheon's mind about taking this assignment, but when all was said and done, M.D. remained unmoved.

"I'm going in," he had told Stanzer.

Stanzer both disagreed and disapproved, but finally relented. "I guess no man can save another from himself."

"I'm the one who has to live with the decision. I'm the one who has to live in this skin."

"*Live* being the key word," Stanzer replied. "But I guess you gotta do what you gotta do." The colonel extended his arm for a shake. "Good luck, son. You know how to find me if ever you need me. My door is always open."

Those were the last words Stanzer spoke to McCutcheon before he had walked away.

A little melodramatic, M.D. thought. Then again, goodbyes were always awkward.

"You really think I'm lying about this car, don't you?" Puwolsky said.

"Ready when you are," McCutcheon answered.

Puwolsky lunged and M.D. flinched, but the colonel's meaty hand passed over McCutcheon's lap and yanked open the glove box. "G'head. Check the registration."

Puwolsky threw the car's papers into M.D.'s lap, and sure enough the registration proved the car belonged to a Ms. Madeline Vina on 13579 Sycamore Street.

"I tell the truth, kid. I ain't perfect by any stretch, but anyone who works for me—excuse me, works with me—knows I tell the truth." M.D. put the papers back in the glove box as Puwolsky threw the car in gear and got ready to pull away. McCutcheon turned his head and looked out the window. Larson flipped him the bird.

M.D. didn't respond.

"Your colonel," Puwolsky said as they exited the parking lot. "Lemme guess. He doesn't think you should do this, does he?"

McCutcheon rolled his eyes, the answer too obvious for words.

"Did he tell you why not?" Puwolsky asked.

"'Cause you're a dirty cop with a history of being investigated by Internal Affairs."

Puwolsky snapped his head around at the mention of Internal Affairs and opened his mouth to spit out a fiery defense of his actions. However, before any words escaped from his lips, Puwolsky reconsidered his response and spoke in a subdued tone.

"Done some research, I see."

"Always."

"Then you've seen that nothing big's ever stuck?"

"That's because Detroit's too fucked up at the top to get anything right."

"Exactly," Puwolsky said. "And that's why sometimes we gotta break the rules. It's the only way to get shit done. Me and your colonel, we're not so different like that, are we?"

McCutcheon ripped open a package of raw almonds. Getting some energy in him before entering the state prison struck him as a good idea.

"I gotta feeling you are," M.D. replied.

"You're right, we are. We are very different, son." Puwolsky sped down the highway driving like most cops do: as fast as he wanted, with little regard for the rules of the road they expect civilians to follow. "I've burned through three marriages; your idol's never been hitched once. I got four kids; he's got zip. I coach a basketball team for inner-city youth down at the rec center; he wouldn't know how to identify a volunteer if she lifted her blouse and waggled her bazungas at him."

"What's your point?" McCutcheon asked.

"My point is that you've been played, son."

M.D. shook his head. "Whatever."

"Listen to me," Puwolsky said. "You do not have to do this. I mean that. You are still free to say no. Just give me the word."

They drove along in silence, each man thinking many thoughts, neither speaking to the other. Puwolsky turned the speed of the windshield wipers from medium to high as the intensity of the rainstorm grew. Forty-five minutes passed without a word between them until a white sign, its letters written in simple black print, appeared on the side of the road.

APPROACHING JENTLES STATE PRISON

WARNING: DO NOT PICK UP HITCHHIKERS

"My offer still stands," Puwolsky said. "'Cause once you cross through those gates up there, son, it's an entirely different world."

"What do you mean, Stanzer played me?" M.D. asked.

Puwolsky exited the highway, turned left, and drove up the long, single lane service road exclusively used by the prison.

"I betcha he said you had to let the girl go, didn't he? Fucking people who have never opened their hearts to love, they just don't get it, do they?"

M.D. stared at the wipers zip-zapping across the windshield, throwing spray off the glass.

"Betcha he also said you needed to make your own decision about this, too. That he couldn't make 'em for you," Puwolsky continued. "Guys like him, they get off on getting in your head and making you feel like they really tried, but in the end, also making you feel like you have to make your own choices in this world. Thing is, all this guy has is his career. No marriage, no family, no kids... his career means too much to him—it's his entire life—and now that his little experiment with you has gone to piss, he knows he might fry."

M.D. wrinkled his brow, the look on his face clearly saying, *What do you mean, gone to piss?*

"The reason I am telling you this is 'cause I only work one way: I shoot straight, tell the truth," Puwolsky said. "You're just a pawn to guys like Stanzer. Always have been. He loses you, it's just another chess piece. He loses his job, however, and he loses his complete identity."

To M.D., Puwolsky was a jerkhead whose words didn't add up. Stanzer had never been like that with McCutcheon. No, his colonel might not have supported this choice, but Stanzer had never done anything to make M.D. believe he could not be trusted. "I know you don't believe me. If I were you, I probably wouldn't believe me either," Puwolsky said as the vehicle cruised up the service road and silver spirals of barbed wire fence appeared on the horizon. "But that's because you don't know all the facts."

"What facts?"

"Me, I told you the truth from day one. I told it to you straight about the death of your gym buddies. I told it to you straight about the fact that your father sits inside those walls up ahead. And I told it to you straight about the danger to your girl. But Stanzer, he's Mister Fucking Mind Game. Been lying to you since the beginning."

"What beginning?"

"The very beginning. The get-go. What, you need a map?" Puwolsky said. "They had their eyes on bringing you in to do their undercover dirty work ever since that day Freedman called in, playing the '*favor-for-an-old-friend*' card."

"You know Mr. Freedman, my old high school science teacher?" M.D. asked.

"Me, no. But my department was looped in on the search for your sister when she was abducted, and I know that it wasn't just an accident that you got plunked into Wit Sec soon thereafter. Usually it's the middle class or even the rich folks that get that kind of protection. Families from the ghetto? No offense, but we don't have the resources to protect all the people from the 'hood who need an angel to look out for them. Your ticket got punched because they saw value in you."

"Who saw value in me?" M.D. asked. For the first time, Puwolsky's words did make sense. When Gemma had been abducted, McCutcheon turned to the only person he could—Mr. Freedman, his high school science teacher—and Mr. Freedman was the one who brought in the FBI.

That's how Gemma was saved. That's how Sarah was found. And that's how McCutcheon ended up in a white van bound for Bellevue.

"Lemme guess: not soon after you were taken away to some new city you'd never even heard of, they fed you that 'Come fight for the red, white, and blue' shit. The 'do your duty, higher calling, America needs your service' line. That how they get you?"

Puwolsky read McCutcheon's face, a furrowed brow telling him everything he needed to know about the answer.

"You were played, son. You were their target before you even knew they existed, an experiment to see if teenage operatives in the field of battle could work at a realistic level. Before you knew left from right, I bet you were raced through training, told how great you were, and sent off on missions to see if your boat could float. The downside? Not you being wounded or even dying. No one gives a shit about that. The downside has always been awareness. Notoriety. Recognition. A public knowledge that our government is willing to risk the lives of kids by placing them in the line of fire."

The prison's guard tower came into sight. Two men wearing green rain slickers carried high-powered rifles with scopes as they walked across a catwalk one hundred feet above the ground. "But your boat did float," Puwolsky said. "Which turned out to be great and terrible. Great because you kicked ass but terrible because word got out, and now some suits in D.C. want to get one hundred more kids just like you up and running. But other suits in D.C. still believe in the Constitution. That second group went bat shit and now they need someone to flambé for all this. Stanzer's career is on the doorstep of being a political piñata unless you never existed. Everyone is in full denial mode right now. No more missions, no more targets; the program is going to be shut down."

M.D. remained silent.

"That's why you're in this car now, son. Because Stanzer is cutting you loose. If he had any more assignments for you, do ya really think he'd have let you go? Your unit is over, your papers have been burned, and your entire existence is being washed off the map."

"You saying he wants me dead?"

"Nah," Puwolsky answered. "Not at all. Guy probably cares about you. But know this...he cares about himself, too."

The Cadillac pulled up to the front gates of Jentles State Penitentiary, an institution built in 1896. It started as a rectangular facility of three hundred cells able to hold up to six hundred prisoners, and operated on the "Two Bucket System." One bucket for human waste, the other for fresh water. The only rule: don't mix the buckets.

Prisoners who caused the guards any grief would have their buckets mixed.

In the late nineteenth century Jentles gained fame as one of the worst penal institutions in the United States, and since that time it had done little to lessen its reputation.

Many had tried to shut it down. Many times, too. But the D.T. was like a nonstick frying pan; no matter how much the heat had been turned up, nothing stuck. Lawyers filed lawsuits, journalists did exposés, and at one point, even the church refused to send any more clergy inside to provide spiritual guidance for the prisoners after two of their fathers were beaten by gang members for refusing to play the role of drug mule, so the fiends inside could score their dope.

Inside the D.T. a chicken bone became a shank, mice became meat, and year after year mentally healthy people entered but institutionally deranged madmen came out. Over and over the case had been made that the D.T. violated the Eighth Amendment of the U.S. Constitution, specifically the prohibition against cruel and unusual punishment against those in detainment. As one of the briefings said:

"An epidemic of beatings by deputies as well as by inmates, barely edible food, poor sanitation, and inadequate medical care puts the jail's residents in a constant state of risk and harm."

Like most lawsuits against Jentles, it was still being shuffled around in someone's case file inside the Court of Appeals.

The D.T. stood as a house of monsters housing monsters who had committed and were still committing horrible crimes. Yet, where were all these monsters supposed to go? Without an answer to that question, the D.T. just kept right on rolling on, business as usual. Eighteen hundred men called the Devil's Toilet home, and while indoor plumbing, electricity, and telephone lines had arrived since the gates first opened, the guards still ruled the complex with the same mentality as they did more than a century ago.

Old habits die hard.

Puwolsky waved his badge at an armed guard standing in a gray box, and a sheet of metal ground its way open, allowing the Cadillac to pass through the perimeter. A second gate with a second guard box stood inside the first. Beyond stood an unmistakable stench of violence, abuse, and death oozing from the prison's walls.

M.D. spied a chimney in the back corner, smoke rising from its bleak stack. A place so primitive, M.D. thought, they still burned their trash.

"You may not like me, may think I'm a fuck, but from day one I have told you the truth," Puwolsky said. "Your father is inside. That is the truth. The High Priest is inside. That is the truth. Your father sold you out to the High Priest and if you don't go inside and take his life he's going to kevork up your girl. Detroit can't stop that. Only you can. That is the truth."

Puwolsky pulled up to the guard manning the second gate.

"Name's Puwolsky, I'm on the list." The colonel had to practically shout to be heard through the downpour. "Notify Krewls I'll meet him in back by delivery."

The guard checked his clipboard, found Puwolsky's name, and waved the vehicle through. "Make a left at the fork," the guard shouted as rain crashed down on his slicker. Puwolsky rolled forward again and M.D. watched as the gate closed behind him.

"What's that mean, they're gonna kevork her?" McCutcheon asked.

"You know, kevork. Jack Kevorkian, that Doctor Death physician-assisted suicide guy," Puwolsky said. "Some of his muscle will grab her and make the murder look like a suicide. Probably tie it to her love for you to make it seem all the more legit."

M.D. swallowed hard, feeling as if he might puke.

"Don't be so shocked. This is D-town, post bank-ruptcy, and there's a war going on for the soul of the city," Puwolsky said. "The High Priest, his kind of ruthlessness is unprecedented. That's why he needs to be stopped. That's what I'm doing here. That's what you're doing here. It's black and white."

M.D. looked to his right. Cement, brick, iron, and steel. Not a blade of grass, not a tree, not even a rebellious weed.

"Look, kid, I knew you didn't know any of this stuff, and I ain't gonna hold it against you if you say no to me and want to turn around right now. You say the word and we're gone, because the truth is, if you go in there, I can't protect you. All I can do is yank you out once you say you've had enough," Puwolsky told him. "But your first chance to pull that plug won't come for at least three days. That's seventy-two hours from now. In one way it's forever and in another, it's not that long at all."

"Why three days?"

Puwolsky reached under his seat and pulled out a file. On the front cover a seal read STATE OF MICHIGAN, DEPARTMENT OF CORRECTIONS.

"Because Lester Rawlins, who is doing forty-five years to life for two counts of murder one, needs to be processed. Jentles doesn't own the most efficient prisoner intake system in the world. It'll take you a little bit to get things settled."

M.D. opened the contents of the file and saw a picture of himself next to his new name.

Rawlins, Lester Alfred
Prisoner ID# 8765KT76Z
Eligible for Parole: July 2063

Though the documents were forged, they looked real to McCutcheon. As real as it gets.

"You have my word that if on Thursday you want out, I'll pull you. Remember, I'm the guy who tells the truth."

The Cadillac made its way around the side of the prison and drove past a kennel of black hounds living under a thin, silver roof behind a chain link fence. At the sight of the vehicle, the dogs started barking, raging like feral beasts. If not for the metal fence keeping them quarantined, M.D. was sure, these huge animals would have attacked the car, biting bumpers and trying to break through windshields. These weren't puppies, these were people chewers; and as soon as M.D. caught sight of the dogs he felt sure that more than a few unfortunate prisoners had been on the wrong end of their teeth and claws.

The car came to a stop at the loading dock in the back and one thing immediately seemed clear to McCutcheon: Jentles State Penitentiary was a place where what happened inside remained inside.

"So what's it gonna be?" Puwolsky asked. "Are you going to go for the...?"

"Cuff me."

M.D. extended his arms. Puwolsky paused for a moment before taking any action.

Kid's brave, he said to himself. *Ain't no doubt about that.*

After parking the car by the loading dock, Puwolsky reached under the seat and lifted a set of silver handcuffs.

"Everyone said you're a warrior, kid." Puwolsky clicked the steel bracelets over McCutcheon's wrists. "They weren't lying."

TEN

On the outside, McCutcheon appeared calm, cool, and collected, but on the inside fear screamed through his veins. The sound of the handcuffs clicking shut triggered a massive surge of terror.

He hadn't expected the suffocating feel of the steel shackles on his wrists to set off his internal panic alarms they way they did. Especially not as suddenly or as quickly or as deeply.

But they did.

He took a slow, deep breath and reminded himself that in a fight-or-flight world, fear kept people alive. Sometimes fear pushed people to great heights. But sometimes fear paralyzed.

Ultimately, as McCutcheon knew, fear boiled down to choice. Fear could devastate him or it could propel him. Fear, as the martial arts taught, was nothing more than energy. The challenge for its students became to properly channel it.

A very real sense of dread continued to grow in the pit

of M.D.'s stomach. He knew he had to slow his inner world down, reflect on his feelings, and remind himself that there was only one proper way to deal with this torrent of terror.

No, he could not control whether the fear existed, but he could take responsibility for his reaction to it.

Stay here, he told himself. *Breathe into it. Sit with this fear, don't run or deny or hide from it. Listen to its message.*

Yes, this fear felt immense. But also, M.D. reminded himself, it would not last. No emotion was ever permanent.

What was permanent then? McCutcheon asked himself. *What existed past the clutter, beyond the ups and downs, beneath the seas of emotional turmoil?*

He answered immediately: *My strength.*

Nothing had transpired yet. Nothing at all. McCutcheon was merely sitting inside a Cadillac wearing handcuffs he'd voluntarily put on and could still ask to be removed. For all the horrors his imagination could have created, all the anxiety he could have manifested by focusing on all the potential terror of entering an ominous prison as an undercover agent on a lone-wolf mission, as of that exact moment nothing at all had yet occurred.

Love, he knew, was stronger than fear. Always. *Did he still want to go in?* McCutcheon asked himself.

Yes.

Am I sure?

Yes.

Why am I sure?

Because my motivation stems from a place of love.

So how, M.D. asked himself, was it best to go in, like a scared little child filled with worry and dread or like a brave and noble warrior owning courage, purpose, and strength?

On the inside, M.D. felt a surge of power rise up inside of him. Being anxious would negatively affect his ability to execute this mission. Did he want to be anxious?

No.

Did he need to be terrified?

Alert, yes. Terrified, no.

Was all this negative energy of any actual use to him?

Energy is just energy, which means this fear can be a gift if you rechannel it.

His inner power began to grow.

My body is ready, I am in the best shape of my life, and I am motivated by the purest reason that exists. I will be okay.

McCutcheon repeated the last line to himself a second time, knowing that once inside, the power of his mind would be his sharpest sword.

I will be more than okay. I will succeed.

He breathed in and breathed out, slowly, patiently, deeply.

Thank you, fear, McCutcheon said. *Stay if you like—or go—but know that I hear and appreciate your concerns.*

Poof! The terror vanished. In its place was a reservoir of confidence, power, and poise.

"Hey," Puwolsky asked, snapping his fingers. "Hey kid, are you okay?"

McCutcheon blinked his eyes open and they shined with the light of a wolf. He turned to the colonel.

"I'm ready."

Whoa, Puwolsky thought. Who is this kid?

"Yeah, um...sure," he said.

Puwolsky flashed his car lights as a signal to someone on the inside, and a few seconds later the back door by the loading dock cracked open.

A man approached. A skinny guy with bad teeth and yellow hair named Major Daniel Krewls. He was not particularly tall, not particularly muscular, but he stomped his black boots with authority through the foreboding puddles on his way to meet the car.

Puwolsky rolled down the window. Krewls stuck his chin in the vehicle and looked around.

"LeRoyce didn't make the trip?"

"LeRoyce is no longer with us."

"Too bad."

"Shit happens."

"So they say. This the guy?" Krewls shined a flashlight on McCutcheon's face. "Seems a little young to play with the big boys."

"I wouldn't underestimate his abilities."

"Where's my money?"

"Where are the details?" Puwolsky began. "The story goes that..."

Krewls interrupted. "The detail that comes first is my motherfuckin' money," Krewls interrupted.

There was a stalemate but it was brief, and Puwolsky relented. He reached into his jacket. "You're like one of the damn prisoners, making sure you get paid first before anything happens." He passed Krewls an envelope.

"I'm worse than the prisoners," Krewls said as he fingered through a sheaf of hundred-dollar bills. "'Cause I got a badge."

Wardens run state penitentiaries, but Jentles's warden, John Jeffrey Johannsen, had suffered a mild stroke and didn't want to lose his retirement package, so he went on temporary sick leave in order to protect his benefit plan.

That was three years ago.

Six months after Johannsen stepped away from his desk, Deputy Warden Steven Elliot found himself indicted for stealing from the prison employee fund. Next in line would have been the associate warden, but the state of Michigan, in its infinite wisdom, decided to eliminate the position of associate warden from all of the correctional facilities, in order to trim the budget and cut down on bureaucracy. Major Krewls, a man with nineteen years under his belt at the time, turned up next in line in the chain of command.

"Eight thousand," Krewls said. "That's it? I deserve a bonus."

"Go hump a turtle," Puwolsky answered.

Krewls soured his face. Clearly, this was not a negotiation.

"All right," Krewls said stuffing the cash inside his jacket. "What we got?"

"This prisoner's name is"—Puwolsky passed the file over to the major—"Lester Alfred Rawlins. Story is he was sentenced to forty-five to life but escaped from Longacre Penitentiary upstate, and is now being transferred here."

"Forty-five years? *Whew-weee*," Krewls said. "That's a long time for a young buck like you to do a bid up in here."

"It's just three days," Puwolsky said with a glare in Krewls's direction. "We're starting there."

"Oh yeah, right." Krewls took the forged paperwork from Puwolsky's hands. "Three days, gotcha."

The seamless way in which everything went down between the two men made M.D. wonder just how many other people had been sneaked in through the back door and railroaded into the prison, without ever having seen a trial, a judge, or a jury. Certainly, the scheme ran far too smoothly for it to be the first time Krewls and Puwolsky had ever pulled it off. No nerves. No anxiety. No signs of concern about being caught or discovered.

Too much assurance M.D. thought. Too much arrogance. All signs of weakness, he knew. The overconfident were always vulnerable. McCutcheon filed this knowledge away in case he needed it later.

"Anything else I need to know?" Krewls asked.

"Yeah, read that."

Krewls scanned the materials.

"Hmmm, I'm thinking Think Tank."

"Don't fuck around with this, Krewls. You know why he's here."

"I'm just saying," Krewls answered. "You'd bet on him, right?"

"I'm warning you, don't mess around."

"Come on, Puwolsky," Krewls says. "With the chump change you're paying, I could use the extra cash."

"Why are you always bitching about money?"

"'Cause money rules the world," Krewls said. "Just tell me, would you bet on him?"

While the eight grand was supposed to get M.D. into a position whereby he could execute his mission, Puwolsky knew that dirty officers like Krewls always liked to make a little extra something-something for themselves whenever the chance presented itself. Smuggling in phones, looking the other way during a beat down, there were scores of ways that prison guards could puff their pockets. Besides, once M.D. exited the car and entered the D.T., Puwolsky knew that Krewls was going to do what Krewls was going to do anyway; he was lord of the realm, so the colonel figured it was better to simply tell the truth in order to try to move things along as quickly as possible.

"I'd bet the fucking farm on him," Puwolsky said. "Just make sure a certain someone has an encounter and ends up in the morgue truck sooner rather than later."

Krewls smiled, his crooked teeth ready to take a big bite out of this new opportunity. "Nothing to worry about." Krewls tapped the cash in his pocket. "You, son, are fixin' to triple this for me, ain't ya?"

McCutcheon didn't answer. He hadn't come to Jentles

make crooked prison guards smile. He was here for other reasons and he knew he had to keep those reasons front and center in his mind.

Puwolsky reached over, opened the passenger door, and McCutcheon climbed out of the car and into the rain.

"So you're a little soldier, huh?" Krewls stepped nose-to-nose with McCutcheon. "Just remember who the general is and we'll get along just fine."

Even though Puwolsky had always suspected Krewls might put M.D. through a few extra challenges before he'd be placed in a position to take out the High Priest, the colonel hadn't mentioned any of this to McCutcheon. In fact there were many things Puwolsky hadn't mentioned to McCutcheon about this mission.

Of course, there were a few things M.D. hadn't mentioned to the colonel, either. Like the fact that he had absolutely zero intention of murdering D'Marcus Rose.

"I'll see you in about three days," Puwolsky said.

"Yep," M.D. answered. Krewls grabbed McCutcheon by the elbow and began leading him inside.

"Right this way, son," Krewls said. "Let's go get you set up all nice and cozy."

Puwolsky turned the key, the Cadillac roared to life, and all three men took the next step forward in their lives, thinking about their own individual schemes.

Each just having lied, lied, lied to the others.

ELEVEN

"**M**ove it, ass breath!"

Major Krewls hauled McCutcheon into a gray-and-white intake room that smelled of piss and fear and slammed him into a chair with four other cuffed felons.

"Now, wait!"

McCutcheon understood Krewls's show of roughness. In prison, eyes are everywhere, and if even a sniff of the idea surfaced that M.D. was anything other than a convict, he'd be shanked before dinner, and Krewls himself would burn. Sure, the major wanted the envelope full of money that came with backdooring M.D. into his institution, but Krewls also knew it could cost him his badge, his pension, and maybe even his freedom.

For all parties involved, the stakes were high.

Krewls popped a roasted sunflower seed into his mouth, separated the shell from the nut using only his teeth, and then spit the gnawed husk onto the floor. A moment later he locked M.D. to a hard steel seat and then bashed him with a baton.

"*Uunnnnggghh*!" M.D. groaned as the shot drilled him in the ribs.

"Just a reminder, fucko," Krewls said, making sure every other prisoner in the room heard him. "You're cookin' in my kitchen now."

Krewls marched out of the room, and three of the four handcuffed inmates awaiting processing into the facility eyed the new fish in the tank. The fourth, bound in a restraining jacket made of unchewable cloth and fitted with leg irons and a waist chain, gazed at the walls as if there was an animated cartoon playing on them. M.D. noted a hint of drool dribbling from the guy's bottom lip, and a zoned-out daze in his eyes. Behind this prisoner's head, McCutcheon spied some graffiti scribbled on the wall.

WELCOME TO THE DEVIL'S TOILET, A POEM

WELCOME 2 THE DEVIL'S TOILET
KILL URSELF NOW
IF U HAV THE CHANCE.
AND NO DIS DON'T FUCKING RHYME

Really inspirational, M.D. thought.

"Y'all know we're fucked, right?" said a skinny guy with big teeth making herky-jerky twitches. "Fucked like rabbits about to be stew. Screwed like turkeys about to be dumplings. Cooked like cows about to be hamburger pie."

"I ain't fucked," came the booming voice of the

bald-headed convict sitting next to the motor mouth. "Night Train is the guy who does the fucking. The fuckin' up of people that is." Night Train kissed his left bicep then his right, each arm a boulder. "Ain't nobody want a piece of Smith and Wesson."

"Too true," Motor Mouth said. "Ain't no one want a piece of Night Train."

Suddenly the eyes of the restrained prisoner turned wide and crazy and he began smashing his head against the wall and screaming.

"*Aaaeerrgggh!*" Thud. "*Aaaeerrgggh!*" Thud. "*Aaaeerrgggh!*" Thud.

"Aw, shit, we gotta a banger," Motor Mouth said. "Yo, guard! Get this boy some meds."

"*Aaaeerrgggh!*" Thud. "*Aaaeerrgggh!*" Thud. "*Aaaeerrgggh!*" Thud.

No one came.

Then as abruptly as he started, Banger stopped. No rhyme, no reason, no explanation. He simply returned to staring at the walls.

"Just a damn shame how there be so many peoples with mental unhealthiness in our prisons," Motor Mouth said. "A damn shame." Motor Mouth twitched two more times and then turned his attention to the guy on his left. "Hey, Timmy, what you in for?"

A twenty-three-year-old white kid, no tattoos, no facial hair, looked up with a *Who me?* expression.

"Yeah you," Motor Mouth said. "What you done?"

"My name's not Timmy."

"Well, you look like a Timmy to me. Lemme guess. Drugs?"

The guy not named Timmy didn't answer.

"I knew it!" Motor Mouth exclaimed. "What you slangin', X? Shrooms? Young fella like you might be pushing a little blow but definitely not the Big H."

The guy not named Timmy kept his mouth shut. He'd taken a course on *How to Survive in Prison* paid for by his father before heading out to the D.T., so he'd been coached on all the rules of how to act in order to make it through his bid.

Keep your eyes in your own head. Don't take any favors from anyone cause nothing is free in lockup. Since many attacks happen when you are using the toilet, always piss while sitting on the shitter with your pants all the way off, so in case you're targeted, you can defend yourself without having your prison chinos trip you up at the ankles while you fight.

"And remember," his coach told him. "One rule trumps all others: Show no fear. Poop your pants on the inside but on the outside you gotta wear the mask of a stone cold killer." Weak prisoners would be exploited.

The guy not named Timmy practiced his cold, dispassionate, "Don't mess with me" face for two solid weeks before entering the D.T., yet less than three hours into a twenty-two-month sentence, his hands trembled, his mouth dried, and his eyes blinked at more than twice the normal rate.

"Aw, wouldya look at this," Motor Mouth said. "Young

buck here about to dookie in his pants. Just please don't tell me you in for *mareee-juana*? A damn shame the way society'll take minor little trafficker like you and toss 'em in a place like this. Tsk, tsk, tsk," Motor Mouth said, smacking his lips. "The D.T. ain't no place for a dude like you, in here with murderers and armed robbers and sickos who'll take your manhood quick as they'll take a muffin off your breakfast tray."

Motor Mouth leaned forward and looked compassionately at the guy not named Timmy. "Baby, you wanna know what's gonna help you survive in here? Do ya?"

Motor Mouth leaned gently forward and spoke slowly, making sure to clearly pronounce each of his words one at a time.

"Not. A. Damn. Thing."

A grin, big and wide, grew across Motor Mouth's face. "You need to abandon all hope, motherfucker, 'cause baby, you about to enter a place from where you ain't never gonna return. Haaa-haaa-haaaaa!"

"Aaaeerrgggh!" Thud. *"Aaaeerrgggh!"* Thud. *"Aaaeerrgggh!"* Thud.

Motor Mouth cackled like the Wicked Witch of the West, Banger smashed his head against the wall, and McCutcheon watched as a new wave of whiteness washed over the face of the guy not named Timmy.

"And what's your deal?" Motor Mouth asked, turning his attention to M.D.

McCutcheon didn't reply.

"Oh, the strong, silent type, huh? I bet you're one of

those bitches who thinks he ain't even did nothing wrong to be in here."

M.D. glared, wordless and fierce.

"*Ooh-weee*, you got a mean mad-dog stare on you, don't ya now?" Motor Mouth said, practically feeling the energy ooze from McCutcheon's chest. "Well, that'll help you some in here, but ain't nothing gonna save you from the food. They be serving toes in here for lunch."

"*Aaaeerrgggh!*" Thud. "*Aaaeerrgggh!*" Thud. "*Aaaeerrgggh!*" Thud.

Krewls stomped back into the room and smashed Banger in the gut with his baton. "Cut it out. You're giving me a headache." Banger doubled over from the blow. It was abusive but it worked, and Banger stopped banging.

"Can I just say how much I hate these lawyer paper jockeys always sweating us for overcrowding? Okay, listen up," Krewls announced. "I only have four beds right now and one's in the infirmary. But my problem is ain't a one of you need the infirmary."

Krewls looked up from his chart. "Yet," he added, as a sinister smile crept across his face.

The major looked around at his five charges. "Okay, which one of you wants to send another to the hospital for me?" he asked. "Come on, come on, I ain't got all day."

Night Train surveyed his peers then nodded his head. "Smith and Wesson'll do the honors for ya, boss."

"Great, we have one volunteer. Who's next?" The other four prisoners, Motor Mouth, Banger, the guy not named Timmy, and McCutcheon, all stayed mum.

"Okay, if that's the way it's going to be." Krewls tucked his chart underneath his arm, walked into the center of the room, and began tapping each of the remaining prisoners on the top of his head.

"Duck. Duck. Duck...GOOSE!"

Krewls's hand stopped on the guy not named Timmy, and the new convict's eyes practically popped out of his head.

Me? the look on his face said. *You want me to fight this animal?*

"I'll do it," M.D. suddenly blurted out.

Krewls shook his head back and forth. "Oh, no," he said in a disapproving manner. "Please don't tell me I just boated a fish with a conscience."

"I said, I'm in," McCutcheon replied.

The guy not named Timmy looked up at M.D. with wide, thankful eyes.

"All right," Krewls said. "I guess I get to road test my new ride to see what I got under the hood before the big show begins."

Krewls uncuffed M.D. and then Night Train. Both stood.

Night Train, three inches taller, seventy pounds heavier, stepped nose-to-nose with McCutcheon.

"I'm gonna fuck you up."

"I don't have a beef with you."

"You will in a sec."

"I don't want to fight," M.D. said in a calm and tranquil voice. "We do not have to do this."

"Shit, if I were you, I wouldn't want to fight me either," Night Train said. "Prepare to meet Smith and Wesson."

Night Train rolled his neck in a wide circle, raised his fists, and kissed each of his biceps one at a time. Fifteen seconds later, he lay crumpled on the intake room's floor, blood running from his nose and mouth, the center of his face looking as if he'd been smashed in the middle of his grille by a metal pipe.

Muscles without speed were like birds without wings for M.D.: nothing but target practice.

Krewls rubbed his chin. He'd seen a lot of prison fights in his time, but this kind of quickness, strength, and precision? The major smiled. "You gonna make me some genuine cash-o-la, ain't you?"

M.D. spit, sat back down, and reminded himself yet again that he'd only come to the D.T. for one reason, and it wasn't to assassinate the High Priest. His aim was to save Kaitlyn. Nothing else mattered. He owned a plan to do it, too. A plan that did not involve murdering D'Marcus Rose. But he hadn't shared it with anybody. Not Puwolsky. Not Stanzer. Not Krewls.

They weren't the only ones who could scheme, he figured.

Unconscious on the floor, Night Train, in a pool of his own blood, spasmed. McCutcheon hadn't wanted to hurt him. He didn't want to hurt anybody on purpose. Not ever again. It went against his code. But seeing the guy not named Timmy get his head kicked in would have been like driving past a car accident with a pregnant lady trapped inside a burning vehicle, without stopping to help. He simply had to stop it.

McCutcheon reflected on the fact that his entire identity now revolved around helping those who could not help themselves. It had become his life's mission. This is why he knew that despite Stanzer's words, he felt the colonel would never completely abandon him, no matter what happened with Puwolsky. McCutcheon wasn't stupid enough to fully trust a man who could not be trusted. Yet he knew in his heart he could trust Stanzer.

There was just no way, M.D. told himself, that Stanzer would simply forget about his prize young soldier and cut him loose. M.D. had done too much good work, proved himself too talented, shown too much of his deep value as an asset to the program. Sure, Stanzer may have been a salty prick at times, but the guy was loyal.

McCutcheon felt confident that if push came to shove, and things went sideways with Puwolsky, he always could count on his colonel. Even if his colonel had led him to believe otherwise.

"Don't get too comfy, sugar pies," Krewls said as two guards wearing rubber gloves to protect themselves from blood hoisted Night Train up, lifting him by his Smith and Wessons. "A few more minutes and then it's off to your new home."

A few more minutes, M.D. thought, and the mission inside the mission would begin.

TWELVE

"Strip!"

McCutcheon yanked his shirt over his head, removed his shoes, and took off his pants. After stepping out of his underwear he waited for his next directive.

"Bend and lift your sack." The correctional officer's direct, impersonal tone communicated two different messages at the same time. Message one: *Do what I say and we will not have a problem.* Message two: *If you do not do what I say I will use force to resolve our problem.*

McCutcheon knew there was no point in fighting with the guards, so he complied and bent over. Entirely naked, his bare feet pressed against a cool floor, the officer probed M.D.'s rectum with a cold, gloved hand. At most state penitentiaries, a visual inspection was more than enough for inmates just entering lockup, but at the D.T. the guards always probed. Not for extra security but in order to flex their power. The D.T. operated on a "no negotiation" policy, which meant that if an officer was ever taken hostage in a riot situation, the institution would refuse to bargain with the prisoners in order to secure an officer's release.

No negotiation. One hundred percent of the time. All the guards who worked at Jentles knew this stood as an absolute. This meant that all of the guards who worked at Jentles also knew that each and every convict who crossed through their front gate might be the man who one day takes his life.

Establishing an upper hand right from the very start became a psychological tool to help ensure compliance.

As the guard searched McCutcheon's anus for contraband that he knew didn't exist, M.D. reminded himself once again that his greatest enemy from this point forward would be his own mind. The system would seek to dehumanize him, mentally break him down in order to get him to submit like a tamed animal to the will of their sick, deranged culture. *No matter what*, M.D. vowed to himself, *I cannot let this happen.* As an institution the D.T. turned men into beasts and beasts into savages.

McCutcheon would determine who McCutcheon would become. No one else.

"Spray."

M.D. straightened up tall, lifted his arms and the guard blasted him with a stream of delousing vapors.

"Turn," the guard ordered. M.D. did as instructed, spun, and closed his eyes. The second blast of disinfectant sent fumes into his nostrils that caused his eyes to water and his cheeks to burn, while leaving the taste of stale copper pennies in his mouth.

"Dress." The guard ripped his blue rubber gloves off of his hands and tossed them in the trash. Though the state employee felt no sympathy for McCutcheon, McCutcheon felt a moment of sympathy for the guard. This officer was a man whose career consisted of looking into the anal cavities of society's lawbreakers. And he acted as such. His compassion for prisoners had vanished long ago. To M.D., an ass search felt personal; to the staff member, it was just another day at the office.

Life had beaten him down.

McCutcheon deposited the civilian clothing he'd worn to Jentles into a clear plastic bag, and then slipped on a pair of white boxers and a T-shirt that smelled of cheap soap and bleach. Next he put on a navy-blue prison jumpsuit with a thick orange stripe running across the shoulders, which sported a patch that said INMATE on the back. Though the black letters had no significant mass, McCutcheon could feel their weight. A pair of starched white socks, a pair of laceless orange slip-on shoes, and the ensemble was complete. Once Motor Mouth, Banger, and the guy not named Timmy had gone through their cavity search and re-clothing process, the four men were fingerprinted, photographed, given a bagged lunch, and returned to the intake room to await transport.

None of them had eaten in hours. M.D. opened his sack. A sandwich, an apple, and a cookie. McCutcheon loved apples. Crisp, crunchy ones. But the mealy, soft ones that had no snap grossed him out.

As soon as his finger made contact with the fruit's skin, M.D. knew he wouldn't be eating it. The squashy, red lump of bruised mush didn't even deserve to be called an apple.

M.D. tossed the inedible red oval back in the bag, fumbled past a cookie he knew he wouldn't touch, and hoped the sandwich might offer some protein that would prove chewable.

The cellophane wrapper described it as TURKEY ON WHITE, but after McCutcheon opened it up he thought a better description would be FATTY RUBBER ON FOAM. Not starving due to the raw almonds he'd smartly snacked on before departing, he closed the bag.

"Want my cookie?"

M.D. raised his eyes. The guy not named Timmy was holding out his dessert.

"Keep it," M.D. said. "And keep your spirits up, too. Gonna be rough on all of us in there. Remember, your spirit is your strength."

"Thanks," the guy not named Timmy said. McCutcheon set his bag down on the chair next to him, figuring if he got too hungry later on he'd suck down the mustard package for energy.

"It's go time, sugar pies!"

M.D. took a deep breath and centered himself. Though already harrowing, his journey into the penitentiary was just at its beginning.

A white metal door with blots of orange rust peppering the frame screeched open, and McCutcheon crossed into the main detention area of the D.T. He'd expected the prison to smell bad, serve horrible food, and host rats, roaches, and lice. What he hadn't expected was the noise. Prisons were hard, tough places built with hard, tough materials designed to lock away hard, tough people, and Jentles sounded exactly that way.

Whenever architects constructed a home, a school, or a library, they took acoustics into consideration. Whenever architects designed a lockup facility, their aim was containment. No one cared about the way sound bounced off the walls; preventing society's scum from escaping was all that ever mattered, and when it came to keeping the rabbits corralled, no facility in the nation owned a better record than the D.T.

Not a single inmate had escaped from Jentles in the last fifty-five years, the longest current streak in America. Trying to break out was virtually impossible, and it had even become a running joke among the cons.

Only two ways out of the D.T.: front-door parole or back-door parole. Front-door parole means you get your walking papers. Back-door parole means the morgue truck. Ain't no third option.

Rabbits, the slang word prisoners use to describe jailbreak artists, had no chance once they arrived at the D.T. "Aw, look at the lil' bit of sweetness we got right here," a shirtless, tatted-up prisoner yelped out as a guard escorted the four new fish down the central corridor. "Hey, honey bunch, you got plans later tonight?"

McCutcheon ignored the catcalls and kept his eyes straight ahead, one foot in front of the other, alert, focused, and present. Behind him Motor Mouth waved hello and gave shoutouts to old friends, while Banger, forced to take two small steps to every one the guard took due to his leg chains, dragged his feet. As for the guy not named Timmy, M.D. hoped he could keep his eyes in his head, his face expressionless, and his ears tuned out to all the chatter on the cell block.

He couldn't. McCutcheon glanced over his shoulder and his insides melted. He could feel the guy not named Timmy's fear from fifteen feet away.

As could every other man in the institution.

"Yo Bug, give that one to me."

"I see me some dinner."

"Somebody gonna split that boy like a wishbone."

"Keep it moving, keep it moving," the guard ordered to the guy not named Timmy. But it was too late. Not five minutes in and he'd already shown his cards. All those weeks of preparation that his father paid so much money for were down the drain.

Convicted felons who've circulated through the penal system a few times knew that one of the worst things about entering a new facility was the cellmate lottery a prisoner faced upon arrival. Would your new cellie be a serial killer? An unpredictable psycho? A son-of-a-bitch suffering from some kind of untreated mental illness? Lockup saw all kinds. Self-mutilators who try to hurt themselves so that their physical pain drowned out their emotional devastation. Gassers who took shits in their own hands, and then smeared it across their own bodies or threw feces at the guards. Most feared, however, was the bull homosexual, the prison wolf on the prowl for fresh meat. Two grown men. One small cell. For the weak, things could get ugly fast.

Of course, inmates didn't come with warning labels stapled to their foreheads. Some had a short temper. Some loved pain. Some were just plain bad. Even an average size, average looking con, who appeared steady, calm, and rational could quickly turn out to be the most homicidal man on the cell block. The stress of incarceration ate psyches like termites ate wood, rapaciously and with no quarter. Everyone was damaged. Everyone was unpredictable. Everyone was a threat.

None could be trusted. This was the first and last rule of survival for anyone who entered the Department of Corrections, and McCutcheon knew it well. To trust meant risking death.

"This is you," the guard said to M.D.

Beyond the iron bars lay his new home, a six-foot by eight-foot cell with a steel sink, a steel toilet, two metal shelves, two metal bunks—one on top of the other—and one fellow prisoner, already inside lying on the bottom bed.

The guard opened the cell's door and M.D. stepped forward, unsure of what to expect. He imagined a snarl or some profanity. Maybe a whole bunch of rules about how and when he could use the toilet.

Rules he might have to renegotiate with his fists.

"Welcome. Been expectin' you."

The cell door slammed behind McCutcheon and an involuntary shudder wormed up his spine. The sound of iron bars locking him into a cage felt more haunting than he ever expected.

"Come on in. Make yourself comfortable. Plenty of space. Wanna cuppa coffee? Name's Fixer."

He had hair the color of snow, a slender frame, and arms that flabbed even though he wasn't overweight. Guy seemed seventy, at least.

An old man? M.D. thought.

Fixer held up two pieces of exposed wire from a snipped brown extension cord that had been plugged into an electrical socket at the back wall, and McCutcheon watched as his new cell mate dipped both ends of the shiny coil into a plastic bowl filled with water. By the time M.D. tossed his gear onto the top bunk, eyed the chipped paint on the ceiling, and spied the dismal spot where he'd now be brushing his teeth, tiny bubbles started to rise from the bottom of Fixer's container.

"They sell them hot pots in the commissary, but they don't get hot enough for the water to boil," Fixer said. "In a way, they're kinda like my penis, supposed to do one thing but they don't." The old man reached for two packets of instant coffee and two cups. "Guy like me supposed to be able to get a stiff one, you know, raise the ol' flagpole, but not anymore. Can you believe I ain't been laid in forty-seven years? Hell, if I saw me a vagina right now, I'd have to trade that sucker in for something more practical, like a good pillow. You gotta a girl?"

McCutcheon didn't reply. Instead he stood in the middle of the cell, stretched out both of his arms, and extended his fingetips. Each brushed the opposing wall and M.D. realized that yes, he could indeed touch both sides of his new home at the same time.

"Thing about them hot pots is, if you boil up some liquid that there could be used as a weapon. Throw it at a guard or an enemy or something. That's why they sell hot pots that don't get hot. Also why we gotta make ourselves these here stingers." With the water furiously bubbling, Fixer reached for a paper cup. "You want sugar with your coffee?"

"I don't want coffee at all."

Fixer, about to pour a fresh cup of prison java for his new cell mate, froze, stung by McCutcheon's ungrateful, blunt reply. To M.D. it seemed fairly obvious that a worn-out old timer who lacked muscles, speed, or strength did not own the skills to be any kind of threat to him.

Then a second thought crossed McCutcheon's mind as he watched the old guy remove the stinger's wires from the boiling water.

Or maybe he did?

THIRTEEN

"**F**ine, you don't want coffee, no problem. But I'm sure you wanna eat. You gotta be starved by now."

Fixer crossed to his shelf and pulled down a package of instant ramen noodles.

"I'll cook us somethin' dandy."

"They gave me something to eat right here," M.D. said, referring to the brown bag he brought with him.

"Oh, you don't want to eat S.O.S."

"S.O.S.?"

"Same ol' shit," Fixer said. "They been serving that rubber turkey since 1952. Don't even know why they call it turkey. At best, there's kitten meat in there."

Fixer tore open the package of dry food and searched his shelf for another bowl.

Ramen noodles? How many nights had I been forced to eat those with my sister, M.D. thought.

After putting the noodles in a plastic bowl and pouring the unused hot water from the coffee over the top of them, Fixer crossed back to his shelf and sifted through some personal items. Though hungry, the smell of bland ramen noodles boiling in prison water that had been heated by the tips of exposed metal wires, didn't exactly rev M.D.'s taste bud engines.

BAM! With the heel of his shoe Fixer stamped down on a package of peanuts and twisted his foot side-to-side grounding the contents of the packet into smithereens. Once satisfied with his efforts, Fixer took another plastic bowl and two spoons down from his shelf and began moving around his small space like an actual chef: nimble, fluid, and in total command of his kitchen.

Fixer mixed the seasoning packet from the ramen noodles together with a squeeze of mayonnaise and then dropped a few fat plops of Furnell's Furiously Flamin' Hot Sauce into his evolving concoction. After a dash of something M.D. couldn't quite make out, Fixer added the package of smashed peanuts to the bottom of the bowl and began blending all the ingredients together with a ladle that he'd obviously stolen at some point from the penitentiary's commissary.

"This one of my specialties right here. I call it Prison Pussy Pad Thai." Fixer smiled wide.

M.D., unimpressed, didn't return the grin.

"And now, for the highlight." McCutcheon's new cell mate crossed back to his supply shelf and pulled down a small silver tin. "White chicken meat. On a special occasion like this, nothing but the best."

M.D. wrinkled his brow. "Why a special occasion?"

"A new cellie of your stature? This is practically a holiday for me."

"What do you mean, 'my stature'? How do you know about me?"

Fixer gazed at the ceiling as if it were a blue sky in a sunny meadow. "Little hummingbirds. They flutter everywhere in here. You just need to know where to listen."

Fixer waved his hands magically across the sky and then shuffled to the sink. After draining some water from the ramen noodles into the toilet he opened the can of white chicken meat and combined everything from the two bowls into one.

A surge of steam, spiced and flavorful, exploded from the hard plastic dish as the hot water and noodles hit the mashup of Fixer's ingredients.

"*Mmm-mmm*, you gonna love this."

An involuntary swallow of saliva swelled in McCutcheon's throat. "Why would I love what I'm not going to eat?"

"And why ain't you eating?"

"I don't want to owe anyone for anything."

"How can you owe for what's already been paid for?"

M.D. squinched his eyes. "Paid for by who?"

Fixer shook his head, turned, and reached into a basket under his bed. "So many questions. I guess for young people"—Fixer held up a shiny red apple—"a piece of fruit like this is so much more than just a piece of fruit. But for a geezer like me, with a penis that doesn't know how to sing the 'Star-Spangled Banner' anymore"—Fixer bit into the luscious red fruit and a spritz of juice sprayed from his mouth—"an apple is just a fuckin' apple."

Fixer extended his hand. "Wanna bite?"

McCutcheon stared at the offering. The apple looked crisp and sweet, but M.D. didn't reach out to accept the gift. In prison, *free* did not exist, and owing debts was a sure recipe for problems down the road. Convicts had been shanked over as little as the nonrepayment of a candy bar. Best to keep to his own, M.D. thought. Stay focused on the mission.

"I'm good."

"Toss me your mustard."

"What?"

"Your mustard? From the S.O.S. It's the only thing worth a shit in there, anyway."

M.D. reached into his bag and handed over his two mustard packets. Fixer grabbed them, went back to his shelf, took down a metal plate, and then set a flat silver dish on top of the stinger's wires.

"Fried mustard'll make my penis play the electric guitar."

"Is everything about your penis?"

"Pretty much. Ever since it died, that is. Then again, don't all of us want what we can't have? Have I mentioned I haven't been laid in over forty-seven years?"

"You did."

"Well, that'll tell you all you need to know about the cruelty of incarceration."

Fixer turned his attention to the mustard and meticulously squeezed every last drop from each of the packets onto the hot plate. Following proper jailhouse protocol, he then reached out his arm and offered the empty packets back to M.D.

"Suck?"

M.D. waved the old man off .

"Suit yourself." Fixer put the mustard in his mouth and extracted every last bit of flavor he could from each of the already empty packets. "In due time, everyone starts to suck. Ooh..." Fixer turned his attention back to the mustard crackling on the makeshift cooking pan. "Here we go."

Like a sous-chef in a five-star restaurant, Fixer mixed the sizzling mustard into the ramen noodle dish, twirled the contents in the bowl, holding two spoons in one hand like a man who'd graduated from a high-end culinary institute, and then blended everything together with musical smoothness, as if keeping a regular rhythm to his twirls enhanced the flavor of the food somehow. Once satisfied with his creation, Fixer unplugged the stinger and served up two evenly divided, heaping portions of sizzling hot grub.

The old man plunged a spoon into the bowl of the simmering jailhouse cuisine and then offered a nice, big serving to M.D.

"Dig in."

McCutcheon didn't reply. Instead he stared at the wafts of spiced scents rising from the dish that hit him in the nostrils and caused him to salivate against his will.

"No owe. You contributed the mustard," Fixer said. "So if it makes you happy, you can just eat the parts touched by that."

McCutcheon understood the logic behind Fixer's words. Since the mustard touched everything, M.D. could eat the entire bowl without feeling indebted. His new cellie hadn't just identified M.D.'s problem; he'd offered a solution, too.

But why, M.D. wondered. No, an apple was never just an apple.

On one hand, Fixer might have just been friendly, an old man with too much time on his hands, hungry for conversation and a sense of camaraderie. On the other hand, perhaps this was all a scheme, a way of manipulating M.D. into letting his guard down.

For what, an attack? M.D. considered the age of his new bunk mate.

Not likely, he deduced.

"What'd you do?" M.D. asked as he accepted the bowl of food, grabbed a seat on the edge of the bed, and loaded up his spoon. "You know, to get locked up."

"Murder one. Two counts. Gonna be fifty years next May," Fixer said. "And I know you're next question: how'd I do them?"

"Yeah, sure," McCutcheon answered.

Fixer's eyes narrowed as he watched McCutcheon take his first bite of food.

"I did it the old-fashioned way," Fixer replied. "With poison."

Suddenly, a surge of heat blazed in McCutcheon's mouth. Liquid fire.

M.D. spun his head around and immediately realized his new cell mate had not yet taken a bite of his meal.

"There, there, relax into it," Fixer said. "The pain won't last that long at all."

FOURTEEN

A guard's voice bellowed down the corridor. "Lights-out, Tier Three!"

Like a warehouse factory being closed for the evening, a switch flipped from on to off, and the overhead fluorescent lights in every cell on the block shut down for the night with a staticky buzz.

Darkness in the cages, however, did not mean there'd be silence.

"You fill his tank, old man?"

The thin and angled face of Krewls appeared between the weathered and worn bars of McCutcheon's cell.

"I believe he is satisfied."

M.D. found the word satisfied to be an interesting choice of terms. His body lay on the cot with only a thin piece of flattened foam serving as a mattress, and the scratchy gray blanket he'd been provided with smelled of mold and vinegar. Yet he'd just eaten one of the most delicious meals he'd tasted in years. The hot sauce burned his tongue like lava with the first bite, but seconds later the heat gave way to a delectable spice that left M.D.'s taste buds yearning for more. So yes, in one way McCutcheon felt extremely satisfied. In most others, however, he did not.

"Good," Krewls replied, spitting out the shell of another sunflower seed. "Get some rest tonight, sugar pie. Tomorrow's a big day."

Prisoners at the D.T. outnumbered the guards by a ratio of two hundred and sixty to one, which meant that no matter how much control the officers were supposed to own over the facility, the reality was the inmates were always but a moment away from being in complete and total charge. This is why Puwolsky couldn't have just staged an "accident" for the High Priest. To do so would have initiated a large-scale uprising from the largest gang in the institution, and Krewls knew that neither he nor his men would survive if something fishy occurred to D'Marcus Rose, while the High Priest was in their custody.

Shotcallers in the penitentiary didn't just simply fall down and bump their heads in the shower, and with soldiers protecting him on every inch of the yard, rival gangs couldn't get to D'Marcus, either. Ironically, in one of the most dangerous places in the United States, the High Priest enjoyed exceptional safety.

However, if M.D. punched his ticket, all bets were off.

"Yep, sleep tight, sugar pie," Krewls said, dreaming of all the money he was going to make. "And let me know if you want us to get you a li'l teddy bear to snuggle up with. We provide those, too." Krewls cackled as if he'd told that joke to new fishies a thousand times.

After the major vanished down the hall, McCutcheon

closed his eyes. Lots of different thoughts wanted to swirl through his mind, but M.D. knew nothing would be more beneficial to him than shutting down his tired brain and getting some rest. He'd been awake for more than thirty-eight hours. Taking advantage of the quiet before the storm made the most strategic sense. To expend energy tomorrow, he'd need to replenish energy tonight.

M.D. relaxed his body with a series of full inhalations and exhalations, progressing from slow and deep four-counts to slower and deeper eight-counts. He'd started meditating a few months earlier. Like most new students to meditation, McCutcheon found that his mind often raced from thought to thought. If he focused on his breath, however, with patience and single-mindedness, he learned he could penetrate beyond the bouncing thoughts and get to a deeper, more soulful inner space.

A place of spirit.

Relax, he told himself. *Be at peace. The wars will come soon enough and you will be ready.*

Suddenly, a bloodcurdling scream rang through the corridor.

"Nooooooooo!"

Its voice unmistakable.

"Ssstttooopppp! Pleeeaaassse!" McCutcheon sprang from his bed.

"Somebody. Heelllppppp! Oh my God, noooooooo!"

M.D. strained to see down the hallway, but the bars prevented him from acquiring a view.

"Guaaaard!! Heeeelllppp!! Pleeeeeeaaase!"

McCutcheon looked to Fixer for an explanation.

"There are three reasons new guests don't sleep during their first night in the D.T.," the old man said in a calm and even voice from his reclined position in the lower bunk. "Number one is fear. Ain't no bigger enemy than your own mind inside of prison. Ain't no greater ally, either. Kind of a puzzle, no?"

"SOMEBODY! PLEEEEAASSE!!"

Acoustics caused each plea to bounce like a rubber ball off the walls. Begging pinged from the left. Crying careened from the right. Screams for mercy, yelps for rescue, shouts for savior and relief popped off the ceiling, bars, and floor.

But no help came.

"OOOOWWWWWW! NOOOOOOOOO!"

Fixer reached under his bed, took an orange from his basket, and began to peel its skin.

"The second reason a new fish doesn't sleep on their first night in prison," he continued as he plopped a chunk of the fruit's juicy flesh into his mouth, "is unaccommodating cell mates."

M.D. paced the cage like a tiger, his stomach turning. The guy not named Timmy screamed and screamed, but to no avail.

"Your buddy got tossed into Cell One One Three. Too bad."

"Why doesn't somebody help him?"

"A person can lose their humanity in this zoo," Fixer said. "In fact, most do. Men come in; animals come out."

"But why don't the guards help him?"

"Help him?" Fixer asked. "They're the ones who put him in there in the first place. That end of the pod, they call it the Think Tank."

McCutcheon spun around. He'd heard that phrase before.

The Think Tank stood as a medieval theater in the round where the guards staged prison cockfights for gambling, sport, and fun. Conveniently located next to the Think Tank was Cell One One Three, a dwelling designed to motivate the gladiators, because the loser of a fight would sometimes find themselves tossed into the domain like a bloody fish thrown into the tank of a shark should the fighter's performance not be up to snuff.

If Krewls didn't think a combatant showed enough heart, guts, or effort, the con earned himself a little vacation time with Pharmy and Goblin, the longtime residents of Cell One One Three.

Pharmy was short for Pharmaceutical. As a six-foot eight-inch, three-hundred-eighty-pound mentally retarded inmate serving a life sentence without the possibility of parole for stabbing an emergency room nurse to death with a ballpoint pen, the penal institution had been experimenting with pills on him like a human lab rat since the early 1990s. Some inmates felt Pharmy wasn't even a real person any more; he was more like a forgotten creature existing in the bowels of the penitentiary like some sort of subterranean beast in a horrifying fairy tale.

He only listened to one person: Goblin, his four-foot two-inch dwarf cell mate who served as Pharmy's master.

Outside of lockup, Goblin, orphaned by his parents at the age of two and raised in sixteen different foster care homes over the next fourteen years of his life, struggled to survive in society. In jail, however, Goblin flourished. As a sadistic dwarf with yellowed teeth he'd self-sharpened into fangs and a wandering eye, Goblin owned no moral code and felt no remorse. Like Pharmy, all the years in the pit of the D.T. turned him from a person into a creature, and the two misfits became tied to each other like peanut butter and jelly. Goblin owned the wits and the will, Pharmy owned the brawn and the mass, and as an inseparable team they lived in the intestines of the D.T. as the unofficial regulators of the inmate population.

Push any of the guards too far and a convict went to solitary. Push a guard even further and an inmate might find himself vacationing for a night or two in Cell One One Three.

"Every now and then when things have been running dry, Krewls tosses them a bone," Fixer said.

"But why him?"

"'Cause every predator has to feed, and your friend, well . . . he just wasn't ever going to make it in here anyway. Somebody was gonna get him," Fixer said. "Krewls probably just decided to toss a cookie to his pets."

"HELLLLLPPP! PLEEEEAASSE!!"

"But they never gave him a chance," M.D. said.

"You should get some sleep."

"Fuck you."

"You wouldn't like it," Fixer said. "I just lie there."

McCutcheon continued to storm back and forth across the cell.

"You can't control what you can't control, kid," Fixer said. "You got your destiny, I got mine, your friend has his. Best, I learned, to just tune out."

Tune out? Impossible, M.D. thought. And even if he could, he knew he would never want to. Only a man who'd lost his soul could ever do such a thing, and McCutcheon felt he'd rather die than become that cold and unfeeling.

The screams continued.

"If it's any consolation," Fixer said, "it usually stops in about forty-eight to seventy-two hours."

"Why? What happens in forty-eight to seventy-two hours?" M.D. asked as the whimpering continued to ring up and down the halls. "They get bored?"

"Bored? No. Goblin's far too evil to get bored with a human toy," Fixer said. "What'll happen is your friend will be offered some shoelaces when Pharmy and Goblin get their hour in the yard for rec."

"Shoelaces?" M.D. looked down at his orange colored prison sandals. Most state facilities provided laceless footwear to convicts so they couldn't hang themselves.

With shoelaces.

"Krewls'll offer your friend an option," Fixer said. "Many who've been sent to Cell One One Three take it. Especially the new fish."

"This has been going on for a while?"

"Years," Fixer said. "Way I see it, not necessarily a

shameful thing, either, ya know? In here, a person's gotta do what they gotta do to survive, and ain't a man in this hell ain't thought at one time or another about ending their own life."

The yelling continued. Each time it died down, McCutcheon prayed for it to end, but then a new shriek would come—a different pitch, a different volume, a different tone—and the skin of McCutcheon would crawl again.

M.D. gripped the bars so tightly, the white of his knuckles looked as if his bones might burst out from underneath his skin.

"The don't call this place the Devil's Toilet for nothin'." Fixer rolled over onto his side, seeking to go back to sleep. "Really, try to get some rest, kid. Tomorrow, you're gonna need your strength."

"Would you help him if you could?"

"I can't."

"But would you?" McCutcheon asked needing to know.

Fixer shook his head. "This here ain't no place for these kind of questions, kid. In prison you do what you gotta do to survive."

The cries continued. All night. Hour after hour of wailing, begging, and screaming for someone, anyone, to put an end to the horror.

An end that never came.

Hour after hour passed with M.D. standing at the bars of his cage, wishing there was some way he could get out. How can he sleep? M.D. wondered as he looked down at

Fixer. *How can anyone in this whole place sleep?* There had to be hundreds of other men listening to the same cries as he was.

"What's the third reason?" M.D. asked.

"Pardon?" Fixer said, waking from his slumber. The old man tried to approximate the time. It had to be about three in the morning.

"You said there were three reasons a new inmate doesn't sleep during their first night in jail. What's reason number three?"

Fixer took a long, deep breath before responding. He could see that his new cellie still had a lot to learn about living in the world of incarceration.

"Reason number three is because they still have a conscience," Fixer answered. "But don't worry, kid. Soon, yours will die, too. Jail eats everyone's soul."

"SOME-BAH-DEEEEE HEEELLLLLLLPPP ME!!"

"Only one thing matters in here," Fixer said. "Your own survival. Remember that, kid. And just be thankful that it ain't you down there."

M.D. tried to open the bars of the cell door again using all his might. Yet it was all for naught. McCutcheon wasn't Superman, and he wasn't able to bend iron with superhuman strength. His cage remained locked, and no one would be coming to open it, either.

"PLEEEEAASSE HELP ME!"

"Ain't but two ways out of the D.T., kid," Fixer said. "Parole or the morgue truck. Till one of those days comes, every last one of us has to do what we gotta do to survive.

No apologies needed. Now get some rest. Or at least shut the fuck up so I can."

The cries bounced from wall to wall all night. By the break of day, begging turned to groaning and by sunrise groaning turned to silence.

Around 5:00 a.m. the wailing stopped. McCutcheon climbed into his bunk and finally laid his head down. As he closed his eyes, he realized the silence turned out to be the most disturbing sound of all.

FIFTEEN

McCutcheon didn't get a wink of sleep. He'd entered the D.T. voluntarily and remained determined to make his way through this mission with honor. Values, he knew, didn't change according to the environment. A good person remained a good person regardless of where they were. Locations did not matter; principles did.

"Why you goin' to breakfast when breakfast has already come to you?" Fixer reached into his box of goodies and withdrew a couple of hard-boiled eggs. "We got plenty."

"'Cause I'm not looking for food," M.D. answered.

Fixer stared at his young cell mate. "A guy who goes to the cafeteria not looking for food must be looking for something else."

"Conversation."

"Or trouble," Fixer said. "Then again," he added. "Sometimes, they're the same thing."

"Maybe."

M.D. stepped out into the hall and placed his hands behind his back, one wrist holding the other. Adapting properly to prison life meant taking cues from other inmates.

They would be his teachers. Head up, eyes scanning the perimeter, gaze not invading other people's personal spaces, yet also not leaving himself open to unforeseen ambushes, a cold, hard scowl at all times.

As a new fish, he'd certainly be tested. Where and when he could not know. After the night he'd just endured, however, M.D. felt eager to take on any man with the guts to try him. The first inmate to take a run at him would be the last.

Scores of prisoners marched single file to the left, hands behind their backs obeying the institution's rules like broken-spirited horses. M.D. began swimming upstream against the flow of traffic to the right.

"Where the fuck do you think you're going?" a guard's voice bellowed.

McCutcheon knew exactly where he was going: to Cell One One Three. He didn't care what kind of monsters lurked there; justice beckoned to be done.

But not on this guard's watch.

"Fall in line!"

M.D. remained exactly where he stood, fists clenched.

"I said, fall in line!" The guard reached out and grabbed McCutcheon by his arm with a show of blustery force. Unfortunately for the officer, his grip demonstrated zero technique.

Bad move, M.D. thought. Kimura time.

Over the shoulder, around the elbow, a snare of the wrist, then a motorcycle rev, and *snap*, bye-bye elbow joint. Six months in a sling, twelve months before this guard could even turn a door handle open without the use of a second hand to help. Another set of fingers suddenly grabbed McCutcheon from behind a moment before he struck. Now two would be headed for the infirmary, M.D. thought. He knew there'd be consequences for his actions—dire ones—but McCutcheon didn't care. Throw him in solitary for thirty days, sixty days, ninety days, it did not matter. Someone needed to stand up for the people who could not stand up for themselves. To M.D., he'd rather die for a cause than live with no code at all.

"Pardon his misdirection, Officer Clume," Fixer said, tugging McCutcheon's right wrist. "He's just a new fish. Doesn't know his ear hole from his asshole."

M.D. looked into his new cell mate's eyes. The old man stared back with directness and calm.

"It's the cafeteria you want, kid," Fixer said, not breaking eye contact. "That hunger in your belly, you can't fill it down that way."

Officer Clume, still holding on to McCutcheon with his tough-guy grip, glared at M.D. with no idea as to how close he stood to losing the use of his right arm for the next calendar year.

McCutcheon deliberated what to do. As a boy, he had been exploited a thousand times over in a thousand different ways. By the streets. By society. By his very own father. Now, as he stood on the precipice of being a full grown man, M.D. refused to be victimized anymore.

Nor would he allow others to remain hapless victims. McCutcheon took a personal vow that he would not sit idly by should the strong prey on the weak. If they did he promised himself that they'd be able to count on someone as dependable as tomorrow's sunrise to make things right.

Justice needed to exist.

The cafeteria stood to the left. Cell One One Three stood to the right. All eyes waited to see the direction in which McCutcheon would walk.

"My bad," M.D. said, heading left. "Guess I was going the wrong way."

"Damn right you were," Officer Clume replied. "Now move." M.D. began walking in the opposite direction of Cell One One Three. Not out of fear or abandonment, but rather because he remembered what the ancient texts always said about warfare.

He who knows when the time is right to fight—and when the time is not—shall be victorious.

Fixer was correct. McCutcheon would never make it to Cell One One Three before a swarm of guards tackled him, pepper sprayed him, and then smashed a few of his bones. Sure, he might be able to take on one or two or even four of the staff, but eventually they'd overpower him and make him pay.

Any battle would be for naught. No matter what his strategy, he'd lose. Though his heart burned with fury, his cool head needed to prevail.

M.D. fell in line, placed his hands behind his back, one wrist grabbing the other, and began walking in the same direction as all the other broken-spirited horses.

"I don't need you to save me," he said to Fixer as they approached the front of their cell.

"Sometimes it's best to go around walls rather than through them," Fixer said as he entered their cell. "Come on, let's eat and make jokes about my penis."

"Can't," M.D. said, continuing down the corridor. "I have a few other things to do."

"Busy morning, huh?"

"For a guy who can't get an erection, you certainly seem to have a hard-on for my business."

"Hey, I'm a nice guy like that," Fixer said with a toothy smile.

"No, you're not," M.D. said. "You're a survivalist. That means there's something in this for you. Don't think I don't know that, old man."

The grin melted off of Fixer's face.

"But don't worry, I have other fish to fry, so whatever li'l hustle you got goin' on, I won't mess it up for you. But know one thing: don't you dare fuck with me. Got it?"

Without another word McCutcheon jumped into the stream of prisoners and followed the train of convicts through a maze of walls and doors to the cafeteria, a large mess hall where all the silver chairs were attached to all the silver tables and all the silver tables were attached to all the yellowed floors. In Jentles, anything not securely attached would become dislodged and fashioned into a weapon. The prisoners knew how to make crossbows from dental floss, nunchucks from chair legs, and papier-mâché shanks from used toilet paper rolls.

In a population where more than eighty-five percent of the people had dropped out of high school, the D.T. housed scores of violent derelicts who functioned like Ivy League engineers.

M.D. grabbed a tray of slop he planned not to eat and scanned the room for the right place to sit. The whole scene reminded him of high school. At Fenkell, the cool kids sat in one area, the band kids in another, nerds on the left, misfits on the right, and so on. In Jentles, the same general rules applied, except people didn't group themselves by personality; they grouped themselves by gang affiliation.

Spotting the Priests required little effort. Being the largest army in the D.T. they commanded the best real estate: off to the back, in front of the bathroom, where no one who needed to take a shit could pass without gaining their permission.

McCutcheon, tray in hand, approached their province.

Three tatted-up soldiers rose from their chairs as M.D. walked forward. No one who was not a Priest was welcome in this area. M.D. knew this but still he continued straight ahead. The three Priests formed a human wall and the prison guard by the southernmost door, sensing a developing situation, placed his hand on his two-way radio in anticipation of a dispute. Five more soldiers rose as M.D. neared.

Still he walked forward.

It would be eight on one. McCutcheon continued forward, angry and fearless. Cold, hard eyes locked in on M.D. from all angles.

"Let 'im pass," a voice from the back commanded.

The wall of soldiers, not needing to be told a second

time, parted and McCutcheon stepped forward to the breakfast table of the High Priest.

"Well, looky fuckin' looky. Yo, Demon," D'Marcus called out. "Check out how the world just turned."

McCutcheon's father, sitting at the High Priest's table eating oatmeal, raised his eyes. The sight of his son in a prison jumpsuit stung him, but like all prisoners quickly learn in lockup, Demon kept his emotions hidden behind an unreadable wall.

"Fuckin' Bam Bam," the High Priest said. "Now what brings you to my li'l section of town?"

D'Marcus laughed and six of his lieutenants chuckled. M.D. remained stone-faced, in no mood for games.

"I will fight for you."

"You will, huh?"

"And I will win."

"I bet dat's true."

"But leave her the fuck alone. That's nonnegotiable."

McCutcheon set down his breakfast tray and extended his arm for a deal-sealing shake. Not a fist bump or a high-five but a traditional, classic, man-to-man handshake, as old-school as it gets.

Puwolsky might have wanted D'Marcus Rose assassinated because of all the mayhem he was bringing to the city of Detroit, but McCutcheon entered the D.T. with an entirely different objective. His only aim was to save Kaitlyn. Nothing else mattered.

In the big scheme of things, M.D. knew Kaitlyn's life

didn't really mean anything to the High Priest. Of course, M.D.'s life didn't really mean anything to himself if harm came to Kaitlyn because of his own entanglements with these gang members, either. This is why McCutcheon felt a negotiation could be brokered. M.D. would fly their colors in the Think Tank, take on whoever was thrown at him, win back the reputation of the Priests as the baddest boyz in the big house, and then collect his payment in the form of his girl being forever removed from their hit list.

Once this deal was made, M.D. knew D'Marcus would live up to his word, too. How? Because McCutcheon knew something that Puwolsky clearly did not.

Priests always pay.

McCutcheon had heard this expression hundreds of times during his years in Detroit. *Priests always pay.* It was the gang's motto, a creed they passed down from gangster to gangster, generation after generation over the course of their forty-year history. As hoodie-wearing businessmen running a multimillion dollar underground network of drug dealing, prostitution, bookmaking, extortion, and embezzlement, the Priests built their reputation on the simple fact that their word was their bond. If you were owed something from them, you got what you were due. Paid in full, proper, no shortchanging, period. Of course the Priests always got paid, too, and if you owed them a debt, they always collected, whether it be in terms of cash, favors, or blood.

Yes, the Priests may have been entirely vicious sociopaths, but also they were the most honorable group of criminals in America. Sometimes, M.D. knew, the logic of the streets made for a strange type of math.

D'Marcus stared at McCutcheon's outstretched arm, noncommittal and filled with thoughts he felt no need to share. Soldiers to his left and right awaited orders. If their shotcaller commanded McCutcheon smashed, eleven of them would have pounced before M.D. even had a chance to raise his arms.

McCutcheon understood the consequences of this gamble. He'd spent hour upon hour going over it in his mind, weighing the risks versus the reward. Ultimately, he knew the odds were not in his favor. Shotcallers didn't make deals; they dictated terms, and those who didn't follow orders—especially in prison—would eat a shiv in the shower.

Yet for Kaitlyn, this bet seemed worth it. His money down, the roulette wheel of his life spinning in front of him, M.D. waited to see where the ball of his destiny would land.

The High Priest took a last lick of oatmeal off his spoon, set it neatly down on his tray, and extended his hand.

"You have a deal," he said, shaking McCutcheon's hand man-to-man.

"Good," M.D. replied. "See you tonight. Oh, and one more thing."

"What's dat?"

"Keep him"—McCutcheon pointed at his father—"the fuck away from me."

D'Marcus smiled at the seriousness of the request.

"What, we ain't gonna have no father-son reunion over prison porridge?"

"I hate oatmeal," M.D. said, with a burn in his eye aimed squarely at his dad. "Like a lot of things around here, makes me want to puke."

Demon remained motionless and refrained from a reply.

The High Priest plunged his spoon back into a large plop of mushy brown hot cereal, and M.D. turned to leave, but then stopped as he spotted Night Train sitting at the table. Though Night Train's face looked like he'd been in a car accident, the prison infirmary had already cycled him back into general population, having swapped him out of the infirmary for a different convict riddled with lesions as he slowly died from the H.I.V. virus.

McCutcheon didn't know Night Train was a member of the Priests back in the intake room when he blasted him. Then again, it didn't matter to him much, either.

"Just pray I don't get my chance to run at you, li'l youngin'," the gangster said. "Night Train got a memory like an elephant."

"An elephant, huh?" McCutcheon answered. "Then you should be able to recall what happens when you fuck with Bam Bam."

His business done, M.D. walked away. Demon, having seen the exchange between his son and the muscle-bound gangster, smiled, but did it slyly, so that no else at the table could see his grin.

That's my boy, he thought.

"Demon, a word," D'Marcus barked. McCutcheon's

father rose from his chair and sat down right next to the High Priest.

"Yeah, boss."

D'Marcus rubbed his chin. "What the fuck was that all about?"

Demon watched as M.D. weaved his way back through the crowd of hardened criminals, the word INMATE plastered on his back.

"I ain't got no idea."

SIXTEEN

As McCutcheon lay in his bunk staring at the cracked ceiling of his cell it wasn't the thought of his upcoming war that ate at his mind; it was his father.

How did he even land in here? And how did Demon square his debts with the Priests? The last he'd heard his father had turned state's evidence against D'Marcus Rose because the High Priest had issued a green light on Demon's life, as a result of a few hundred thousand dollars' worth of gambling debts.

Yet now the two of them, the snitch and the shotcaller, were eating oatmeal together side by side like good old breakfast buddies? It didn't make any sense.

Of course, with Demon, little ever did.

McCutcheon worked to put the various pieces of the puzzle together. D'Marcus acting as if he had no idea that M.D. would even be arriving. Demon comfortably protected by a crew that once wanted his spinal column chainsawed in half like a piece of firewood. To McCutcheon, figuring everything out felt like assembling a model airplane that hadn't shipped with all the parts.

How in the world could he have—

A high-pitched alarm suddenly pierced the air and blared through the facility. Startled, M.D. spun his head around and saw three guards racing down the hall.

"Riot?"

"Nope," Fixer said, lying back on his bunk casually and reading a magazine on international cuisine. "Someone did the Dutch."

"Did the Dutch?" M.D. asked.

"It's slang," Fixer replied as another trio of black booted guards flew past their cell. "For committing suicide."

Suicide? M.D. thought. Who?

But before the question even fully formed in his mind, McCutcheon already knew the answer.

"Shoelaces?"

"Probably," Fixer said. "They work a lot better than bedsheets, which have a tendency to unravel."

Two more guards made their way toward the scene, but instead of racing they trotted with a lessened sense of urgency. Dead was dead, they figured. No need to hurry.

McCutcheon hopped down from his bed and tried to gaze down the corridor, but the iron bars prevented him from gaining a decent line of sight. Once again, he began pacing his domain back and forth, step after step, a trapped animal at the mercy of his captors.

Forty-five minutes passed, one torturous tick at a time, and then a small squeak became more and more audible. Soon a gurney appeared, its right front wheel wobbly, and it rolled past the front of McCutcheon's cell. Twenty minutes later the gurney squeaked past the cell again, but this time from the opposite direction, with a motionless body lying lifeless under a wrinkled sheet. The only thing M.D. could make out on the corpse were its shoes.

Orange, rubber-soled, and laceless.

Fury swelled in McCutcheon's heart. He wanted to rampage. To fight. To tear somebody's head off and make them bleed. Shark-versus-shark battles were one thing, but what had just happened to the guy not named Timmy was something else entirely.

A nerve had been touched deep inside him. Injustice was his button, his inner trigger, and a flood of rage, liquid cancer, toxic and lethal, began racing through his veins.

"Jail eats everyone's souls." M.D. didn't believe it at the time Fixer said it and he didn't believe it could ever happen to him. Now it was. The anger, the hatred, the fury, it made him feel...

Dare I even say it? he thought.

Murderous.

McCutcheon's inner beast awakened from its slumber, a giant rising from the depths of hibernation. M.D. felt its power, its strength, its energy. Most frightening of all, he felt its capacity to turn homicidal.

McCutcheon closed his eyes as waves of red and violence crashed through his chaotic mind. *Breathe, M.D. Breathe.*

He needed an antidote. Something cooling to douse the flames that threatened to engulf him. But what? What could bring him back from the edge of this dark and perilous abyss?

The squeak from the gurney's wobbly wheel faded from earshot, and McCutcheon searched for something to slow the stream of inner venom before it consumed him entirely.

Stay focused, M.D. Keep searching. Do not give in to the forces of hate.

An answer appeared. Love. Kaitlyn.

Focus on her. Focus on her now.

For convict after convict the thought of a special someone on the outside—an image, a dream, a memory, optimism for the future—represented the last rope to sanity an inmate could clutch. Whether real or imagined, to a con doing hard time, a person on the outside must be brought to the inside in order for the inside to remain a viable, livable place.

Hope would be the remedy. He must mentally go to a place beyond the perimeter, a world beyond the walls, a destination at which he would one day arrive with his soul still intact.

McCutcheon closed his eyes and saw Kaitlyn's shining face. Her green eyes flecked with sunshine. Her warm smile. The little wrinkle at the corner of her lip.

Perhaps it was a way of coping. He knew this. Perhaps it was a way of simply making it from one moment to the next. Whatever it was, it didn't matter. M.D. needed Kaitlyn now more than ever.

Just like she needed him.

Ever since M.D. arrived at Jentles, he'd told himself

not to think of her. Thought it would be too unhealthy to dwell. He needed to be disciplined, he thought. To stay focused on the world inside the walls so that he could stay alert, achieve his aim, and find the seam in the structure to escape. Puwolsky getting him out served as Plan A. Stanzer coming through for him somehow (even though they'd never discussed anything of the sort) served as Plan B, because he knew the colonel would never leave him hanging out to dry. Yet tucked away in the back of McCutcheon's mind was the knowledge he might also need a Plan C as well as a Plan D.

Trust no one was the rule. Except yourself, of course. Ultimately, M.D. knew, it might fall entirely up to him to find a way out of this hell.

Despite his initial plan to keep Kaitlyn away from his thoughts at all costs, a new voice in his head now cried out and begged for him to hold on to the vision of Kaitlyn, like a life raft in a sea of growing blackness.

Yes, she needed him but he, too, needed her.

Don't fight it, he told himself. *Think of her inner beauty.*

The beast within began to calm as McCutcheon began to remember he hadn't come here to fight for himself. He came to fight for her. The only reason he'd even ventured into this pit of despair was because he'd listened to the most golden part of his heart.

Now that gold, in his darkest hour, would need to sustain him.

Though uncertain about the existence of God, McCutcheon dropped to his knees and said a small prayer for the guy not named Timmy. He never had a chance, and now he was gone. What kind of God allowed for things like that to happen?

An answer did not arrive, but McCutcheon remained on his knees. Was it out of respect for the victim? Out of fear of nothingness? M.D. wondered if perhaps he needed to believe in God simply because he'd feel too hopeless about life without the knowledge that there was a good, loving, logical force behind all the things in this world that made absolutely no sense.

McCutcheon opened his eyes and found Fixer staring at him. "I gave up on God a long time ago," the old man said. "But to be fair, God gave up on me, too." McCutcheon rose from his knees. "And my penis," Fixer added. "God gave up on that as well, so if you're keeping score he's winning, two to one."

Fixer smiled but the grin was short-lived because a wooden baton clanked at the iron cage's door.

"Okay, sugar pie, hope you're ready for tonight," Krewls said. "'Cause in a few hours, it's time to rock-'n-roll."

SEVENTEEN

Krewls spit the gnawed shells of a few salted sunflower seeds onto the cold, concrete floor and reached into his pocket to reload his supply. Aside from the two guards who had escorted M.D. to the Think Tank, no one else had yet arrived for the midnight festivities.

McCutcheon surveyed the battle terrain. Hard walls. Hard floors. No impediments or perimeters, just a square-ish end of a poorly lit corridor with no windows, furniture, or phones.

Pretty straightforward, he thought. The only potential danger: the entrance to Cell One One Three lurking toward the back.

M.D. could see the front bars of the cage's door but little else as a result of the darkness engulfing the interior of the room. Cell One One Three looked more like a cata-comb than a standard prison cell. In the late eighteen hun-dreds the space housed the state's most mentally deranged inmates. Not much since then, it seemed, had changed. He knew evil lurked inside—M.D. could almost feel its presence—but more than this he could not yet tell.

McCutcheon made a mental note that no matter where the fight took him he needed to keep away from the front of those bars. Hands could reach out—maybe even teeth— and a win could turn to a loss if he found himself ambushed from behind.

As his eyes scanned the room searching for other clues that might help lead to victory, a door handle turned, and the sound of scratchy metal reverberated throughout the room. Seven prison guards emerged from a behind the door, each wearing red and green uniforms with black patches on their sleeves that read MOORLY. A felon, blond hair, hands cuffed behind his back, thick and taller than McCutcheon, followed behind.

M.D. immediately deduced that these guards had come from a different institution. McCutcheon had expected a war against a prisoner from Jentles. Instead, he realized, tonight would feature inter-penal system battle.

"No big crowds tonight, sugar pie. Just a private show- ing for me and some of my buddies down the road. That man right there," Krewls said, in reference to the prisoner M.D. would be forced to fight. "His name is Thrill Billy. A real wild one. Doesn't just like to beat opponents; likes to take their teeth."

Krewls withdrew a thick wad of hundred dollar bills from his pocket.

"But I got a feeling you like to chew that tasty food Fixer been fixin' for ya," Krewls added. "And me, well . . . my aim is to thicken this here stack and enjoy myself while I do it, too. Let's both head back to our beds happy tonight, shall we?"

Krewls spit out another sunflower seed and walked off to greet the men from Moorly, a three-and-a-half hour van ride from Jentles with no traffic. McCutcheon didn't pay much attention to the officers from the other facility, however. His opponent, Thrill Billy, captured all of his concentration.

The guards uncuffed Thrill Billy, and once liberated from his steel bracelets the convict shook out his wrists to get rid of the stiffness he felt from wearing handcuffs for so long. A moment later he yanked off his shirt without a care in the world for the frigid chill hanging in the air. A sea of blue ink covered his dense, puffy chest. McCutcheon knew a guy didn't get that swollen in lockup without having spent years on the yard.

McCutcheon studied Thrill Billy looking for any small insights he might pick up that could help him form a fight strategy. The skull tattoos, the spiderweb inked around the entirety of his neck, the letters E-W-M-N etched across each knuckle on his right hand, a prison acronym that stood for Evil, Wicked, Mean, and Nasty. Thrill Billy's whole body stood as a living, breathing painting.

A painting, McCutcheon realized, that told the tale of his personality. All color, rage, and in-your-face aggression. M.D. began to calculate his approach to the upcoming battle. The more he watched Thrill Billy warm up, the more convinced he became that he understood the best, wisest path to victory.

Thrill Billy threw a hurricane of strong, powerful left-right-left combinations and then rolled his head around on his neck with a big, wide, aggressive swirl. Not small rotations but rather full swivels designed to not only loosen up his body, but impress everyone with his thick, powerful torso. Each motion seemed exaggerated, every action occurred with a sense of pomp and confidence.

"Aaaaarrggghh!" Thrill Billy suddenly yelled, and then he smashed himself in the face with back-to-back open-handed slaps. The guards from Moorly smiled at the sound of their fighter's hands cracking his face. They liked their man's spirit. Liked it a lot.

Krewls crossed back over to McCutcheon, having locked in all the bets. M.D., knowing the time drew near, pulled off his shirt, folded it up neatly, and set it down on the floor off to the side where he expected it wouldn't get mussed up.

Krewls squinched his eyes. *Folding a prison shirt?*

The major looked his fighter up and down. McCutcheon sported no tattoos, threw no warm up punches, and made no show of aggression whatsoever.

"Aren't you gonna holler or something?" Krewls asked.

McCutcheon slowly turned his head and shot an ice-cold glare at Krewls. The major had been glared at by thousands of prisoners over the course of his career, but there was something different about the way M.D. lasered in on him, and Krewls felt his stomach sink. McCutcheon offered no words, but the major could feel the presence of a dangerous energy. Having already seen a taste of M.D.'s capabilities, he liked his fighter's chances.

Liked them a lot.

M.D. knew how Thrill Billy wanted to fight even before they traded their first strikes. He'd come out of the chute like a tornado, a bull rushing forward looking to storm his opponent. No fear. No hesitation. A cyclone of violence and rage.

Sure, M.D. could choose to stand and bang with him. Or he could hop on his bicycle and dance, peppering him with shots from the outside till a bigger opening to land a significant blow appeared. But the most strategic way to beat this opponent, M.D. knew, would be to get in his head. To frustrate him. To use Thrill Billy's own energy and aggression against him.

It was a classic judo mentality, and the more McCutcheon considered it, the more confident he felt it would work.

Clinch him up, lock him in tight guards, boil his blood and get him agitated. Once Thrill Billy began feeling constricted and tense in McCutcheon's confining holds, M.D. knew his opponent's anger would grow.

And with anger he'd lure Thrill Billy into a mistake. Set a trap. Snare his prey.

McCutcheon would use patience to battle his opponent's impatience. Use his mind to battle his enemy's brawn.

McCutcheon knew his battle plan. Fighting strength and aggression with strength and aggression is what Thrill Billy wanted. Clearly, power was his strong suit. But did he have the temperament to roll around on the ground for seven or nine minutes with his arms tied in knots and his legs wrapped in a tangle of locks, without the ability to strike, kick, or punch? How would he feel snarled on the ground, unable get more than three inches of separation between his hulking upper body and M.D.'s chest?

Thrill Billy wanted a striking war, so M.D. would take him to the ground and like a snake, slowly and patiently tighten his coil, until aggravation clouded his opponent's better judgment and he made a mistake. Once he did, M.D. would take advantage and finish the fight.

Perhaps an Achilles lock? Maybe an arm bar? Even something as simple as the snaring of the wrist that would lead to McCutcheon putting unbearable amounts of pressure on his foe's tiniest joints. No, it wouldn't be a sexy win with a big knockout punch and lots of blood, but M.D. owned no ego when it came to how he triumphed. What mattered most was victory—it was the only thing that mattered—and as McCutcheon watched Thrill Billy jump up and down like a hyper-caffeinated teenager who'd just swallowed a quadruple espresso, he knew his opponent had already lost the fight long before they'd even begun their dance.

He'd meet the storm with calm. The fury with serenity. Inevitably, cool waters always prevailed over hot seas.

"All right, my li'l darlings," Krewls called out with a gleam in his eye. M.D. prepared for war the way he always did, with a final slow, deep and patient breath. Amateurs tensed up before battle; professionals knew the value of staying relaxed and fluid. "Time to put your big-boy pants on, fellas, 'cause once again it's..."

"I know this is not what it looks like!"

All eyes spun toward the open end of the corridor. Walking up the hall, his black boots clicking with each step forward, came Major F. Franklin Mends, a newly minted major who'd recently transferred to the D.T. with the very clear goal of cleaning the place up.

Everyone knew the rumors. Everyone knew the gossip. F. Franklin Mends owned a master's degree in public policy and a second master's degree in criminal justice. He came to Jentles with a purpose. An idealist. As a man who believed in the power of reform.

An officer ready to put his money where his mouth was, too.

As many of his superiors knew, Mends could have pursued his agenda from the comfort of an air-conditioned office in the state capital of Lansing, but instead he chose to walk a beat.

"But why?" his wife asked when he informed her that he'd decided to take a position at Jentles.

"Because all reform must be started by people who have experience where the rubber meets the road."

"But we have kids, honey. Twin three-year-olds."

"It's not as dangerous as the media makes it seem."

"No, it's more."

"Jamie," he said taking his wife by the hand. "These are people I am trying to help. Human beings that are being treated like animals. I can do some good."

"Do your good at home, Franklin. I'm begging you."

Despite his wife's pleas, Mends took the position. She thought about leaving him over it. She knew he'd make no friends and be at constant risk every time he crossed through the front gates of the prison. F. Franklin Mends wasn't merely seeking to change a penitentiary; he sought to change a culture. His ambitions seemed too high, too risky, too fraught with danger. Jamie didn't have the stomach for it.

Franklin did.

"It'll be okay," he told her. "I promise."

She did not believe him.

"You're on the wrong block there, Major," Krewls said in an authoritative tone. "I know you're new here, but this area, my team, we already have it covered."

"Do not make me respond to this in an official capacity," Mends warned. "Times are changing, but I'll do the right thing tonight and give you a chance." Mends looked at the guards from Moorly. One report and multiple officers from multiple institutions would fry.

The Moorly guys held their tongues and looked to Krewls to make the next move. He was supposed to have his end entirely handled, and he didn't. Far as they were concerned, this was Krewls's mess and he needed to deal with it.

"Our friends have come a long way." Krewls peeled off five one hundred dollar bills, crossed the room, and stuffed them into Mends's pocket. Handling matters might cost a bit more than Krewls anticipated, but he figured he'd make it up on the back end by riding his new pony M.D. a little harder later on down the line. "Your shift, I believe, it's on Cell Block D. Right, Major?"

Mends removed the cash from his pocket and tossed the bills in the air. Everyone watched as the money fluttered like rectangular green birds crisscrossing their way down to the floor.

"*FSSSSSSSHHHH!*" came a sinister hiss. Mends spun around, and the face of a dwarf with a triangular nose and glowing eyes popped his head through the iron bars.

"You're in over your head, Major Mends."

"You're in up to your neck, Major Krewls. All of you are."

The two men glared at one another. A standoff. Krewls's eyes told Mends he needed to wander back up the hallway he'd just walked down, and go disappear behind some paperwork. Mends's eyes said that he'd snitch on every last one of his crooked comrades if this nonsense did not stop right away. Goblin and Pharmy began banging on the bars of their cell and howling like monkeys in a zoo. The Moorly officers, knowing their place, remained silent. Both Thrill Billy and M.D., still shirtless in the center of the room, remained where they were, neither knowing what to do next.

"I guess our brothers drove a long way for nothing," Krewls finally said.

"Not really," Mends answered. "They drove a long way to learn that they ought never drive this way again."

The seven men from Moorly glared. If a prisoner would

have set Mends on fire just then, not a one would have spit on the man to extinguish the flames.

"You," one of the Moorly staffers called to Thrill Billy. "Let's go."

Two minutes later the door slammed behind them, seven hours' worth of driving all for nothing. Mends, after picking up the neatly folded prison shirt sitting on the floor, tossed it to McCutcheon.

"I'll escort this gentleman back to his quarters," Franklin said. "You men can relax and finish your shift in peace."

Mends grabbed M.D.'s arm by the bicep and led him down the hall. Not in a domineering way, though, more like a caring son might lead an aging father by the arm with a strong but compassionate grip. Thoughts of reversing the hold and locking Mends into a Kimura never even crossed McCutcheon's mind.

"Don't worry, son, you won't have to do this again." Mends opened the door to M.D.'s cell. "You're not an animal. You're a human being entitled to fairness and dignity. The system needs to remember that. Going forward, we're gonna try." M.D. stepped inside his six foot by eight foot space and the door locked behind him.

"Get some sleep," Mends said. "I'm sorry it's gone so far."

Major Mends walked away, his black boots echoing softly through the prison with each receding step. M.D. turned around and saw Fixer staring at him. The old man inspected McCutcheon top to bottom, checked his face for injuries, his fists for signs of impact, his body for any markings of battle at all.

"Hmmm," Fixer said. "An interruption, I presume?"

M.D. didn't answer.

"The new guy, Mends?"

McCutcheon hopped into his bunk.

"A guy who thinks he is going to change the system is admirable," Fixer said. "But what guys like this usually find is that it's the system that changes them."

EIGHTEEN

Hostility and tension permeated the atmosphere of the prison like dampness does the air just before a rainstorm. At every turn the potential for violence existed. Inmate versus inmate. Guard versus inmate. Inmate versus guard. And now even guard versus guard. In a facility used to being on edge, a new edge existed, and each man in the penitentiary felt the tension of an invisible, threatening vibe.

Secrets didn't exist in lockup. Word had spread about McCutcheon, Mends, Thrill Billy, the guards from Moorly, and Krewls, and by lunchtime the only thing that remained unknown was how the conflict would be resolved. Disputes between gangs got settled on the yard or in the showers. But battles between guards? Would it be a war of paperwork or something more? No one knew.

Yet everyone felt this was just the beginning, not an end. Krewls had ruled too long and too viciously to simply walk quietly away.

Over the next twenty-four hours McCutcheon felt an eerie calm following him as he made his way through the

D.T. He took breakfast and lunch in his cell with Fixer, read about forty pages of a book the old man owned about a woman who quit her life to travel to Italy in order to eat, drink, and find the meaning of life, did an hour in the yard for rec with some stretching and a light workout, and then went back to his cell where he passed the time with a nap as well as intermittent visions of upcoming dream dates with Kaitlyn.

The entire day passed without incident. At each turn M.D. felt the gaze of many others following him, but obviously someone with significant influence circulated the word to leave McCutcheon alone.

Clearly, the request was being honored, too. Not a soul in the facility batted an aggressive eye in M.D.'s direction. He felt almost invisible.

"I didn't invent the prison campfire," Fixer said as he barbequed a few links of summer sausage on the thin silver poles of an old radio antenna. "But I definitely perfected it."

"It's delicious," M.D. said taking another bite.

"Making us some dessert, too." Fixer began pulling a few different packages down from his shelf. "I swear, if it wasn't for whippin' up food, I'd have gone nuts years ago."

Fixer rummaged through his supplies. "Commissary privileges what done saved me. I ain't eaten S.O.S. in over thirty-five years. Hmm, let's see." Fixer studied his resources. "Okay," he said with a smile. "Got it. In here, they call this Correctional Cake."

Fixer began walking M.D. through all the steps of cake

making, penitentiary style. "You start with some Oreos, but ya gotta scrape the cream out and set it aside, 'cause the cookie part, once ya crush it, becomes your dry crumb crust. I like to hold it all together with peanut butter." The old man held up a tube. "This stuff's gold. Run ya nearly fifteen smokes if you want to trade for it on the black market."

"I don't smoke."

"Neither do I" Fixer said. "Shit'll affect the performance of your penis."

M.D. laughed.

"Then ya mix the peanut butter with the inner cream of the Oreo and a dash of vanilla extract. Of course, some folks who ain't got my talents for securing ingredients just use water, but I got connections." Fixer carefully tended to the creation, his attention locked on the dessert with the same love for his work as that of a fine bakery chef. "Once I spread this wet mix over the top of the chocolaty crumbs, I crush up some M&M's and then do it all over again to make a second layer. Top it off with a few Hershey's Kisses, a little banana, and voilà! We're in business."

Fixer presented a cake. It looked as if it could win a contest on one of those cable TV cooking shows.

"I'm very impressed."

"Wait till ya taste it," Fixer said as he flipped a spoon around to slice it, using the handle of the utensil as if it were a knife. "*Mm-mmm!*" Fixer passed M.D. a piece.

"No, thank you."

"What? You ain't eatin'?"

"I keep to a pretty strict diet."

"Then why'd you let me make the damn thing?"

"'Cause I could see how much joy it brought you."

Fixer cocked his head sideways. "How much joy it brought me?" Fixer looked at the slice of uneaten cake. "You are acting way too civilized for a person facing more than four more decades in here."

"You know my bid?"

"Little hummingbirds," Fixer said. "They tell me everything." The old man set down the plate. "You know, you ain't never told me if you got a girl out there."

"Yeah, I got a girl."

"You in love?"

"The worst kind," M.D. said.

"I was, too," Fixer said. "She's the reason I'm in here. Two guys raped her at a dance club but they never even got charged. Prosecutor said my gal was dressed too sexy, dancing too suggestively, had been drinking too much, and was basically asking for it. Courts didn't even try the case."

"So you took them out yourself?"

"Poisoned their pizza pie. People gotta eat, and there are a million ways to slip some shit into a person's food if you know what you're doing."

Fixer took a bite of his dessert.

"Judge wanted to make an example out of me. Murder was one thing, but revenge killings based on the fact that the justice system had already weighed the evidence, and since I didn't like the outcome I took matters into my own hands, and, well...he said society needed to know vengeance like that could not be tolerated."

Fixer reenacted his judge's final words.

"'As defenders of the Constitution we must uphold the Constitution.'" Fixer balled his hand into a fist and smashed it onto his knee as if hammering down a gavel. "The court has spoken."

"How many more years you got to go?"

"I woulda been out five years ago but I had some time added to my sentence for bad behavior."

"How much time?"

"Seventy-nine years."

"Whoa! What'd you do?"

"Killed four more people," Fixer said, without a sense of remorse in his voice. "Not all at once, of course. At different times and in different ways. In here you do what you gotta do to survive. It was me or them. Well, guess who's still here?"

Fixer took another bite of cake. "There's a lot of ways to ice a guy in lockup. Beat a man till his brain gives out. Strangle him. It's hard to stab a guy to death, though. The human body is a lot tougher than you'd think," Fixer said. "Shanks are dangerous, but unless you get a strike directly into the skull, heart, or neck, the best strategy is to just go for the leg, that F artery."

"The femoral artery," said McCutcheon, a longtime student of human biology.

"Exactly," Fixer replied. "Stopping the hemorrhaging

with an ambulance on its way out in society is hard enough, but you slice that baby in here, it's a long way to a doctor. Go for the leg and have a fella bleed to death, that's my strategy. They never see it coming."

This old man has taken six lives, M.D. thought. Wow. Put Fixer in a delicatessen and dress him in a collared shirt and you'd think he was just a regular Joe eating a pastrami sandwich.

"Seventy-nine more years till I am eligible for parole, ain't that something?" Fixer picked up his cake and then set it back down, having suddenly lost his taste for dessert. "Only two ways out of the D.T., parole or the morgue truck. Me, I've known how I'll be leaving this place for a long time now."

A moment of silence passed before M.D. pried a little further. Usually, McCutcheon would have given the old guy his space, but M.D.'s next question tugged at him so hard he needed an answer.

"So what happened to your girl?"

"In my heart, I know she loved me, but then, well . . . she moved on." Fixer raised his eyes. "Once ladies come to terms with the fact that a guy ain't never coming back, like any other creature they got needs, and they move on."

Fixer walked over to the sink and set down his dish. "And really, who can blame them?"

McCutcheon, clearly not wanting to think about this possibility, hopped up into his bunk and lay down.

"Sorry," Fixer said noting M.D.'s sudden change of mood. "Guess I shouldn't have said that. Young fella like you probably still holding on to the illusion she'll wait for ya."

"It's not an illusion."

"Sure thing, kid. Sure thing."

A guard's voice rang down the hall. "Lights-out, Tier Three!" A moment later, darkness arrived.

"Can I ask you something?" M.D. said.

"Shoot."

"What's it like to kill somebody?"

Fixer scraped the uneaten cake on his plate into the toilet and began rinsing off his dish. The rest of the cake he kept on the shelf. Perhaps he'd use it to trade tomorrow for some packets of soy sauce.

"What you discover about killing folks is," the old man said, "that once you done one, there ain't much difference between adding on a second, a third, a fourth, or a sixth."

Fixer climbed into bed.

"And if the time comes to do number seven, you figure you'll go on do that one, too."

NINETEEN

lick! The cell door unlocked. It was just after midnight.

"Rise 'n shine, sugar pie. Time for some late-night fun."

Krewls, along with two other uniformed officers from the night before, stood at the front of McCutcheon's cell, waiting to escort M.D. to the Think Tank. Fixer remained in his bed, eyes closed, feigning slumber. He fooled no one, yet still he lay there motionless.

After granting M.D. a moment to take a piss and slap some water on his face, the guards led McCutcheon to the same place where the prior night's festivities were supposed to have been held. Again no audience awaited, no auditorium full of prisoners stood in attendance to cheer on their favorite gladiators in the hall. Instead, this match would be for the guards and the guards only. Seven of them. Unlike the previous evening, however, when the group stood by the near wall, the guards now waited on the opposite side of the arena, closer to the entrance of Cell One One Three. Other than that, everything looked very much the same.

M.D. spotted his next opponent, an angular Latino with buzzed hair and dark eyes. Not a big guy, M.D. thought. Wiry, with long arms for his body. Probably a boxing background. McCutcheon took a closer look at the convict's hands and saw knotted, weathered knuckles.

A boxer for sure.

"And so we try again," Krewls announced. "I do expect a far different result this time, however."

A couple of the guards from Jentles smiled as if an inside joke had just been passed, and then one of the officers pushed M.D. forward with a hard shove.

"G'head. Get going."

M.D. stepped into the center of the Think Tank, eye to eye with his opponent. A heartless glare stared back at him, made all the more intimidating by three small teardrop tattoos dotted beneath his foe's left eye, the universal prison sign for *I have killed before.*

McCutcheon, calm and poised, glared back, no fear on his face, no fear in his heart. "I do not want to fight you," M.D. said even though he understood the inevitability of conflict.

"Wouldn't want to fight me, either," the man replied with a broken toothed smile.

M.D. shook his head. *Does everyone in this place use the same line?*

"Gentleman, I think you know the..."

"I cannot fucking believe this!"

Mends stormed up the corridor his index finger pointing squarely at Krewls.

"You think I'm messing around?" Mends grabbed the Latino prisoner by the arm and barked an order at one of the lower ranking guards.

"Take this man back to his cell right now."

Silence filled the air. No one moved. Fury from Major Mends rose from his chest like hot steam. Clearly, he could not believe the audacity of these men. Particularly Krewls. For F. Franklin Mends, this was the straw that broke the camel's back.

"I said now!"

After a look to see what he should do, Krewls nodded and the guard began escorting the Latino prisoner back to his cell.

"And you," Mends said spinning around to face Krewls. "You are going to burn for this."

Krewls didn't reply. Instead he just stood there smug and quiet, like he knew something Mends did not.

"You think this is a game? You think I am going to allow this to slide again? I warned you. I warned all of you that—"

Suddenly, the door to Cell One One Three popped open, and like a bat flying from its cave, Goblin leaped onto the shoulders of Officer Mends and bit his ear.

Pharmy stormed forward next, like a bull seeing red. Mends, not having seen either of the attacks coming, took a thunderous forearm from Pharmy to the back of the head, and the major was stunned.

Though two prisoners attacked one of their fellow officers, not one of the remaining six guards in attendance made a move to help. That's when McCutcheon realized there was never going to be a fight. It was a trap, and Mends had fallen into it. Teach the do-gooder a lesson, send a message about how things really work in the D.T., that kind of thing. The fighters were merely bait, and now the fish was on the hook.

Pharmy clubbed the reform-minded Mends with a second forearm shiver to the head. Then a third. The impact of each blow from the nearly four-hundred-pound man hit the major like a sledgehammer, and Mends's eyes clouded.

A fourth blow rendered him unconscious.

"*FEEEEEEEEE!*" Goblin hissed. Pharmy, slow and lumbering, grabbed Mends by the collar of his shirt and began dragging him across the floor toward the entrance of his cell.

Goblin hopped over Mends, popped inside, and smiled deliciously as if tonight would offer him unprecedented joy. He and his cell mate had been fed many a man before, but never a guard. Extraordinary torment awaited.

McCutcheon scanned the faces of each of the guards as they watched their peer being dragged to doom.

"Dangerous patrol this corridor, huh?" Krewls chuckled. "Dang old cells; weird how they sometimes just don't stay locked."

Of the six remaining officers in the Think Tank, three smiled, one remained stone-faced, and two others wore looks of soul-wrenching concern.

Should we stop this? Go help him? Their faces revealed an inner struggle, a battle between the light and dark part of their hearts. *How had it gotten this far*, they wondered. *How deeply had they sunk?* Neither of them ever imagined something like this would ever occur, yet now it had, and they had no idea what to do.

Frozen by a combination of indecision, cowardice, and fear of reprisal from their corrupt and criminal peers, the two guards simply watched as a monstrously large mentally retarded inmate dragged one of their own into the prison's darkest dungeon.

Goblin licked his lips.

Mends regained a bit of consciousness and looked up with frightened, pleading eyes. Brave as he was, Mends was not so brave that he was ready to face this. He looked to his partners, an appeal in his eyes, the sad look of a terrified boy on his face imploring his daddy to help, to please stop this whole thing from happening before the Boogeyman became all too real.

His allies, led by Krewls, did nothing. Mends offered a last bit of struggle, a final attempt to crawl away, but Pharmy cocked another large right hand and punched Major Mends in the back of his head. A *boom!* rang out. Mends went unconscious. Again.

There would be no more resistance.

McCutcheon led with a side-kick to the back of Pharmy's leg, and followed with an elbow to the giant's ear that caused him to yelp and release his grip on Mends. The major fell like a sack to the floor, and the eyes of each of the guards from Jentles bulged from their heads, shocked by the sight of what they'd just seen.

He's gonna help him?

Like a demon, Goblin pounced from the darkness into the center of McCutcheon's chest, and the dwarf's momentum carried M.D. to the floor. With fanged, sharpened teeth Goblin bit down on McCutcheon's shoulder the same way a feral coyote would bite down on the neck of an innocent deer.

McCutcheon screamed in pain as blood ran from the dwarf's mouth, but Goblin's success was short-lived. M.D. threw the dwarf off him with a surge of strength that sent the dwarf flying nine feet high in the air. He landed with a thud and groaned. Seeing Goblin hurt, Pharmy stormed forward, an angry rhinoceros, and smashed McCutcheon like an offensive lineman mashing a football sled. M.D. took the hit at full speed and the ferocious tackle bounced M.D.'s skull off the concrete floor, bringing cobwebs to his head. Staggered and instinctively sensing trouble, M.D. jumped to his feet, knowing he needed to use his speed. Rolling on the ground to battle this monster would be a terrible strategy.

But it was too late. Pharmy snatched McCutcheon's leg and pulled him to the ground.

Squirm away. Get to your feet. Do not stay on the floor with him.

The weight of Pharmy, however, proved too much for M.D. to move. The gigantic man, understanding his advantage, used his leverage to roll his big belly onto McCutcheon's face, and before M.D. could slither away the man smothered his foe with flab. M.D. turned his head to the side, struggling to breathe, and Pharmy bounced his balloonish gut up, then down, purposefully using his stomach's immense girth to slam McCutcheon's head into the floor.

M.D. shot a laser beam strike at the big man's ribs, but he couldn't get much leverage on the punch to create any meaningful impact, and Pharmy used his weight once again to slam McCutcheon downward.

Another tremendous boom echoed off the walls and M.D. lost his wind. The beast prepared for a third, a fourth, and then a fifth up-and-down collapse.

"Should we stop it?" one of the guards asked. "You know, keep your boy fresh for some of the big money wars we talked about?"

Krewls popped a sunflower seed into his mouth and considered the question. "Gimme five hundred bucks on the hero."

"Against Pharmy and the troll?" the guard replied. "I thought the plan was save the kid to fight bigger fish?"

"'Round here," Krewls replied, "people gotta save themselves."

"Fuck it, I'll take that action."

"Me, too," another guard said.

Krewls pulled out a wad of bills from his pocket. "I've always been a sucker for the underdog anyway," he said. "Plus, with the stakes this high, well...I'm bettin' this kid's gonna get resourceful."

"You got it, sir."

The guards worked out their bets.

"I really wish we had some chairs, boys," Krewls said looking around. "'Cuz I got a feeling this one here will be worth a seat."

TWENTY

M.D. had fought large and heavy opponents in his life but never anyone this gargantuan. From such a weakened, vulnerable position, he knew his only play would be to go for the vitals—eyes, throat, or groin—but Pharmy already had M.D.'s arms pinned to his sides, and the fat of his gigantic stomach prevented McCutcheon from being able to either strike or squirm away.

Even breathing was a battle.

Pharmy, using his weight smartly, continued to attack M.D.'s head with big booming falls. Both of the fighters knew it was only a matter of time before M.D. suffered one too many slams and concussed. McCutcheon fought as best he could, wriggling to his right each time Pharmy hoisted himself upward, but still found himself unable to slide away before yet another colossal detonation of flesh smashed down onto his skull. M.D. took heaps of abuse, unsustainable abuse, with each new crash reaping even greater consequence for his opponent. Giving away nearly a foot in height and two hundred pounds of weight in a ground war, offered McCutcheon almost no odds for success.

"Ooh," a guard said to Krewls after yet another belly flop smashed into McCutcheon's face. "That's gotta hurt."

"And smell, too," another officer added. "I mean, when's the last time any of you have seen the big fella shower?"

A couple of laughs escaped their lips as they watched Pharmy continue to smother and pound M.D. Though he struggled with all his might, McCutcheon could not get to any of Pharmy's vitals.

So he decided to let Pharmy's vitals come to him.

The huge beast set himself up for another immense collapse, but this time, instead of spinning to his right, M.D. broke the pattern, wriggled to his left and bent his leg at the knee.

Pharmy, with irreversible momentum, slammed down with another huge explosion, but instead of slamming into McCutcheon's face, he jammed his own testicles into the top of McCutcheon's knee.

Upon seeing the impact each of the guards instinctively grabbed their groins and averted their eyes. Pharmy's eyes rolled to the back of his head and he flopped over breathless and immobilized. McCutcheon staggered to his feet and shook the cobwebs from his head, but before he could drop-kick Pharmy in the face, Goblin jumped onto his back and bit him for a second time in the same shoulder from which he'd already taken a huge chunk.

M.D. screamed in pain and his blood began to boil. Something about being bit snapped M.D., turned him from conscious fighter into primal animal, and a moment later, seething with rage, McCutcheon reached around his back, reversed the position on the dwarf, and grabbed the evil dwarf by the sides of his head.

Then twisted.

A crack echoed off the walls. Goblin's eyes bulged wide, then froze, open and hollow. McCutcheon, shirtless, sweating, blood running down the front of his rippled torso, released his grip and the dwarf fell to the floor.

Lifeless.

M.D. took a step backward, sucked some wind in order to get his body the oxygen for which it starved, and readied himself for the next phase of Pharmy's fury. He expected unprecedented wrath from the beast, a level of ferocity the likes of which he'd never yet seen in an opponent. Collecting his wits he resolved to stay on the outside, on his feet, too, with a plan to dance and strike. Speed and quickness would be the path to victory. When the opportunity appeared, he'd go for the eyes or throat. Maybe even fishhook Pharmy's mouth or jam a finger three inches deep into his ear hole. Rules were gone. Ethics were out. Survival was all that mattered.

He'd have to defeat this foe by any means necessary. Nobility in warfare had just become a luxury he could no longer afford.

Head shots, head shots, head shots were the only thoughts that ran through his mind.

Pharmy climbed to his feet, but in a move that surprised everyone, did not storm forward. M.D. raised his fists and waited for the rage, but noticed that the look of violence and anger had disappeared from Pharmy's face. Instead, the giant softly limped to his fallen cell mate, dropped to his knees, and tenderly tried to arouse Goblin from his sleep.

"Brutha, Wake. Brutha, wake now. Wake."

Pharmy poked at Goblin with his thick index finger, but the midget lay motionless on the floor, entirely unresponsive.

"Brutha, wake now. Wake."

Like a puppy trying to lick its mommy's nose after she'd just been run over by a car, the human beast hunched over the only person on the planet that he'd ever loved.

Or who loved him back.

"Wake please, Brutha. Wake."

McCutcheon's heart fell into his stomach. *What have I done?*

Mends eyes blinked open and slowly he sat up.

"You oughtta check those locks a little better next time, crusader," Krewls said to Mends as he prepared to walk away. "Me and my first lieutenant will each mention it in our incident report how the two inmates must have jimmied the thing during your hallway patrol. And the midget slipping on the wet floor, well . . . we really oughtta get that leak in the ceiling fixed, too."

"Brutha? Brutha?" Pharmy said, confused by Goblin's unresponsiveness.

"Here's your cash," one of the guards said to Krewls as he handed him a stack of neatly arranged bills.

"Yep, really oughtta fix that leak," another of the guards said to Mends.

Krewls took a deep sniff of the green paper. "Ah, I love the smell of money on a Tuesday night."

TWENTY-ONE

The guards threw a weary and worn McCutcheon back inside his cell, and as the door locked behind him the words of Colonel Stanzer echoed through M.D.'s head: *You've been spared so far, but at some point every last one of us who does this kind of work gets bloody with stains that don't wash off.*

Stanzer always wanted to turn me into a killer, McCutcheon thought. He always wanted me to taste blood, to bury my naïveté, to slay my dragon.

Well, fuck him. Fuck him for ever dragging me into this.

Fixer wetted a washcloth and reached out his hand. "Here, try…"

M.D. snared his cell mate's throat. "Do not touch me, old man. And do not say a goddamn word, either. I don't want to talk. Especially about your penis."

Fixer lowered his arm, M.D. released his grip and then hopped into his bunk. He wanted to rest, sleep, vanish, disappear. But of course, he couldn't. Only one thought raced through his head.*What have I just done?*

TWENTY-TWO

At six the next morning a bell cried out, signaling the start of a new day. Fixer, as usual, remained in his cell, choosing not to go to the cafeteria for breakfast. M.D. stayed, too. There was nothing out there for him anymore. Nothing at all. So he went back to sleep for another three hours. When he woke, he saw the old man smiling and stirring a cup of tea.

"Oh, the hummingbirds are flapping today."

"Fuck the hummingbirds," M.D. said rolling back over.

Even before all the oatmeal had been plated in the cafeteria, word spread throughout the entire prison about how McCutcheon defeated Pharmy, snapped the neck of Goblin, and saved a guard. It made for great breakfast time conversation. It also created an incredibly large problem for M.D. Taking the side of a screw over a fellow inmate carried a price.

The penalty of death.

When McCutcheon saved Mends he signed his own death certificate, because in the world of prison it was always the convicts versus guards. Anyone who violated this law of life behind bars required swift and immediate payback. In a culture with no values, rules were still rules. Us against them. Always. Saving a guard was worse than snitching.

"Good still flickers in your heart," Fixer said admiringly. "Prison extinguishes that in most men."

"There's no good in here, only darkness. I was a fool to come."

"You didn't choose to come. It was your destiny."

"My destiny?" McCutcheon still felt numb about the idea he'd taken someone's life. "That's what I'm afraid of."

"You're a special one, kid. All my years I ain't never seen nothing like it. Got me so inspired, I feel forty years younger. Only thing is," Fixer said as the sound of boots stomping up the hallway grew louder. "I think the games for you have just begun."

Five guards stormed to the front of their cell.

"And perhaps for me as well."

The cage door flew open and a black-booted officer slapped the tea from Fixer's hand, sending the cup of hot liquid rocketing against the wall.

"Toss this place. Now!"

After roughhousing M.D. and Fixer out of the cell, the guards, following Krewls's orders, began attacking every personal item in the small domain. Bit by bit they threw all of Fixer's things onto the floor. M.D., of course, owned nothing.

"Contraband!"

They smashed his cooking ladle.

"Contraband!"

They smashed his collection of spices.

"Contraband! Contraband! Contraband!"

Each and every item Fixer owned got tossed onto the floor and mashed into fragments by the heel of hard, black, steel-toed boots. From the cache of fresh fruit to the chocolate chip cookies, from the plates to the cups to the spoons. They even destroyed his beloved stinger.

Krewls nodded approvingly at the dismantling of Fixer's life. Then, discovering one more thing that required attention, Krewls reached out, removed the pair of black eyeglasses from Fixer's face, and dropped them to the floor.

SMASH! His boot slammed down on the spectacles and blasted them to smithereens.

"I'm sure once we requisition another pair, the order'll be filled in what, eight to ten months?"

"Fuck you, Krewls!" Fixer cackled. "You can't get to me. The kid beat you. The kid owns you. The whole prison knows it, too." Fixer turned and shouted at the top of his lungs so the entire cell block could hear. "THE KID KICKED YOUR ASS!"

BAM! Krewls bashed the old man in the gut and Fixer fell to the ground, grabbing his stomach. Just as it wasn't a coincidence that the guy not named Timmy ended up in Cell One One Three, it also wasn't a coincidence that M.D. ended up sharing a cell with Fixer. The old guy was supposed to guide the kid. Teach him the rules. Keep his belly full, his body healthy, keep him out of trouble, and make sure the young stud toed the line.

Saving a guard hadn't just pissed off the entire inmate population; the guard M.D. saved was a guard Krewls had set up. Hell needed to be paid for the defiance, and the first person to make good on the debt was the old man to which Krewls had granted lots and lots of leeway.

It took a moment for Fixer to catch his wind but once he did the old man raised his eyes and glared at Major Krewls.

"You can beat our bodies, but you can't beat our spirit. And the kid," Fixer said. "He just reminded us all of that. Reminded the entire population." After forty-seven years in lock up, Fixer realized he had sold his soul. It never bothered him either, because every last con he'd ever encountered eventually ended up selling theirs, too. Except McCutcheon. M.D. hadn't and he wouldn't, and that inspired Fixer to see his world in a whole new light.

The old man struggled to his feet and began to chant.

"Long live the kid! Long live the kid! Long live the kid!"

"Throw him in ad seg," Krewls said.

"For what?" the guard asked.

"Defiance."

"But he's a geezer, Major. Guy ain't gonna make it through a long bid in solitary."

"I said throw him in ad seg!" The officer clearly didn't want to do it, but like every other guard on the staff, he knew that Krewls ran the ship and he feared the major's power.

"Let's go, Fixer," the guard said with a soft tug of the old man's arm.

"The kid beat you, Krewls. No matter what you do

from here, the kid beat you." Again Fixer began shouting at the top of his lungs. "We are human beings! We are people! You can take our bodies but you can't steal our souls. Uprising! Uprising! Long live the kid! Long live the kid!"

Krewls pushed M.D. back inside his cell and locked the door. "Clean this mess up," he said to M.D. "Or not," Krewls added. "I don't care what he says about 'Long live the kid' or about how badass you think you are, the chances of you making it to see dinnertime three nights from now fall somewhere between fuckin' nada and nope-er-rooskie."

"Long live the kid! Long live the kid!"

Fixer's shouts became more faint as the guard escorted him down the hall and into solitary confinement. A moment later Krewls walked away, but it didn't escape McCutcheon's attention that not a single other prisoner on the cell block joined in on Fixer's chorus.

Not because the other cons didn't understand Fixer's sentiments. Not because they didn't agree with these sentiments, either. The reason that no single man offered even one peep of support came because of only one thing.

Fear of retribution.

A green light had been issued on McCutcheon, a command that called for his death.

A green light that had been issued by the High Priest.

TWENTY-THREE

Since McCutcheon would have been flying the colors of the Priests in the Think Tank, it fell on the Priests to handle their own man. Otherwise, if another gang had to do the deed of keeping a renegade convict in check, the Priests would be seen as "punk-ass bitches" who'd broken the unspoken code of life behind bars.

In lockup, all gangs self-regulated their own people. If they didn't police their own when a code was broken and another gang had to do it for them, rivals gangs would consider this absence of retribution an act of war. The Priests may have been the largest gang in the facility, but if all the other gangs united against them, any battle was sure to be bloody and costly.

For their part, the Priests had no real reason to stick by the side of M.D. anyway. And there was every reason in the world to sell him out and make him pay.

All the shotcallers agreed: M.D. had to go. The High Priest concurred, as well. In fact, he even saw it as an opportunity to prove his unrivaled supremacy. D'Marcus would make the hit on McCutcheon more notorious and more infamous than any other hit ever executed in prison. Cons would talk about this icing for decades. Not only would the Priests take out McCutcheon, but D'Marcus decided that he'd make Demon seal the deal.

"Make a father kill his own son," D'Marcus boasted. "Now that shit shows POWER!"

He decreed the order. Word spread through the prison. No one was to touch M.D.

No one except Demon.

Later that afternoon, the High Priest handed Demon an eight-inch silver shank fashioned from the leg of a broken bed frame. Its spiked end had been sharpened to a fine triangular point. When Demon was first handed the weapon, he thought it looked like something that could kill a vampire.

"I have spoken," D'Marcus said. Demon held the shiv in his hand and felt its weight. With masking tape wrapped around the back half of the shank the weapon owned a firm and solid grip. A strong tool, indeed. Capable of great destruction.

"We'll rush as a mob, hold him down and then you'll strike. Am I clear?"

"Clear."

"You got any reservations about what you're gonna do?"

Demon raised his eyes, confident and alert. "None at all."

"Good." The High Priest smiled. "I can't wait to see this shit. We'll roll at chow time tonight."

But M.D. didn't go to dinner that night, and though

the S.O.S. offered little that he liked, the bag of food that Mends provided got McCutcheon through the evening.

And the next got him through breakfast, and the next got him through lunch, and the one after than got him through dinner the next day. The Priests didn't have a chance to get to M.D. out in the open at all, and after twenty-four hours of inaction, the other inmates in prison started getting restless.

After thirty-six hours, rival shotcallers began to question the intentions of the High Priest. Maybe this was a power play, a way of showing every other con on the yard that the biggest dog in the park got to make its own rules? A big fuck-you to everyone else. The whole prison grew tense and looked at risk of descending into chaos. Something had to be done. Krewls knew it. He understood that the whole facility stood on the edge of anarchy.

"Mends thinks the guards are in charge," Krewls told one of his lieutenants. "We don't take action, this whole place is gonna blow and we'll be living in a shit storm for months."

Of course Mends didn't live at the jail and couldn't monitor everything twenty-four hours a day, so on the third morning after McCutcheon had saved the major from Pharmy and Goblin, while Mends rolled on the carpet of his town house with his twin three-year-olds rolling on top of him, Krewls arranged for M.D. to have a little rec time on the yard, whether he wanted to go or not.

McCutcheon knew he'd been set up. He understood that he'd been tossed into the rec area where the ad seg guys got their daily hour of court-ordered fresh air, a twenty-four-by-eighteen-foot pen, on purpose. There was only one way in and one way out, and after the guards brought M.D. into this rectangular steel cage and told him to enjoy his workout, he knew to expect trouble.

Twenty minutes after he'd been locked alone in the steel enclosure, no other prisoners around, no other guards on duty, Mends at home spending some time with his family, McCutcheon saw a door open.

In stepped seven Priests. Night Train first, four other beefy, hardened soldiers behind him, then Demon, and finally the High Priest.

McCutcheon backed up, took off his shirt, and neatly folded it up before placing it on the ground.

"This is gonna be delicious," D'Marcus said with a beaming smile.

Five Priests fanned out before rushing at McCutcheon, while Demon and D'Marcus held their position in the back. M.D. knew there was no way possible for one man to fight five guys—but he also knew he didn't need to fight five guys.

He only needed to fight one guy. Five different times in a row.

He landed an elbow in the center of Night Train's face, and re-smashed the nasal cavity he had already hammered in less than a week earlier. Night Train crumpled to the ground, and M.D. knew that after a blow like the one he'd just delivered, Night Train would not be getting up.

Stay outside, M.D. thought. Fight the guy on the edge and keep pushing him away.

The huddle grew tighter around him and McCutcheon shot low and outside to the left. His punch landed right above the groin of his second target, and the gangster buckled forward from the impact. M.D., however, instead of following up with a shot to the face, pushed the second Priest to the inside, causing him to block the path of his fellow attackers.

The obstruction worked, but only for a moment, because McCutcheon ran out of room. The fence behind him cut off the rear, and the fence to his right left him no space to maneuver to the north. A third Priest rushed forward and ate a big fist, but attacker four and attacker five each landed clean, heavy blows. M.D. tried to trade with them, but there were too many assailants and not enough space, and thirty seconds later McCutcheon found himself unable to hold off the assault.

They had him and they began to make him pay.

They drilled M.D.'s ribs, face, and head with thunderous blows and then, once wobbled, the Priests held M.D.'s arms up against the fence, laying the center of his chest bare. Demon stepped forth, reached behind his back and withdrew the long, sharp killing device.

McCutcheon, bleeding from his face, made eye contact with his father. Demon's gaze looked empty, cold, and soulless.

"Daddy brought you into this world," D'Marcus said. "And now Daddy's gonna take you out."

The four Priests restraining M.D. smiled.

"I seen a lot of men die," D'Marcus continued. "But this memory is gonna last a lifetime."

Demon raised the shank, its edge poised to strike.

"Die, motherfucker!" His heart filled with rage, Demon struck with all his might and nailed his target exactly where he aimed, driving the metal spike five inches deep into the soft flesh of his victim's neck.

The High Priest staggered backward and gagged, blood gushing from his jugular like an uncapped oil well spouting a red stream of liquid gold high into the air.

Stunned by the sight of their leader being stabbed in the neck, the four Priests restraining McCutcheon instinctively relaxed their grip. Demon led with an overhand right and then followed with a crisp left cross, landing two stone cold shots, just like he used to do back during his days as a professional boxer. Each blow hit its mark, and the Priest holding McCutcheon's right hand crumpled to the ground. With a newly freed arm, M.D. smoked an elbow that cracked a Priest on his temporal lobe, and the man on his left crumpled, too.

Four on two turned to three on two and three on two quickly turned to even odds.

Son fought by father, side by side, and before another two minutes had passed, the Daniels men were the only ones left standing inside the steel cage.

Demon and his son stepped over a fallen enemy and headed for the door, leaving a gaggle of bodies bloody and battered in their wake. D'Marcus spasmed as he tried to pull the spike from his neck, but it had been lodged too deep, and with each passing moment he lost more and more blood.

Demon slapped M.D. on the back as they exited through the doorway and smiled.

"Good to see ya, son."

TWENTY-FOUR

When Demon and M.D. stepped out onto the main courtyard where all of the general population inmates took their daily free time, Krewls's mouth fell open. He'd been expecting D'Marcus and his crew of felonious henchmen to walk through the ag seg door he'd opened for them fifteen minutes earlier. Instead, he saw McCutcheon and his father and no one else.

"A few of dem guys musta slipped back there," Demon said as he sucked a small stream of blood running from the knuckle of his right hand. "I myself didn't see much but I can only imagine a fall like that gotta be mighty painful."

McCutcheon and Demon continued forward and walked over to an unoccupied cement bench far away from every other con on the yard. Moments earlier eighteen hundred prisoners had been doing push-ups, playing checkers, or shooting the breeze, but the sight of M.D. still on his feet after all the bragging and boasting the Priests did about how they were going to orchestrate a father taking out his very own son, caused man after man on the yard to stop, stare, and wonder.

If McCutcheon was here, then who was in there? Eyes scanned the ad seg entranceway, but no one else appeared. Suddenly small huddles began to form across the yard. Krewls popped a sunflower seed into his mouth and tried to project a calm, in-control demeanor, but his fellow officers felt tension seize their chests, and they started making small and nervous moves like re-tucking in their shirts and adjusting their belt buckles. High-stakes political strategizing began to take place right in front of all the officer's eyes, each gang recalculating their level of status and power on the yard.

It wasn't the formations of small scheming teams that unnerved the guards; it was the knowledge that after their strategy sessions would come action.

A fight broke out over by the pull-up bars where the Priests took their rec, and Krewls watched as a swarm of convicts formed a large circle around two warring men. Perhaps the two bulls would be the only ones to go to battle, Krewls thought, so he let the fight go on without interference. The major's highest hope was that once the conflict ended, a new leader would emerge, assume control of the Priests, and everything else would remain status quo on the yard.

It didn't happen that way at all.

Inside the wall of bodies, legs kicked and punches got thrown, but mixed loyalties led to multiple Priests taking sides and jumping into the fray, and a single fight turned into a medium-sized brawl.

Then a few more Priests jumped in. Soon the crowd

surged to forty people. This was much more than a personal conflict; this was civil war.

Sensing their opportunity, the East Side Mobsters rushed at the Priests. The E-S-M had been getting punked by the Priests for far too long, and when they saw the weakness in their enemy, they decided to take a crack at hitting back at the soldiers who'd taken so many unfair shots against them.

Then the Princes of Mayhem attacked from the flank, taking their cue from the E-S-M, but the Princes' biggest enemy, Hellz Reaperz, saw a chance to move up the totem pole with the Priests, so they jumped in to help their part-time allies. In less than one-hundred and twenty seconds, hundreds of men were fighting. A fallen prisoner took a stomp to the side of his head. Four men beat on a guy's open face. An inmate's eye socket had been broken open so badly that his optic nerve dangled from his head like a white yo-yo on a chunky, bloody, fleshy string.

Krewls blew a whistle, waved to the tower, and shots rang through the air. Per prison protocol, the guard in the sky fired a series of warning rounds high in the air, but since the rubber bullets were not aimed at anyone, the inmates kept fighting, more blood flowing with each passing moment.

Horns blared. Sirens screamed. Guards, fearing for their own lives, counted the moments until reinforcements arrived. More shots rang out and rubber bullets flew. The inmates fought on.

Then came the tear gas.

Scores of men began to gag and then fell to the ground, lying on their bellies spread-eagle in a sign of submission. Striving to cover their eyes and mouths with their shirts, they moved from battling to one another, to battling the vile fumes.

Despite the gas, the fighting raged on.

A dozen guards dressed in riot gear raced toward the action sporting helmets and masks that prevented the tear gas from affecting their breathing. Wielding shields, batons, stun guns, and pepper spray, they began unleashing every tool in their arsenal against any man who remained on his feet.

More shots ricocheted off the ground, but as the situation escalated from Level Orange to Level Red, the snipers moved from shooting the earth to shooting at prisoners. Convicts began taking rubber bullets to the chests, arms, and legs. Even the ones lying down. The shooters didn't care. Neither did the guards. With the institution in such disarray, no one was safe and no amount of force would be deemed too excessive.

A slug hit a Priest in his ear and he fell to the ground, permanently deaf on the left side of his head. Another bullet hit an E-S-M in his testicle and caused it to swell to the size of a grapefruit. The prisoners on the yard lay in a fog of fumes and smoke, praying for a strong gust to whisk the chemicals away. Demon and M.D., far away from every other person, huddled close together and made sure no one attacked. Both knew they were targets. Both also knew that from this point on, they would only have each other.

As the gas, bullets, and batons began to take effect, the number of convicts continuing to war diminished, and the number of men fighting dropped from thirty to twenty and then to ten. After another hailstorm of clubbings, Tasers, and pepper spray, the guards regained control of the yard, and every inmate out for rec time lay spread-eagle on the ground.

All choked, many bled, but nothing had been settled, which, as Krewls knew, could mean only one thing.

There was more war yet to come.

It took the guards more than three hours to get all the prisoners securely locked back in their cells. Not long after everything settled down, McCutcheon had a visitor.

"You just fuckin' up my whole little enterprise, ain't ya?"

M.D. didn't reply.

"Well, Puwolsky did tell me to feed ya to the birds once your work was done. Guess it's now time to put some pepper on ya." Krewls spit out a seed. "Pepper up both you and your dad."

M.D. sprung up at the mention of Puwolsky.

"What, you thought he was coming to save ya? *Shee-it*, he and his partner, they set you up from the get-go, and once we get some order restored 'round here, your ass, sugar pie, is all mine."

Krewls popped another sunflower seed into his mouth and ambled down the hall. "This is my prison, hero. You seem to have forgotten that, but I'm gonna make you remember."

TWENTY-FIVE

Every inmate in the institution spent the next four days on Level Red lockdown without access to a shower, the commissary, the phones, or the rec yard. Especially not the rec yard. Administration canceled all family visitations, eliminated the high school equivalency classes in the library, and even prevented cons from going to Sunday church service. On day five, after yet another round of S.O.S. bags for breakfast, lunch, and dinner, McCutcheon's heavy door slammed open. Being the first prisoner to see a hallway in over one hundred and twenty hours didn't make M.D. any new friends. Most of the cons, in fact, blamed him for the lockdown in the first place.

Why don't he just die like a regular bitch? was the question most asked. *Who's he kiddin'? Everyone knows that at some point he gonna get got.*

McCutcheon, of course, held a different opinion.

"Come with me," a voice said. "And grab your stuff."

A long walk through a winding series of buzzers and locked doors led McCutcheon to a distant wing of the facility he'd not yet seen.

"This is you and there's your new cellie." Mends knew that easier ways existed for a man with his credentials to earn a paycheck, but money, he tried to remind himself, didn't drive his actions; living a purposeful life, one marked by integrity and self-respect, did.

"For the time being," Mends added. "The two of you should be out of harm's way in here."

"With the fuckin' Cho Mo's?" Demon snapped.

"It's the safest unit on the grounds," Mends replied. "This wing has been specially designed to keep inmates from being attacked by fellow inmates."

"But the Cho Mo's?" Demon said again and then he yelped out at the top of his lungs. "I get my hands on any one of y'all and I am gonna BEAT YOUR ASS!"

The words *BEAT . . . YOUR . . . ASS* echoed through the corridor.

"Calm down, Demon," Mends said. "The child molesters are serving their time just like the courts ordered them to do. They're paying their debt."

"Fuck 'em!" Demon said. "Ain't nothing burn me worse. YOU SICK FUCKS!!!"

McCutcheon and his father had been placed in Cell Block F, a tier that demanded highly restricted access in order to keep its residents, mostly reserved, middle-aged men, safe. These were not the thugs of the main yard; Block F was home to scores of inmates with non-calloused hands and slouching shoulders who knew how to do things like fill in Excel spreadsheets or calculate amortization rates on home mortgages. Few knew how to street fight—at least before coming to prison—but perhaps that was why they preyed on young, defenseless children in the first place.

"I'LL SMASH 'EM UP!" Demon said yet again, making sure his words rang out loud and clear. Though at least fifty other prisoners were within earshot, not one of them dared to reply.

"I'll be back," the major said after double-checking the cell door. No one stood lower on the totem pole of incarceration than child molesters. Even serial killers looked down on them as unworthy moral scum.

As Mends walked away, McCutcheon tossed his gear on the high bunk and stretched his arms out wide. No, he could not touch each of the opposing walls at the same time.

Only the government, he thought, would build a system where child molesters got more space than people who committed insurance fraud.

Behind him, M.D. felt his father's eyes burning a hole in his back.

"Is there a problem?"

"Why you in here?"

"Why are you?" M.D. snapped, in no mood to hear a damn word from Demon about how to live an honorable life.

"Hey, I'm still your father. Speak to me with respect."

"Fuck you."

"Fuck you."

"Fuck you back," M.D. said. McCutcheon already fought his father a little less than a year earlier and kicked his ass, and he knew he could do it again at the drop of a hat, too. After all the years of his dad slapping him around, treating him like a servant, punching his mother in the face, and threatening his little sister, M.D. felt more than ready to crack his father's jaw at a moment's notice. In fact, he itched for a reason to do it.

"Aw, I can tell this is about to be a whole lotta of fun," Demon said, running his mouth. "It's like father-son camping, Detroit style."

A surge of anger swelled in McCutcheon.

"Why'd you even do it?" M.D. said, in reference to Demon saving him.

"You gotta ask?" his father answered. "*Sheee-it*, I'm hurt by the question."

"You know, the only goddamn reason I'm in here is because of..." M.D. stopped midsentence before uttering his next word. He was about to say *Because of you*, but then McCutcheon realized this might not actually be the case.

"Lemme ask you a question," M.D. said, changing directions.

"Yeah?"

"Were you and the Priests ever going to kevork my girl?"

Demon cocked his head. "What the fuck does kevork a girl mean?"

M.D. exhaled a deep sigh. "That's what I thought."

Krewls told him the truth: he'd been set up from the get-go. Kaitlyn was never in danger; the Priests hadn't summoned him to the D.T. to fight on their behalf, and

Puwolsky wasn't ever planning on coming back to yank him out of Jentles.

It was all a trap. A ruse. Deception. But who ambushed him? And why?

M.D. started pacing the cell trying to figure out the riddle. Only one explanation made sense.

Stanzer set him up.

The more M.D. kicked the idea around, the more he realized it was just like Puwolsky said to him when he emphasized how McCutcheon's entire existence posed a gigantic threat to Stanzer's whole career. If the colonel got caught using underage soldiers to participate in covert missions, the politicians would roast him like a duck on Chinese New Year, and then serve him up on a polished platter.

Stanzer, his barrel chest and bold, patriotic tattoos, practically brushed his teeth with the American flag, so losing his career would feel like more than merely being fired from a job and publicly humiliated; he'd be losing his entire identity. The guy never took a wife, never had kids, and never viewed his personal destiny as anything other than that of being a wartime soldier, even during eras of peace. Wearing a uniform stood as Stanzer's sole reason for living, and to lose that right would mean losing his life's purpose.

Who is he if he is not this? M.D. wondered. McCutcheon couldn't find an answer, which led him to believe that Stanzer didn't have one. The whole enigma began making more sense.

Stanzer got desperate. He found his back against a wall with a well-armed enemy closing in. People go to great lengths to protect what's most important to them when push comes to shove. McCutcheon knew that. M.D. also knew he was always an experiment. A trial. A research project to see if future operations such as these were viable. Stanzer had told him all this a thousand times. Clearly, the experiment had gone awry somewhere, and the whole scheme was simply a way of burying M.D. in a manner by which no one would ever find him.

The fake papers, the false IDs, the back door into a state penitentiary far off the grid where anarchy ruled and the law's long reach seemed practically nonexistent. All of it bore the markings of Stanzer.

McCutcheon collapsed on the bed and realized he was nothing more than a pawn. Adults had been playing chess with M.D. his whole life. His dad. The Priests. Now the colonel. The more things changed, the more they stayed the same.

M.D. started from the beginning and began replaying all the events in his mind that led him to the D.T. in the first place. It all made sense. The hostility between Colonel Stanzer and Colonel Puwolsky when Puwolsky first showed up to inform M.D. about the threat to Kaitlyn.

All lies. Collusion. All made up.

The reverse psychology of Stanzer's visit to Bellevue to convince McCutcheon *not* to take the mission.

All lies. Schemes. All made up.

The "slay your dragon" talks about the girl he thought

he loved. Those conversations were never about trying to convince M.D. to let Kaitlyn go; they were about constantly reminding M.D. of his affection for her. They needled him, poked him, kept him edgy. By constantly telling McCutcheon to forget his feelings for Kaitlyn, Stanzer was actually reminding M.D. how crazy he was for her.

How could I be so stupid? he thought. And then a final realization came to him, one that crashed like thunder.

Kaitlyn is gone. She is totally and entirely gone.

McCutcheon wanted to kick himself for being so naive. Kaitlyn was hot, rich, smart, and talented, and her boyfriend disappeared like a ghost ten months ago. A line of guys from Detroit to Texas would be vying for her attention and, truth be told, if the tables were turned and a chick had dumped M.D. as coldly, cruelly, and inexplicably as M.D. had dumped Kaitlyn—no words, no explanation, no contact in nearly a year—he would have moved on, too.

With a "Fuck her" attitude to boot.

Stanzer said it many times: "If we gotta cut you loose, we will." McCutcheon had always taken it as a joke. A little ribbing. Some good-natured camaraderie.

Turns out it was the truth.

Everyone knew the military functioned as a cold, impersonal machine that calculated all of its decisions on a plus/minus basis. When M.D. represented a benefit to the machine, they kept him on and kept him well fed. When he became a liability they severed their ties and burned their tracks. The math didn't add up any more for Stanzer to keep his little pet project alive, so Stanzer took the necessary steps in order to save his own ass.

The colonel had even taught him that in warfare doing the unthinkable to your opponent is one of the surest ways to attain victory. It was unthinkable that Stanzer would set him up and sell him out.

That's why it worked so beautifully. McCutcheon never saw it coming.

He played me, M.D. thought.

Demon saw rage starting to burn in his son's heart, the toxic kind that gnawed at a person's soul, and he wanted to help. He wasn't mad at his boy. Wasn't upset with him at all. Though he still didn't know why or how McCutcheon arrived in the D.T., Demon knew in his heart that the reason must have stemmed from a miscarriage of justice. His boy never shoplifted, never bullied other kids, always did his homework, and constantly said *please* and *thank you* his entire life. Getting locked up in a hellhole like the Jentles? There had to be a story behind it, one that he wanted to hear. Maybe a little friendly conversation, he figured, something light and easy, would open things up between him and his son.

"You mentioned your girl," Demon said. "You two still a thing?"

McCutcheon almost attacked his father right on the spot, but he refrained. For the first time in M.D.'s life, his dad had not done anything. The question he'd posed was entirely innocent.

M.D., however, didn't answer. Instead he rolled over in his bunk and took an inadvertent whiff of his flat, smelly pillow.

If I thought I had problems before, I'm super fucked now.

Demon, however, wasn't ready to give up that easily.

"Hey, son. You remember when I told ya relationships'll just fuck a fighter up?"

"Yeah."

"I was wrong," Demon said. "That was an addict talkin'. Lockup is a crazy place. Like this shit is the worst nightmare a man could ever go through, and yet being here and seeing you, well...it's like the best thing that's ever happened to me. Prison cleaned me up. Got me sober. I ain't used in four months and I'm thinkin' clear for the first time in more than fifteen years."

"Real happy for ya, dad."

Demon could feel the sarcasm dripping from M.D.'s comment, but he didn't let it affect the words he wanted to say. Some addicts never get a second chance to clear the air with their kids. If this was Demon's, he planned on taking it.

"Relationships, doesn't matter who you are, M.D." Demon put his hand on McCutcheon's shoulder. "Relationships are everything in this world."

"Sounds like you found God in here."

"Don't know about no God, but what I did find is peace." Demon jumped up onto M.D.'s bunk so he could look his boy in the eye. M.D. realized that one side-kick to the chest would send his old many flying.

"So, tell me, you still with that girl?"

McCutcheon rolled back over and saw a shine in his father's eye, a light he'd never before seen. It was warm, caring, and human. Instead of kicking his dad and sending him flying across the cell, M.D. sat up.

"Naw, we're done. Totally and completely done."

It was true, too. McCutcheon knew that in order to move forward with his life—to save his life—he would have to give up all his fantasies and delusions. Starting with the ones he held about Kaitlyn.

"Too bad," Demon said, patting M.D.'s leg. "I know you cared for her."

McCutcheon felt like snapping at his father. Felt like reminding his dad of the time he'd done all he could to get Kaitlyn to break up with M.D. because he felt she was bad news for him, bad news for his future, and would fuck up McCutcheon's cage-fighting career, a career that represented Demon's only source of income. Pimping out his kid to pay for drugs, hookers, and steak dinners wasn't going to count in the father-of-the-year vote tallies.

But McCutcheon held his tongue. He knew dwelling on the past would do nothing to help either of them at this point.

"So you gonna tell me how you got in here?" Demon asked.

"You first," M.D. replied.

Demon smiled and reclined against the wall. "Okay, sure."

TWENTY-SIX

"You read the papers?"

"Do they even make newspapers anymore?" M.D. asked.

"It's an expression. It means, do ya follow the news?"

"Sometimes."

"Remember that crazy big drug bust in D-town about eight months ago? Four tons of powder and fourteen mil in cash. Hear about it?"

McCutcheon shook his head. "No."

"Well, you got smartness, do the math," Demon said. "A pound of coke costs about seven thousand dollars. That's fourteen million dollars a ton, wholesale. Multiplication that times four tons, and you talking about fifty-six million dollars."

M.D. reached his arms over his head and rotated his neck around in a full circle. At some point soon he'd need to spend some time putting his body in motion. Moving some energy, working some muscles, raising his heartbeat—he needed to stay sharp.

"Is there a point to this?" McCutcheon asked.

"O' course there's a point," Demon said. "Five-O bust up a drug deal, get four tons of powder, but only about fourteen mil in cheese at the drug buy? Where's the rest of the cheddar?"

"You mean, where's the rest of the..." M.D. took a second to figure it out. "Forty something million dollars?"

"Forty-two million, three hundred eighty-seven thousand, six hundred fifty-two dollars and no cents."

"You know the exact figure?"

"Of course I do. It's mine, ain't it?"

M.D. paused. Then he let loose with a big laugh.

"Man, I've heard some bullshit out of you before but this has got to be the biggest bullshit yet."

"Fine, fuck you then. Don't believe me," Demon huffed. "And you're welcome for saving your ass, too."

"I never needed your help."

"Not what it looked like to me."

The two stopped talking and Demon, frustrated, tried to peek his head down the hall to see if he could spy any other inmates. Though he couldn't, he knew the pedophiles were out there.

"Can't believe they got me in here with the Cho Mo's," he screamed out. "YOU SICK FUCKS! Better hope I don't get a chance to get these hands on you!"

Demon's words echoed down the hall, but none of the prisoners replied. They'd heard these sorts of threats a thousand times before and most were used to living with a perpetual target on their back. No one felt sorry for them. No one would help them if attacked. Most people in prison, as well as in society, would be happy to see them dead.

First beaten, wounded, and severely abused, then dead.

Time in lockup passes more slowly than it does on the outside. Each tick of a clock's second hand feels heavier, more methodical, more plodding and pronounced. After ninety minutes with nothing to do and his curiosity piqued, M.D. reignited the conversation.

"G'head, finish your story."

"My story?" Demon asked.

"Well, what would you call it?"

"Factualness."

"Whatever," M.D. replied. "I'm listening."

Demon stood up and began acting out his tale as if he were doing a performance of Penitentiary Theater.

"So I go to the feds, ya see, to turn in the High Priest and make a deal, 'cause the Priests was all up into my ass since you lost that fight against Seizure."

"I didn't lose," M.D. replied.

"Oh yeah," Demon asked. "What happened?"

"I threw the fight."

Demon shook his head. "Pretty fucking lame. There's other ways to conversate with your old man, ya know. Ways to clear the air without trying to get me murdered and shit." Demon couldn't help but laugh. "Man, we got us some family dysfunction, don't we?"

M.D. gazed at the iron bars surrounding them.

"Ya think?"

Demon smiled. Prison humor always made for dark and funny jokes.

"Yessir, the moment you lost I was under water for like two hundred g's," Demon continued. "I mean, *shee-it*...I was done! Priests always pay but they get paid, too. Those fellas don't mess around."

"So you snitched?"

"I survived. Ain't the same thing."

It's a matter of perspective, M.D. thought, but he didn't see the point in arguing about it.

"Keep going," M.D. said.

"Turns out the High Priest ain't what the lawmen really wanted. I'm like, 'How da fuck you not want the biggest boss in the city?' But they were like, naw...we need a sexy bust. Something to feed the media."

"The media?"

"They needed some front page action cause of all the bad press they been taking since the city of Detroit declared bankruptcy," Demon explained. "Cops ain't even bothering to stop average robbers anymore, and with all the budget cuts and eliminated services and shit well, every day TV news just be eating their ass. Especially near where we rest, by Zone Seventy-five, near Fenkell."

"So they wanted some propaganda?" This part of Demon's story made sense to McCutcheon. Detroit's crime, corruption, and general despondency seemed like the lead story on local news every night. A story about the cops winning the war on drugs certainly couldn't hurt anything.

"So I told 'em about this drug buy that was coming up,"

Demon said. "I knew about this monthly flip when I was in all good with the Priests during your fightin' days. Figured I'd tip the coppers off to throw them a bone and be on my way to go figure some new shit out for myself. Didn't know it was gonna be *that* big of a drug buy, though. I mean, this shit turned out to be international."

Demon crossed the cell to take a leak in the toilet. "Just a shame how a person has to use the can in lock-up. I still ain't comfortable taking a dump in front of another man. Treat us all like a bunch of fucking animals, they do."

When he finished whizzing, Demon turned back around.

"You gonna wash your hands?" M.D. asked.

Demon adjusted his nuts. "I can't seem to find the moist towelettes."

M.D. shook his head. His father was never much for hygiene in the first place. "G'head, finish," M.D. said.

"You don't believe none of this, do ya?"

"I can't think of any reason in the world why I'd ever doubt you, Dad." M.D. had been lied to so many times before by his father that he knew that only a fool would consider this made-up fantasy real. Yet he had to admit, he was interested to hear what kind of crazy final explanation his father would cook up to tie this whole cock-and-bull story together. Demon was one of those bullshitters in life who had a gift for making a person want to hear the rest of his nonsense, even though they knew it was all pure make-believe. He owned a gift for it, like the kind of guy who could sell mud in a rain forest, and even his own son surrendered to his enchanted ways.

"So what happens was," Demon continued, "the cops show up, but they ain't got enough men, and a crazy-ass gun battle breaks out. These South American motherfuckers got Uzis and shit. Dealers gets shot, buyers get shot, a few officers get blasted. Looked to me like that shit was cop on cop, too. All hell broke loose."

"Wait a minute—you were there?"

"Yep."

"Because the cops brought you?"

"Hell, no. They didn't know I'd be lurking," Demon answered. "I showed up 'cause sometimes a mouse can find a bit of cheese after busts like this. You know, dudes throw bags into the bushes and shit, when they are running and tryin' to get away. I was hoping to catch me maybe a quarter ounce of powder or something, just to feed my own habit."

"Like a scavenger?"

"Yo, watch your tongue," Demon said. "I'm not so sure I like your attitude and all, and considering you're gonna be my beneficiary."

"Your beneficiary?" M.D. laughed. "So like you got an estate planner now? Dad, this is so good."

"No, I didn't buy any real estate," Demon said, scrunching up his face. "But I might."

"With the forty million dollars you have, right?"

"Forty-two million, three hundred eighty-seven thousand, six hundred fifty-two dollars and no cents."

McCutcheon shook his head. This was classic Demon Daniels. Tell a lie and then stick to the story so sincerely that no one could ever refuse to believe you.

"You are one in a million."

"Don't I know it." Demon grinned proudly. "Okay, so like at the end, people scatter in all directions, but the cops win, and get a nice couple of photographs with four tons of powder and a hunk of cash laid out on a brown picnic table for all the D-town media to drool over."

"And you had a front row seat to all this?"

"Ain't that something? During the chaos—and I mean this shit was like Iraq—I grabbed two huge duffel bags and hauled ass outta there. I know some dirty cops gotta be looking for their money, too. They probably think one of the gangstaz done took it. Want payback, too. But what they don't know is, it was me."

Demon laid back, stretched out comfortably and folded his hand behind his head.

"Now that shit's my buried treasure."

TWENTY-SEVEN

McCutcheon stared at his father reclining on the prison bed as if it were a lounge chair by a tropical beach.

"You are a lying motherfucker."

"It's true," Demon said. "How you think I got my juice in here? I done laid low for like two months, then went back to the Priests after shit settled down and gave 'em double what I owed them. Told 'em I won big playing the ponies in Atlantic City."

"And they believed you?"

"Those motherfuckers don't care. A bitch walks in with four hundred grand in cash and says here ya go, clear my name, they take that shit and say, 'Thank you very much, would you like one of our hoochies to lick your Popsicle?'"

"And they had no idea it was their drug money you were giving back to them?"

"That's the sweet part; it wasn't their drug money," Demon said. "The Priests were just brokering a deal for some rednecks out of Canada. People think Canada is all polite and clean and shit, but they got some big powder-lovin' fools up across the border. It wasn't Priest money I took. It was Canadian cash."

"You stole Canadian dollars?"

"Is you stupid?" Demon asked. "Of course not. Who buys cocaine with funny looking Canada money? These real American greenbacks, I got. Green as they come. For once in my life, I was in the right place at the right time."

McCutcheon looked down the hall and wondered when food might be coming. Like every other prisoner he hated the S.O.S., but hunger was hunger. No signs of a meal delivery, though.

"So how'd you end up in here?" McCutcheon asked.

"Jaywalking."

"Huh?"

"You heard me. Jaywalking."

"This story just gets better and better."

"What happened was I got drunk in Vegas and decided to cross from Caesar's Palace to the Paris Hotel right in the middle of Las Vegas Boulevard with two hotties, one white, one Puerto Rican, on each arm. Oh, you shoulda seen them titties," Demon bragged. "But some junior Nazi policeman busted me and found out I had a warrant for my arrest, 'cause I'd done violated my parole by not checking in with my P.O. for a few months back in D-town. Got cuffed on the spot, extradited back to Michigan, and the bitch-ass judge gave me nine months to teach me a lesson. Been here for five, only four more left to go."

"And then you're gonna take your buried treasure and go to, let me guess, the Cayman Islands?"

M.D. always knew it was his father's dream to one day retire a wealthy man in the Cayman Islands.

"Indeed," Demon answered. "Or at least I was till you showed up."

The cell got quiet, the fun and lightheartedness of Demon's story giving way to the cold reality of their current circumstances. Demon, reflective, crossed to the front bars of the cage and picked at the chipped white paint. Four months left on a bid was practically nothing to a con. An easy stretch. On the other hand surviving four months in the D.T. after double-crossing the Priests was an eternity. It's one thing not to have gone through with the hit against his own kid; it was quite another to put a knife in the neck of the main head shotcaller. Demon knew that being quarantined with the Cho Mo's might offer him some protection, but M.D.'s father was also a realist, and he knew chances were high that he was already a dead man.

At any moment, a hit could come.

M.D. started inspecting the cell and studying the environment. He'd been well-trained in the art of urban warfare and had been taught that if a way existed in, a way always existed out. "This prison's too old not to have weaknesses," McCutcheon said, surveying the domain. "You been here for months. What have you heard?"

"There's only two ways out of the D.T.," Demon said. "Parole or the morgue truck. Everyone knows that."

McCutcheon used his finger to peel away some of the aged concrete in the back corner of the cell and started ruminating over the how the plumbing lines ran vertically down the southern wall and then under the floor. The water supply had to flow in from somewhere, which meant that where there were pipes there was crawl space.

"There's gotta be a way," M.D. said. "There's always a way."

He tested the strength of the toilet to see if he could pull it off the wall. It gave a bit, but M.D. didn't want to yank it with full strength until he formulated a plan. Just ripping a shitter off its anchors would get him nowhere. Brains before brawn. Always.

Demon studied McCutcheon as McCutcheon studied the cell and couldn't help but admire his son's optimism and grit. In the cage, his son always had more heart than any fighter Demon had ever seen. M.D. never gave up, never surrendered, and never believed he was ever out of a fight as long as there was still time left on the clock to battle. In so many ways, McCutcheon demonstrated perseverance, honor, brains, bravery, and goodness. In so many ways, McCutcheon demonstrated all the qualities that Demon himself did not.

"I done made a lot of mistakes, M.D.," Demon said to his son. "Lord knows I was a terrible dad. But you've always been my boy, and you gotta know one thing."

"Yeah, what's that?" McCutcheon retested the strength of the sink. Perhaps if they both pulled at the same time a big enough hole could open so that . . .

Demon suddenly spun M.D. around and spoke in a sincere voice, his eyes wet with tears.

"I always loved you, son. I mean that. I always did."

McCutcheon listened to his father's words. Heard every last one of them and then took a long moment to consider his response.

He decided to say nothing. He didn't hug his father. He didn't smile at his father. He especially did not say *I love you* back.

Demon had hoped his boy would forgive him. Hoped his sobriety and changed ways would translate into a new and vibrant relationship with his kid. He wanted McCutcheon to put the past in the past, and see the true essence of his old man's heart. See his goodness, his light, his deep love. Demon searched M.D.'s face for some sort of sign that his unspoken apology for all the hurt he'd caused, all the pain he'd brought into this young man's life, would be accepted.

Could what was done be done?

M.D. wasn't stupid and clearly saw the searching in his father's eyes. Saw his hunger and his hopefulness and his regret for all the thousands of mistakes he'd made in the past.

He looked away.

McCutcheon carried too many wounds from a shattered, tattered childhood to forgive his father for being such a selfish piece of shit. Maybe one day he could let it all go, perhaps he could forgive and forget and move forward, but for M.D., now was not the time.

Even though it may be the final time he'd ever have a chance.

As Demon slowly recognized forgiveness for his sins would not be forthcoming, he decided to do something very un-Demon like and not pursue the issue further. Instead, he removed his hands from M.D.'s shoulder and decided to let it go. A lump formed in his throat. A lump caused by the fact that he completely understood his son's perspective.

In fact, Demon thought to himself, I don't know that I'd forgive me either. Demon wiped his eyes and gulped down the truth, but like all truths this one felt hard and exceptionally difficult to swallow.

McCutcheon returned to surveying the cell. Certainly, a large hole would open if he and his father pulled the toilet off of the wall at the same time, but every prisoner in lockup had probably thought of an escape route exactly like this before.

Which made the plan lame. The more M.D. contemplated yanking out the john, the less he liked the idea. Too clumsy. Too uncertain. Too much cloudiness about where to go, which direction to turn, which path to take. And this was assuming they could even create a hole big enough to slip through. Besides, he knew, escaping the cell wasn't the goal; escaping prison was. A broken toilet breakout plan felt like a fantasy.

Only two ways of the D.T.; parole or the morgue truck.

McCutcheon knew he needed to stay strong. Keep his eyes on the prize and not give in to despair. Part one of any plan would be remaining certain he could pull something off. If hope died, any plan beyond that would fail.

He began telling himself the things he knew he needed to hear. *Relax. Be patient. First ideas are rarely the best ones anyway.*

Stanzer had taught him that. Stanzer, the guy, should McCutcheon ever get out, who'd pay.

Like any fight, keep pressing but also remain patient. Solutions will come.

McCutcheon turned around, ready to hunt for a new approach.

"You been staying sharp?" Demon asked, prison slippers on his hands as if they were focus mitts for boxing.

His dad waved him forward, challenging him to see what he's got. Did M.D. still remember all the things Demon had taught him back when they trained together at the gym?

McCutcheon looked at the sandals on his father's hands and knew what his father wanted. Demon always loved working out. Back when his father was an up-and-coming boxer Demon epitomized the term *gym rat*. Then drugs got to him. But even after that, some of Demon's best father-son memories consisted of training little M.D. to throw hooks, jabs, and pinpoint right crosses. No one had ever seen a five-year-old counterpunch like Demon Daniels's kid. He was the apple of daddy's eye in the gym. Some fathers never forget the day they teach their children to ride a bike. Demon never forgot the day he taught his son to smoke the hell out of a speed bag.

Training like a monster was a genetic trait that ran through both of their bloodstreams. Did M.D. still have it like he used to?

McCutcheon took in the dimensions of the small space and then yanked off his shirt.

"Do I still have it? Always."

Demon smiled. "All right then, let's see some combinations."

M.D. began teeing off on the sandals with fists that flew with the speed of a hawk. One wrong move and he'd smash his father. Or perhaps accidentally hammer the edge of the metal bed frame, which stood way too close to where the two of them were trying to box. Any misstep would surely shatter the bones in McCutcheon's fist. Though practically no room existed to maneuver, the two of them had been doing this balletlike dance together for years, and once they started up again, a musical, thundering *rat-a-tat-tat* boomed through the halls. The entire cell block reverberated with the echoes of their violent, rhythmical opera.

Sweat began to stream down both of their bodies. M.D.'s rippled torso glistened in the yellow light, and for a moment, a brief and shining and liberating moment, neither of them was incarcerated.

They were free. Free from Jentles. Free from the Priests. Free from their dark and violent pasts, and free from their dark and violent futures.

"You gotta keep your mind strong, son," Demon said. "No matter what shit comes at you in this lifetime, you gotta keep your mind strong. You hear me?"

"Yes, sir."

Deep wisdom existed in Demon's advice. M.D. also understood deep irony existed as well. Sometimes, M.D. thought, people with the most fucked-up lives offer the sharpest knowledge.

McCutcheon picked up the pace, his striking ability off the charts.

"Damn, you got world champion skills, son. You gotta be thinking about getting back in the cage one day, no?"

"In case you hadn't already noticed, Dad, I'm in a cage right now."

Demon scanned the cell. "Ya got me there."

More sweat dripped and the pace moved even faster. M.D. struck with focus, ferocity, and extremely bad intentions. Demon tried to push his son to his limits, but struggled to keep up. The *pop-pop-pop* of McCutcheon's hands smashing the sandals reverberated like cannon shots down the hallway.

Suddenly, Demon stopped.

"You saved a fucking guard?"

M.D. heaved in and out, his lungs screaming for oxygen.

"I saved a person."

"But why?" his father asked. "No con takes the side of a screw. Not in this prison. Not anywhere. Ever."

"Because doing the right thing feels like the only thing I know how to do."

Demon nodded. His son always marched to the beat of a different drummer when it came to principles.

"You're ten times the man I'll ever be, son," Demon said. "But you know what that means, don't ya?"

"What?"

Demon slowly removed the prison slippers from his hands.

"Because of it, you're fucked."

McCutcheon smiled.

"You mean we're fucked, don't you?"

Demon sat down on the edge of the bed and wiped a stream of sweat from his brow. "This, my boy, is very, very true."

TWENTY-EIGHT

"**L**ong live the kid! Long live the kid!" The chant echoing up the halls caused M.D. to stir from his bed. "Long live the kid!"

"What the hell is that?"

McCutcheon smiled. "Just a crazy old man."

"Well, I hope he shuts up soon," Demon said.

"No," M.D. replied. "What you hope for is that he brought us food."

"Long live the ... hey, there ya are? How's the penis, kid?"

Fixer walked up to the front of M.D.'s cell pushing a gray cart made from hard plastic. On it McCutcheon spied orange juice, bananas, a few bags of mixed nuts, and a couple of covered dishes, food Fixer probably prepared himself.

"Anyone's tank need a refill?"

"You know this old-timer?" Demon asked suspiciously.

"I do."

"And you trust him?"

"Of course he doesn't trust me," Fixer replied. "He

ain't dumb. You can't trust anyone in here, not even your own father."

Demon did not smile.

"That was a joke. Get it?"

Suspicion blazed in Demon's eyes.

"How you come to get down here, old man?"

"Yeah," M.D. said. "How'd you get out of solitary?"

"How do you think I got out?" Fixer tossed McCutcheon an apple, ripe and juicy. "The new major. It's a new day."

M.D. crunched a bite from the piece of fresh fruit. Delicious.

"Thank you."

"No, thank you," Fixer said. "Change is coming. Everyone can feel it."

"Yeah?" Demon asked. "What's the word?"

Fixer offered Demon a box of Pop-Tarts but he didn't accept them. Demon loved Pop-Tarts—they were his favorite item in the prison commissary, and these were raspberry, his number one choice.

Yet still, he made no move to accept the gift.

"What you want for those?"

"Nothin'."

"Bullshit. Ain't nothin' for nothin' in here. I got money on my books. Plenty of it. Name your price."

"Kid's already paid for 'em," Fixer said. "The change out there, it's all because of him. Smart guys in here, we know who we have thank for that."

"And the dumb guys?" M.D. asked. "What do they think?"

"They think you need the morgue truck," Fixer answered, not pulling any punches. "But ain't exactly a consensus about much going on right now. Not about nothing."

Fixer re-offered the Pop-Tarts to Demon and M.D.'s father stared at the box. A moment of indecision passed, and after McCutcheon crunched another bite of apple, Demon decided to accept the offering, even though he knew that by doing so he was probably setting himself up for trouble.

But he was already in trouble, he figured, and these were raspberry, well worth the risk.

"That riot woke a sleeping giant. The D.O.C. is gonna review the entire facility. Warden Stroke is out. Deputy Warden Moron gettin' replaced, too, and Krewls's time as the lead dog around here is limited. He knows it, though, which makes him real dangerous right now. Y'all watch your ass around him, ya hear?"

The more Fixer spoke, the more credible he became to Demon.

"Paper pushers are slow, though," Fixer continued as M.D.'s father wolfed down the first Pop-Tart in two gulps, and headed toward the second in its shiny silver bag. "Ain't no one expects nothing immediately, but there's gonna be new leadership, that's for sure. My guess is Krewls'll survive. The system isn't gonna go back and right any past wrongs, but moving forward his leash'll be reined and things for every con in here will be way better. That's 'cause of you, kid."

Fixer picked up one of the plates of food.

"What about the yard?" Demon asked.

"Nothing settled yet out there, neither. Whole facility still on Level Orange, doing twenty-three hours a day in their cells. But they did reopen the commissary, church, and library, so things are slowly getting back to normal. Major Mends is talking about getting all the shotcallers together to broker a peace communal. Or at least prevent another riot."

"What's up with the Priests?" Demon asked.

"Chaos. Civil war. You done threw them into a power struggle ain't no one can predict the outcome of. Apparently there wasn't no kind of succession plan in place," Fixer said with a laugh. "What's the word? Contingency. Y'all ain't had one."

The old man lifted the flat plate that covered a large bowl, and a waft of spiced steam rose through the air.

"I wouldn't worry though," Fixer said to Demon.

"Why's that?"

"'Cause either way, you ain't gonna have any friends on that team."

Demon nodded. He knew the old man's words were true.

"Y'all want some ChiChi?"

"ChiChi?" M.D. asked.

"Sweet and spicy. This here got beef jerky mixed with salted nuts, a dash of my famous hot sauce, and a bag of Texas beef ramen," Fixer passed the heaping plate to

McCutcheon. "Warning ya, though, this batch got some kick."

M.D. didn't need to be offered the food a second time. Hungry as a bear, he plunged a spoon into the strange but wonderful concoction.

"*Mmm,*" he said after his first bite. "So good."

Demon cocked his head to the side. "This old man cook for you the whole time you been down?"

"Whole time," McCutcheon replied.

The scent of the food hit Demon's nose like a seductive lullaby hits a baby's ears, and after a moment of deliberation he reached over and grabbed M.D.'s plate. "Let me taste that shit."

His verdict arrived immediately.

"Damn, old man, your ass is a magician."

Fixer grinned. "Wait till you taste the cake I made."

M.D. took his plate back from his father, walked a few steps backward, and sat down on the lower bunk ready to shovel more food into his mouth. "You know I don't eat that stuff, Fixer."

"Well, pass it to me," Demon said eagerly. "'Cause I sure as hell do."

Demon extended his arms through the bars and took the cake in both of his hands. It was big and lopsided and required Demon to figure out a way to slip it back between the bars.

McCutcheon, glad to be finally eating, plowed another spoonful of ChiChi into his mouth and gazed at the dessert.

It looked amazing. Three layers. Chunks of candy bars and cookie crumbles. Fixer must have used a ton of Oreos just to make the frosting, he thought. Clearly, a lot of effort had gone into this creation. It was the most ornate dish M.D. had yet seen Fixer make.

But why?

McCutcheon paused.

Fixer knew he would never touch a bite of the cake, so why make it?

M.D.'s spoon froze midair. "DAD WAIT!!" he cried out dropping his bowl. The ChiChi crashed to the floor.

No, M.D. would not touch the cake. But Demon would.

His father spun his head to see what M.D. wanted but McCutcheon's warning arrived too late. With Demon's arms fully extended out of the cell and his waist propped up next to the bars, Fixer pulled out a hidden shiv from behind his back, went low, and ripped a six-inch gash across the top of his father's thigh near the groin area.

Right at the femoral artery.

Demon dropped the cake and it shattered on the floor. Then he staggered backward as a stream of blood spouted from his thigh like an oil gusher. M.D. lunged and the tips of his fingers wisped past Fixer's shirt, the old man proving just fast enough to back away and prevent himself from being snagged.

The bars that separated them had saved him.

Demon fell to the ground, not quite sure of why he'd been stabbed in the leg instead of the stomach, head, or chest, but he knew he'd been sliced deep. Fixer stared at the work he'd just done, then raised his gaze. He and M.D. made eye contact, a silent question burning on McCutcheon's face.

Why?

The old man spoke in a low voice. "Krewls. Guy was gonna bunk me with Pharmy."

M.D. shook his head and gave Fixer a look of disappointment that sliced through the old man's heart worse than the old man's shiv had just sliced through Demon's leg.

"Hold on, Dad. We gotta wrap that thing." McCutcheon ripped off his shirt and began performing triage. "Gotta keep pressure on the wound."

"Pharmy," the old man mumbled, his shoulders sagging off his small and shriveled frame. "What could I do?"

"GUARD!" M.D. shouted. "GUARD!"

"A person has to do what a person has to do to survive in here, don't they?"

"GUARD! SOMEBODY GET A GUARD!"

"We ain't all as strong as you, kid. We ain't all..." Fixer searched for the word. "Brave."

"GUARD!" M.D. cried out as he applied pressure to the wound. "GUARD!!"

Fixer stood in front of the cell and watched as blood from Demon's leg pooled onto the floor, and a thought crossed his mind. A thought he'd never had after each of the prior murders he'd committed.

If I could rewind the clock, just rewind it to as little as thirty seconds ago, I swear I'd make a different decision.

But life did not work like that. Clocks never got rewound, and during his moment of truth Fixer realized his own darkest fear had just come true.

Prison had eaten his soul. Left in its place: cowardice.

Fixer slunk off, knowing he'd now have to live the rest of his days with this knowledge.

"GUARD! GUARD! GUARD!!!" M.D. howled.

Shoelaces, Fixer thought as he heard McCutcheon's screams echoing up the corridor. What I wouldn't give right now for a pair of shoelaces.

TWENTY-NINE

"You know what I'm thinking about right now, son?"
"Just hold on, Dad. You gotta hold on. GUARD! GUARD!"

"White sandy beaches." A faraway look drifted across Demon's eyes. "Those Cayman Islands got some damn beautiful white sandy beaches."

"Don't give up, yet, Dad. Keep fighting."

Despite McCutcheon's best efforts to suppress the wound, life slowly drained from the body of his father. M.D. had propped Demon's legs up so they were above his heart, and with his father's back against his own chest, wrapped his arms around his dad's midsection so he could cradle his father in his arms and hold him upright while continuing to apply steady pressure to the wound. Every bit of cloth, toilet paper, and so on that M.D. could get his hands on had been used to fashion together a makeshift field dressing, but all of it was sopped in red from a faucet that could not be turned off.

McCutcheon's improvised first aid might have helped a

little, but both of them knew it was a losing battle. Demon needed the infirmary and he needed it right away.

"Guard!" M.D. cried out, praying that someone would finally answer his calls. "Guard!"

Suddenly, the sound of boot steps could be heard walking up the corridor.

"GUARD!" M.D. yelled. "HELP!!"

A gnawed sunflower seed landed in the pool of dark red liquid and swirled around in a concentric circle, like a leaf after the wind had blown it into the stillness of a quiet, tranquil pond.

"What's all the commotion, sugar pie?" Krewls tilted his head sideways to inspect the damage. "Ooh, that little scratch might need it a Band-Aid. Hell, might even bleed out unless we get him to the infirmary."

"How much do you want?" M.D. asked.

"How much can you get?"

"Don't give him shit," Demon sputtered.

"Bet on me. Bet it all!" McCutcheon said. "And do it twenty times over. I'll come through each and every time, I promise."

"I believe you will," Krewls replied. "But I also think that's gonna be true whether a bed opens up in the infirmary right now or not. Survival instincts and all." The major spit out another shell. "That's assuming you're still around after you get sent back to g-pop. You ain't got many friends back that way, you know. This right here," Krewls said, nodding at Demon's leg, "this a favor I'm doin' for one of 'em. Me and the man who wants to be the new High

Priest, we already got us a new, whatchya call it, business arrangement. I help him, he helps me; that's how things work 'round here."

His inspection over, the major began to walk away.

"Krewls, please. I am begging you."

"Don't beg that scum for nuttin'."

"Perhaps when your friend Mends returns for his next shift the occupancy rate in the infirmary will have changed." Krewls looked at his watch. "Only 'bout four more hours to go."

"Fuck you," Demon said to Krewls.

"Die slow, Mister Daniels. And know one more thing before you go to your final destination."

"What's that?" Demon said defiantly.

"Your little boy is next." Krewls laughed. "I just wanted to give him a front-row seat to your demise. And now that I hear these words leaving my mouth, you know what else? I'm thinking, 'Ouch. That's gotta hurt.'"

M.D. looked down the hall to see if perhaps another guard could be located, someone whose humanity might still remain accessible.

But no one else was around.

"I told you whose prison this was, sugar pie. Ya shoulda listened."

After popping yet another seed into his mouth, Krewls ambled away.

"KREWLS!" M.D. called out. "KREWLS!"

"Forget him, son, he's gone," Demon said. "And..." Demon took a moment to catch his breath. "So am I."

"No you're not, Dad. You're not!"

"Just listen to me. I gotta tell you something."

"Don't talk. Save your strength. GUARD!"

"You were always righteous, M.D."

"GUARD!" he called again, and the tears McCutcheon had held back for all these years started to flow.

"And I believe you were born to do something special with your life," Demon said. "To make things right."

"Save your energy, Dad," McCutcheon said, crying. "Someone is going to come any minute now, I know it. GUARD!"

"Don't matter no more." Demon swallowed, but little saliva existed in his throat. "My destiny is to die in here, a forgotten piece of shit. I've done too many bad things in my life to count."

"Don't talk, Dad."

"But your destiny is to make shit right in this world. That's your fate, McCutcheon. Go make shit right."

"GUARD! Where the fuck are they?"

"Listen close to me now, son. There's a house. Seven seventy-five Fenkell Avenue. It was bulldozed 'cause it used to be a crack house. But they ain't bulldoze the cellar. Find that house. That's where my buried treasure is."

"You're gonna get your buried treasure, Dad. Don't give up."

"Listen to me, son. Seven seventy-five Fenkell Avenue. Repeat it."

M.D. repeated the address. Not because he believed

anything actually existed at the location, but rather simply to please his father.

"Seven seventy-five Fenkell Avenue."

"Good," Demon said. "Now, go to the house that's no longer a house when you get out of here—I know you'll find a way—and take this buried treasure." Demon stammered, the light in his eyes beginning to dim. "Take this buried treasure and go make shit in this world right."

"Hold on, Dad. Please, I'm begging you."

"I'm proud of you, son, and always remember one thing." Demon smiled, peace shining in his eyes. "I've always loved you."

His eyelids closed. Forever.

THIRTY

When Mends saw McCutcheon cradling his bloody, lifeless father, tears still running down M.D.'s face, his stomach sank.

"What's this, an assault? A full investigation must be launched right away."

Krewls popped into the hallway and spit out the shell of a roasted seed. It was as if he'd been waiting for Mends to show the whole time. "I'll get my officers on it," he said. "After I make arrangements for the morgue truck to stop by tonight, that is." A cackle escaped from his sideways smile.

Krewls spit another shell onto the floor, his message clear: *My jail.* And he'd just proved it yet again.

Mends considered himself scrappy. Resilient. A fighter. No one got the better of him. Not in the high school locker room. Not in his college fraternity house. Not while pursuing his multiple graduate degrees. Mends fought for what he believed in. He knew who he was and he knew what he stood for.

Until he arrived at the D.T. He'd almost quit after the incident with Pharmy and Goblin, but after lying to his wife about how he sustained his injuries and screwing up his courage, he returned to work determined not to be scared off from the immensity of this task so quickly.

Yet now, seeing this, Jentles State Penitentiary had just proven every assumption Mends held about his own identity wrong.

I came here to change the system, but the system has beaten me. I can't do this.

Mends dropped his head, defeated.

Krewls reached for the radio mike he wore on the upper left shoulder of his uniform and barked out a command. "We gotta a D.B. on Cell Block F," Krewls said. "Send a table, but first we'll need the X team before we can remove the body."

"An extraction team? Why?" Mends asked. He didn't like the idea of six guys in full body armor storming the cell to subdue an already subdued McCutcheon.

"Because we're dealing with an extremely violent offender," Krewls answered. "I mean, who do you think committed this horrible crime? That D.B. didn't slip by the sink. This is clearly a homicide scene, cell mate on cell mate."

Krewls pulled a plastic bag from the inside of his jacket and held up the bloody shiv Fixer had used to murder Demon.

"Found this over there. He musta tossed it."

"You're serious?" Mends asked.

"Absolutely," Krewls replied. "And the moment we open this door to extract the D.B., this prisoner might go berserk. We need to be prepared. Officer safety, as I think you know, Major Mends, is always a top concern around here."

M.D. remained on the floor, cradling his father, dazed, drained, and sopped in blood.

"Look at him," Mends said. "This inmate isn't a threat. This is a person with no more fight left in him."

"Just like a black widow," Krewls replied. "They lull their victim to sleep and *bam!* They pounce. Can't take that chance."

Krewls smiled at McCutcheon with a smirk that said, *That's right, son, the bad guys have won.*

M.D. did not reply.

"Nah," Krewls repeated. "Ain't gonna take the chance at all."

When the black-booted X team arrived with their helmets, clubs, and high-octane attitudes they expected a heated fight, but McCutcheon offered no resistance and submitted to being cuffed without incident. Standard procedure for X team extractions meant a set of full restraints, including cross-arm tiebacks and leg shackles, like the kind worn by Banger when McCutcheon first arrived at the intake room.

With each step M.D. took forward, chains rattled.

"The D.B. goes to the infirmary for storage until the morgue truck arrives later tonight, and the prep goes to the hole," Krewls ordered. "Unless you have any complaints you'd like to register about the manner in which we are serving due process, Major Mends."

All eyes turned to Mends. After a pause, he answered softly.

"No complaints at all."

"Good," Krewls said. "You men get the body and you men take this scum away."

Three guards with helmets began leading M.D. toward ad seg, but before they rounded the corner, Krewls added a final word.

"My shift's over, sugar pie. And tomorrow is a day off for me. But I'll see ya soon, and then you and I can have some more fun. Don't miss me too much." Krewls spit a sunflower shell that landed on the side of M.D.'s cheek, the wetness from Krewls's spit causing it to stick to M.D.'s face.

McCutcheon slowly turned his head. His eyes blazed. For a moment, though entirely restrained and protected by six other guards in riot gear, Krewls felt a cold shiver run up his spine. Something about McCutcheon's glare let Krewls know he'd messed with the wrong person; and even though the major knew he held almost every card in the deck, and owned no logical reason to be afraid, he swallowed an involuntary gulp of fear.

As long as McCutcheon could still breathe, Krewls knew this story was not over, and his instincts told him that the kid's situation would need to be addressed sooner rather than later. The longer M.D. lived, the more dangerous he became, and if heaven forbid McCutcheon ever did manage to get free, Krewls understood the young prisoner's liberty would be his own end.

Krewls shook off his fright because logically it made

no sense. This was his jail. His command. He owned the kid's ass outright.

Yet still, something gnawed at him.

"All right, let's go," Krewls barked. "Take him away."

On the outside Krewls projected strength and conviction in his orders, but McCutcheon understood what Krewls was really feeling on the inside. And with good reason, too, M.D. thought, as the guards marched him away.

Because as all who walk the earth know, no one can escape their destiny.

THIRTY-ONE

In the early 1800s the United States of America led the world in the innovative practice of incarcerating their most violent inmates in isolated cells. Authorities believed that by denying prisoners human contact or any external stimulation, the state's most troublesome offenders would discover the error of their unlawful, antisocial ways. Solitary confinement, the system assumed, would lead to rehabilitation.

They were wrong, and the results were disastrous. With overwhelming evidence condemning the practice as inhumane, the strategy of using solitary confinement was all but abandoned by the U.S. government for the next one hundred years.

However, in the latter part of the 1900s, solitary confinement made a comeback, but with a new twist. Instead of torturing prisoners by tossing them into dark and dingy holes, inmates were placed in well-lit, sterile boxes. Cramped, concrete, windowless cells outfitted with a sink, a shower, a toilet, and a slot in the door wide enough for a meal tray to slip through was the new version of solitary confinement. Prisoners, deprived of phone calls, commissary privileges, and family visitations, would remain in their unit for twenty-three hours a day, their only break being rec time, which involved being escorted in shackles to another solitary pen, where convicts could pace alone for an hour before being returned to their original cages.

The psychological damage proved to be exactly the same. Correction officials, however, defended the practice as necessary to protect guards as well as other prisoners. A new category of inmate was born: the V-S-Ps.

Violent Super-Predators.

This became McCutcheon's new classification in Jentles: a V-S-P.

Some V-S-Ps had spent a decade in solitary, their minds slowly rotting away.

Time itself evaporated. And with it, an inmate's sanity.

A loud *SLAM!* locked the box and McCutcheon, free from his restraints but restrained from his freedom, took a seat. Not on the bed, but cross-legged on the floor.

Is there any reason for hope, he asked himself. *Any reason at all?*

No was the obvious answer. But M.D. knew a strong mind would look for the positive, the hidden unknown. McCutcheon, determined to find a satisfactory answer, repeated the question to himself.

Is there any reason for hope, he asked himself again. *Any reason at all?*

A small but clear inner voice told him that there was, and although the thought might be far-fetched, the whole idea that hope still existed brought M.D. all the relief he needed at the moment. Instead of succumbing to panic, M.D. simply reminded himself to breathe in and breathe out and accept his new circumstances one moment at a time.

Fear, he reminded himself. *Welcome it. Do not push it away. Make the energy of fear a friend instead of a foe.*

But where was the hope? What possible reason could M.D. find to still believe in a future beyond blackness?

The answer, McCutcheon realized, stared him directly in the face, and once he realized it, it even caused him to laugh. *In a world so strange as to deliver me to this destination, the world could still prove strange enough to deliver me out of it, too.*

Perhaps it would take a week. Perhaps a month. Perhaps a year. Maybe a decade. But M.D. knew he would not spend the rest of his life locked in this box. Therefore, he told himself, it was not a matter of *if* he'd ever be released from solitary confinement, it was only a matter of *when.*

His moment came at midnight on his very first evening.

"I thought you'd like some closure," Mends said opening the cell door. "You know, view the body and say good-bye."

Mends tossed McCutcheon a set of clothes.

"After a shower, that is."

M.D. looked down at the bag he'd just been passed. It wasn't a prison uniform; they were the clothes from when he first arrived at Jentles.

He raised his eyes.

"Come on," Mends said. "We don't have much time."

McCutcheon blasted on the water, quickly cleaned the blood off of his body, and carefully followed Mends through the winding prison halls down to the room where the penitentiary burned their trash.

Raging heat from the fire blasted the two men in the face as they stepped inside the incinerator room and closed the door behind them. Next to the furnace door a body lay on a gurney covered by a white sheet.

"I myself have always felt I'd rather be cremated as opposed to buried anyway. You?" Mends asks.

"Never gave much thought to it."

"Seems purer in a way," Mends said. "Like a funeral pyre for a Viking or something."

McCutcheon shook his head. Leave it to Demon Daniels to exit this life like a gallant Viking.

Mends opened the incinerator's cast-iron door and the two men stared at the fire, its hypnotic flames dancing and flowing and waving as if to supernatural music.

"What about the morgue truck?" M.D. asked.

Mends removed the toe tag off Demon's foot and handed it to McCutcheon.

"They say there's only two ways out of the D.T., parole or the morgue truck. Looks like this guy just found the third." Mends pulled back the sheet and reached underneath Demon's arms. "Come on, help me lift the body."

McCutcheon put two fingers to his lips, kissed them, and then touched his father's chest, right over his dad's heart. Without words or tears or any other sign of emotion,

McCutcheon lifted his father by the feet, and on the count of three he and Mends tossed Demon's corpse into the fire.

Mends closed the furnace door as the flames began to eat Demon's flesh.

"Jump on. I'll cover you up and I'll roll you out to the loading dock."

M.D. ripped off his shoes, hopped up on the gurney and placed the toe tag DANIELS, DAMIEN PRISONER ID #475S869LZ on the big toe of his right foot.

"Here," Mends said, passing M.D. a final gift. "You might need this."

McCutcheon reached out and accepted the offering. It was an Al Mar S2KB SERE combat knife, 8.5 inches long butt to blade, designed for the Special Operations Command Units out of Fort Bragg, North Carolina. The acronym SERE stood for Survival–Evasion–Resistance–Escape. Mends had just passed McCutcheon a blade that could battle a bear.

"I'm transferring out, tomorrow," Mends confessed. "Thought I could make a difference here. I can't."

He hung his head, sad, defeated, and shamed. M.D. opened the folding blade, fingered the razor-sharp edge and then reached out and grabbed the major by the arm.

"You can still make a difference," McCutcheon said. "And you are. Don't surrender your power."

The two men looked one another in the eye.

"And never give up," M.D. added. "We all have our destiny."

A surge of inspiration suddenly began to flow through

the major's veins. Maybe he still could make a difference? Maybe he still could reform a system that cried out for healing? Maybe there were other paths, other roads he could try? Perhaps one closed door would lead to an open window, he thought.

Maybe I shouldn't give up, he told himself. *I never have before. He's right, why now?*

"Thank you," Mends said. "I don't know what your story is or how you got here, but you're certainly not a middle-aged man named Lester Rawlins, and I definitely owe you a debt of gratitude."

M.D. closed the blade of the SERE and hid the knife in the lining of his pants.

"You just paid it," McCutcheon said. "Now it's time to go make shit right."

"Who, me?" Mends asked. "Or you?"

"Both of us," M.D. replied.

M.D. adjusted his toe tag, pressed his shoes tightly to his hip on the left, and laid back on the gurney so that Mends could cover his face with the sheet.

Ten minutes later, he was in the morgue truck.

Twenty minutes after that, he was beyond the prison's gates.

THIRTY-TWO

cCutcheon lay strapped to a gurney underneath a white sheet, feeling the soft *bump-bump-bump* of the road passing beneath the vehicle's wheels as it cruised down a lonesome highway in the middle of the night. The morgue truck wasn't so much a truck as it was an oversize wagon with an extended rear cab, and though the space in the back offered capacity for two lifeless bodies, M.D. lay alone and unaccompanied. In a way, the path he'd discovered out of Jentles felt fitting, because a part of him was now dead. A young man went into prison; an entirely different young man was coming out.

Using the knife Mends had given him, M.D. sliced through the white sheet, cut the tan restraints that belted his body to a cushionless wooden board, and freed himself using slow, methodical, quiet movements each step of the way. Having paid close attention to even the smallest of details, M.D. knew he'd been loaded into the vehicle feet-first, which meant that his head pointed backward toward the rear spilt-panel door of the black car. This, he knew, would be advantageous, because he'd be able to inch the sheet downward below his eyes without the driver up front detecting anything suspicious.

Then again, the guy behind the wheel most probably felt no obligation to check for anything suspicious. People who transported live prisoners stood at high alert during every inch of the journey; people who transported dead ones might as well have been delivering bushels of carrots.

It took M.D.'s eyes a moment to adjust to the blackness in the back of the vehicle, but once his vision sharpened into focus, he saw that the coroner's wagon, unlike an ambulance, was bereft of any supplies. No tools, no cords, no clothing, nothing of any value existed that might help McCutcheon execute the next phase of his plan. Having an array of medical instruments to build an arsenal of tools and weapons would have been helpful, he thought, but at least there was no divider separating the front seat from the backseat of the car.

Good, M.D. thought, pulling the sheet back up over his head. Patiently, having scouted the terrain, he formulated the next stage of his attack.

Make noise, he thought. *Noise, for sure.*

McCutcheon knew that pouncing into the front seat and putting a blade to the driver's throat would certainly allow him to successfully hijack the vehicle, but he also knew that a dead body springing to life from the back of the wagon might spook the driver so much that he'd run right off the road and possibly flip the car.

Yet a *bang*. A *clank*. A noise that would cause the driver to scratch his head and wonder if maybe the rear door had not been properly locked, or a restraining belt had possibly unbuckled, all would ease the man's attention into the back of the vehicle.

M.D. knew a small noise that grew more audible was exactly what he needed to create in order to *not* scare the living daylights out of the driver. Taking control of the vehicle didn't pose a problem; doing so without giving the man behind the wheel a heart attack did.

McCutcheon used the heel of the knife to make a soft tap against the side of the metal gurney's silver bar. A few seconds later he made another. Then after that, two more, each a bit louder than the previous. After the fourth noise the driver turned down the volume of the car's radio and listened more closely.

Maybe he had something in his tire? Maybe a gurney's wheel wobbled loose? Was that noise he'd just heard inside of the car or out? He listened closely.

Slowly, patiently, M.D. waited without making any more noise in order to allow the silence to seep in. After a few seconds of stillness passed, the driver reached for the radio's knob, turned up the volume, and an easy-on-the-ears country-western song resumed playing, the driver figuring, "Eh, was probably nothing."

BINK! McCutcheon banged on the metal again, and the driver spun around to scope out the back of his truck. That noise, he knew, had definitely come from inside.

"Continue. To. Drive." M.D. said. M.D. sat up, deliberately avoiding sudden moves, but also deliberately making sure to show the driver the burn in his eyes and the sharp tip of his long, dangerous blade. "If you want to make it home tonight, you'll do exactly as I say."

The driver, fifty-eight, gray hair, beach ball belly covered by a white dress shirt and light black jacket, felt his chest tighten. No one had ever broken out of the D.T. before.

No one, he realized, until now.

Not only did the driver understand what was happening, but he also understood that he had no contingency plan. Assistant coroners didn't carry guns. Assistant coroners hadn't been trained in prisoner protocol. Assistant coroners shuttled corpses from Point A to Point B like furniture trucks carried sofas; the stuff in the back was merely cargo.

McCutcheon hopped into the front seat and the driver realized he was as prepared as a florist would be to deal with an escaping con.

"Repeat after me," McCutcheon ordered. "There was no body at the prison."

Instead of repeating the words as he'd been told to do, the driver searched the road, instinctively looking around for help.

Empty highway. No police. No alarms or panic buttons on the vehicle for him to sound.

The driver's only possible means of assistance, he realized, would come from his cell phone, and his eyes scanned downward. Sitting in the cupholder next to an empty bottle of diet soda was the device that represented the only chance for him to have any communication with the outside world.

The driver looked at the phone. Looked at McCutcheon's knife. No chance, he thought. Not even worth a try.

"I said," M.D. repeated, "repeat after me. There was no body at the prison."

"There was no body at the prison."

"Major Mends made a mistake about the pickup."

"Major Mends made a mistake about the pickup."

"Major Mends has all the details if you need."

"Major Mends has all the details if you need."

"It was all a miscommunication, a wild-goose chase. You know the D.T., they're always fucking up."

"It was all a miscommunication, a wild-goose chase," the driver said. "You know the D.T., they're always fucking up."

M.D. reached into the cupholder and picked up the driver's cell phone, a newer model device with lots of bells and whistles.

"I would have called but I lost my cell."

"I would have called but I..." The driver watched as M.D. studied his phone. McCutcheon, not hearing the entire sentence repeated exactly as he'd demanded, raised his eyes. One look was all it took for the driver to understand the stakes for which he was playing.

"I would have called but I lost my cell."

McCutcheon knew he only owned two options as far as the driver was concerned. The first would be to leave no witnesses. Just put a knife in the back of the guy's skull, scramble his brain like eggs, and leave a hard-to-find carcass in a shallow grave somewhere far away from where people would be likely to look. Sure, he'd buy himself maybe a week's time with that approach, but M.D. wasn't about to kill an innocent man who'd just happened to have chosen the wrong night to work the graveyard shift at the county morgue.

This left option two: prepare the driver with a viable story and then scare the shit out of him so he followed every command without question.

McCutcheon reached across the console and held up the driver's phone.

"Unlock it."

In the world of mobile technology, cell phones that required user thumbprints to activate, provided exceptional digital security. Much better than passwords by leaps and bounds. Unfortunately once an unwanted guest got the past the iron gate of thumbprint verification, few, if any, defensive measures existed to keep a trespasser from penetrating nearly every level of cyberdata a person owned. During M.D.'s training, Stanzer had taught him all the dirty tricks. Now McCutcheon planned to use them in order to hunt down his former boss.

The driver placed his thumb on the screen and the phone buzzed to life.

HELLO JEFFREY

"Jeffrey," M.D. said. "I want you to pay attention to the road and listen closely, because I am now going to explain some things about where your life stands."

"Where am I going?" the driver asked.

McCutcheon leaned over and checked the gas gauge. Still half a tank. "For now, just stay on this highway and do not exceed two miles over the speed limit. Clear?"

Jeffrey nodded.

M.D. turned his attention to the driver's phone. "You'll notice that as I scroll through your cell all of your apps are logged in for your convenience. Bad move, Jeffrey. For example, your e-mail is open." McCutcheon started tapping on the screen. "E-mail is the gateway to everything, because I can now log in to all of your personal sites and request password resets. For instance, I see you use this app right here to bank online." M.D. tapped the screen. "Forgot my password... password reset request being sent ...I toggle over to your e-mail account and then I reset your password... new password set... Perfect. I am now in your checking account." M.D. looked at the screen. "Oh, I see you paid $127.60 to your cable company two days ago. That bill feels a bit pricey, doesn't it, Jeffrey? You probably get HBO. Wait, let me log in and take a look.... Oh, you do. Plus, you have two other cable boxes in your house, your home address being 7271 Almond Avenue." M.D. raised his eyes. "How'm I doing so far, Jeffrey? You understand where this is all going?"

Jeffrey remained silent, eyes on the road.

"I can get into your credit cards, I can get into your retirement accounts, I can get your social security number, driver's license, and four-digit PIN for your ATM card. I can get it all," M.D. said. "And, worst of all, I can lock you out. Do you know how hard it will be to prove you are you after I put a whole series of fraud warnings out that some loony guy is pretending to impersonate me, by claiming he had his phone stolen and all his passwords changed? Just a total nightmare, huh?"

Jeffrey felt his chest get even tighter.

"But you know what's most frightening of all, Jeffrey?"

"Wh-wh-what?"

"I now have your contacts page and all your photos. Oh, look," M.D. said. "Those must be the grandkids."

M.D. showed Jeffrey a picture of three young ones smiling at a park.

"I now have access to your entire life, Jeffrey. Your wife, your kids, your money, everyone's address, birthdays, I own it all and all because I own your cell phone. Spooky, isn't it?"

Jeffrey remained silent, wishing for the good ol' days of pen and paper.

"What do you want?" Jeffrey asked.

"Just your silence," McCutcheon answered. "If word of a prison break gets out, you're the only possible source for it and . . . hey, is that your dog, Jeffrey?"

M.D. held up a picture of a fluffy white poodle loping around in the grass of a backyard barbecue.

"Ask yourself right now, Jeffrey," McCutcheon said as he tapped the screen with tip of his knife. "Is risking the safety of all these people really worth it?"

Only the most desperate of soldiers ever stooped to the level of hurting civilians, and while M.D. had been pushed past his breaking point, he also knew he'd never go through with any of the threats he was making. Yet, if he was going to be able to let Jeffrey walk away from this evening scot-free, McCutcheon knew he needed to make sure Jeffrey left the car pissing his pants.

"What else do you want?" Jeffrey asked, tears welling in his eyes.

"Just your silence, Jeffrey. Everyone will remain safe as long as you can follow the story and remain silent. Seem like a fair deal?"

Jeffrey wiped the tears from his eyes. "A very fair one."

"I agree," M.D. said turning his attention back to the phone. "I'll let you out soon, but right now I have a few more things to do, so for the moment, just continue to drive."

For twenty minutes the coroner's wagon cruised along in silence. The longer they drove, the more calm Jeffrey felt. In his heart he knew he would hold up his end of the bargain one hundred percent, and for some strange reason that he could not quite identify, he also felt like the escaped prisoner who was now calling all the shots would do the same. After thirty-five miles of road passed underneath the car's wheels, he no longer felt panicked. Perhaps he realized he was just a guy in the wrong place at the wrong time. Or perhaps he felt put at ease by McCutcheon's calm demeanor. This wasn't an edged-out psychopath sitting in Jeffrey's front seat; this was a calm and poised person who knew how to work a cell phone like a technological witch doctor.

"Wh-what else can my phone do?"

"You're asking me questions?" M.D. replied.

"I, uh," Jeffrey said, quickly turning his eyes back toward the road. "I just had no idea my cell could do all those things."

"This isn't a phone, Jeffrey. This is a weapon." McCutcheon tapped the screen and began downloading some obscure mobile software. "And right now I am headed to the mysterious and dangerous regions underneath the World Wide Web, a place called the DarkNet."

THIRTY-THREE

To turn from prey to predator, to shift from hunted to hunter, weapons would be required. While physical arsenals had fortified mankind's armies for thousands of years, McCutcheon knew that modern-day warriors required cybertools. Fists, guns, and knives could only take a soldier so far in contemporary times; digital warfare, however, could leave a cascade of carcasses in its wake. All anonymously.

As a theater for battle, DarkNet represented the new frontier.

"Where are we going?"

"Keep driving."

"When will we stop?"

"I'll let you know."

The destination did not yet hold any importance to M.D. Before anything else he needed time to download TOR.

Part of Stanzer's covert training included a detailed module on how to use The Onion Router, otherwise known as TOR. As a suite of software and hidden online networks,

TOR enabled people all across the globe to use the Internet anonymously, protecting them from traffic analysis, network surveillance, and, most importantly, location discovery. From online pirates to pornographers, hackers to whistle blowers, military personnel to journalists to terrorists, TOR had been originally developed with the U.S. Navy in mind for the purpose of protecting government communications. Instead it had evolved into a widely used means by which law enforcement officers, activists, criminals, and many others could conceal their identities, as well as their business from the rest of the world.

With TOR at his disposal, M.D. could find out everything he needed about anything he wanted without anybody being able to find him. The Onion Router was a place where bad people went to do bad things and good guys went to stop them.

And vice versa.

Once Jeffrey's cell phone had been successfully converted into an anonymous digital cyber slave, McCutcheon began to hunt for data. In the DarkNet, all of M.D.'s searches would be impenetrably cloaked.

"Take the next off-ramp and head west," McCutcheon said, looking at the map he'd brought up on the phone. "You're gonna drop me off somewhere."

Thirty-six minutes later, after a series of left-right-left directions, M.D. ordered Jeffrey to stop the car in a dark and grimy alley.

"Out of the car. And go open that black Dumpster."

Panic seized Jeffrey. He had thought he was safe, but now he wasn't so sure. Being ordered to open the lid of a Dumpster at four forty-five in the morning, in a shadowy alley on a street in the middle of nowhere, triggered every panic alarm in his nervous system.

This is how people are murdered, he thought. He made me think I would be okay, but he fooled me and I am now going to die.

"I said, pop the lid," M.D. demanded. Jeffrey, his heart pumping with fear, opened the lid of the black Dumpster, feeling like a man who had just been passed a shovel on the way to digging his own grave.

The lid clanked open with a soft *bang*, and Jeffrey wished for a moment that he'd thought to throw it open with greater force in order to create a noise and possibly draw the attention of some sleeping neighbors. But he hadn't, and he regretted it. This led Jeffrey to deliberate whether he should fight or not. Perhaps he needed to throw a right cross to try to save his own life. As M.D. opened the rear of the wagon, Jeffrey balled up his fist behind him. With McCutcheon's back turned, this could be his last, best, and only shot.

"You don't want to do that, Jeffrey," M.D. said, as if he had eyes in the back of his head. "What you want to do is grab the stretcher. All we're tossing in the Dumpster is the gurney, not you."

Jeffrey exhaled a deep sigh of relief and uncurled his hand. Thirty seconds later the stretcher lay at the bottom of a garbage bin and they were back in the car on their way to a new destination.

"Jeffrey, do you remember what we've talked about earlier tonight?"

He nodded.

"Get the flu. Call in sick to work. Don't tell your wife jack shit, and do not replace your phone until seven days have passed. These are easy directions. Are you prepared to follow them?"

Jeffrey gulped. "Yes."

"Remember, everything you do, I can see. Do nothing and nothing will happen. Do something and..."

McCutcheon let the words hang in the air. He wanted Jeffrey's imagination to run wild for a moment.

Which it did.

Grandkids. The dog. His home address and wife. The safety of all his loved ones flashed through his mind. Not only could he remain silent, he would.

"Pull over behind that gas station," M.D. ordered. "And keep the car running."

Jeffrey did as he was told, and when the vehicle came to a stop, M.D. opened the passenger door. "One last thing." McCutcheon reached into the glove compartment. "I'm gonna need your phone charger. Not a problem, is it?"

"Uhm...no."

"Disappear, Jeffrey. In a week, this will all be over."

M.D. hopped out of the car and then vanished into the dark of night. Jeffrey just sat there for a moment behind the steering wheel wondering what had just happened. He had no idea who had just kidnapped him, nor any idea of where the escaped convict was going.

But M.D. knew his next destination. He was off to break into the home of Major Henry Jacob Krewls.

THIRTY-FOUR

Wearing only a stained white T-shirt and pair of tightie-whitey underwear, Krewls sat down in a worn brown reclining chair and zapped on the television with his black remote control.

Day off, he thought. Cartoons. A shower. Shop for bananas and toilet paper in the afternoon, then home for online porn. He had the whole day planned.

Then he saw McCutcheon. Krewls, still seated in his chair, dropped his spoon and a dribble of white milk ran down his chin. He had three firearms in the house plus a Taser, a nightstick, and a blackjack. The only thing within his reach: a box of Fruit Loops.

M.D. scanned the room and took in the depressing details of Krewls's solitary, blue-collar, single-guy life. Shitty furniture. Crooked paintings. The faint smell of lingering farts trapped in the air. It was a home without happiness, but McCutcheon had expected as much. More than expected it; he understood it. Krewls's joy didn't come from the house where he lived; it came from work. Abusing power fulfilled all of his earthly needs.

Krewls waited for M.D. to speak. Waited for M.D. to flash a weapon. Waited for M.D. to give a command, bark an order, or make a monstrous gesture.

He didn't. McCutcheon just stood there, ice in his eyes. Each moment that passed unnerved Krewls more and more, until finally, unable to take the tension anymore, he spoke.

"Please, I'll, uh, do whatever you..."

"Ssshh," McCutcheon said, raising a finger to his lips. He pointed to the kitchen and walked out of the room, leaving Krewls alone in his chair.

Krewls saw his opportunity to dash. To dart into his bedroom, grab the 9mm sitting by the side of his dresser, and blow a series of holes in M.D.'s head and chest. The hollow-points in his gun would create caverns in the kid's torso big enough for a squirrel to crawl through.

But he didn't. Not because M.D. stopped him. McCutcheon was already in the other room. Krewls didn't because he didn't have the guts. He just couldn't move his feet and muster up the will to make the dash for his arms. Like all bullies, once confronted, Krewls turned into a cowering sissy. He had a chance to make his move, he was being given a shot, and all he could manage to do was walk into the kitchen without even putting up a fight.

"Sit," McCutcheon ordered. Krewls did as he was told. M.D. reached behind his back and pulled out his knife. Raising it into the air, he twirled the blade around, reversed the handle so that the tip of the SERE pointed toward his chest, the grip toward Krewls, and set the weapon down on the table. The message was clear.

G'head. Pick it up.

Krewls looked at the blade, looked at McCutcheon, and lowered his gaze, shame filling his heart. This wasn't an intruder who had broken into Krewls's home; it was his karma—and as the old saying goes, *Karma's a bitch.*

"Let's have a talk," M.D. said. Using a dirty dinner plate as a makeshift tripod, McCutcheon propped up Jeffrey's cell on the kitchen table. Once satisfied he'd framed his shot the way he wanted it to look, M.D. pushed the record button on the phone's video camera.

"State your name."

"Uhm...Henry..."

"Louder!"

"Henry Jacob Krewls."

"Occupation?"

"What are you doing?"

M.D. glowered. Krewls, still unsure of where all this was headed, decided to continue.

"Commanding guard at Jentles State Penitentiary. Known unofficially as the D.T."

"How long have you been an employee of this facility?"

"Nineteen years."

"Henry, have you ever physically abused a prisoner?"

"Look, kid...let's talk about..."

M.D. raised his eyes. One glare was all it took. Krewls gulped then continued.

"Uhm, yes. I have occasionally abused the rights of prisoners."

"How many times?"

"I don't know."

"How many times, Henry? Ten? Twenty?"

McCutcheon sought honesty and Krewls knew it.

"More than that." Krewls hunched his shoulders. "Hundreds of times. Maybe thousands. May I have a drink of water?"

"No."

Silence fell over the kitchen. Fifteen seconds of it, the video camera recording each passing tick of the clock. Krewls shuffled in his chair, leaned his elbows on the table, and gazed downward, growing visibly more uncomfortable moment by moment.

"Have you ever arranged for sexual violence to occur against any of the people in your custody?"

The question hung in the air like a gray cloud, and Krewls, still looking downward at the cheap, floral patterned tablecloth, swallowed hard. A moment later he raised his eyes and looked directly into the camera.

"Yes."

"How many times?"

"I don't know."

"Henry..."

"Many times. Many, many times."

The first few minutes were long and tedious, but McCutcheon had been trained by Stanzer in the principles of criminal interrogation. Television cop dramas sexed up the art of grilling a perp and made it seem like a little glaring, a few hard slaps, and a couple of large, looming threats were all it took to get a lawbreaker to admit to their crimes.

McCutcheon understood that the best tactic to get what he wanted from Krewls lay in exploiting his psychological weakness. The art of effective interrogation offered a variety of strategies for this. Sometimes policemen used the ploy of "good cop, bad cop," whereby one officer played the role of friend, one the fearsome foe, and a criminal would admit their sins to the good cop in order to keep the bad cop from dropping the hammer on them.

Another common strategy was the technique of maximization, whereby a litany of horrible consequences would be laid out in such gory detail that an accused perpetrator would spill his guts in order to reduce the harshness of their inevitable sentence. They knew they did the deed, they got caught for doing the deed, so, as opposed to trying to maintain the lie that they were innocent, they'd choose the path of bargaining for a lesser, "not maximized" consequence.

Scholars estimated that almost fifty percent of suspected criminals confessed to their crimes under the duress of interrogation. Why did it work so well? Fear.

Fear made people talk, and while Krewls was most certainly terrified by the sight of an ex-con he'd horribly abused standing alone in his living room with a large knife, M.D. understood that to get Krewls to really sing he'd need to tap the prison guard's deepest, darkest inner fears in order to get his plan to work.

What was Krewls most afraid of? M.D. asked himself. Deep down inside, beyond all the masks and all the bravado and all the outwardly tough-guy appearances, Krewls was nothing more than a scared little boy filled with shame.

McCutcheon saw evidence in the details of Krewls's home: in the cartoons on the television, in the sugary cereal with milk, in the messy room. All so childlike. McCutcheon saw evidence in his body language: in the way Krewls sagged his shoulders, looked at the floor with downcast eyes, and spoke softly. But the cross on the wall next to the picture of his deceased mother proved to be the final piece of the psychological puzzle.

Why would a man who believed in God act in such an ungodly way? Why keep a large photo of your stoic-looking dead mother on the wall, staring out into the room with a look of disappointment and disapproval with the dates of her birth and death etched on the picture's frame? Krewls wasn't a heartless Hitler; he was a wounded little boy carrying an immense amount of guilt.

He didn't start as a monster. He probably didn't even view himself as a monster. It had all just sort of snowballed, which let M.D. know that it wouldn't take much to get Krewls to snap. He'd even probably been hoping to get caught. When McCutcheon put the video recorder in front of Krewls, he wasn't offering the man punishment; he was offering the prison guard a chance to cleanse his soul.

Krewls took it, and much to his surprise, but not to M.D.'s, once Krewls started to confess, once he began talking, he found it nearly impossible to stop.

He began to tell tales of horror. Of things he'd done to Pharmy. Of things he'd had Pharmy do to others. He told stories about purposefully bringing in spiders and wasps and bees to spook the men in solitary. There were tales of requesting prisoner's wives to perform oral sex on guards in order to enter the visitation room. From cockfights to contraband, negligence to nastiness, Krewls spoke for almost forty-five minutes, pouring out story after story of abuse, neglect, and consciously concocted trauma.

It went beyond a mere admission of guilt; holding on to all the hateful things he'd done had been toxic to his heart, and by speaking his truths to the camera Krewls began to experience the liberty of confession. Tears came. Tears of shame, hurt, and sadness. He admitted to feeling lonely, scared, and threatened. He wasn't a bad person, he claimed. Just a sad one, and he'd done all these things as a means to cover up all the pain he felt inside.

But he was done with all that now. A new man, he swore. McCutcheon had shown him the way, and Krewls vowed that from this day forward he would nevermore be the tyrant he once was.

It felt good to get this off his chest. He felt lighter. Better. Even spiritual, he said. This confession would help Krewls turn a new page in his life. And help Jentles turn a new page in its own forward-looking history.

"Thank you," Krewls said, his face wet from crying. "Thank you. From this point forward I am a changed man."

McCutcheon turned off the camera and checked the

cell phone to make sure he'd gotten everything. Fifty-eight minutes worth of footage. All of it perfectly recorded.

"What are you going to do now?" Krewls asked rubbing the tears from his eyes. Wow, did he feel better.

M.D. tapped the screen and began navigating his way through the TOR software so that any digital footprints he might leave couldn't be tracked.

"YouTube," M.D. said as he hit the upload button.

The words smashed Krewls in the head like a hammer. McCutcheon didn't need to explain how the rest of the events would unfold. Krewls could easily piece it together.

YouTube would lead to media attention. Media attention would lead to journalists. Newspeople chasing the story would lead to more media attention, which would ultimately lead to an official investigation to determine whether or not any of the activities described in the video were true.

Which they were.

Krewls would be arrested, indicted, and tried in a court of law.

Then sentenced.

To prison.

Maybe not the D.T. but most certainly a dark and loathsome penitentiary, and on the hierarchy of prisoners in jail there was only one rung lower than Cho Mo in any facility.

Former cop or prison guard.

There was no way around it. Krewls could try to go on the lam and run like a fugitive, but he knew he'd never make it past McCutcheon.

M.D. reached into his pocket and pulled out a thick wad of cash. "I found this in your drawer. Eight thousand dollars in cash. Seems like a bit of an underpayment but still, I'm taking it."

Krewls remained frozen with fear. M.D. picked up the cell phone.

"There. Uploaded. Wanna see?"

McCutcheon flipped the phone around and showed the screen to Krewls. He read the title of the video.

REAL-LIFE PRISON GUARD CONFESSES
TO YEARS OF HORROR & ABUSE
WARNING: VERY GRAPHIC!

Krewls turned his attention to the lower right hand corner, underneath the black edges of the video, and saw the viewer count change from two to three. In under a minute, three people had already clicked. Krewls started praying. Perhaps the footage would disappear into oblivion? Maybe it would die an undiscovered death like so many other videos posted to YouTube that never draw even a handful of clicks? Krewls began to convince himself about his fairly decent chances. With so much white noise out there on the Internet, so many people uploading so many crazy things each and every day, perhaps no one would be intrigued by the title M.D. had selected.

The view count clicked to five. Then eleven. Before another sixty seconds had passed, twenty-three people had already clicked on Krewls's confession.

Krewls took his eyes off the screen and looked at McCutcheon. Krewls had played a role into turning M.D. into a killer, but McCutcheon wanted to choose a different path for exacting his vengeance.

A bloodless revenge, served cold.

I don't want to take his life, M.D. told himself before he'd broken into Krewls's house. *I just want his destiny to unfold. But Stanzer...*

McCutcheon picked up his knife and put the eight thousand dollars in cash back in his pocket.

"Where's your cell phone?" M.D. asked.

"On the counter."

"I need it."

M.D. scooped up Krewls's phone and looked at the screen. Guy didn't even use a passcode lock. McCutcheon put it into his pocket. Krewls reached out and grabbed M.D.'s arm.

"Please," Krewls said. "Don't." His eyes were red and bloodshot.

M.D. glared at the hand that clutched his sleeve, and the memory of the guy not named Timmy flashed across his mind.

"Remove your fingers or I will snap every joint in your hand."

Krewls, unable to offer anything more than puppy dog eyes, released his grip and McCutcheon headed for the door, a ghost about to disappear.

Target one, executed.

McCutcheon left the house and vanished.

Krewls, still at the kitchen table, dropped his head into his hands, no idea what to do. Then he spied something. A small item. Sitting on the cheap floral tablecloth, an option for his destiny revealed.

There they were, lifeless yet profound. A pair of shoelaces.

THIRTY-FIVE

Three hours later McCutcheon sat in the corner booth of a red-and-white diner in the city of Lansing, Michigan, making sure to face the front entrance at a diagonal angle so he could see every patron that either left or entered the establishment. To his right, thirty feet away, a path to the restroom. Beyond that a swinging door that led to the kitchen, which was sure to have a back exit to the street.

From this point forward, any place he entered would need at least two ways out.

He eyed the menu. Chicken-fried steak. Deep-fried catfish. French-fried potatoes, home fries, mozzarella sticks, deep fried.

A waitress approached.

"May I please have a large salad, no dressing, no croutons, extra tomatoes, carrots, and cucumbers?"

"Sakes alive, that sure is healthy." The waitress's laugh caused her rosy cheeks to jiggle. "Sure you don't wanna try the meat loaf?"

"Just a salad, please. But a big one." M.D. smiled. "I'm kinda hungry."

"They ain't that big."

"Can you make it a double?"

"You want two of 'em?"

"Yes, please."

"A double it is." The waitress jotted down a note and scooped up the menu. "That sure is one heck of a memorable order. Most folks who come in this time of day are looking for taters, beef, and gravy."

McCutcheon held the grin on his face, but behind his smile he knew he'd just made a mistake. Being remarkable, standing out in any way, was not what he wanted to do. Being notable made him memorable, and being memorable made him easier to track.

Hunger, he realized, had clouded his judgment. So had a lack of sleep. He ought to know better than to order something so atypical in a place like this. It was an amateurish slip-up, a silly blunder, but serious enough to cause M.D. to hit the pause button and take stock of his situation. Yes, he wanted to go, go, go, but upon deeper reflection he knew he couldn't continue at this pace. If he did, more errors would continue to stack up. Avoidable ones. The kind that might cost him his life.

Sometimes, he realized, the fastest path forward required putting on the brakes.

M.D. took a deep breath. *Slow down*, he said to himself. *Take some time, recuperate, and think things through.*

In the Notes section of Jeffrey's cell phone, McCutcheon opened a new, blank page and typed in the word "NEEDS."

Underneath, he typed the letters F, R, T, and P, each on its own line.

F stood for *Food*. His body needed nutrition. Check. Though he'd slipped up in the way he'd ordered his salad, M.D. knew a plump, pleasant waitress in an unexceptional part of town that he'd never been to before would not be his downfall.

No need to be paranoid, he thought. No one was chasing him. At least not yet.

R stood for *Rest*. Best plan would be to jump on a bus so that someone else could do the driving, and he could shut his eyes for a few hours on the way to his next destination. Not a bus out of Lansing, though. After the gaffe with the salad, M.D. decided it would be safer to depart for his next destination from a different city. This led to the *T* section of his list: *Transportation*.

After eating he'd steal a car, drive somewhere within a two-hour radius, dump the vehicle, and catch a Greyhound. He'd have to be careful about where he stepped off the bus, though. Best for it to be a city he'd never previously visited. This meant he'd need yet another form of transportation afterward. But what, steal another car? No, something more efficient, more nimble, and stealthy. A motorcycle. Yeah, that sounded good. But not a hot one. A bike that he'd purchase. But how?

He looked at Krewls's phone and decided to deal with the details of this part of things a bit later.

Overall, each move McCutcheon plotted would allow

him freedom and mobility, but changing the mode of how he would get from place to place three times in the next twelve hours felt like a smart way to cover his tracks. It was the Squiggly Line Theory, no direct paths from A to B. No patterns, no footprints, no discernible sequences, or designs. Move, vanish, move, vanish, move vanish, then appear.

Puwolsky and Stanzer would never know what hit them.

M.D. looked back down at the *P* section of his list. The *Plan* required more attention. McCutcheon sat back, closed his eyes, and allowed the worn padded cushions of the oval restaurant booth to support his full weight. He was tired. He was hungry. He had much to do. He also hoped the waitress would hurry up and deliver his salad. With a little luck, she'd be smart enough to bring him a nice, tall glass of water, as well.

The diner's front door opened and three men dressed in jeans, long-sleeved shirts, and work boots entered. They grabbed a booth four spots down from McCutcheon and debated about whether to go for the chicken-fried steak or the meat loaf. Nothing to worry about, M.D. thought, and he returned to considering his plans. Pinching a car would be easy, he knew, because all security measures were only as strong as their weakest link.

What was an automobile's weakest link? Its key, of course.

M.D. had been taught that once automobile manufacturers began installing engine immobilizer systems into all their vehicles, stealing cars had become ridiculously hard.

It's why Stanzer never bothered to train McCutcheon in the art of hot-wiring a ride. Modern cars contained uniquely programmed microchips in their ignition keys, a technology super tough to crack or circumvent. No key, no start, no way around it.

Yet even though technology had advanced leaps and bounds, people (Stanzer explained) were as gullible as ever.

"Why steal a car?" Stanzer said. "All you really need to do is have someone hand you the key?"

"And how do you do that?"

"Through social engineering."

"Never heard of it."

"It's the art of exploiting human vulnerabilities," Stanzer said. "And for the modern-day soldier, it's a must-have tool in your arsenal of weapons."

Hour upon hour of studying behavioral psychology made Stanzer believe he understood most people better than they understood themselves.

"Still not sure I get it," M.D. said.

"Look at it like this," Stanzer replied. "Think of yourself as a hacker of humans. What three qualities do most human beings possess?"

"Eyes, ears, and a nose."

"Very funny," Stanzer said. "Number one, most people view themselves as good. Number two, most people view themselves as helpful. And number three, most people want to be liked. Choose your target according to these parameters and then exploit that person's weakness."

McCutcheon shook his head. "You're evil."

"I'm effective," Stanzer replied. "There's a big difference." Stanzer went on to explain how lots of people possessed car keys, and that all M.D. needed to do if he ever found himself in search of a ride was to find someone to hand him a key. McCutcheon scanned the restaurant.

Hmm, maybe the waitress?

"Here's a double-size salad for you, honey. I combined it all into one large bowl to make it easier for ya. That okay?"

"Perfect," M.D. said. "Thank you."

"And for some reason, I don't have you fixed for a soda pop," she said handing McCutcheon a tall glass of water.

He smiled. "With a wedge of lemon. You've got my number, don't you?"

She returned the grin. "Yes I do. Need anything else?"

"Actually," McCutcheon said, "would you mind changing the channel? Stories like this depress me."

The waitress spun around and looked at the television screen hanging off the wall.

BREAKING NEWS: JAILS IN CRISIS:
RAMPANT ABUSE, RAMPANT NEGLECT

"You got it, hon," she answered. "World's got some good stuff in it, too, but you wouldn't know it from watching the TV."

"That's true," M.D. said.

"Me, I try to look for the good in folks," the waitress said. "Try to do it each and every day. Flat out lose my mind on this planet if I didn't."

She clicked off the television and M.D. thought about her last words. *Looked for the good in people every day, did she?*

"Oh, one more question," M.D. began before she walked away.

"Sure thing," the waitress said. "Anything, honey."

McCutcheon took a second before making his next request. "What's the biggest hotel in the area? You know, the largest one that's nearby?"

"Oh, that would be the Grand," the waitress responded. "Only a few blocks away."

"Think they're full today?"

"Well," she said, "there's a dentist convention down at the Lansing Center this week. Few thousand folks talking about teeth for the next three days. They might have some rooms left. You want me to call for you?"

"You're too nice," M.D. said with a grin. "But I have my phone right here. I'll just Google it. And by the way," M.D. added as he punched his fork into a big bowl of leafy greens. Scamming the waitress out of her car wouldn't be right. Only a jackass would socially engineer a working woman like her. "This looks really good."

"We aim to please," she said before disappearing back into the kitchen. McCutcheon plunked a bite of food in his mouth and gazed back down at the screen of Krewls's cell phone.

Eat slowly, he told himself. *All the answers will come soon enough.*

It wasn't long before M.D. cooked up a plan to score a

car and then drive it to the bus station in Kalamazoo, 75.8 miles away. Obtaining a motorcycle afterward, he realized, would be something he could easily take care of on the Greyhound via the Internet before he napped. Still there was the bigger issue of how to ensnare Puwolsky and terminate Stanzer. Each would be difficult, he knew. Each for different reasons.

M.D. plugged the phone charger into the wall so he could juice Jeffrey's cell to max capacity, and then set up a news alert on Krewls's phone. If any information bubbled up across the Web about a prison break, the cell would flash an immediate notification.

So far it appeared Jeffrey had remained quiet. Probably would for a while, too, but M.D. knew it was only a matter of time before Stanzer discovered McCutcheon had escaped. To orchestrate a plan to eliminate a covert operative guaranteed that the colonel would follow up in order to make sure all the i's had been dotted and t's properly crossed. M.D. might be free for the moment, but the clock was undoubtedly ticking.

His best defense, he knew, would be to play offense. Attack the two men and bring the battle to them. After a few more of forkfuls of salad, McCutcheon began to cobble the ideas together. His first order of business, however, before he could launch any sort of offensive, would be to cover his flank. He knew he wanted to attack his enemy's greatest weakness, but he also knew that their first order of business would be to attack his. Stanzer, once he got news about McCutcheon's escape, would without a doubt be thinking in this manner.

Before advancing any further, M.D. would need to double back.

He thought about calling home, but couldn't risk the phone lines being tapped, so for the next thirty minutes M.D. toggled back and forth between his two cells and his fork, setting into motion details of a new plan as he ate his meal. Having cell phones, he realized, was far more valuable to him than owning guns. Funny, he thought, how the aims of battle had remained the same for centuries, but the weaponry with which warriors could attack had changed greatly.

M.D. finished his food, paid his check, and left the waitress a hundred-dollar bill for a tip. Krewls would have wanted it that way, he told himself with a smile. Next, he exited the diner and walked three blocks east to the Grand Hotel, a large beige-colored building with tall, vast columns and stately archways. M.D. spent ten minutes in the opulent lobby, a bustling place filled with bellhops in uniforms and businesspeople walking across marble floors. He searched for his target.

A middle-aged man graying at the temples? No.

A husky guy, early thirties, wearing glasses? Possible, not ideal.

Then he appeared, the guy he wanted. Male, red vest, wavy hair, early twenties, looked like a guy who smoked pot on the weekends.

McCutcheon studied his mark for eleven minutes to get a sense of his workflow. In a hotel this busy with such a steady stream of people checking in and checking out, the sense of organized chaos would be an ally in his quest to dupe the Grand Hotel's valet parking attendant. Three minutes later the right moment appeared and McCutcheon sprung on his prey.

"Hey, man," M.D. said briskly, approaching the wavy haired valet. "My boss just left a file folder in the trunk."

The twenty-something-year-old looked sideways at McCutcheon.

"The blue Chrysler," M.D. said. "You just parked it."

The parking attendant looked down at his hands. He held three different sets of keys.

"Yeah, that one right there," M.D. said pointing at a black key ring with the Chrysler emblem blazing from the center. "Don't you remember me, we just pulled up?"

"Uhm, you got the ticket?" he asked.

M.D. searched his pockets. "Aw shit, I didn't get it from him. Look," M.D. said. "All I need is to get in and out of the trunk." McCutcheon flashed a Can-ya-help-a-fella-out look. "Be back in like two minutes."

The valet considered what to do as more cars lined up waiting to be parked.

"Here ya go," the attendant said handing McCutcheon the keys. "It's on the third floor."

"Third floor? Got it. Thanks."

"No problem." The valet hustled off to the next car.

"Just leave the keys on the counter if I'm not here when you get back."

"You got it, dude," M.D. said with a friendly wave. "Appreciate it, buddy."

McCutcheon took the stairs to the third floor, beeped the key ring to unlock the door, and turned on the ignition, the proud new owner of a navy blue Chrysler. By the time the hotel had even noticed the car was missing, M.D. figured, he'd already have dumped the car and be sitting on the bus.

He exited the garage, turned north on Elm Avenue, and made his way toward the highway heading east. It was just like Stanzer had said: "Why hot-wire a ride when you can simply find a mark to hand you the keys?"

THIRTY-SIX

tanzer pulled out a chair, wooden, no cushion, and set down his drink on the brown table. His skim-milk latte, steam rising from the top, would need a few moments to cool. Stanzer hated skim-milk lattes. Thought they were for pansies. He'd only ordered it so that he'd have a beverage in his hand that would enable him to blend in with the rest of the café crowd. The colonel missed the days of shadowy garages and get-togethers late at night under freeway overpasses, but they'd long since passed for the men who ran covert operational units for the federal government. In the modern era, the murky world of black opps ran on caffeine.

"This is why the world hates us," Stanzer said to the man he was meeting. "Because we invented five-dollar cups of coffee. All war boils down to economics. Who the hell can afford these things?"

"A tip has come in."

"A tip?" Stanzer said taking a seat. Three-star general Montgomery Evans took a sip off of his double-shot cara-mel macchiato and nodded his head.

"If word of your unit gets out," General Evans continued. "It would be, how shall I put this? Unsavory."

"It's not getting out."

"But if it does…"

"Don't worry," Stanzer said. "It won't."

A pretty woman with long legs and shapely hips swished by in a blue dress. Both the general and the colonel remained quiet until she completely passed.

"This tip," Stanzer asked. "I assume it's been safely intercepted?"

"*Safely* is a dicey word when it comes to the Web."

"Where'd it come from?"

"That's what bothers me," the general said. "It was almost too easy to trace."

"Yeah?"

"Came in from Detroit," the general said. "Via an e-mail off the desktop computer of a DPD narcotics unit."

Stanzer raised the latte to his lips, took a sip, and then put it back down, a scowl of disapproval for the entire coffee industry on his face.

"You traced it right to the machine?" he asked.

"Directly," the general replied.

"And it's not a setup? No Internet relay schemes to make it appear as if it came from a location that it really didn't originate from?"

"It's been confirmed," the general said. "Completely legit. Came straight off one of their officer's desktops."

"Odd," Stanzer said weighing the news.

"You'd at least think cops would know how to mask

their communications if they wanted to remain anonymous in this day and age," General Evans replied. "This guy used a fake Gmail address and thought that'd be enough to keep him in the shadows."

"No DarkNet? No TOR? You're people are sure?"

"No browser bundling whatsoever. Just a straightforward fake Gmail account created under an assumed identity. Username was..." General Evans extended his arm and showed Stanzer a piece of paper. "'TTheTTerminal TTerminator.' Double *t*'s everywhere."

"Catchy," Stanzer said.

"So the question I'm asking myself is," General Evans continued, "why would a DPD narcotics officer rat you and your clandestine operation out by name? It's like some sort of whistle-blowing attempt."

"They cited me?" Stanzer said.

"Specifically," the general answered. "Put a white-hot spotlight on you. It's the absolute intent of this message. Its author clearly wants you torched."

Stanzer considered the information. A DPD narcotics officer. An attempt to out his unit. Stanzer targeted by name. There could only be one link.

McCutcheon. Too coincidental to be anything otherwise. Stanzer rose from his chair.

"If you'll excuse me, sir, I had better go direct my full attention to this matter."

"Indeed," the general said. "And for God's sake, man, make sure it stays quiet. We need to keep what we're doing around here buried. With all this hacking going on every-where I'm personally considering going back to pagers."

"Understood, sir," Stanzer said. "You have my word."

■　　■　　■

"Colonel, could you please make sure you speak your answers into the microphone," the senator from Nebraska said. "Remember, we are filming this."

"I said," Stanzer repeated, leaning closer to the mike, "there are currently no active agents under the legal age of eighteen years old working under my authority."

Stanzer, dressed in his full uniform, pressed pants, pol-ished shoes, shiny bars on his collar, sat at a beige-colored conference table in a chilled room taking questions from a panel of three—two men, one woman—each dressed in a shade of navy blue, the standard Washington, D.C. color for business attire. Though there was no one else in attendance, a video camera captured every word of the proceedings.

"But you did have such an agent, once upon a time, cor-rect?" asked the senator from his center seat.

"Is that a question or an allegation?" Stanzer replied.

"It's a question."

"Because if it was an allegation it would require proof," Colonel Stanzer said. "And I am quite confident that there is no such proof that any agent of the sort you are describ-ing exists."

"Well, where did he go?" asked the man on the right. His gold-rimmed spectacles and a neatly trimmed mustache gave the impression of a meticulous person, the kind of bureaucrat who paid close attention to details and took particularly exacting notes.

"Where did who go?" Stanzer asked.

"Stop the games, Colonel. They are tedious."

"We have a name, you know," said the female member of the panel from her chair on the left. "McCutcheon Daniels. Known as 'Bam Bam' on the streets. He served in your unit, correct?"

"Is that question or an allegation?" Stanzer said. "Because, if that is an allegation, it would require proof in the form of . . ."

Senator Ackersleem slammed his hand down on the desk and his nameplate went flying.

"You know what really sickens me about all this, Colonel? As a former military man myself, it's the fact that as a leader you are supposed to care about your men. You are supposed to have their backs. But you," the senator raged, "all we see here in this report is a person who appears to have buried his own man somewhere in the great unknown, because the thing he cares most about is his own career. What do you have to say to that?"

Stanzer leaned forward to make sure his words would be clearly recorded by the microphone.

"I have no connections, nor have I ever had any connection, to any agent named McCutcheon 'Bam Bam' Daniels."

The senator threw up his arms in disgust.

"Are there any other agents in this covert unit?" the woman asked.

"What unit?" the colonel replied.

"Have you trained any other underage soldiers for the purposes of war?" asked the man on the right.

"What soldiers?" the colonel said.

"I am deeply troubled by this whole thing," the senator said. "Who is looking out for this child's welfare right now? Who is providing for his safety? What is he doing, who is he working for, where is he?"

"As the records clearly show, whoever this McCutcheon Daniels once was, he has now disappeared, Senator Ackersleem," Stanzer said in a smooth and even tone. "But if you'd like me to try to find him..."

The senator pointed to an armed guard by the door. "Get this officer out of my face."

Stanzer rose from his seat, turned, and calmly made his way toward the exit.

"And shut that damn camera off, would you," the senator barked. Eight seconds later the screen went black.

THIRTY-SEVEN

Stanzer rang the doorbell of a green-and-white, five-bedroom, four-bathroom house in the Detroit suburb of Plymouth. It featured a three-car garage and pool in the backyard. After forty-five seconds of no one answering, he pressed the bell a second time and stared up into the security camera that gave eyes over the front door. Though it took another twenty ticks off the clock before someone arrived, a man with a damp towel draped over his shirtless shoulders finally answered, a displeased look on his ruddy-cheeked face.

"I got a problem."

"It's Sunday," Puwolsky said, his beer gut sagging over his wet red bathing suit.

"These kinds of dilemmas don't wait."

Puwolsky rubbed his hands through his hair and stepped aside, his body language signaling for Stanzer to come in.

"Didn't mean to pull you out of the Jacuzzi."

"How'd you know I was in the Jacuzzi?"

"Too chilly to swim in the regular pool, too cloudless not to want to be outside today. Nice place you got here."

"My wife," Puwolsky said escorting them to chairs in the study. "She does well on the Internet."

"Oh, yeah. What's she sell?"

"You got a point to this visit?"

"I do," Stanzer said.

"Daddy, Daddy, can I play on the iPad?" A seven-year-old girl in a yellow bathing suit rushed to her father's side.

"Can you get a towel please?" Puwolsky snapped. "How many times do I have to tell you about wet feet in the house?"

"But I want to play on the iPad."

"You know the rules; it's an analog weekend. No screens for the entire family."

"But it's so *bo-rrrring*," the little girl moaned.

"You don't see me checking my e-mail, do ya?"

"But daddy..."

"You have my answer; now scram. I have company."

"Hmmph."

After a stomp of her foot, the little girl turned and made her way back across the room to the sliding glass door at the rear of the house, a trail of wet pitter-patter footprints smattering the floor in her wake.

"Kids," Puwolsky said. "They'll run all over you if they smell an inch of daylight."

"Kind of like United States senators," Stanzer replied.

Stanzer reached into his pocket, tapped the screen of his cell phone, and turned the device around so Puwolsky could see the images. After a moment of buffering, the video of his testimony began to play.

"Colonel, could you please make sure you speak your answers into the microphone. Remember, we are filming this."

"I said, there are currently no active agents under the legal age of eighteen years old working under my authority."

Once Puwolsky had seen enough to get the gist of the tape, Stanzer tapped the face of his phone and the screen went black.

"You do have a problem," Puwolsky said. "What are you thinking?"

"What do you think I am thinking?"

"Hey, you came here," Puwolsky replied. "Speak your mind, Colonel."

Stanzer scratched an itch at the back of his head, a resigned look on his face. "I'm boxed in," he said. "There are no other plays."

"You could own it. Fall on the sword. Take it like a man."

"I could," Stanzer said. "But they'll ruin me. These glory-seeking gasbags will burn everything I've ever built to the ground."

"You got more of these kids in your unit?"

"No."

"He's the only one?"

"Yes."

"I find that hard to believe," Puwolsky said.

"He's the prototype. Always a first, isn't there?" Stanzer flicked some imaginary lint off of his shirt. "These paper pushers don't know what it's like out there. They don't know what it means to be on the front lines like me and you. Sometimes people like us, good people, we have to do some very bad things. Do you understand where I am coming from on this one, Colonel?"

Puwolsky leaned back in his chair and thought about how true these words were. How many times had he been forced to go past the edges of the law in order to enforce it?

"Who ratted you out?"

"Still working on confirming it," Stanzer said.

"How'd they pull it off?"

"Internet tip. Pretty sure it was a fake Gmail address. Very hard to trace. Not optimistic at all we'll ever find the person who sent it."

Puwolsky nodded. Whether it was a nod of admiration for the whistle-blower's digital acumen or just approval of the overall circumstances, Stanzer couldn't tell.

"So what do you want from me?" Puwolsky asked.

"I think you know," Stanzer replied.

"I need to hear you say it."

Stanzer leaned forward. "I need you to help me make the kid disappear once and for all."

Puwolsky narrowed his eyes, nodded his head and moved in for the kill.

"What's it worth to you?"

Puwolsky knew federal guys like Stanzer owned pockets that ran deep. This Sunday visit, he began to think, might not turn out to be too bad after all.

"And might I remind, you, Colonel Stanzer," Puwolsky

added with unabashed bluster, "based on what I see in that video, you'd better bring a beefy answer to the table right now. Something significant and concrete."

"Concrete?"

"Like cement."

Stanzer took a moment before replying. "How about, as a reward for helping me out I save your fucking life."

Puwolsky chuckled. Then he stopped. Stanzer was entirely serious.

"I don't follow."

"That guard, Krewls?"

"Yeah?" Puwolsky said.

"Committed suicide."

Suicide? Puwolsky thought. That didn't sound like Krewls at all.

"You haven't seen any of the news about the D.T. on television?" Stanzer asked.

Puwolsky shook his head. "Analog weekend. No screens for any of us. Good for the kids' brains."

"Well, bad for you," Stanzer said. "'Cause I have more news, too. McCutcheon escaped."

"No chance. How do you know this?"

"I don't for sure. It's an educated guess."

"Impossible. There's only two ways out of the D.T.," Puwolsky said. "Parole or the morgue truck."

"I don't know how he did it, I don't even know *that* he did it, but I've been doing this a long time," Stanzer said. "This many coincidences this close together are not a coincidence at all. Someone is orchestrating something."

Puwolsky considered the angles. The more he thought about it, the less he liked the way things were adding up. Yes, he knew the High Priest was dead. That was good, real good, because he and Dickey Larson both knew that the death of D'Marcus Rose meant the death of their biggest problem. Yet, if McCutcheon had actually escaped from Jentles, a whole new set of issues now existed.

"If what you're saying is true, he'll be coming for me," Puwolsky said.

"He will."

"And Larson, too."

"Maybe."

"Where is he now?"

Stanzer shrugged.

"You don't know?" Puwolsky said. "But you trained this animal."

"He's not an animal, he's a soldier."

"I tell you what he is," Puwolsky said. "He's a ghost. And how the fuck do you prevent being attacked by that?"

"Easy," Stanzer said as he confidently reclined in his chair. "You attack his greatest weakness."

THIRTY-EIGHT

Riding the bus allowed McCutcheon to get some much needed rest, but he didn't doze easily because an itch still gnawed at him to pick up the pace. There was no way he could take the Greyhound all the way to Bellevue. That would be like gift-wrapping himself for Stanzer. The game of cat and mouse with the colonel was on, even if Stanzer didn't yet realize M.D. was free. Though no news about a prison break had yet hit the Web, the large amount of media attention regarding all the corruption at Jentles State Penitentiary would surely catch Stanzer's eye.

M.D. knew he might be invisible for the moment, but his instincts told him it was best to operate as if his secret about having escaped was already out. Stanzer, he knew, possessed too much mental firepower to believe in coincidences.

When it came to concern about Puwolsky and his Neanderthal thug Larson, however, McCutcheon held a different point of view. Whether they knew he was out mattered little. They were fools, he thought. Just dirty cops and small time thinkers with an overinflated sense of their own abilities because they operated out of one of the most bank-rupt and dysfunctional police departments in the nation. Sure, the crap they pulled might fly in Detroitistan, a city with a long and infamous history of guys with badges act-ing like crooks, but in the world of the F.B.I. these two clowns would be bagged, gagged, and smoked in a D.C. minute. Just a bunch of amateurs, M.D. thought. Showing McCutcheon the white Cadillac's car registration on the ride into the D.T. had proven it, too.

Ms. Madeline Vina. 13579 Sycamore Street. The address was almost too easy to remember. All odd numbers in order.

Small details. How many times had Stanzer emphasized their significance? Gather enough small details and they always paid off.

Puwolsky, M.D. felt, was anchored, arrogant, and sloppy. Larson, with his love for steroids and street brawls, might prove to be a formidable fistfight, but tracking him would be work any twelve-year-old with access to Wi-Fi could handle. Finding these two bozos would be easy, M.D. thought. But how to locate Stanzer was a nut McCutcheon still had not cracked.

The colonel had no woman in his life. No kids or fixed address, either. He lived as a nomad, a wandering war-rior protecting his nation by sacrificing his own personal desires for the greater good of the country. Yes, he'd been in love before. Told M.D. about a girl named Jamie in fairly extensive detail during one of his "You gotta slay that dragon" speeches, too. But Stanzer had walked away from her years ago.

He walked away in order to serve his nation.

"I loved the girl," Stanzer said. "But my destiny was to make a different choice."

McCutcheon wasn't so sure he bought what the colonel was selling. Maybe the girl had just dumped him and the colonel was too much of an egomaniac to own up to it. However Stanzer, when pressed, argued that there was another aspect to his thinking.

"A reverse side to the reverse side," as he put it.

"What's that mean?" McCutcheon asked.

"About me being fair to her," Stanzer said. "Forget my own wishes for a minute; think about Jamie, knowing that every time I walk out the door I might not come home for weeks on end. Or maybe when I do, it's in a body bag. Sure, soldiers do it all the time, but don't pretend it doesn't eat the person on the other end of the door alive."

Stanzer explained that walking away was actually an expression of love for the lady who'd stolen his heart.

"With the dark work I was being asked to do, I just couldn't put her life at risk like that. To be with me meant she'd always be a target. To have a life together meant we'd have to have a home. A resting place. An address to call our own. Remember, these fuckers I hunt, they hunt me back."

It's not that Stanzer didn't want to be with her, he said; it's that he felt that if he chose to be with her, chances were too high that she'd get hurt.

Emotionally. Physically. Maybe both.

"When I said good-bye I broke her heart," Stanzer said. "But I did it while she still had a heart to spare."

"What'd you tell her?" M.D. asked.

"I told her to go find an accountant or a professor, someone who'd come home at night. But a man like me, well... I just wasn't right for her. Wasn't right for anyone."

"How'd she take it?" M.D. asked.

"She fucking hates me," Stanzer said. "But to this day I am convinced I made the right decision."

"You never wanted kids?" McCutcheon asked.

"I wanted them bad."

"You never wanted a relationship?"

"I have plenty of them. Just not the romantic kind."

"What about sex?" M.D. asked.

"Ladies love the uniform," Stanzer replied. "I have no problems in that department whatsoever."

McCutcheon still didn't buy it. He thought Stanzer was using his work as an excuse to protect himself from getting close to anyone. Everyone in the colonel's life was at arm's length, and to M.D. this seemed like a way Stanzer could keep this girl Jamie there as well. Yet, now that McCutcheon sought to stalk the colonel, and couldn't find a string anywhere to grasp, he realized how smart Stanzer's strategy turned out to be. There were no threads to his life anywhere.

Unlike his own.

"There can be only one lover for a guy like me," Stanzer said. "And that's Lady Liberty."

Even though he'd shown it to McCutcheon before, Stanzer extended his arm, rolled up his shirtsleeve, and let M.D. read the tattoo on his left forearm once again.

People sleep peaceably in their beds at night only because rough men stand ready to do violence on their behalf.

"It's not just ink," Stanzer said. "It's a code."

The more McCutcheon thought about it, the more he realized he had no leads with which to go after Stanzer. And he knew there wouldn't be any, either. His only chance, he realized, would be to make the colonel come to him.

But how? When the Greyhound stopped at the Trailways Depot in Davenport, Iowa, M.D. still did not know.

He exited the bus and entered into the station's large and open lobby. Linoleum floors, shined to the point of almost being too clean, reflected white lights bouncing off the ceiling. The optics of it made the whole space looked like an indoor ice skating rink, where one false move might cause a person to slip on the glistening floor.

M.D. scanned the benches and saw his target. Dusty, six-foot two-inches, twenty-four years old, in weathered jeans and a shirt advertising a local bar named Shoobie's. Dusty eagerly eyed all the passengers departing the bus, a look of hope and excitement beaming on his face.

McCutcheon approached.

"I'm Terry."

"You're Terry?" Dusty said wrinkling his face. "I thought you was a girl."

"You sellin' it to me or not?"

Dusty deliberated what to do.

"You already took my money," M.D. added. "But I can easily cancel the transaction." McCutcheon raised his cell phone. A few taps and the credit card payment M.D. had charged to Krewls's Visa account would be reversed.

Disappointed, Dusty rose to his feet.

"Yeah. Come on."

Through Jeffrey's phone M.D. found a guy on the Internet in Davenport who was selling what he wanted. Through Krewls's phone and a PayPal account M.D. paid for the item. But McCutcheon needed a ride to go pick up the merchandise, so he made himself appear to be a buyer named Terry. A buyer named Terry who liked to party and might or might not have really large breasts. Dusty, who also liked to party—and most certainly liked really large breasts—volunteered to come pick Terry up from the bus station to, as Dusty said in his e-mail, *Make it a right bit more convenient for ya.*

So nice of you to offer, Terry had replied.

Good ol' Dusty proved true to his word. Wore a Shoobie's shirt just like he said he would, too. The guy from Iowa paused before opening the door to his white pickup truck.

"You ain't one of them Internet homos, are ya?"

McCutcheon smiled. "Sex has nothing to do with why I'm here."

Dubious, Dusty opened the door and climbed into the driver's seat.

"Well, just so you know, I ain't into that freaky-deaky stuff, and if you try some shit with me..." Dusty reached under the seat and flashed M.D. a set of black nunchucks. "I took karate in high school."

McCutcheon grinned and buckled his seat belt. "No freaky-deaky stuff, promise."

Fifteen minutes later the white pickup pulled into the driveway of a one-story house that had dirt instead of grass for a front lawn. Dusty opened the garage.

"This thing move?"

"Partner, this thing hauls ass."

"I prefer Harleys."

"Me, too," Dusty said. "But these rice rockets ride a lot quieter. I'm flipping it so I can get me an ATV."

"Sell me that gear, too?" M.D. asked.

McCutcheon nodded at the black leather jacket, gloves and helmet sitting on the work bench.

"Well, I wasn't really planning on..."

McCutcheon pulled out a fan of hundred-dollar bills. Dusty stopped talking midsentence.

"A grand sound fair?"

"Partner, you are my kind of customer."

M.D. set the money down on top of a red toolbox and used a wrench as a paperweight to make sure the bills didn't fly away.

"See, no freaky-deaky stuff."

After slipping into the black leather outfit, which perfectly matched the black two-wheel rocket he'd just bought with Krewls's money, he fired up the bike's engine.

"Pleasure doing business with you," M.D. said as he slapped down the tinted flap of the helmet's visor. McCutcheon screamed away. Behind him Dusty counted the stack of hundred-dollar bills in his hand, delighted with the idea of how he'd be drinking some mighty fine whiskey later on that night.

The ride to Bellevue only took four and a quarter hours, but M.D. didn't want to show up at his house until after sunset. It was true that he preferred Harleys, but McCutcheon wanted a Japanese engine because he knew it would allow him to cruise through the quiet neighborhoods of suburban Nebraska with more stealth. Hogs were great rides, but quietness wasn't one of their top features.

At 8:05 p.m. M.D. rode past the front of his town house. Then again at 9:20 p.m, 10:10, and again at 11:15. Each time he checked for surveillance vehicles, suspicious work crews, and open windows in neighbors' homes across the street that might have scopes or cameras looking out.

He discovered a good news–bad news scenario. The good news was that no surveillance existed. Perhaps he was wrong, but M.D. felt pretty confident he'd be able to identify any outlying elements on his home turf, and after four different passes from four different angles he felt fairly confident that he would not be walking into an ambush.

Yet the bad news outweighed the good by miles. Each pass by the house caused McCutcheon to grip the bike's throttle tighter and tighter. There was no activity inside. No lights. No silhouettes moving past windows. Nothing.

From just after sunset to just before midnight not a soul stirred.

On a school night.

Finally, at 11:45 p.m., McCutcheon parked the bike three streets away, jumped over a series of backyard fences, and circled to the rear of his garage. Under a potted pot he'd hidden a key. He used it to open the back door and discovered the thing he most dreaded finding.

Emptiness. There was no one home.

THIRTY-NINE

During one of their many meals together Stanzer and M.D. once talked about what life would have been like for the two of them if they were lawmen battling bad guys in the Wild West.

"No doubt," Stanzer said. "I'd shoot my enemy's horse."

The idea irked McCutcheon.

"Shooting the horse is out of bounds. You can't kill an innocent animal."

"The horse is part of the theater of battle."

"It didn't sign up for it," McCutcheon argued. "The animal got dragged in. I'd never shoot the horse."

"In is in," Stanzer replied. "War is chess and if you are going to survive, if you're gonna win, you have to manipulate every piece on the board to your best advantage. No compassion, no sympathy, no mercy."

"That go for civilians, too?" M.D. asked.

"Depends," Stanzer said. "In war, the overriding question is, 'What's my best play?' If I am battling a bunch of bank robbers in a Wild West shootout, taking down their horses makes good strategic sense. My enemy is demobilized. At the very least I disconcert and destabilize them, creating new opportunities for me as well as new hardships for them. After you take out the horse your odds are improved significantly. Most definitely," Stanzer reiterated. "I shoot the bastard's horse."

"What about morals?"

"In fact," Stanzer continued disregarding M.D.'s question. "I probably shoot it first before I even bother to aim for the guy riding it, now that I think about it. It's a much fatter target."

"You are a cold man," M.D. said.

"Don't worry," Stanzer replied. "One day you will be, too."

McCutcheon didn't like Stanzer's answer. Not at all. But it told him a lot about the colonel's character. He was a man who'd shoot the horse.

Which meant he was a man who would go after Gemma.

Fuck! M.D. thought to himself. *I went for food and rest when I should have pushed the pace. Fuck! Fuck! Fuck!*

McCutcheon knew the colonel's best strategic play was to go after his sister. It made the most sense because it was a move that, as Stanzer would put it, would disconcert and destabilize his opponent. Gemma, Stanzer knew, was McCutcheon's greatest weakness, and taking her to God-knows-where completely threw M.D. into a tailspin.

McCutcheon had no idea of her location. Had no idea if she was safe. Had no idea the lengths to which Stanzer would go to use her as a pawn to get McCutcheon to come to him.

On Stanzer's own terms and in Stanzer's own way.

Just like that, the situation had flipped. The predator was once again the prey.

Fuck! McCutcheon thought again.

M.D. took a deep breath and tried to clear his head before rage and fear consumed his mind and stole his ability to reason.

Okay, what does the evidence prove? Don't sulk, don't get emotional or distraught. Find out what the evidence proves.

M.D. crossed to the refrigerator. Milk still fresh, three days more until the expiration date. He opened the bottom drawer of the crisper. Lettuce still firm, nothing wilted or soggy.

He felt the fruit. All still edible.

He closed the refrigerator and searched around for signs of a hasty departure. Nothing in the town house seemed ransacked. No signs of struggle.

He surveyed the entirety of the room. Nothing seemed even the slightest bit out of place.

He checked the bedrooms. Looked through clothes and closets. Gemma's purple travel bag was gone. He went into the bathroom. Her toothbrush was missing, too.

Evidence proved they went somewhere. Evidence proved they packed. Evidence also proved that the home wasn't invaded. The whole atmosphere was too serene and organized.

This wasn't a kidnapping; this was voluntary departure. But to where? And with whom?

McCutcheon pulled out Jeffrey's phone and dialed Sarah's number. It went straight to voice mail without even ringing, which told M.D. that her cell had been powered off.

Not a good sign.

Then again, it was late. Maybe she'd already gone to sleep?

There was only one way to ascertain the final piece of evidence, the proof that would either confirm or deny M.D.'s greatest fear. McCutcheon didn't want to tip his hand and play this card unless he absolutely had to. But he truly had no choice. He'd made the calculated decision to stay in northern Michigan and complete his business with Krewls before zipping home to shore up the safety of his sister. He knew it was a risk, but the odds seemed exceptionally low that he'd be able to have a clean go at Krewls if he'd gone back to Bellevue first. Krewls, he knew, would show up at work, discover M.D.'s absence, and then alert Puwolsky and Stanzer to the situation, thus eliminating the best weapon M.D. had at his disposal.

The element of surprise.

McCutcheon felt that if he exacted his revenge on Krewls swiftly and efficiently, he'd be able to get home in time to lock down Gemma before anyone yet discovered he'd broken free from the D.T.

He was wrong. He'd gambled and lost.

How could I be so stupid?

Rage began to burn. Self-loathing. Every time love

factored into his decision making, Stanzer had taken advantage of McCutcheon. With Kaitlyn. With Gemma. Even with the affection he felt for the colonel. M.D. practically looked to Stanzer like the positive father figure he never had. Loyal. Honorable. Righteous. Worthy. For months they'd trained together side by side, and now it was all a lie. A scheme and a betrayal. All proof that the student had not yet become the master.

McCutcheon logged into TOR. He and Stanzer always communicated through the DarkNet to relay messages to each other. That's how they'd remained in contact while hunting Al-Shabaab soldiers in New Jersey, it's how Stanzer had trained all his field agents to transmit confidential data, and it would also be how Stanzer would relay any message to M.D. should he now be seeking to communicate with him.

The upside to logging into TOR would be that McCutcheon would soon know the answer as to whether the colonel had taken his sister. The downside would be that by pinging in, the colonel would know M.D. had access to the Internet, which meant that if Stanzer did not already know that M.D. had escaped from the D.T. he would now. In a best-case scenario, Gemma and Sarah had simply gone to a friend's house and M.D. would merely be tipping his hand. In a worst case scenario . . .

McCutcheon didn't want to think about that.

It took a moment for Jeffrey's phone to pick up the satellite relays. Once it did, M.D. stared at the screen and found his answer waiting in his secret inbox. It arrived in the form of two words.

RENDEZVOUS POINT.

McCutcheon's heart dropped. He'd just received an encrypted message from the guy who shot horses.

FORTY

Red numbers glowed from the face of the black digital clock hanging on the wall. 3:15 a.m. A time for sleep. Unless, of course, a trap was being set.

Stanzer and Puwolsky, alone in a soundproof room, readied their attack.

"Think he'll show?" Puwolsky asked, a Glock 9mm in his right hand.

Stanzer, his weapon holstered, crossed to pick up a bar stool.

"Yep," he answered.

"How can you be so sure?"

"'Cause I have the only thing he cares about."

"The girl?" Puwolsky asked, sliding his finger from the barrel of the Glock down to the gun's trigger.

"Naw," Stanzer replied as he moved the stool into the center of the room and calculated the optimal spacing between the seat and some folding chairs off to the left. "My guess is he already slayed that dragon."

Puwolsky considered Stanzer's words and then moved his finger off the Glock's trigger.

"Good answer," Puwolsky said. "You pass."

"Didn't know there was a test."

"Indeed there was," Puwolsky said. "'Cause there ain't no way you grabbed his girl."

"Yeah, why's that?"

"Because I did."

A surge of adrenaline rushed through Stanzer's veins, but he long ago mastered the art of not reacting outwardly to disturbing news. Calm, poised, and patient he moved a small table from the center of the room to the far wall without missing a beat.

"As an insurance policy," Puwolsky continued. "And if you would have lied to me just now, it would have told me you were in cahoots with the kid."

"Cahoots, huh?"

"With you fuckin' military guys a fella never knows who's lying, who's telling the truth, and who's setting the stage for a double cross." Puwolsky raised his weapon. "A wrong answer and you woulda had to meet the Double T?"

Stanzer wrinkled his brow. "The Double T?"

"That's what I call her," Puwolsky said, kissing his Glock. "The Terminal Terminator."

"What a coincidence," Stanzer said. "That's what I call my cock." Puwolsky glared then cracked a grin. "Very funny, Colonel. But one call from me and the girl eats a bullet."

"Well, I hope you already made it, because I just jammed all the phone lines. Whole network is down. Wi-Fi. Cell towers. Everything."

Puwolsky looked down at his phone. No signal.

"Gotta keep everything within a hundred yards offline for at least six hours," Stanzer said.

Puwolsky tapped a few icons on the phone's screen. Nothing.

"Why?"

"What do you mean, why?" Stanzer said. "To a soldier like the one we are about to do battle with, a cell is a weapon. Probably more useful to him than a gun at this point. Can't risk it. Who knows what he's cooking up."

"Well, if Larson doesn't hear from me in the next forty-five minutes," Puwolsky said, "he's gonna pop the little lady."

"Tough shit for her then, isn't it?"

Puwolsky stared. Was Stanzer serious?

"You gotta open the phone lines," Puwolsky said.

"Nope, can't risk it."

"Look, I ain't above a little collateral damage when an operation goes sideways," Puwolsky said. "But icing an innocent teenage girl for no good reason? We even took the precaution of having the Priests grab her so she doesn't know who's behind it all. My hope is, softy that I am, to get her back home safely when this is all said and done."

"That's your problem, not mine."

"Open the phone lines."

"Nope."

"Open the goddamn phone lines, would ya?"

"I told ya," Stanzer said. "We need a wide circle of blackout coverage on the front end of this operation as well as on the back. No telling what crazy cyber-scheme he might have created. The kid could be out there stalking us right now for all we know."

Puwolsky tapped his phone again but to no avail.

"You don't understand. I gotta get in touch with Larson. He's not like me, he's a lunatic, he lives for breaking heads. Me, if I have to take a life, I do it with remorse. Him, he's a stone-cold killer."

Stanzer thought about it.

"I'll give you sixty seconds," he said. "Tell your boy we need a safety net after the scheduled rendezvous time because we have no idea what traps might be waiting. Just to be sure, tell him he might not hear from you again until noon."

"All the way till noon?"

"If he's that trigger-happy, let's give ourselves some latitude," Stanzer said. "And by the way, I am only doing this once. That's nonnegotiable."

Puwolsky shook his head. "You spooks and your fucking tech. Me," he said. "I just stick with regular old e-mail."

"Could be your downfall," Stanzer replied.

"Doubt it," Puwolsky said. "I'm pretty good with computers and passwords and shit."

Stanzer reached into his pocket, pulled out a small black device, a militarized version of a mobile phone, and tapped in a code.

"You've got one minute and then all wireless devices are back to being paperweights, so be efficient."

Puwolsky called a phone number. Larson answered.

"Yeah, it's me," he began. "Look, change of plans."

As the two talked Stanzer stared down at his device's screen. A phone number appeared. The number Puwolsky just dialed.

He did a location search. A map popped up, GPS tracking. Larson's exact coordinates.

Stanzer waved at Puwolsky and gave him the signal to hurry up. He now had what he wanted.

FORTY-ONE

With the furniture properly situated and the space locked down, Stanzer and Puwolsky sat in beige folding chairs on opposite sides of the room laying in wait. A violent confrontation seemed inevitable, but with more than an hour to go before M.D.'s arrival there was little to do but remain patient.

Puwolsky played a game on his phone, a silly little flying pig app where the point was to swim around dropping anvils, no Internet required.

"Hey, Puwolsky," Stanzer said. "Let's you and me clear the air a minute. Man to man."

"What?"

"I don't like you very much," Stanzer said. "In fact, I think you're a prick."

Puwolsky lifted his eyes from the screen. "You ain't the first," he replied.

"But we're sort of partners now. Wouldn't ya say?"

"For the next few hours at least," he said. "Yeah, sure."

"Then tell me something," Stanzer said. "I know why I need the kid to vanish. It's his ass or mine. And I know why you now need the kid to vanish. 'Cause if you don't hunt him down, he's gonna hunt you."

"Pretty much," Puwolsky said.

"But why'd you even target him in the first place?"

Puwolsky lowered his eyes and returned to playing his game. "I told ya," he said dismissively. "To take out D'Marcus Rose, the High Priest."

"But you just snatched McCutcheon's girl last night, and the High Priest bit the bullet five days ago," Stanzer said. "To me, this means that the Priests were never really after his girl in the first place. Otherwise, they'd have taken her out right after D'Marcus Rose had his final chip cashed in as payback against M.D."

Stanzer raised his eyes again and smiled. "You'd make a good detective."

"Don't flatter me, fuckwad," Stanzer said leaning forward. "We're about to conspire to kill an undercover operative together. This isn't dating; this is marriage, and I need to know who I'm sharing a bed with. You know my story, now what's yours?"

Puwolsky closed out the flying pig game and put his phone back in his pocket.

"D'Marcus thought I betrayed him in a drug deal gone bad between some Canadians and South Americans," Puwolsky said. "My unit was greased to provide security, make sure no cops showed, but cops did show. The feds. My team had no idea. Whole thing turned into one big clusterfuck, and D'Marcus saw the bust all over the evening news." Puwolsky spread his hands across the sky. "D-town nabs huge cocaine shipment!" he said. "Was on every channel, like a 'score one for the good guys' type of story. The High Priest thought I set his associates up."

"Did you?"

"Not at all. I have no idea who tipped the feds off. But D'Marcus was crazy. He blamed me, and this whole 'Priests always pay' shit sent him over the edge. One of my partners died at the scene, they took out another, and they tried to ice both me and Larson twice. We figured our only play was to find a way to whack his ass before he got to us, and then broker a new deal with the next in line to become the High Priest."

"So you picked McCutcheon to do the dirty work?" Stanzer asked.

"First, I struck a deal with a thug named Puppet. We agreed to go back to the way things always were, cops playing nice with gangsters, and he agreed to call off the green light on me and Larson, if I could manage to get someone who could punch D'Marcus's ticket in lockup for him."

"A coup d'état?" Stanzer said. "With this Puppet character lying in wait?"

"Exactly," Puwolsky said. "The way D'Marcus dined off the carcass of the people in the Detroit projects didn't sit well with a lot of the Priests. I mean these were their cousins, sisters, and brothers that were having the screws turned on them. Of course, we knew there could be problems with future Priests if things didn't break Puppet's way, 'cause when a gang leader falls you never really know who is going to be the next in line, but hey, we were desperate. Worth a shot, right?"

Stanzer considered the information. "But how'd McCutcheon even bubble up on your radar?" Stanzer said. "He'd vanished. Gone underground."

"The girl."

"The girl?" Stanzer said. "You mean Kaitlyn Cummings?"

"Yep," Puwolsky said. "This chick, I tell you, she became like the running joke of every detective on the DPD. First month your man was gone she showed up every hot-damn day wanting to file a missing persons report about her cage-fighting boyfriend, who mysteriously disappeared into a white van with some guys in suits. The second month she still showed up, five days a week barking the same fairy tale. Month three, too." Puwolsky chuckled. "Hell, she still shows up every Wednesday at four forty-five p.m. like clockwork after all this time. I got no idea what your boy did to this little honey, but wow, she spiraled."

"What do you mean, spiraled?"

"I mean she tanked," Puwolsky said. "On her way to becoming a Rhodes scholar, bound for the Ivy League, then fears that the love of her life didn't really dump her, but instead fell into some sort of grave danger, and she just loses her shit. Started to mope. May or may not go to college, decided to take a year off and shovel lattes at Starbucks while waiting for her knight in shining armor to return. Rich girl like that with the world at her feet gets doinked by Cupid and the princess entirely collapsed. I kid you not, she came in every single day for months."

Stanzer scratched his head. "I still don't see the connection. Where's the link?"

"Larson."

"Larson?" Stanzer said. "How?"

"He's got a brother named Oscar who works for the New Jersey Office of Homeland Security. That's where all the funding is these days, fighting America's boogeymen."

"And?" Stanzer asked.

"And so he's on this stakeout trying to catch some Al-Shabaab techno kid and the shit is just boring. Day after day of just sitting in a room filled with screens for weeks. The Larson boys, they're the type that like to go out and bust heads."

"So?"

"So one day on the phone Oskee and Larson are catching up, telling one another about what they're each up to, and Oskee gripes about how he's on the world's lamest stakeout, one that supposedly revolves around some kid, a youngin' from Larson's part of the world, Detroit, who's turning into some kind of urban crime fighting legend. Some underage MMA cage fighter from the projects that's been recruited to secretly hunt terrorists, like a myth."

Stanzer nodded his head, finally seeing it. "So that's when it clicked?"

"I figure it's got to be the same kid, right?" Puwolsky said. "And my reasoning goes that if a girl like this is so hot for him, he's gotta be twice as hot for her. I mean this little honey was just WAY out of his league so that's the card we played. The threat of danger to her was just bait to lure him in." Puwolsky laughed. "Never underestimate the stupidity of teen love, right?"

Stanzer didn't respond.

"So I go on a little fishing expedition to discover more of the facts. After that, you know the story. A payoff to Krewls, I bait a nice hook on the assumption the kid still cares about her, he bites, takes the mission, and voilà! My problem's solved."

"So she really loved him, huh?"

"Still does, I'm sure," Puwolsky said. "Gonna be both of their fucking downfalls."

Stanzer nodded and reflected on what he'd just heard. It made sense. Puwolsky needed someone who could get into Jentles and take out the High Priest. If M.D. failed, no big deal. Puwolsky had no real ties to McCutcheon, and couldn't have given a shit if his soldier died behind bars. Yet if the person Puwolsky sent in to the D.T. succeeded, then he and Larson's big problem with D'Marcus Rose disappeared and they'd be back in business with a new High Priest. Plenty of upside, little downside.

"Gotta give it you," Stanzer said. "It's pretty clever."

"Damn right it is," Puwolsky said. "You F.B.I. gumps ain't the only ones with brains. You know what your problem is, Stanzer?"

"What's that?"

"You thought you could keep your mysterious little unit a secret," Puwolsky said. "Only failures can be kept secret. When you succeed, people hear about the shit."

"All right, so lemme ask ya," Stanzer said. "How many other guys you railroad with Krewls?"

"What, you mean like backdoor into Jentles?"

"Yeah."

"Seven, maybe eight, each for a different reason. Some rival gangsters of the Priests. A few businessmen who wouldn't play ball with our other various enterprises. What's that you say?" Puwolsky said. "Sometimes good people need to do some very bad things. Krewls had this special cell he'd toss the guys into and we'd never hear from them again."

Puwolsky smiled, but Stanzer didn't return the grin. The colonel remained stone-faced. Disapproving, even.

"What?" Puwolsky said. "You never took justice into your own hands?"

Stanzer checked to make sure he had a full cartridge in his handgun. "What do you think I'm doing here right now?"

FORTY-TWO

At five forty-five a.m., McCutcheon stood outside of an unremarkable building in an unremarkable suburb of Detroit with the morning wind howling through the streets. Rain began to fall in the predawn blackness. Using the back entrance, M.D. went through a door, climbed three sets of stairs two at a time, and stopped at suite 310. Home of Bump-n-Grind Soundscapes.

A rinky-dink music studio, M.D. thought. Classic Stanzer. Soundproofed walls. Single-entry access. Guy had probably already jammed all the Wi-Fi and cell tower signals within a hundred-yard radius, too.

McCutcheon checked his phone. No bars. Yep, clearly a trap. A trap, McCutcheon knew, he had to walk into.

"Ssshh," Stanzer said to Puwolsky, his eyes fixed on the door handle as it began to turn. "He's here."

Dressed in black, M.D. entered the room. Puwolsky, safety off the Glock, slid his finger from the barrel of his weapon down to its trigger.

"Be a long time before anyone finds a body in there," McCutcheon said, nodding toward the recording booth on the other side of a long rectangular sheet of double pane glass.

"Oh, they'll find it eventually," Stanzer said. "Yet not with any trace of who's behind the deed, of course. Go on in and sit."

Stanzer made sure to remain a minimum of five feet away from McCutcheon at all times. Pressing a gun against the head or chest of M.D. would be exactly what McCutcheon would want, because it would give him an opportunity to seize, spin, and strike. But leaping sixty inches or more to disarm the colonel before he could pull the trigger—not even the fastest of the fast could cover that type of ground quickly enough to avoid eating a bullet.

M.D., however, didn't move.

"I said go," Stanzer repeated.

"You'll free her?"

"Of course," the colonel replied. "We don't take out civilians. Part of the code."

M.D. sniffed. *Code. Yeah, right.*

Stanzer used the barrel of his Crimson Trace Sig Sauer P226 to point to the inside of the recording booth, the red targeting beam's laser showing the exact spot where he wanted M.D. to go. The Sig was a good weapon, accurate and powerful, but Stanzer brought another firearm with him, too, a Colt .25 strapped to his ankle. Out in the field he could never be too prepared.

"Now," Stanzer said to M.D.

The large padded recording booth on the other side of the black-and-gray mixing board was about the size of a large bedroom. The space could easily accommodate a choir of ten. M.D. studied the particulars. Eight chairs had been configured in a semicircle near the back wall, and there were three floor lamps, all turned on, each emitting a soft, yellow light. There was a single brown stool, too, tall like the kind found at a bar, front and center, where a lead singer would most probably sit.

Definitely the place where M.D. would be told to go.

"Right there," Stanzer said, using his Sig to nod toward the bar stool. Before taking his seat McCutcheon squatted and tapped the ground.

"What's that?" Puwolsky said, his Glock at the ready.

"It's called tapping out. I've never done it before." M.D. rose to his feet. "But now I have. I assume you want this?"

M.D. reached behind his back and withdrew a handgun. Both Stanzer and Puwolsky tightened their grip on their own respective weapons, but M.D. fingered his piece delicately making sure not to wrap his palm around the gun's handle. His move wasn't meant to be aggressive. He wanted Gemma returned home safely, and with no route other than submission available for him to achieve his aim, he surrendered. Not with shame in his heart, though. He'd been fighting in the cage long enough to know that eventually even the best get beaten.

Besides, McCutcheon always knew he'd die a violent death. It was the only thing that made sense after having lived such a violent life.

"Shut the door," Stanzer said. Puwolsky sealed the room and Stanzer moved to a secure position directly behind M.D. He raised his weapon. Pointed it at the back of McCutcheon's head. An infrared dot projected a glow on the center of his young soldier's skull.

"I never like to kill a man unless he knows why he's dying," Stanzer said, his Sig at the ready. With his free hand Stanzer reached into his pocket and handed Puwolsky his phone. "G'head. Show him."

Puwolsky raised Stanzer's cellie, tapped the screen, and handed McCutcheon the screen. A video started to play.

"Colonel, could you please make sure you speak your answers into the microphone. Remember, we are filming this."

"I said, there are currently no active agents under the legal age of eighteen years old working under my authority."

Puwolsky reached for the phone, but Stanzer waved him off because he wanted the entire video to play. The recording only lasted a few minutes and M.D. watched every single frame. When it ended, McCutcheon raised his eyes and spoke to Stanzer through the reflection he saw in the glass partition that separated the recording booth from the mixing table, much like the way a man would address another man through the rearview mirror of a car.

"I guess sometimes," M.D. said, "good people have to do some very bad things."

"I think our next moments together will certainly prove that point," Stanzer replied.

M.D. nodded and waited for his bullet. He debated whether to cross himself. Whether to bow his head, raise his finger, touch his forehead then his chest then his left pectoral muscle then his right pectoral muscle and finally his heart.

Did God even exist? In these last few moments McCutcheon owned as many doubts as ever.

Puwolsky pressed his gun against the side of McCutcheon's head. "You want me to take the shot?"

"Don't matter to me," Stanzer said. "But my piece is clean." He tilted the Sig sideways. "Numbers gone. Untraceable. Part of our burner cache, so that the bodies we leave behind can't ever be tracked back to the weapon that was used."

"Then best for you to take it," Puwolsky said. "The Double T is my personal sidearm." He kissed the barrel of the Glock. "The Terminal Terminator. It finishes foes."

Puwolsky took a step backward and smiled.

Sniper school taught shooters to fire a weapon from the stillness to be found at the bottom of an exhalation because it improved a marksman's accuracy by leaps and bounds. Stanzer calmly adjusted the beam of his Sig, blew the last bit of air from his lungs, quickly rotated, and squeezed the trigger. *Bam!* He fired two more rounds. *Bam! Bam!* All three head shots. The sound of gunfire exploded through the room, but none of the noise escaped beyond the padded walls of the soundproofed recording studio.

Puwolsky crumpled to the floor, a trifecta of hollow points cratering his skull.

McCutcheon swung out of the chair, ripped a hidden blade from his belt, and darted low. He dashed for the legs. Closed the distance of five feet quick as a cougar, and before Stanzer pointed the barrel of his weapon downward, M.D. was holding an 8.5-inch Al Mar S2KB SERE combat knife up against the top portion of Stanzer's upper thigh.

Right at the femoral artery.

FORTY-THREE

"**D**rop the gun."

"Son, you don't know what you are doing."

"Yes, I do," McCutcheon said. "One slice and you'll bleed out. Li'l prison trick I learned. No chance of survival."

"That's not what I mean."

"I'm done with words. Drop the gun."

Stanzer did as he was told. McCutcheon kicked the gun away, spun the colonel around, and violently rammed him up against the wall. *Smash!* He pressed his elbow into the center of the colonel's back, and Stanzer groaned. M.D. swung the knife around to the front of the colonel's throat, and then held his blade up against his prey's jugular.

"Other weapons?"

"Of course," Stanzer said, his ear being painfully pressed into the recording studio's wall. "Ankle holster sports a .25, belt buckle holds a Blackhawk Mark 1 combat knife."

M.D. disarmed the colonel and frisked him top-to-bottom for additional arms. He'd told the truth; he held no other weapons. McCutcheon picked up both guns, stepped backward five feet, and turned the Sig on his former boss, the red laser targeting beam pointed at the center of the man's chest.

"Where is she?"

"You heard him," Stanzer said. "Kaitlyn's still in Detroit."

"Don't mess with me. I mean my sister."

"She's safe."

"That's not an answer."

"Norman, Oklahoma. Horseback riding camp. Having the time of her life."

McCutcheon glared.

"Just put the fucking gun down so we can talk a sec, will ya?"

M.D. raised the red beam from the center of Stanzer's chest to the center of the colonel's forehead.

"I'm done talking. Mind games are over."

"It was all a ploy, McCutcheon. A ruse to smoke him out."

"I'm done with tricks."

"There is no Senate inquiry. It was all a lie."

M.D. shook his head. Didn't believe a word of it.

"Google it," Stanzer said. "There is no senator from Nebraska named Ackersleem. It was all staged. Four actors, an empty conference room, one video camera, limited perspective. Easy stuff to do."

M.D. considered what he'd seen in the video. Cautiously, he took two more steps backward to create even more distance between the barrel of his handgun and Stanzer, in case the colonel tried anything. Using Jeffrey's phone, he went online. Or at least, he tried to.

"No signal," McCutcheon said. "Very convenient."

Stanzer nodded toward his pocket. "May I?"

M.D. debated whether or not to allow the colonel to reach for his phone jammer. Since Stanzer had blocked all the signals, it was probably the only mobile device in the building that worked. However, as M.D. knew, if he permitted the colonel to access this device, Stanzer might shoot out a stealth call for backup, an alert of some sort to the cavalry.

"No," M.D. said, knowing he couldn't risk it.

Stanzer rolled his eyes, incredulous. "I know you think I—"

"Turn around," M.D. ordered, cutting Stanzer off. The colonel did as he was told and McCutcheon cautiously removed Stanzer's phone from his pocket. After taking three steps backward, he stared at the screen.

"No passcode lock?"

"I left it open 'cause I knew you wouldn't trust me."

"I still don't."

"That's smart. You shouldn't. I haven't earned it yet. But think for a minute," Stanzer said. "Why would I take him out instead of you?"

"To eliminate all connections to every part of this operation."

"Perhaps. But the rule of thumb is, you always take out your most dangerous enemy first; and who represented a bigger threat to me, you or him? Why didn't I search you when you came into the room? Why didn't I fire on you when you lunged at me? Think about it, son; I could have punched your ticket many times over already. The reason I didn't is because I never planned to."

M.D. didn't reply.

"I'm on your side, McCutcheon."

He still didn't say anything.

"For God's sake, just Google it."

M.D. looked at the phone, then back at the colonel. "Keep your hands up."

Stanzer did as he was told and McCutcheon searched online. Sure enough, there was no senator from the state of Nebraska named Ackersleem.

Stanzer read McCutcheon's eyes as McCutcheon read the information on the screen.

"I told you, it was all a lie."

"I want to talk to Gemma."

"Fine," Stanzer said. "In the recent calls section of the phone you'll see a number with a four-zero-five area code. Dial it."

M.D. went back to Google and searched to see if 405 was in fact an area code for Norman, Oklahoma. It was, but McCutcheon knew it could still be a trap. Stanzer was a master of crossing his *t*'s and dotting his *i*'s, and routing a fake call through the city of Norman, Oklahoma, would be child's play to him.

"Just dial it," Stanzer said growing annoyed.

M.D. did. A woman's voice answered. "Hello?"

"Sarah?" McCutcheon said. "It's me."

There was an awkward pause. "Oh, uhm, hi. You, I guess, want to speak to Gemma?"

"I do."

M.D. knew that Stanzer might be able to con his mother into covering for him, but there was no way the colonel would be able to get his sister to maintain a lie. If Gemma felt threatened in any way, it would take McCutcheon less than five seconds to figure it out.

"Hi, Doc!" rang a bubbly voice.

"You okay, Gem?"

"I love it here!" she exploded. "I got to polish a saddle and then they let me ride a pony, and now I know how to trot and brush a mane, and cleaning the stalls smelled like poo-poo but it was also kinda fun," Gemma said all in one breath. "Can we get a horse, Doc? Please, please, please?"

"Put Mom back on."

"I love you!!"

"I love you, too."

"With gobs of heart and sunshine!!"

McCutcheon heard Gemma say, "He wants to talk to you" as she passed the phone to Sarah.

"Hello?"

"You in Norman, Oklahoma?"

"Ride 'em, cowboy."

"I'll be in touch."

Click. M.D. hung up, stared at Stanzer.

"You believe me now?" the colonel asked extending his arm. He wanted his weapons back.

M.D. considered what to do. He came to the rendezvous

point expecting to encounter a man who had betrayed him. And so that is what he saw. But what he expected to see was now getting in the way of what he was actually witnessing. Stanzer hadn't made any attempt on his life. Stanzer had been forthright about the weapons he carried. Stanzer had just put him on the phone with his sister, who, not coincidentally, was currently whooping it up at an equestrian center far from Bellevue.

Why so far from Nebraska? Because Stanzer knew that's where Gemma would be safe.

McCutcheon passed Stanzer his gun.

"'Bout time," the colonel said, holstering his Sig. He pushed past McCutcheon, reached under the bar stool, and yanked free a quart-size bag of white powder that had been secretly duct taped underneath. Four ounces of premium Columbian blow.

Stanzer, still wearing gloves, meticulously placed Puwolsky's fingerprints on the bag of coke, tore a seam in the plastic, and then mixed the white powder together with the red blood that had spilled from Puwolsky's brain. It only took a moment to ruin the usability of the drugs by creating a concoction of pink and sticky paste.

Stanzer picked up the Glock, placed the Double T in Puwolsky's right hand, and fired off two rounds into the wall, so that once the coroner's unit discovered the body they'd be sure to find gunpowder residue on the dead man's fingertips. As Stanzer applied the finishing touches to the fabricated crime scene, M.D. gazed downward at Puwolsky's lifeless eyes staring at the ceiling. They were empty and cold. Without emotion, M.D. reached into the dead man's pocket, removed his cell, and rolled Puwolsky's inert thumb over the screen.

"Good thinking," Stanzer said.

With the phone unlocked, M.D. went into the Settings section and commandeered control of the device.

"Now come on," Stanzer said after executing the final details. "Time to go get this prick Larson. Clock's ticking."

Stanzer quickly fired off a series of coded text messages through the DarkNet.

"Why's the clock ticking?" M.D. asked.

"Because," Stanzer said. "They grabbed Kaitlyn."

FORTY-FOUR

Stanzer weaved through traffic doing eighty-five miles an hour while the rest of the cars on I-75 cruised at an average speed of sixty. The colonel slalomed through vehicles, zigzagged between lanes, and crossed double yellow lines, like a running back on a football field looking for daylight. Everyone on the road, alarmed by the nut in the white Chevy four-door, all thought the same thing: *Asshole's driving like a maniac.*

"Where we going?" McCutcheon asked.

"Eaton Street. A few blocks off of Livernois."

"Livernois?" M.D. said. "That's Priest territory."

"Correct." Stanzer took a hard right and did a four-line lane change, ignoring the horns that blared at him. "Puwolsky brokered a deal with a new shotcaller named Puppet. Ever heard of the guy?"

"No."

"Well, I'm sure he's heard of you... Bam Bam."

McCutcheon nodded. His whole life the price for being an underground cage warrior had always been a tax he never wanted to pay. He loved the sport but the notoriety that came with being the best of the best fit him like a poorly tailored, brightly colored suit: uncomfortable to wear and something that drew far too much attention. Even now, a long while after he'd left the MMA war tour, the myth of Bam Bam the Conqueror still affected his life.

"How do you know all this?" McCutcheon asked.

"It took some doing."

"And *when* did this doing get done?" M.D. asked, placing extra emphasis on the word *when*.

Stanzer merged from the I-75 onto the M-10 and checked the GPS coordinates of his destination. Before heading to the site, the colonel knew he'd need a place to settle and craft a plan. Where, he wasn't yet sure, but maybe, he thought . . .

McCutcheon suddenly swiped the homing device from Stanzer's hand. "Colonel!" he snapped. "I need to know."

Stanzer nodded. He knew what he was being asked. McCutcheon wanted to know what the hell had happened to him and why.

"I knew it was a mistake to let you go into Jentles," Stanzer began. "But I also knew it would have been a bigger mistake to stop you because you would have been damaged goods after that. If something really did happen to your girl, you'd have resented me for the rest of your life."

M.D. didn't say a word.

"I only knew what you did at the start, anyway: there was a threat to Kaitlyn, these Doper cops were tainted, and the prison scenario was a tactical nightmare. But I had no idea it was all a setup. I tried to get some eyes on you inside the penitentiary, but planting a mole like that takes time."

"What finally clued you in?"

"A tip came in via e-mail. Ratted me and my unit out by name," Stanzer said. "We tracked it right to his desk in Detroit. After that it wasn't hard to piece everything together. Puwolsky knew I'd go looking for you at some point over the course of his scheme. This meant that at some point he knew he'd have to deal with me."

"You mean to get rid of you?"

"Yes," Stanzer said. "Before I figured out the truth and began hunting him."

"So how'd he find you?" McCutcheon asked. M.D. had tried himself but come up empty.

"He didn't. No one does," Stanzer said. "So he tried to blow the whistle on my operation. As you know, we're not exactly authorized."

"So he figured that was his best angle to take you out?" M.D. said.

"Exactly," Stanzer said. "Without the ability to snuff me out, he went for the next best thing: make me fight a different war on a different front, a bloody one. It's a classic military strategy."

Stanzer ran right up on the tail of a silver BMW and flashed his lights, his bumper only inches away from the sleek luxury sedan. The Beemer, driving at a normal speed, moved a lane over to the right so Stanzer could fly past.

"Puwolsky figured leaking the existence of the Murk to the do-gooding bastards in Congress would swamp me in red tape and bureaucratic muck. Hell, using minors to fight domestic enemies might even get me tossed in jail. He would have loved that."

Stanzer zipped around a blue minivan and accelerated toward Exit 9.

"Certainly a congressional inquiry would bog me down far too much to chase after you," Stanzer said. "He figured there was just no way I could deny your existence under the glare of D.C.'s spotlight and pursue your whereabouts at the same time."

McCutcheon shrugged. "Not a bad attack."

"Not bad at all," Stanzer admitted. "Except the guy completely underestimated how deeply the FBI can crawl up anyone in America's digital ass. Not just the FBI, but the CIA, the DEA, the NSA, and so on. If a U.S. citizen sends an e-mail using anything other than the DarkNet, we can find out every last detail about the user, to, from, location, content, etcetera within a matter of minutes. It's fucking child's play at this point."

"So you tracked the e-mail to his desktop computer, put two and two together, and then created a fake Senate panel to make it look like you were in deep shit."

"Correct."

"But why did you shoot him?"

"What do you mean?"

"You know what I mean," McCutcheon said. "You had him. Why not let justice take it from there?"

"Justice did take it from there, son," Stanzer replied. "I'm just its angel of execution."

M.D. didn't offer a response. Didn't comment one way or the other, but by not saying anything, he clearly communicated a sense of disapproval.

"Dirty lawmen burn me," Stanzer added. He gripped the wheel much tighter than necessary. "I mean, where's the goddamn code?"

The colonel exited the highway at the Livernois off-ramp and slowed the Chevy to twenty miles per hour as they entered the heart of the 48204, one of the three most dangerous American zip codes year in and year out. Stanzer knew that a guy like him, in a car like the one they were driving, stood out like a red tomato on a plate of green lettuce, so he stayed clear of the final destination until he and McCutcheon could get on the same page about the plan.

The white Chevy rolled past a three-story brick auto parts building, its top floor burned completely off. The place looked as if a bomb had been dropped on its roof. Then they passed a vacant lot with long, tall, overgrown grass. The space hadn't been tended to in years. Then they passed a decently kept home with two red tricycles sitting in the driveway. Then they passed a charred house. Then they passed another decently kept home and then another scorched house, its frame a mixture of exposed brown wood and black singe marks. As rain began to fall, Stanzer inspected the property more closely. The house's windows had been broken out, two crater-size holes gaped where a chimney used to exist, and a white sign, clean and visible from the street, had been taped to the smashed front door.

DEMOLITION SCHEDULED
Warning: STAY OUT

The residence was just one of hundreds, maybe thousands, in the greater Detroit area on a list to be bulldozed. As M.D. knew, there were simply too many structures slated for destruction for the city to keep pace with the volume, but the longer these abandoned homes stood, the longer the heroin addicts had a place to shoot junk, the hookers had a place to turn tricks, and the curious little seven-year-olds had a place to go investigate cool, interesting urban artifacts like soiled condoms and used hypodermic needles.

Stanzer peeked down the driveway.

"This'll work."

"How close are we?" M.D. asked.

"There's an abandoned market—you know, beer, wine, lottery, that type of thing—three blocks up to the east," Stanzer said. "Blue walls, covered with gang graffiti, well fortified, shuttered tight. She's in there."

Stanzer put the car in reverse, looked over his right shoulder, and backed the Chevy down the long, gravel driveway. After parking he cut the engine.

"Tell me," the colonel asked, reaching behind him. "Are you ready to do the things we might have to do once we go in there?"

Stanzer flipped open the lid of a DU-HA weapons storage box sitting on the floor of the backseat and revealed a cache of arms: another Sig Sauer, a Ruger SR9c, two Smith & Wesson .357s, a Mossberg 590 A1 short barrel shotgun, and an M40A1 bolt-action sniper rifle with a special 10 power Unertl scope.

"Because there are other options for you, son. I already have a team positioned five blocks down at the ready."

"A hostage rescue team?" M.D. asked.

"No," Stanzer said. "This team, well... we're not looking to make any arrests."

M.D. weighed the words he'd just heard. He knew three items stood on the colonel's agenda for this operation.

Number one: Larson would exit the building.

Number two: It would be in a body bag.

Number three: Save Kaitlyn.

Number one and number two were locks, but number three was only a hope, an aspiration for Stanzer. Though the colonel didn't say it aloud, the hard truth was that, considering the circumstances, Kaitlyn might not be savable.

With Larson standing as the last link to possibly blowing the cover off of the Murk, Stanzer needed the corrupt cop's silence guaranteed. The colonel knew that to arrest Larson meant that a greaseball lawyer would most likely, at some point, seek to trade his client's secret knowledge about Stanzer's activities for a plea deal. What kind of bargain would be made, Stanzer wasn't sure, but he knew General Evans well enough to know that if the choice came down to either letting a crooked city cop walk, versus shuttering a cutting-edge covert military unit with an outstanding track record for nailing high-profile targets, Evans's decision would be a no-brainer.

The general would let Larson skate.

Guy probably wouldn't even get prison time, Stanzer thought. After all, his lawyer would argue, it was just way too dangerous for a cop like Larson to do time in a state penitentiary. It'd practically be a death sentence. Stanzer knew if he brought Larson back in cuffs, the charges would get bargained down to the point where he'd merely be forced to surrender his badge. Beyond that, it'd be a bunch of stupid negotiations back-and-forth about whether or not the bastard could keep his pension plan.

Dirty lawmen, they burned Stanzer. Burned him bad. But if Larson never saw a pair of handcuffs . . .

Stanzer picked up a .357 Magnum, extended his arm, and offered McCutcheon the handgun.

"You don't have to come with us. In fact, considering your emotional attachment to the outcome, it could be a mistake," Stanzer said. "But on the other hand, I feel you've earned the option."

M.D. stared at the large, powerful revolver. He shook his head. He didn't want the gun.

"Not only have I earned the option, sir"—M.D. reached past the short barrel shotgun and grabbed hold of the Sig Sauer—"but I am exercising it."

McCutcheon lifted the Scorpion TB model Sig 1911 with a Houge G-10 grip. It featured a 4.2-inch barrel, a low profile night sight, and a modified 16 mag capacity filled with Speer Gold Dot 185 grain jacketed hollow-points. He'd chosen a tactician's weapon, the kind favored by Marine elites.

"So what happened to your principles?" Stanzer asked.

M.D. cocked the gun.

"I have new ones."

FORTY-FIVE

tanzer packed the Ruger SR9c into his belt loop, grabbed the custom-made sniper rifle manufactured in Quantico, Virginia, and he and McCutcheon exited the car. After jumping a series of fences and crossing three streets, they took cover behind an abandoned red pickup truck sitting lifelessly on cinder blocks.

Stanzer put his earpiece in and spoke into a thin black radio mike that extended to his mouth.

"Everyone in position?"

No one spoke. Instead, six men offered hand signals. McCutcheon hadn't seen any of them at first, each soldier having blended into the environment with almost seamless precision. A gloved hand went palm up by a tree. Another from behind a house. Two more appeared behind an ambulance that sat unattended in the far eastern corner of the parking lot, and another two flashed their ready signs on opposite sides of a large bush. The invisible squad turned visible, but only for a moment so that Stanzer could gain a fix on their positions, and then each vanished again into their camouflaged positions.

Stanzer assessed the situation. The element of surprise would be their strongest weapon. The rain helped, too. The harder it fell, the less the visibility. The abandoned liquor store, boarded and beaten up, advertised cheap cigarettes and beer in faded paint, but the business had long ago stopped operating. It was now a large square box with a potholed parking lot. Nothing more, nothing less, a target easily taken by highly trained operatives.

If the operatives felt willing to accept casualties. Without windows or doors through which to peer inside, any assault the colonel initiated would start off blind.

"On my signal," Stanzer said.

McCutcheon, like all soldiers, had participated in this training activity many, many times. The first two members of the team would pry open the plank being used as a front door with an alloy Halligan bar, and then a third man would blast the entranceway open with a battering ram to create ample passage for the men behind. Two marksmen, weapons at the ready, would follow on their heels, and a moment later, just like in any of the video games being played at home by young kids, it would turn into a shootout.

Aim for the bad guys, save the girl, avoid getting blasted. Pretty straightforward stuff.

"Colonel, wait," McCutcheon said. "Let's go for wits over brawn." M.D. knew that a straightforward assault didn't offer the best odds for ensuring Kaitlyn's safety. "We can play to our strengths."

"How?" Stanzer asked.

"Instead of storming in?" M.D. replied. "What if we can get them to just bring her out?"

"Speak to me."

McCutcheon reached for Puwolsky's phone. "We send a text that everything's fine. Make up a story about a new rendezvous point, and when they move her to that car, we pounce."

M.D. nodded toward a late model Cadillac with a shiny black paint job.

"A car like that in an area like this, most probably Larson's," M.D. said. "Puwolsky drove a tricked out Caddy, too. Can't be a coincidence."

Stanzer considered it. "Well, it's better than blitzing a hornet's nest."

Inside, they both knew, could be a nightmare. They had no idea how many Priests they'd face, no clue as to how many of the enemy soldier's were armed and not an inkling about the type of weapons they might encounter. These weren't petty shoplifters; these were urban gang members and they'd likely be armed to the teeth. Thirty years ago, kids on the mean streets carried low-caliber handguns; nowadays they slung fully automatic Kalashnikov assault rifles.

The biggest problem with a full frontal assault, as McCutcheon saw it, was that no one had eyes on Kaitlyn. She could be tied to a chair or chained to a pole or in any one of ten different compromising positions. Larson might have even set up a scenario where, should they be attacked, she'd be used as a human shield. M.D. knew Priests would die and Stanzer's squad would win the day. The girl he loved, however . . . her well-being was a different story.

"Definitely worth a try. Let's map it." Stanzer spoke into the radio mike. "Hold your positions."

They formulated a battle plan. Stanzer would lay hidden on the northeast side of the building with the high-powered rifle aimed at the front door. Once Kaitlyn exited, Stanzer would keep the rest of the enemies pinned inside the building by putting bullets on the exit. An attack like this would leave only the men who'd already walked out of the liquor store in front of Kaitlyn to do battle with the team.

Before initiating action, M.D. would head down to the side wall to play the point and spring from the blind side of the store's front entrance. By remaining off to the right and only five yards away, McCutcheon would have the ability to leap in and go man-to-man in close combat, or stand his ground and fire on targets from close range, depending on what the situation called for. Stanzer and his soldiers would snipe, M.D. would ambush, and even if five guys exited the building prior to Kaitlyn, the team would have numbers on their enemy in addition to the element of surprise.

All angles were covered. Approximate mission time after the first shot rang out: fifteen seconds. Fifteen seconds, M.D. thought, and Kaitlyn would be safe.

McCutcheon put a wire in his ear so he could communicate with the rest of the team, and after getting the thumbs-up signal, he dashed through the rain and sidled up next to the store's western wall. He pulled out Puwolsky's phone and prepared to send a text.

"Got eyes on me?"

"With this scope? Perfectly."

"Sending it now."

"Copy," Stanzer said.

M.D. composed a message on Puwolsky's cell phone and fired it off.

> mission done – all gold – meet at detroit
> historical museum on woodward ave in 1 hr,
> southeast side, parking lot B – bring girl

"Message sent," McCutcheon whispered.

"You know if they don't bring her out we're gonna have to go to in," Stanzer said.

"You mean Plan B?" M.D. asked.

"I mean Plan F," Stanzer replied. "*F* standing for *Fucked.*"

M.D. stared at the phone and waited for a reply.

"Well, I guess we're about to see how smart these guys are," he said.

A reply buzzed in. McCutcheon looked down at the screen.

> how many french fries do fifth graders eat?

M.D. wrinkled his brow.

"What's it say?" the colonel asked.

"It's a code," McCutcheon replied. "A verification query."

He gulped.

"And the answer could be anything."

FORTY-SIX

M.D. reread the text message from Larson and tried to cook up a plausible response, but guessing the proper reply felt impossible. It could be *peanuts sit in tall bushes* or it could be *basketball players smell like blue barns* or it could be *mad little mice.*

There was no way to tell. Worse, there was no way to crack it. Certainly not in the limited amount of time in which he had to reply.

"Shit!" McCutcheon said. Underestimating the intelligence of Puwolsky and Larson might have just cost Kaitlyn her life.

M.D. put the cell phone back into his pocket and pulled the Sig from the small of his back. Time for plan F, he thought.

Then a new idea struck him.

"On my signal, jam all cell phones," he said into the radio mike.

"Roger," Stanzer said not questioning why. The colonel knew there was a time to lead, a time to follow, and a time to shut the hell up and trust the man in the field. He'd gone this far with McCutcheon, so now he'd have to go the whole way, and only hindsight would prove whether it was a mistake.

Stanzer removed the black case from his pocket and readied his interference device. M.D. composed a text.

hello?

He counted to twenty and then composed another.

hello? you get that?

Larson replied twice via text, but McCutcheon ignored both responses. Instead, he counted to twenty yet again and fired off a third message.

Larson, wtf...where r u?

"Okay, kill it," M.D. said into his mike.

Stanzer tapped the screen, and a moment later all cell signals within a hundred-yard radius went dead. McCutcheon, heading for cover, fell back to his position behind the junked red pickup truck next to Stanzer.

"How much battery life you got left in that thing?" he asked as he slid next to the colonel.

"Maybe ninety minutes," Stanzer said. "Explain your thinking."

"Scenario one," M.D. said. "He thinks the cell towers

are down because of the storm and we toggle back and forth, turning the phones on and off, to create the impression that it's just patchy service he's getting, due to crappy weather."

"And we continue to try to lure him out?" Stanzer asked.

"Correct," M.D. said. "But I can't say I am a big fan of this plan because I know if I was on the other side of that door, I'd be…"

Suddenly, the front entrance cracked open.

"Suspicious," McCutcheon said finishing his sentence.

A hand appeared. Waving a white T-shirt, like a *Don't shoot me* flag. The colonel, M.D., and all six members of Stanzer's team locked on the liquor store's front door.

A tall figure wearing a blue-and-black hoodie stepped out into the rain. Six laser beams suddenly dotted his body with red targeting points, three on his chest, three on his brow.

The man, a thug, a gangster, looked down, saw the red dots, and paused. It was clear the shooters could have already taken him out, but since they hadn't he figured it was okay to step forward. To make his intentions clear, however, he continued to wave the white shirt high in the air.

"Bam Bam!" he yelled into the empty parking lot.

McCutcheon didn't answer.

"Bam Bam!" he hollered again his voice cutting through the rain.

The tall gang member strained his eyes to see, but he couldn't make out any figures in the distance.

"Bam Bam!" he blindly yelled a third time. "He knows you're out here."

McCutcheon held his ground.

"He wants to make a deal."

Stanzer and M.D. traded a sideways look.

"He's crazy, man," the guy shouted. "Says you either talk to me or he starts sending out the girl. In chunks. One bloody piece at a time."

"I have to go," McCutcheon said.

"It's a trap," Stanzer replied.

"Seems to be kind of a theme for me lately." M.D. stepped out from behind the red pickup. "Yo!" he cried out. The Priest turned his head. "I'm over here."

The two met in the middle of the parking lot as rain continued to fall on their heads.

"Who ya got with you out here, SWAT?"

"Do you know what I'll do to you if any harm comes to my girl?"

"Listen up, youngin', this shit ain't got nothing to do with me. That cop in there's fucking crazy," the gangster said. "Me, I'm a straight-up businessman."

"A businessman, huh?"

"You bet your ass," he said. "And I'm in a helluva predicament."

McCutcheon looked his man up and down. "Who are you?"

"My fellas call me Puppet."

"The new High Priest?"

"Not for long if my boyz see me make nice-nice with

you," Puppet said. "I do and my shit'll be floating at the bottom of the Detroit River by sundown."

McCutcheon didn't seem surprised by the news.

"So why are you out here?" M.D. asked.

"This shit was supposed to be just regular business. I deliver a certain person of interest to Larson and he provides me a fat payment for her delivery. Mutherfucker kept a few of the more significant details about who he was runnin' a game on in the dark, and shit's done snowballed like hell on me now."

Puppet gazed down at his sweatshirt and spied the laser beams targeting his chest. "Yo, can you do something about that?" he said in regard to the guns being pointed at him. "Shit's making me nervous."

McCutcheon considered the request and looked over his back shoulder. Stanzer, able to hear M.D.'s entire conversation through the live radio mike M.D. wore, gave an order.

"X the beams."

The red dots peppering Puppet's kill zones disappeared, but Puppet was smart enough to realize the weapons were still being pointed at him. One wrong move and he'd get lit up like target practice.

"How many peeps you brought out here anyway?" Puppet asked.

"Enough to make sure every last person in that building goes home in a box."

Puppet shook his head. "Like I said, we sure got us one hell of a predicament, don't we?"

"Not if you bring out the girl."

"I told ya, I'm a businessman, so we can talk about that, but Larson," Puppet said. "Guy's a fucking psycho. Ain't no way he's letting her just walk right out."

"So betray him."

"I cross him and my men in there will be seeing me do a favor for you. Point-blank, that shit can't happen. My leadership ain't exactly what you call solidified at this moment of time."

"But you'll have saved their lives."

"Priests don't care about dying," Puppet said. "Priests only care about living by a code. On the streets. In lockup. In the fuckin' hearse on the way to the cemetery, the code is the only thing that matters. Makes for a real predicament."

Puppet knocked his head back and let a few drops of rain fall onto his face.

"But I'm a businessman, so I come to ya with a proposal."

"If my girl's safety isn't guaranteed then don't even bother talking. That's nonnegotiable."

"You got it," Puppet said. "But I gotta be able to walk away from this, too. Me and my boys. No one arrested, no one sniped."

Stanzer spoke into M.D.'s earpiece. "Not a problem."

"I don't have a problem with that," M.D. said to Puppet.

"See, I told ya, I'm a businessman," the gang leader replied. "But Larson wants to be able to walk away, too."

"Not happening," Stanzer said.

"Not happening," M.D. repeated.

"He's making a proposal," Puppet said.

"There will be no negotiation," Stanzer said.

"We're not negotiating," McCutcheon said.

"You and him, one on one," Puppet continued offering up the deal. "He makes it past you, he walks scot-free. Back to his former life."

"No way," Stanzer said.

"And if he doesn't?" M.D. asked.

"I said," Stanzer barked into the earpiece. "No way."

"He knows he's cooked anyway," Puppet said. "He figures his partner's dead, he ain't got no more allies, and the only poker chip he owns is your little lady. He's willing to trade her safety for a shot at his freedom. Not for his freedom. He knows y'all won't go for that. Just a shot at it."

Stanzer's voice crackled in McCutcheon's ear. "Okay, make whatever deal he wants. I'll handle Larson later after the girl is safe."

"But just in case you're thinking about handling Larson later after the girl is safe," Puppet added, "you gots to know one thing."

"What's that?" M.D. asked.

"Priests always pay. But they get paid, too."

McCutcheon had heard the saying a thousand times before. "What's your point?" he asked.

"My point is that I'm the guy who picked up your li'l lady. That means I know where she lives. That means I know where her whole family lives. So if you break your word to me and double-cross Larson, my peoples in there are gonna think me and you struck our own little side arrangement. They gonna think I punked out in the face of pressure from the po-po. And that, as you know, would be very bad for me."

"Which means?" M.D. asked.

"Which means I'm gonna have to go back after her again, in order to prove I'm solid and save my own ass," Puppet said. "She's the only insurance policy I got."

M.D. snatched Puppet by the throat.

"What'd you say?"

"Yo, chill man, we just doin' business here."

"This ain't business," M.D. said squeezing tighter. "It's personal."

"Well, you brought her into it," Puppet argued.

"I didn't bring her into anything."

"Yeah, you did," Puppet said. "Soldiers like us can't give a fuck about a chick. They come, they go, but if you stupid enough to care about one, that shit becomes a liability." Puppet pushed McCutcheon's hand away from his neck. "Now let me go, youngin'. We doin' business here. Act professional."

M.D. released his grip but remained locked in on Puppet's eyes, ready to tear the gangster's head off.

"Stay poised, son," Stanzer said into the earpiece. "Focus on the mission."

"So what are you telling me?" McCutcheon asked Puppet.

"I am tellin' you in my line of business, my word is my bond," Puppet said. "You give me your word Larson won't be targeted by whatever fucking Navy SEALs you got out here if he can get past you in a one-on-one showdown, and everyone can head home early and go get us some hot chocolate."

"We can't make that promise, McCutcheon," Stanzer said into the earpiece. "And you know it."

"You got a deal," M.D. said.

"McCutcheon!" Stanzer snapped. "I know you hear me, son. You do not have the authority to—"

M.D. tore out his earpiece and tossed it to the ground. Soon as he did Puppet's chest lit up with red dots.

"What da fuck?" Puppet said.

"All right, Mr. Businessman, we're on." McCutcheon extended his hand for a man-to-man shake. Puppet, still lit up with red targeting beams, paused, not knowing if he was about to be blasted. When he finally realized no bullets were coming, he reached toward the outstretched hand of McCutcheon and accepted the deal.

The two negotiators had come to terms.

FORTY-SEVEN

"That's bullshit! You overstepped your bounds."

"He's a 'roid monster, sir. All ego," McCutcheon said as he took off his watch. "Guy's wanted me from day one."

"This isn't some flyweight piece of shit who's had a couple of community college Tae Kwan Do lessons," Stanzer barked. "We snooped his background. The man's got years of Academy training. Stick, fist, knife, gun, all kinds of certifications. He's not some pussy cop. He's an animal."

"He won't get by me."

"He might."

"No chance."

"Yes, there is a chance. There's always a chance. It's a bullshit deal, and a bullshit move, and it wasn't your call to make."

"With Puwolsky out of the picture, Larson had no other play."

"But we did," Stanzer said. "Didn't you read your enemy? The Priests don't want to fight. That's obvious. You could tell that all they want is a path out. We sweat them for another few hours, stay patient, hold our position, and they'd start to re-think their loyalties. Shit," Stanzer said. "By four o'clock this afternoon I'm sure they would have popped Larson themselves. Especially if he made a move on the girl. Her life is their life now and they know it. You fucked the pooch on this one, soldier."

McCutcheon secured his SERE knife in his belt. "I'm going in there. And Larson is not coming out."

"Admit it. You want to have a go at him."

"I want Kaitlyn safe."

"Naw, you want payback," Stanzer said. "You want payback for being schemed, you want payback for the hell you went through in prison, and you want payback for being treated like a piece of disposable ghetto dog shit."

Anger screamed through McCutcheon's blood. The cool, calm, methodical warrior was nowhere to be found. What raged inside was a beast hungering to be fed.

"And what's your point, sir?" McCutcheon asked.

"My point is," Stanzer said, "I just want to know whose ego it is we're really dealing with?"

The colonel set down his sniper rifle. If McCutcheon was going in, he wasn't going alone.

"He beats me, you have to let him walk, sir. No matter what happens, this has to end for Kaitlyn. Promise me that."

The colonel remained silent.

"Promise me, sir."

Still, Stanzer said nothing.

"So that's how it is, huh?" M.D. said. "Well, pardon my

bluntness, but fuck the unit, sir. I mean what the hell are we fighting for anyway if not for civilian safety?"

Stanzer put on a pair of leather gloves.

"Maybe it's you who ought to look at his ego, Colonel, 'cause to me your priorities right now seem all smacked up."

Stanzer flicked the safety off his Sig and then put the gun in its holster.

"This was not the way I wanted this to play, McCutcheon," Stanzer said. "But what's done is done." The colonel spoke into his radio mike. "Maintain your positions. No one fires without my orders." Stanzer gazed out at the liquor store. "Even if our target walks right out the fucking front door." He turned to M.D. "But you're not going to let that happen now, are you, son?"

McCutcheon replied in a crisp, clear, cold voice.

"Not a chance, sir."

FORTY-EIGHT

"**E**w-weee! I love me a high-stakes matchup!"

As McCutcheon and Stanzer entered the abandoned liquor store, Larson smiled from ear to ear. The Priests—there were seven of them in addition to Puppet—stared at their two enemies with somber, menacing eyes. Some held handguns, others smoked menthol cigarettes, some just kept their hands in their pockets looking mean and trying to keep warm. There were no assault rifles in the room.

For the Priests, this was a war they never hoped to wage. Like with quicksand, they'd mistakenly stuck their toes into the dark puddle of colluding with dirty cops, and then found themselves neck deep in danger. Maybe they'd live to see tomorrow's dawn, maybe not. As street soldiers, all of them knew that every day could be their last—but this day felt particularly more doomed than most.

Yes, they were prepared to shoot it out with Stanzer's team. If they had to. But none of them felt they'd win.

Larson appeared almost giddy. He was a gladiator, and gladiators lived for the moment of battle. Roughly a century before Jesus Christ was born, real men—big, bold, fearless, and mighty men—warred to the death on the sands of the Colosseum floor. Larson always wished he could travel back in time and be one of the lucky ones who got to fight in the majestic stadium. Winning or losing, living or dying, these things didn't drive him; his thrill came from the fantasized glory of participating in a life or death competition, a match of honor. Though Larson could not go back in time to Ancient Rome, he felt exhilarated by the idea that he'd brought Ancient Rome to Detroit.

"Honored guests," Larson said with a gallant bow. "Welcome."

McCutcheon scanned the room. White bulbs dangled from exposed wires in the ceiling, offering lighting that was checkered and irregular. Some areas were bright, others were not, and no real rhyme or reason existed behind the pattern. The fact that the lights worked at all meant electricity still ran through the walls, but the smell of stale beer, mold, and piss indicated that any ventilation system had long ago stopped functioning. There were broken silver racks of old shelves piled in one corner, two overturned freezers lying like corpses in another, and planks of rotted wood heaped throughout. A rat scampered past a discarded beer can and disappeared through a hole. Surely not a lone soldier.

But where was Kaitlyn? Larson, reading M.D.'s mind, stepped behind an archway and rolled her out from behind the blackness. She sat in a wheelchair, arms and legs bound, a hood covering her head.

A wheelchair? M.D. thought. Surely, they hadn't crippled her. No way they'd gone that far.

Larson rolled Kaitlyn to the far end of the cavernous room and set her under one of the working white lights. M.D. suddenly understood the reason for the wheelchair. Larson hadn't severed her spine; the wheelchair was for ease of transport. A chair with wheels on it enabled Larson to roll her wherever he wanted.

Any cop who thought like that, McCutcheon realized, was a cop who had kidnapped before.

"She should see this, don't ya think?" Larson lifted the cloak off Kaitlyn's head as if he were unveiling a statue and she blinked, the sudden light too bright for her green eyes. As she struggled to regain her vision McCutcheon noticed the wounds. A black eye. Traces of a cut lip beneath a white gag. Seeing Kaitlyn's injuries caused his blood to boil.

"She got a li'l lippy," Larson said. "Get it? Lippy?" He laughed. "I tell ya . . ." Larson opened his mouth wide and licked the side of Kaitlyn's face with his soft, fat, wet, pink tongue. "This one's got some pep."

McCutcheon flexed, readied to cross the room and attack, but with an expert flick of the wrist Larson switched open a butterfly knife and put the blade to Kaitlyn's neck.

"*Whoa, whoa, whoa.* Slow down, cowboy," he said to McCutcheon.

M.D. and Kaitlyn made eye contact. Even if they had time to speak, McCutcheon had no words. What could he say? How could he apologize? There was no way to make amends for getting her tangled up in something as horrific as this, and all his excuses of *"I had no idea"* or *"I never meant to"* wouldn't amount to anything, because there she sat, bound, gagged, and beaten. From this point forward he knew he could save her, but he also knew he would never be able to spare her from what she'd already been through.

The realization of the pain he'd inadvertently caused Kaitlyn sliced McCutcheon's heart like a rusty dagger. He knew he'd carry this emotional wound for the rest of his days. So would Kaitlyn. They'd share a pair of scars that would never ever heal. His hurt turned to anger and then his anger turned to rage.

Someone needed to pay.

"Blades or pipes?" Larson asked. Laid out neatly across an old deli counter sat two sets of weapons. On the left, a pair of knives. Stainless steel, black handles, seven-inch blades, identical in every manner. On the right, two pipes. Rusted, not matching, but roughly the same size, weight, and thickness. M.D. noted that neither piece of steel held any sort of obvious advantage over the other, but that, he knew, was because of the gladiator code. Larson didn't just want to battle to the death; he wanted each of the combatants to be evenly armed. A war of honor was the only ethical path.

"I said blades or pipes?" Larson repeated.

"Makes no difference," McCutcheon said.

"To me, either."

Larson picked up one of the two black-handled knives and felt the weight of the gleaming silver blade in his right hand. It was a fine weapon: balanced, heavy, sturdy, serrated on one side for tearing at meat, and razor sharp on its whetted edge for ruthless slicing. Suddenly and violently he spun and hurled the knife through the air. It screamed across the room and exploded into the wall.

All eyes turned. Twenty-five feet away the blade, its tip driven three inches deep into a wooden beam, jutted from the wall. Without words the throw of the knife spoke volumes about Larson's abilities.

"Let's go with these," Larson said in regards to the pipes. "Just more fun to bash shit than poke it, don't you think?"

McCutcheon crossed to the table, picked up the second knife, and gazed at the blade Larson had just used to impale into the wood. Everyone stared. How could M.D. top such a throw? The only way possible would be to hurl his knife and slice Larson's blade right through the butt of its handle, and split the weapon in two like Robin Hood.

Which, of course, would be impossible.

M.D. never spent any time learning to throw knives. He knew how to defend himself against an enemy who might wield one, but beyond that he'd only used them like most civilians did, for cutting food or opening boxes.

Blade in hand, McCutcheon walked to the knife that Larson had just sizzled into the beam like some sort of weapons expert and inspected his enemy's throw. It was a fine fling indeed. M.D. nodded, took off his jacket, and then neatly hung it up on the wall using Larson's blade as a coat hanger.

Stanzer smiled wryly. M.D. peeled off his shirt, folded

it, and then set it down. He turned and his abs rippled. McCutcheon dropped his knife. It fell straight downward. Its tip pierced the wood. Stuck straight up like an erect pencil.

"Let's do this," McCutcheon said.

Larson picked up both pipes, extended his arms, and offered M.D. his choice of weapons. McCutcheon shrugged. Didn't matter to him. Larson tossed the one in his right hand to his opponent; it sailed through the air and M.D. caught it. As McCutcheon's fist wrapped around the pole, he felt the pipe's potential. It was a powerful piece of steel. Strong, thick, certain to cause lots of damage on impact.

Larson, too, pulled off his shirt and his huge, swollen muscles bulged. All eyes in the room stared at his bacne. An unnatural galaxy of red pimples speckled his hulking, mammoth back. Back acne was a common side effect of steroids, much like fits of uncontrollable rage and shrunken nuts. But McCutcheon wasn't there to measure Larson's testicles; he'd come to chop them off.

The two met in the center.

"Like Vale Tudo. Only one of us walks away."

"Just so you know," McCutcheon answered. "I don't want to fight you."

Larson stared into M.D.'s eyes. "Yes, you do."

He was right. M.D. did want to fight him. More than just fight him, McCutcheon wanted to end his life. Adrenaline surged through M.D.'s veins. His inner beast screamed. It needed food, revenge, the spilling of blood.

They raised their pipes.

A look of deviant pleasure glowed in Larson's eyes. He loved the idea of battling in a winner-take-all match. He'd been training for just such a moment ever since he turned ten years old. Larson knew that if he took down McCutcheon, he'd not only save his own life, but also his name would ring out across the far corners of the underground fight world. Larson would be the gladiator who ended Bam Bam, the legendary Prince of Detroit.

No, it wasn't the floor of the Roman Colosseum, but for Larson it was good enough.

"Just so we're clear," Puppet said, acting as de facto master of ceremonies. "No matter what happens," he glared at Stanzer, "you don't pull any bullshit." The colonel, after a moment of eye contact with McCutcheon, rubbed his chin. He didn't like to be told jack shit about what he could or could not do. Especially, by a scumbag gangster. But he nodded. He'd honor M.D.'s wishes. If Larson won, he could walk. As would the Priests, as would Kaitlyn. But if Larson lost, well . . . that would be a different story.

"All right, gentleman," Puppet said, stepping back. All eyes zeroed in on the two opponents. The electricity of impending brutality supercharged the air. "Do your thing."

McCutcheon, pipe in hand, narrowed his eyes. Blood scorched through his veins. Then he had an insight. A sudden realization. One that brought fear and doubt.

He had no strategy.

In all his years of fighting, McCutcheon had never entered into a battle without a well-considered plan. Forethought, tactics, calculated courses of action, and perspicacious blueprints had always been his ace in the hole. He'd defeated scores of opponents over the course of his career who'd been bigger, stronger, and nastier, but he'd only been able to do so by tapping into his own greatest strength: his mind.

For all his skills, McCutcheon was a thinking warrior. He owned a powerful body but an even more powerful spirit— and yet, seconds away from the biggest battle of his life, he had no plan of attack. He hesitated, and concern descended on him like a cloud. His confidence was destabilized.

He had no vision for a path to victory. Worse, he'd run out of time.

Larson, pipe in the air, attacked.

■   ■   ■

Rage had blinded him. Hate had consumed him. McCutcheon's inner beast, crying for carnage, thirsting for bloodshed, driven only by the primal urge of extracting revenge, stole the clarity from M.D.'s mind.

Murder would be nectar. He needed to bash in this man's head and brain him. Nothing less would quench his thirst.

Is this really who I want to be?

Larson roared forward with an overhead right. M.D. deflected the strike with a rising rooftop block and the pipes *PINKED!* as they collided. The explosive sound of metal bashing metal filled the room with a bone-chilling sense of danger.

Pipe fighting was for lunatics. Larson's eyes widened. He'd never had more fun.

Larson swung again. Expertly. Making a figure eight in the air, he advanced on M.D. with three crisp, crashing, consecutive strikes. McCutcheon backpedaled and parried—*PINK! PINK! PINK!*—then hopped to an open part of the room outside of his assailant's strike zone. Lacking clarity on how to proceed, he readied his defenses.

Larson displayed excellent mechanics. His weight was balanced, he did little to telegraph his moves, and he struck with ferocity, power, and technique. Clearly, he'd been well trained. He knew what he wanted to accomplish and why he wanted to achieve it. As a warrior, he was locked in.

The same could not be said about McCutcheon. A part of him wanted to bash Larson's skull. McCutcheon knew just the right spot on the temple to strike to cause immediate brain swelling, too.

But another part of M.D. held back. Violence, his gut told him, wasn't the answer—it couldn't be—and the warrior within knew there must a higher road that he could take. On one hand he hungered to take a life; on the other he yearned to never take one again. Though he'd killed before, having extinguished a person's existence once did not, he now realized, make doing it again any less significant.

McCutcheon, not knowing what to do, was stuck, caught, snared by indecision. And as all warriors knew, the hesitant fighter was always lost.

Larson, sensing tentativeness, raged forward.

Cutting a fierce X through the air, Larson engaged again. Over his left shoulder, a strike from the right, an attack from the hip—*PINK! PINK! PINK!*—he targeted the crown of McCutcheon's head, the side of McCutcheon's neck, and his face.

If even one of the blows had landed the fight would be over. These were immense blows being launched, one after the other. McCutcheon needed to commit, but to what aim? Was he willing to take another life? Was he being forced to murder in the name of self-defense, or was there another path to victory he could embrace without causing death? The questions jumbled one on top of the other, but he had no answers, and he fought like a man plagued by overthinking and indecision.

McCutcheon floundered and Larson gained the upper hand. It became a war of offense versus defense, attack versus protect, assail versus merely ward off. If M.D. didn't take committed action soon, his defenses would surely give way.

Most 'roid monsters were more bulk than athleticism. Not Larson. He had tree trunks for thighs, but he also knew how to leverage them and explode from his hips. In stick fighting, meaningful striking power always came from the hips, and Larson's pipe blasts thundered like bursts from a canon. The more he swung, the more his confidence grew. He was on track to win this war and thus his freedom and the glory. To Larson it no longer was a matter of *if* he'd win, but *when*.

He launched two more blows—*PINK! PINK!*—and smiled. "Gotta say," Larson taunted. "Thought you woulda had more in ya."

He swung again. *PINK!* "Damn, I'm good," Larson said aloud.

With his left palm high and facing inward, McCutcheon used his right hand to wield the pipe and guarded the left side of his head with his free hand. It was a classic defensive posture that allowed him to fend off, parry, and avoid strike after strike. Then a shot landed. A forearm shiver that cracked M.D. in the jaw. Larson followed the shot with a hard knee to the ribs. McCutcheon shot for his opponent's legs, but Larson proved quicker than M.D. had expected and sidestepped the attempted takedown.

With McCutcheon on the floor, after having missed a double leg shoot, Larson spun and crashed down with a monstrous overhead blow. Full speed, full pipe, a mighty man slamming downward from a superior position. M.D. rolled away just as the steel crashed into the floor, and scampered to his feet. It was a miss but a close one.

His lip bleeding, his ribs pounding, McCutcheon steadied himself.

"Just so you know," Larson said with a grin. "There's plenty more where that came from."

It was kill or be killed. *Or was it??*

His inner debate continued.

Larson's onslaught moved forward with another trio of shots. *PINK! PINK! PINK!* The Priests, Stanzer, even

Kaitlyn knew that McCutcheon would only be able to deflect, block, and evade for so long. At some point he'd have to attack with purpose and meaning or he'd be defeated.

McCutcheon searched his heart and the answer became clear: he did not want to kill this man. Why? Because he yearned too deeply to do so.

The battle raged on—*PINK! PINK! PINK!* After another flurry of strikes from Larson, M.D. jumped over a stray bottle, moved into the center of the room, and made eye contact with Kaitlyn. The look was brief but it was also deep and full of meaning.

Suddenly, McCutcheon knew what he had to do, and he switched his pipe from his right hand to his left.

Having spent hundreds of hours in the gym turning himself into an ambidextrous fighter, M.D. changed angles and attacked his foe high-low-high from the left. *PINK! PINK! PINK!* Larson parried the blows, but for the first time in the battle he'd been forced to step backward instead of forward.

McCutcheon attacked again—*PINK! PINK! PINK!*— and while Larson fended off the strikes with a series of defensive blocks, Larson could feel the momentum shifting.

Which is exactly what M.D. wanted. He now knew his strategy. He saw his path to victory. The first phase of McCutcheon's plan—an aggressive assault—would set the stage for the next wave of confrontation. His scheme worked perfectly, too, and M.D. got the exact reaction from Larson that he had expected.

McCutcheon turned up the heat because he knew that

Larson would respond in kind. His foe considered himself an animal, a beast, and Larson's ego would not allow for an opponent to put him on the defensive for very long. Larson, fury raging, went wild-eyed and raised his pipe, now more determined than ever to strike a vital target.

McCutcheon had figured out that Larson deeply wanted one big hit. The home run. A monstrous knockout shot to the teeth, temple, or nose. He didn't just seek victory; Larson sought unforgettable destruction. Only a barbaric blow that would echo through the room with shock would suffice. Aside from a few feints to the knees, everything Larson launched had been high, high, high.

Which allowed McCutcheon to anticipate the next angle.

His quest for the big smash was his weakness. Trachea shots, pipe blasts to the center of the face, blows like this were wonderful paths to victory if they could be landed. However, top stick fighters knew that the most important target area in a battle featuring metal poles for weapons, was the opponent's hands.

A pipe to the knuckles was all it would take. One clean smash and Larson would drop his steel, entirely disarmed. No, it wouldn't be sexiest path to victory, but it would be effective, like taking the fangs from a snake.

McCutcheon timed it perfectly and his metal pipe exploded against the middle knuckle of Larson's right hand, just as his enemy attempted to bring a massive downward strike onto M.D.'s head. The was no *PINK!* Just a muffled *thud*, the sound of steel smashing meat.

Larson's pipe *tink*ed to the floor, and two Priests recoiled in horror as Larson's hand instantaneously swelled to the size of a grapefruit. M.D. went low.

CRACK! He smashed Larson's left ankle and the bone misaligned from the foot. M.D. spun, did a 360-degree turn to generate maximum speed, brought the pipe around the side of his head, and *CRACK!* went for Larson's other ankle.

But missed.

Instead of hitting Larson near the top of his foot, McCutcheon drove his pipe into Larson's lower shin. The steel severed the tibia bone like an ax breaking through a piece of firewood, and Larson's leg dangled off its bone, the bottom still attached to the top only because of the threads of ligament holding the pieces together.

Blood began to seep through his pants. Larson, in shock from the pain, tried, inexplicably, to take a step forward and attack.

He collapsed on his face, his leg unable to support any weight. McCutcheon pounced, dropped a knee into the middle of Larson's back, and forced his enemy's left arm to extend outward from his body in a straight line. With Larson's palm down and fingers extended like a starfish, McCutcheon raised his pipe high in the air.

Fear filled Larson's eyes. He knew what was coming but had no way to stop it. His hand would have to absorb the upcoming blow at full speed unless the plea in his eye could convince M.D. to relent.

McCutcheon gave no quarter. Palm down, knuckles

up, his fingernails pointed toward the sky, M.D. brought down a colassal pipe blow onto the center of Larson's outstretched hand.

The *CRACK!* of shattering bones caused a gangster to gag. If it wasn't for the skin surrounding Larson's fingers, the bones in his hand would have gone ricocheting across the floor like a blast of billiard balls exploding on a pool table. Larson had been defeated, but his life had been spared. Captured yet defanged. No, McCutcheon would not take his life, but also he would not allow this man to pose any further threat. Each appendage of his opponent had been rendered useless, and it might be years before any of Larson's four limbs functioned properly again.

M.D. rose to his feet, victorious. Puppet nodded. The conquest was complete.

McCutcheon dropped his pipe, picked up the knife sticking up out of the floorboard, and swished the blade back and forth across the leg of his jeans in two crisp, clean strokes. He cut the rope tying Kaitlyn to her chair. He wished she hadn't just seen all that, but she had, and M.D. knew he couldn't change that.

When the last bit of twine released her arm, Kaitlyn leaped up and bounded into McCutcheon's arms.

"I'm sorry," McCutcheon said, hugging her close. "This will never happen again."

She embraced him with all her might and tears fell from her eyes.

BAM! A gunshot rang out.

BAM! BAM! Two more.

All eyes turned. Smoke rose from the barrel of the Sig.

"I assume no one has a problem with that," Stanzer asked.

The eight Priests in the room, caught entirely off guard by the gunshots, stared at the huge holes in Larson's chest. Each gang member looked at one another seeking a consensus, as a puddle of dark red began to form around the deceased cop's body. The deal was that if Larson won he'd walk scot-free. No one had said a word about honoring a deal should Larson lose. The Priests had probably expected McCutcheon to end Larson's life anyway. Just like they expected Larson to kill M.D. should he have had the chance. But McCutcheon didn't take the man's life and Larson had lived.

Not anymore.

"Naw, no problem," Puppet said speaking for his people. Priests always pay, but they get paid, too. With the way everything went down, Puppet figured there were no more debts.

"You ready?" Stanzer said to McCutcheon in a nonchalant voice.

M.D. and the colonel locked eyes. Kaitlyn had already seen too much, and now Stanzer had just delivered her a front-row seat to seeing even more.

"You call that justice?" McCutcheon asked.

"Indeed I do. The conclusive kind."

M.D. shook his head, but Stanzer, feeling no qualms about his actions, simply holstered his weapon. He knew who he was, he knew what he stood for, and he knew that this mission required finality.

McCutcheon, arm draped over Kaitlyn, nudged her toward the door.

"Well, ain't that romantic," Puppet said. "Like a Hollywood movie and shit."

A few Priests laughed and rose to their feet. It wasn't the funniest joke they'd ever heard but it broke the tension. Each of them knew they were lucky to be alive and they couldn't wait to get out of there.

Without warning, Kaitlyn released herself from underneath M.D.'s arm, turned, and walked over to Puppet, a soft and gentle look in her eyes.

"I just want to thank you for not hurting me." Puppet towered over Kaitlyn by six inches and probably outweighed her by ninety pounds. "I know you had your opportunity," she said.

Puppet smiled. "Well, that's because I'm not just a businessman, I'm a gentleman."

He grinned. Kaitlyn's eyes turned from soft to fierce and she struck. Spiked Puppet with a straight right hand to the throat. He gagged, and she followed with a knee to the groin, and then a technically perfect hip sweep that sent the gang leader flying over her shoulder, landing flat on his back.

"Oomph," Puppet groaned as he crashed to the floor, completely blindsided by the attack. Kaitlyn pounced like a cougar, pressed both of her knees against the top of Puppet's shoulders and began wailing on him with left, right, left punches straight to the center of his unprotected face. Stunned and caught entirely off guard, Puppet absorbed blow after blow at full strength and his face began to give way. His nose, his teeth. Blood streamed in gushes before anyone in the room had a moment to react.

"You think I'm afraid of you?" Kaitlyn screamed. "Do ya?" She hammered away like a tiger, ferocious, determined, and fearless.

It all happened so quickly that none of the Priests knew how to respond. They all thought she was just some rich, soft, pretty, delicate girl, yet she'd just sucker-punched a two-hundred-pound man and was standing over his body tearing up his face. Three Priests made a move to go after her, but Stanzer quickly drew his weapon and the gang members froze, the colonel's message clear: first one to touch her gets a bullet.

With Puppet's lights turned out and Kaitlyn raging on his face, M.D. jumped in to stop her before she beat him into a coma.

"Okay, okay," McCutcheon said as he dragged her off Puppet.

Kaitlyn scowled at the other Priests, blood running from her fists. "When he wakes up, you tell him a little bitch did this to him. All of you better watch who you mess with. You hear me?"

"Let's go," M.D. said hustling her out the door. "Enough."

"I'm not afraid of you," she screamed. "Not a damn one of you!"

M.D. pulled Kaitlyn out of the room, leaving's Puppet pummeled body lying semiconscious on the floor next to

Larson's corpse. Stanzer, his Sig still drawn, backed out of the building, and five seconds later the three of them were safely outside, protected by the cover of the team in the field. It didn't really matter, however, because none of the Priests dared to follow.

The three of them, Stanzer, McCutcheon, and Kaitlyn, briskly walked to the abandoned house where the colonel had parked the car and then climbed into the Chevy.

Moments later, the white four-door motored away.

FORTY-NINE

They drove in silence, Stanzer at the wheel, McCutcheon in the front, Kaitlyn in back wiping Puppet's blood off of her fists with a small white towel she'd found on the seat. Fifteen minutes passed without a word. They cruised along, dusk falling. The night would be dark and wet. M.D. finally turned around and looked over his left shoulder.

"You okay?"

"You going to tell me where you've been?"

McCutcheon looked to Stanzer. He and M.D. made eye contact, but no words passed between them. McCutcheon looked out the side window without responding.

"And tell me again who this guy is to say no to that request?" Kaitlyn said. "I waited for you, McCutcheon. Waited for months because I knew you'd come back. There were even times while you were away that, I don't know, it felt like you were right there watching me."

M.D. remained silent.

"I'm not afraid anymore, you know," Kaitlyn contin-ued. "I was raised to be afraid. To be scared. To do good in school and follow the rules and go to college and get a job and meet a nice boy and be safe, safe, safe. But it's bullshit. There is no safety. The more secure I try to be, the more I wrap my life in a protected little bubble..." She shook her head. "It's never safe. Just sterilized."

McCutcheon simply stared.

"And when you left I learned..." She paused. "I learned I wanted you."

Kaitlyn suddenly leaned forward and stuck her tongue deep into McCutcheon's mouth. Gave him a huge, passionate, kiss, wet and meaningful and long, and then she plopped backward into the car's rear seat.

"I started taking martial arts classes, too. My sensei has been teaching me to transform my fear into energy," she said with pride. "My whole life I was taught to move cautiously and be afraid, but I am done with that now. Done forever. I have power."

Her green eyes lasered in on M.D.

"And I want to be with you," she said. "I want to be with you more than anything else in the world."

McCutcheon didn't respond. He just breathed in and breathed out, considering what to say. After a few minutes, M.D. glanced over at Stanzer. The colonel knew he was being looked at, he could feel McCutcheon's eyes, but Stanzer still didn't take his gaze off the road in front of him, didn't waver for a second.

"Oh, I'm sorry," Kaitlyn said from the back seat to Stanzer. "With all that shooting-of-an-unarmed-man excitement back there, I don't think I caught your name, mister."

The sarcasm in Kaitlyn's voice wasn't lost on anyone. "Reggie," he said. "Colonel Reginald Stanzer. Nice to meet you."

"A colonel huh? So you're like with the military. You McCutcheon's boss?"

Both men in the front remained quiet.

"What, you some sort of secret agent now?" Kaitlyn asked, her voice full of mockery.

M.D. said nothing.

"Oh, you're not going to tell me anything?" Her anger grew. "You disappear for nearly eleven months and I get the silent treatment. You have got to be kidding me."

M.D. struggled with how to respond. Not knowing what to say he didn't say anything.

"Oh, this is just great," Kaitlyn said. "I spill my heart to the guy who caused me to be abducted, and all I get is a tough-guy look in response. Real brave man you are."

Though she poked him, M.D. didn't take the bait.

"Well, can I at least know where we are going?" Kaitlyn asked after another few moments of maddening quiet.

Stanzer and M.D. exchanged another look. This was McCutcheon's show; Stanzer was just the driver. It fell to M.D. to call the next shot.

"We're going to your parents' house," he said. "I'm dropping you off."

"Excuse me?"

"Go to college, Kaitlyn," McCutcheon said. "All those people were right. Get a degree, find a job, meet a nice guy.

Someone who'll, you know," M.D. said, pausing between words. "Come home at night."

"Didn't you hear what I just said?" she replied. "I don't want a plastic bubble. I don't want a—"

"Look!" M.D. snapped. "You have your destiny and I have mine and they are not on a path to meet." McCutcheon turned to Stanzer, firmness in his voice. "Her parents' house. You need directions?"

"Nope," Stanzer said reaching for his cell. "Got 'em right here."

"Then step on it," M.D. said, turning back around to face front. "I'm sure her family is worried sick."

For the rest of the ride, McCutcheon made sure to only look straight ahead.

Stanzer turned north on the I-75 freeway, merged onto I-94, and looked for Exit 223, because Cadieux Road would take him directly into the heart of Grosse Point. The rain had turned from heavy to light and then to mist, but it fell hard enough for Stanzer to have to use the windshield wipers. Their rhythmic swish filled the car with a lonely, melancholic sound.

Six minutes after exiting the highway Stanzer rolled up to the front security gate of a six-bedroom, 3,600 square foot Tudor-style home. He knew eight different ways to beat the access system if he wanted to, but the colonel merely put the car in park outside the front gate and left the engine to idle.

M.D. exited the car and opened the back door for Kaitlyn. She stepped out and they made eye contact.

"You need to understand," he said. "The world I live in is not made for you. It's too violent. Too dangerous. Too..." He paused. "Unforgiving."

Kaitlyn gently, sympathetically, brushed her fingers across M.D.'s cheek, tender and affectionate.

"Fuck you."

She walked away.

Kaitlyn punched in the access code to the front gate, a heavy click sounded, and the automatic barrier began to swing open.

A light went on by the front porch. The door opened. Two people, a man and a woman, haggard looking, squinted to see.

Was that their girl?

It was. Kaitlyn's mother began crying. Her dad raced to scoop up Kaitlyn and give her a hug. Was she bleeding? Was she safe? Did she need a doctor? M.D. stood by the side of the Chevy, staring, staring, staring, frozen like a statue.

"We'd better go," Stanzer said.

McCutcheon, knowing the colonel was right, climbed back into the car and buckled his seat belt. Tears streamed from his eyes.

"No shame, son," Stanzer said. "No shame at all."

FIFTY

Light taps of rain played like a gloomy sound track against the metal of the car's roof as the Chevrolet cruised along the road.

"Just one question," M.D. said.

"Yeah?"

"Did you turn me into you on purpose?" he asked. "Or are people like us just born?"

Stanzer sniffed. Ran his hands through his hair and extended his arm. Rolling up his shirtsleeve was his only way of answering.

People sleep peaceably in their beds at night only because rough men stand ready to do violence on their behalf.

M.D. stared at the fading tattoo. He knew it wasn't just body paint to the colonel. These words gave meaning to Stanzer's life.

"We off to Norman, Oklahoma?" the colonel asked.

"Drop me at the bus station."

"She'll be back in Bellevue the day after tomorrow,"

Stanzer said. "You take the bus, Gemma will be gone before you arrive."

"Just the bus terminal is fine."

Stanzer stared. Studied his man closely.

"There are others you know. Other people your age in the program."

McCutcheon remained silent.

"They have different skills, various abilities and so forth but, well . . . this thing is growing," he said. "And they need a leader. Someone their own age."

McCutcheon still didn't reply. A moment later, knowing M.D. didn't plan to add anything else to the conversation, Stanzer pressed down harder on the gas and accelerated their speed. The two men drove in silence.

At the Greyhound terminal Stanzer pulled into an open handicap parking spot, figuring he'd only be there for a minute. He wanted to get M.D. as close to the front door as possible now that the rain had picked up. If he parked too far away, the kid would get drenched.

"You know how to reach me?"

McCutcheon rolled his eyes.

"Am I going to see you again?"

M.D. didn't answer.

"Well, can I at least ask where you are going?"

McCutcheon debated whether or not to reply, but then he decided that giving Stanzer an answer would probably be the most strategic way to handle his departure.

"West coast."

Stanzer raised his eyebrows. "West coast?"

"Actually, three stops," McCutcheon said. "Chicago, L.A., then Seattle."

Stanzer did a few calculations. It didn't add up.

"Can I ask why?"

"No," M.D. said. He popped open the passenger door and stepped out into the rain. "But, well...thanks."

McCutcheon closed the door, leaped over a puddle, and darted from the car to the front entrance of the bus station. After shaking off the wetness, he approached the ticket counter and reached into his pocket for some money. There was no line.

"Three tickets, please," McCutcheon said. "Next bus to Chicago. Four days after that I need a bus to Los Angeles. Four days after that I need a bus to Seattle, Washington."

"Express?"

"Of course."

"Need any bag tags?"

"No."

The elderly man behind the Plexiglas window punched up the tickets and M.D. paid in cash.

"The Chicago X don't leave for forty minutes," the old man said.

"Got a restaurant?"

A finger pointed. M.D. noted the worn gold wedding band circling the old man's ring finger.

"They serve salad?"

"S'ppose so."

"Thanks, I'll be in there," M.D. said as he walked away. The old man shrugged. He couldn't give a damn.

McCutcheon ambled through the terminal over to the restaurant, casually using his peripheral vision to glance toward the handicap parking spot where Stanzer had just dropped him off. The blue-lined space was already empty. Yes, the colonel had taken off, just like M.D. expected.

But had he really? Doubtful.

McCutcheon, in no great rush, sauntered past a pair of long, brown empty benches in the middle of the station and entered the sparse eatery. It wasn't so much a restaurant as it was large rectangle where they sizzled burgers and plated them with fries. Place could seat maybe forty-five diners though only two chairs were occupied, both with campers, people who weren't really eating as much as they were just sitting at the vacant spots waiting for their buses to leave. A place like this didn't need two employees. Certainly not at nine fifty p.m on a Wednesday night.

McCutcheon walked behind the eatery's counter and approached a guy in his mid-twenties wearing a Detroit Tigers baseball cap.

"Hey, you can't be back here."

"I'll give you two hundred dollars for your hat."

"What?"

"And another two hundred for your apron."

The employee paused. "You serious?"

"Plus another three hundred and fifty to jump on a bus that's leaving for Chicago in thirty-six minutes. That means my offer's now up to seven hundred and fifty."

The guy, medium height, a bit blubbery, considered it. "Who's gonna watch this place?"

M.D. pulled out a fan of cash. "Close early. We gotta deal?"

It took a moment for the guy to think about the offer. But only a moment.

"Heck, yeah. I love Chicago."

"Good," M.D. said, peeling off a series of hundred dollar bills. "Then enjoy a day on the town tomorrow courtesy of me. Need one more thing, though."

"Wait," the guy asked. "How do I get home?"

M.D. wrinkled his brow. "You, uhm, buy yourself a bus ticket. They're cheap. Like twenty-five bucks."

"Oh yeah, right," he said taking the money. "What else I gotta do?"

"Go step out into the main terminal. Tell me, is there a guy at the counter, in his fifties, looks like a hard-ass, talking to the old man at the ticket booth?"

The guy in the Tigers hat exited the eatery and peeked down to other end of the terminal. Did it stealthily, like a spy.

"Nope."

"What's going on down there?"

"Nothing. Just the old guy talking on the phone."

M.D. took a moment to calculate his next move.

"Tell me when he hangs up."

About twenty seconds passed.

"Okay, he just did."

"All right, stay here," M.D. said. "Be right back."

McCutcheon crossed back through the main terminal, this time with some pep in his step, and re-approached the old man sitting on a swivel chair behind the thick Plexiglas.

"Hey."

"Yeah?"

"So my grandfather, he just call you?"

The old man looked suspiciously as M.D. McCutcheon smiled warmly.

"Come on, I know he did. We just lost grandma to cancer. They were married fifty-four years. Poor guy, he's a good man, but he's worried about me ya know."

The old man behind the counter touched the wedding ring on his left hand almost subconsciously.

"My gramps is former F.B.I.," M.D. continued. "But forgets he's retired. Tracks me like I'm on the most-wanted list or something. It's only because he cares. He ring you?"

McCutcheon looked at the ticket seller with soft, caring eyes.

"Look, you don't have to answer," M.D. said. "I just need to know that you told him the truth. Told him I bought three tickets, the first to Chicago on a bus that leaves in about thirty minutes, then a ticket to L.A., and then a ticket to Seattle. I'm worried about him, ya know. Not sure what he's gonna do without Gram. But obsessing over me isn't the answer. It isn't healthy for him."

The old man looked to the left and thought about his own wife. Thought about what he'd do if he lost her.

"I bet he asked for the bar code on my tickets, too,

didn't he?" McCutcheon said. "Pretended like it was big important Federal Bureau of Investigations business."

The guy nodded.

"Thank you, sir. But don't worry," M.D. said, rapping his knuckles lightly on the glass. "My gramps is gonna be okay."

M.D. cruised back to the eatery.

"Here's your ticket, here's your cash."

"And here's your hat," the guy said, ripping the Detroit Tigers baseball cap off of his head. "I got a spare apron for you back there. A clean one."

"Keep 'em."

"Really?"

"Really," M.D. said. The hat and the apron were just a test to see if the guy was for sale. Once the driver scanned the ticket's bar code M.D. would be back on the grid, just like he wanted to be.

However, as McCutcheon well knew, the only way to stay invisible in the modern world was to create the illusion of being visible. The way M.D. figured it, he'd just bought himself at least six hours, more than enough time to disappear forever.

"Cool. This is my favorite lid anyway." He put his hat back on his head and marched to the two tables where the campers sat dozing. He slapped the wooden surfaces, loud and determined.

"All right, let's go. Time's up. Closing early."

Each of the campers shook themselves awake, gathered

their stuff, and stumbled off to go sit on the benches in the middle of the terminal where they were supposed to be waiting in the first place. Five minutes later, the eatery's iron gate was pulled closed and the place was locked for the night.

McCutcheon zipped his leather jacket and walked out a side emergency exit located near the restrooms. He circled around and watched to make sure that the guy in the Tigers baseball cap got his ticket scanned by the driver. The guy did and then took a seat in the back of the bus. Seven minutes later the evening Greyhound Express to Chicago closed its doors and groaned its way into the dark night, McCutcheon's location entirely known to the Federal Bureau of Investigation.

Or so the Federal Bureau of Investigation thought.

McCutcheon headed down a black alley. He had other business to attend to.

FIFTY-ONE

The morning sun began to rise in a clear and crisp Detroit sky. A brisk wind, some cool air, freshness in every breath. It was a good time of year to toss the football or take a walk in the park. Perhaps even a Saturday boat ride on the blue-green waters of Lake St. Clair for those with the means.

With no more rain in the forecast for the rest of the weekend, today would be a good day.

McCutcheon stepped over crushed beer cans, bags of long-ago eaten potato chips, and packs of discarded cigarettes. He stared at his phone. Looked at the street. Measured up calculations comparing the grid on his screen to the terrain at his feet. Markings were few and rubbish was plenty. It was as if a tornado had ripped through this part of town and everyone who once lived here had vanished. Just taken what they could grab and fled for higher ground.

This once was the Motor City. Still was, too, but the meaning of what that phrase meant had long ago changed.

McCutcheon checked his phone again and approached some rotted wood. He studied the surroundings again and then slipped on a pair of work gloves he'd bought at a hardware store and hunted around. Perhaps there were squatters. Drug addicts or whores or homeless men and women long ago discarded by society and comforted by alcohol and narcotics. But it was too early in the morning for those who prowled the night to be awake at this hour, and though McCutcheon stood tall and easily viewable from more than a quarter-mile away, he also felt alone and unobserved.

M.D. reached for a board. Tossed it to the side. Spun his shoulders around and saw some numbers on a house across the street that ended with a six.

Evens on that side, he deduced. Means odds over here. He checked the grid on his phone again. Calculated. Searched for an address but couldn't find one.

Then he did. Found a plank sitting on the front steps. Read the black numbers. 775. McCutcheon circled to the western side of the burned-out dwelling, yanked at his gloves to make sure they were good and tight, and then began pulling away hunks of decomposed brown wood.

He found a cellar. It was made of battered cedar and the lock was long since gone. It didn't appear as if these cracked, rotted doors to a dark and cavernous underground had been thrown open in forty years. McCutcheon split them apart, hoisted them open, and spied a bag.

Two of them. Duffels. Black and zipped and plump.

He knelt. Opened the first one. Saw brick after brick of clean green cash, stacks of hundred dollar bills wrapped and sorted into tight rectangular bundles.

There were fifties, too. And twenties. McCutcheon stared. It was more money than he had ever seen in his entire life.

M.D. shook his head and smiled, unable to suppress his proud grin.

"Well, I'll be a son of a bitch."